"LORD MONTJOY!" MERCY GASPED. "RELEASE ME THIS INSTANT."

"Only if you can assure me that you do not feel the same way I do." He pressed his lips to her temple. "God have mercy on me. You even *smell* delicious. Exactly as I have been remembering."

Mercy was too busy inhaling *his* scent to explain that it was probably only the rose water Chloe made for her that so attracted him. Enthralled by his nearness and the temptation of the moment, she swayed against him, closed her eyes, and simply reveled in his presence.

"Where is that rogue and rascal who talked me out of my best bottomland and then did not return to do a thing with it?"

Papa's voice in the hall outside the library brought Mercy to her senses. She leapt back from Lord Montjoy as if his touch had scalded her. He merely grinned and turned toward the doorway.

"In here, Daniel—alone with your daughter and trying to convince her that I am *not* a rogue and rascal, after all."

Yes, you are. You are the worst rogue and rascal I have ever met.

SWEET MERCY

KATHARINE KINCAID

Zebra Books
Kensington Publishing Corp.

http://www.zebrabooks.com

For Jessica,
who brings joy into the lives of so many.
May you always know the joy
you give so freely to others.
Love, Mom

ZEBRA BOOKS are published by

Kensington Publishing Corp.
850 Third Avenue
New York, NY 10022

First Printing: November, 1999
10 9 8 7 6 5 4 3 2 1

Printed in the United States of America

PROLOGUE

November, 1773
Collier Manor Annual Foxhunt
Virginia

The red and gold leaves of autumn flashed past Mercy on either side as she leaned forward and urged her horse onward through the flaming woods. Ahead of her, the baying hounds made haunting music: *"Hurry . . . hurry!"* they sang. *"The fox is just up ahead."*

Behind her came another, less delightful voice. "Miss Collier! Mercy—wait!"

The owner of *that* voice was Mr. Lloyd. Oliver Lloyd. Another unwanted suitor. A gentleman who would not take no for an answer—possibly because he had Papa's blessing, as had all her previous suitors. . . . Well, this was her chance to put him off the scent forever. It had worked on others; it would work on him.

"No time to stop!" she shouted over her shoulder. "Come along, Mr. Lloyd! The hounds are getting too far ahead of us."

"Slow down!" he pleaded. "The trees are too close through here. We risk breaking our necks at this pace."

"Cease worrying. I know these woods. Just follow me and try to stay up. When Liberty jumps, prepare to jump your horse. You will be fine. I promise you."

Mr. Lloyd had proclaimed himself an excellent horseman; now let him prove it, Mercy thought, giving Liberty her head.

The mare lengthened her stride and flew through the sun-dappled woods. She knew the game and, like Mercy, reveled in it. A huge log loomed ahead of them, blocking the narrow path. Mercy tightened the grip of her legs to keep herself firmly in her sidesaddle, moved her hands up her horse's neck, and kissed to the mare. Liberty arced her gleaming chestnut body over the obstacle and landed in a full-blown gallop without missing a stride.

"God save us all!" Mr. Lloyd yelled behind her.

Scrambling sounds indicated that his horse had failed to jump neatly. Mercy smiled to herself and kept going. In a foxhunt, it was every rider for himself—or herself. Mr. Lloyd had welcomed the opportunity to take the shortcut through the woods alone with her instead of staying with the other riders. Everyone else had known better and gone around the obstacle-choked barrier. If he thought this last jump was difficult, wait until he came to the ravine with the jumbled logs flanking either side of it.

Liberty crashed through some brush, leapt a small stream, and dodged her way around some boulders. Mercy relished every moment of their mad dash through the woods, but she knew she would have to pull up after the ravine jump, lest they overtake the Master of the Hunt when they came out of the woods. Since her father could no longer ride to the hounds, Colonel George Washington from Mount Vernon had been invited to be Master of the Hunt today, and Mercy respected the colonel far too much to break the rules just to teach Mr. Lloyd a lesson. No one got in front of the Master, his huntsmen, or the hounds.

Since Mr. Lloyd was still managing to keep up with her—albeit hollering over every jump—she decided to take the ravine and logs at full speed, then angle to the left and go round a second time. Two trips should be enough to convince Mr. Lloyd that he was no match for her on the hunt field *nor* in the marriage bed. It had taken one fellow three turns around the woods before he realized he was risking life and limb going in circles and that any woman who would do this to him was *not* the sort of female he wished to wed.

Ah well, some men were more stubborn than others. What they never counted on was how stubborn and persistent *she* was. She would do whatever was necessary to dull a man's interest in her inheritance. If she ever found one who could cheerfully keep up with her, she just *might* marry him. As she kept telling Papa, all a woman had to do to measure a man's true character was invite him to go foxhunting. She could learn more about him in a single morning than by spending an entire week talking to his mother and sisters.

A low-hanging tree limb nearly dislodged her hat for she forgot to duck going under it. For the next few moments, she concentrated solely on her riding. There were no big obstacles in this part of the woods, but the path wove in and out among the trees. Taking it at a gallop required all her attention. Even so, the corner of her riding habit snagged on some branches and tore away with a loud ripping sound that sent Liberty forward as if pursued by demons.

Mercy only laughed. She *lived* for foxhunting. The more challenging the route, the better she liked it. She began to hope Mr. Lloyd *would* last for another go-around. She hadn't had this much fun since the last suitor had been eager to follow her alone into the woods. Men were so gullible. Did they think she was planning a secret tryst with them?

She suddenly spotted the tumble of logs in front of the ravine jump. "Watch out, Mr. Lloyd!" she sang out. "There's a big one coming up."

"Noooo!" Mr. Lloyd cried out. "Stop! I doubt I can make it."

But it was too late for Mercy to stop. She was already airborne. Loath to be separated from *her* horse, Mr. Lloyd's horse came pounding after her.

"Noooooooo!" she heard again.

She brought her mare to a sudden halt and spun her around just in time to see Mr. Lloyd part company with his gelding and sail through the air like a bird. He soared for some distance before smacking into a tree and collapsing in a heap at its base.

God in heaven! She had never meant to *kill* the poor fellow. After all, he had said he could *ride*. If he were dead, she would never forgive herself.

Quickly, she rode back to him and dismounted, half-tripping on her long skirt in her haste. Heart pounding, she dropped to her knees beside him. Hatless, he lay on his back. A red welt creased his forehead, and one eye was beginning to swell shut. With a dazed expression, he gazed up at the tree branches.

"Mr. Lloyd! I am so sorry. Are you all right?"

He turned his head to look at her.

"Oh, Mr. Lloyd! Speak to me. Can you say something?"

His lips moved, and she had to bend closer to hear him. "What? Speak louder, Mr. Lloyd."

"You are greatly misnamed, Mercy Collier. You should never have been named Mercy, for you are a hellion with *out* mercy," he moaned. "If only you will take me home now, I will inform your father I no longer wish to marry you."

CHAPTER ONE

June, 1774
Collier Manor
Virginia

Mercy eyed the magnificent stranger gazing back at her from the full-length mirror and wondered where on earth she was going to hide the little brown toad and the smelly horse apple—generously donated by Liberty—on her wonderfully elegant person.

The toad might fit in the space between the top of her head and the inside bottom of her foot-high powdered wig, but she was uncertain whether the poor creature could breathe in the stuffy enclosure. Besides, she might topple the whole arrangement trying to get him out when she needed him, and everyone would surely notice, spoiling her entire plan.

She had no intention of putting the horse apple on her head, or—perish the thought!—down the front of her plunging neckline, though it would undoubtedly help fill out her sagging bodice.

No, she must find a less conspicuous place, one she could reach without drawing attention to herself. The toad was a busy fellow, even now hopping about in the confines of the small basket in which she had put him—covered with a heavy cloth to keep him from escaping.

"Lud a' mercy, what you got in that basket there?" In the mirror behind Mercy's right shoulder, Chloe's narrow brown face beamed disapproval. "You better not be plannin' mischief, Miss Mercy, 'cause your Pa is determined this time. He intends you should marry before the year is out."

Mercy narrowed her eyes at the friend, servant, and confidante who had delivered her into the world nineteen years ago and considered it her duty to manage her behavior ever since. Chloe's shocked exclamation: "Lud a' mercy, she's got red hair!" had resulted in Mercy being named Mercy. It had also fueled a frantic search of the family tree to reveal that a forgotten redheaded ancestor and not some interloper accounted for her golden-red ringlets.

"What I have in that basket is none of your concern, Chloe. Now that you have succeeded in turning a stable urchin into an English countess, you had better see to your other duties."

"I never seen an English countess, but you do look mighty fine, if I do say so myself," Chloe sniffed. "I still think you should let me pad the front of your gown a wee bit. Doan know why it doan fit you right. Sally took all your measurements b'fore she started cuttin' an' sewin'. You must not be eatin' enough lately."

Mercy suddenly wished she had thought to procure *two* horse apples—one for each side. The smell alone would have kept her latest suitor at bay. She needed to get rid of Chloe, so she could decide where to put the toad and the horse apple. It was past time to make an appearance downstairs.

"Run along now, Chloe. Tell Papa I will join him shortly."

Chloe frowned at her in the mirror. "You tryin' t' get rid of me, girl? . . . Well, gettin' rid of your newest beau is not gonna be so easy. I hear he's been tellin' everyone he's got the nod from your Pa *and* you."

"Reggie Wharton actually thinks I *favor* him? . . . Hah!" Mercy snorted, making her headdress wobble precariously. "If he honestly thinks I do, he understands me about as well as George III comprehends Virginians. I have done everything I can to discourage him—well, not *every*thing, since he has never accompanied me on a foxhunt. But after tonight, rest assured, Mr. Wharton will not be so eager to wed me."

Chloe's black eyes widened, and her brows all but disappeared into the top of her white turban. "What are you plannin' this time, girl? Makes me nervous t' think about it."

"You are the last person I would tell what I am planning, Chloe. Let us just say that tonight, I intend to explore Mr. Wharton's character. Even if he passes my little tests, he will still have to agree not to restrict my activities in any way, consent to separate bedchambers, and—"

"Separate bedchambers! Lud a' mercy! What kind of wife you gonna be if you refuse t' allow the poor man inside your bedchamber? Sounds like you can barely tolerate Mr. Wharton."

"To say I tolerate him is being far too generous," Mercy sighed. "Still, if he meets my requirements in certain areas, I will wed him just to hush you and Papa. As you both so frequently remind me, I need a husband to manage my future inheritance—which involves *your* future too, as well as everyone else's on this plantation. . . . But there is no cause for worry! If I do decide to wed the man, I will be quite loyal and true to him, regardless of how little affection I may actually feel for him."

"Well, you best not forget you need a husband to give you young'uns, too, girl!" Chloe scolded. She brushed a speck of lint from Mercy's sleeve, then rearranged a single long curl on her shoulder. "Why, you oughta have three or four babies by now. Most women of your station have found themselves husbands by the time they're fourteen years old. Why *you* have t' be so particular is beyond me."

"You very well know why, Chloe." Mercy stared hard at her friend's reflection. "A husband could be the greatest impediment to all I have been trying to accomplish here at Collier Manor. He could be more stubborn even than Papa. . . . If it were up to me, you and all the other slaves would have your manumission papers by now. And we would be growing more wheat and corn to feed the Colonies, instead of wasting our time on tobacco. The crop we send to England is only taxed beyond its value, anyway. . . . And what will happen if my future husband decides to support the English, while *I* cast my lot with the Americans? There will be war in my own household. 'Tis all well and good for you and Papa to say I must marry, but when I do, I shall be sacrificing my freedom. A husband could forbid me to foxhunt, as Caroline's did, and I would be bound to obey him!''

Chloe rolled her eyes in exasperation. "But he thought Miss Caroline was carryin' his child, so he was right to forbid her to ride around the countryside chasin' foxes."

"Why? Did he expect her to fall off her horse? Caroline has been riding horses for as long as I have. Until his own mother interfered, William even forbade Caroline to attend our Daughters of Liberty meetings . . . and he refuses to listen to a word she has to say about managing the affairs of the plantation where she has lived for her entire life. . . . Oh, what is the use of arguing? Run along now and make certain things are going well downstairs. Remind Papa that he promised not to make any announcements until *after* dinner. I will be greatly annoyed if he says a word about me and Reggie before or during."

Chloe shook her head. "Poor Mr. Wharton! Suddenly, I am feelin' sorry for him."

"You ought to feel sorry for *me*. If anyone is deserving of sympathy, 'tis a woman forced to wed against her wishes."

"Best not look for sympathy from *me*, girl. I been dictated to all my life. Besides, you gotta wed some time. Might as well be now."

Still shaking her head, Chloe turned away, leaving Mercy to ponder where, on her lovely, emerald-green silk polonaise gown with all its huge flounces and many bows, she was going to hide the only possible means to her salvation: a small, active toad and a kerchief-wrapped ball of horse manure.

* * *

As Ian Montjoy swung down from his horse, he inhaled deeply of the scent of roses. Then he took a good long look at Collier Manor, which he was seeing—and smelling—for the first time. The setting was worthy of a duke's country estate. The house boasted three stories of red brick and had massive, double-storied wings extending from either side. Surrounded by a traditional English maze and many terraced gardens, including one devoted entirely to roses, it stood on a hillside overlooking rolling fields of grain and tobacco bisected by stone fences and a pretty creek.

"Quite impressive, eh, Hiram?" he asked his manservant, who was as much friend as servant. He handed him Thor's reins. "The stable is probably around back. Considering my mission—and also my love for good horseflesh— I would much rather go there with you than set foot inside this mansion, lovely though it is. I hear that the Colliers breed the best thoroughbreds in Virginia."

"Let *me* be the judge o' that, me lord. I shall let ye know what I think of 'em. Meanwhile, just grit your teeth and do your duty. I canna see as ye have much choice."

Hiram took the reins from Ian and calmed the always-restive stallion by placing a gnarled hand on his nose. His own horse—a quiet old mare—stood nearby, her reins looped around a ring in a hitching post until the old Scotsman could return and collect her.

"I have *not* much choice," Ian grumbled. "That is the hell of it. Our beloved monarch did not leave me any— nor did that horde of greedy relatives who cannot seem to survive without clinging to my coattails. If not for them, I never would have had to come to the colonies in the first place. Unfortunately, I need more money to support them all, and America offers the best opportunity for lining my nearly threadbare pockets."

" 'Tis really that nasty entail business, eh, me lord? If not for that, ye could sell some of your land back home to line your pockets."

"The last thing I want is to sell my land back home, but yes, that nasty entail business prevents me from depriving my heirs of a means of sustenance . . . not that I have any heirs to worry about yet. But in case I do one day—especially now that I am betrothed to an heiress—I must think about preserving my assets to hand down to my children."

"Oh, ye will suffer no lack of heirs, me lord—not a virile young stud like yourself. Put to the right mare, ye will sire a whole passel of 'em."

"Not so young anymore, Hiram, and maybe not so virile. The longer I go without a wife, the less I seem to want one. Elizabeth is a tasty morsel, but after an hour in her company I sometimes feel restless."

Ian did not mention that he had already sampled Elizabeth's physical charms; she had made certain he did so before he left England—probably out of some misguided effort to ensure that he return to her. She need not have worried; he had seen nothing yet to make him want to stay in the colonies. Not until tonight, anyway. If he owned an estate like Collier Manor, he might change his mind.

"Once ye wed the lass, that feelin' should pass," Hiram counseled. "Nothin' like a good wife t' settle a man and make him more content with his lot in life."

"How would *you* know? *You* have never been wed."

"No, but I have done a lot of observin' in me many years," Hiram retorted. "Besides, havin' a Scottish mother gave me a sense about these things. I will just be takin' Thor down to the stable now, since ye think I have gone daft in the head."

"I did not say you were daft. But perhaps you should see to Thor now. You need not give him feed; I will not be staying that long. Just offer him water."

"Ye willna be stayin' long?" Hiram wrinkled up his already craggy, wrinkled face. "This affair looks like it will last all night, me lord. Ye should try and have a good time here. 'Tis glad I am ye decided to come separately and not go in the carriage with them folks we are stayin' with. They think themselves better than anybody else—and *him* with a lesser title than your own."

"Yes, and I thought titles would not matter so much over here. Guess I should have expected that anyone the king recommended—a distant relative of Lord North, yet—*would* be stuffy and title conscious. . . . I do not look overdressed, do I?"

Hiram cocked his head and studied him. Hiram was much happier in the stable than in a house, so Ian usually saw to his own clothing. "Not as I can see, me lord. I spotted your host's ladies before we left, and *they* looked ready to meet the king himself."

"The McCallister ladies *always* look ready to meet the king." Rarely self-conscious about his appearance, Ian nonethless brushed the road dust from his coat and wig. Tonight he would be on display, he knew, and must make a good impression. "I hate wigs—and this damned frock coat is much too hot for this time of year in Virginia."

"Ye look grand, though—refined. Exactly how a viscount *should* look. Not gaudy like lesser folks who want t' be someone they are not. If ye ask me, you would look finer still in the garb of a Highlander; 'tis too bad ye were not born a Scotsman."

"Thank you for your unbiased opinion, Hiram. The question is: Do I look like what I really am—a spy for King George III?"

"Tut, tut, me lord!" Hiram glanced around uneasily. A carriage was disgorging its passengers not fifty paces away, the occupants as resplendent as peacocks in their powdered wigs, elaborate gowns, and colorful finery. "Someone will hear ye."

"I almost wish they would. If treason is in the air at this party, I pray *not* to hear it. If I am lucky, everyone who attends will be as loyal to the king as the McCallisters."

"Well, ye havena heard a wrong word from any of *their* friends so far, have ye?"

"No, but I have met few of their friends yet. This is to be my introduction to Virginia society, remember? Tonight, I will meet the first families of the colony—the Lees, Randolphs, Carters, Byrds, and God knows how many others."

"The Colliers, and the Washingtons, too, me lord. Even *I* have heard about all the big Virginia planters."

"Yes, the very people about whom I am supposed to report back to the king. If *these* people rebel against his policies, there is little hope for avoiding war, Hiram. The king expects the common people to be against him, but the Virginia planters are the closest thing to the aristocracy the colonies have. Many of them still have relatives in England, and all of them have friends. The king thinks of even the wealthy colonists as 'rabble-rousing rustics' but he is still counting on them to take his side.''

"Ye havena mentioned it, me lord, but would *ye* take the king's side? Ye've been here long enough now t' form an opinion.''

"Yes, I have,'' Ian said. "But I remain undecided. The trouble is, aside from the McCallisters, I *like* what I have seen here: America is a young, exciting place. Full of new ideas. Bursting with opportunities . . . and England seems far away. 'Tis hard to think that a man who has never set foot on this grand continent should be making all the rules for those who live here.''

Hiram shook his head. "Be careful, me lord. That sounds treasonous t' me.''

"I know it does. I also know I cannot stand here any longer avoiding my duty. Much as I hate it, I must go in that house now.''

"Good luck, me lord. I hope nobody *does* say something that will mark them as an enemy to the crown. Ye will have no choice but to report it.''

"And *you* will have no choice but to pass the information into the proper hands. I am counting on you, Hiram,'' he reminded his old friend. "You are the only person in America I can trust.''

Hiram frowned and shook his head. " 'Tis uncertain I am about *my* part in all this, me lord. 'Tis a bad business— spying fer the king.''

"But we will both meet our obligations, Hiram. I must supply names, dates, and specific incidents, or the king will think *I* am a traitor—and you along with me. We dare not cross him; you know how vindictive he can be to anyone he perceives as an enemy. Why, we could never set foot in England again.''

Grizzled old Hiram straightened his shoulders and looked Ian right in the eye. "My family has *always* done its duty by ye, me lord—and before ye there were yer ancestors. Ye can trust nobody in this world more than me. I do not do this fer the king; I do it fer Lord Ian Montjoy."

"Why do you think I brought you along, old friend? Why you and *only* you? Because no one else knows—or will *ever* know—what the king is forcing me to do here. From the moment he heard I was coming, he started his campaign . . . a most effective one. He knows how to twist arms rather well."

"Beggin' yer pardon, me lord, but will not yer rich lassie be bringin' in enough money t' help ye out?"

"Not quite, Hiram. Her money *will* help, of course, but even if it provided all I needed, I am far too proud to depend on it. I must find my own way to make money here in the colonies. Once, I find it—in tobacco or some other commodity—and set everything in motion, I can return home and marry her."

Thor whinnied just then and began prancing in circles around Hiram. Another carriage had rumbled up the drive, and the noise and commotion were exhausting Thor's patience. He obviously thought he had stood still long enough.

"Off to the stable with him, Hiram. When I am ready to leave, I will send a servant to fetch you both."

"Right, me lord. Have a good evenin'."

Ian sighed and started for the front door of the imposing edifice. He was *not* looking forward to this. But he had to do it; tonight was a perfect opportunity for gathering the information the king required. It was also an excellent time to fish for investment possibilities. At least he would have a respite from the McCallisters. At first, their hospitality had been effusive—until they discovered that he was betrothed to Elizabeth. Apparently, they had been hoping he might take an interest in their daughter, Prudence. The unfortunate girl possessed her father's lean, angular looks and her mother's sharp tongue. Ian would not have been interested in her if she had enough money to keep his relatives solvent for the remainder of their lives.

Gritting his teeth, he prepared himself for an unpleasant evening.

* * *

An hour later, Ian stood in the lavishly appointed drawing room of Collier Manor enjoying a tankard of hard cider in the company of a young man he had first met while riding through Chinn's Crossroads. Thor had thrown a shoe, and Drew Elliot had been most helpful in locating a farrier.

Leaning toward him, Mr. Elliot said in a low voice: "Have they succeeded in betrothing you to Prudence yet, Lord Montjoy?"

Ian suddenly spotted Prudence across the room, surrounded by other sumptuously gowned young women. They were all watching *him,* he realized with a start. From the way they were eyeing him, he might have been a large, delectable insect being stalked by a flock of hungry geese.

"The last thing I knew, I was still betrothed to a young woman who's awaiting my return to England, so we can plan our nuptials," he answered, turning his back on the avid young women.

"You are claimed then? How fortuitous for lesser beings such as my own humble self." Patting the bright golden waistcoat beneath his brilliant blue frock coat, Drew Elliot looked anything but humble, and Ian had to smile at the notion.

"If you need a wife, Mr. Elliot, you should have no difficulty finding one. This room is full of candidates."

"Yes, but there are also plenty of unattached gentlemen with whom I must contend. Few have titles or sufficient funds for grand investments. You outshine us in every way, my lord."

"Ian. Please call me Ian," Ian insisted.

"And you must call me Drew, my lord—Ian. As I was saying, I can hardly compete with you."

"That strikes me as odd—especially considering that I am a stranger here, and this is a precarious time, when everyone is suspect . . . or so I am told."

"Suspect? What do you mean?" Drew looked baffled.

Such an innocent, Ian thought, liking the young man even more. "I mean that everyone is being forced to take sides, and those who favor secession from England have grown hostile and suspicious toward those who do not, and vice versa."

"That is true," Drew conceded, "but there is little mystery about where anyone stands. Why, I could go around this room and tell you precisely who is a confirmed loyalist, who must be regarded as a patriot, and who is still straddling the fence, so to speak."

"Could you really?" Ian felt a stab of guilt. This was going to be easier than he had thought. "Pray do so, if you would, please, Drew. When I make the acquaintance of all these strangers, I should like to know what to say so as not to offend them."

"The McCallisters have not presented you to everyone already?" Drew peered at him in astonishment.

"No, I came by horseback while they took the carriage, so I arrived ahead of them. Besides, I assured them I wished to circulate on my own tonight and call no attention to my title."

"But, my lord, you outrank us all and should be proud of the fact, even here in America."

To hide his annoyance, Ian took another swallow of hard cider. Licking the potent brew from his lips, he leaned closer and remarked: "I thought that here in America rank no longer mattered so much. Do not insist otherwise, Drew, or I will be sorely disappointed."

"But why, my lord? To be a viscount has got to be . . ."

A royal pain in the ass.

"Being a viscount is not all it is made out to be, my young friend. But come now. . . . Tell me about these other guests."

With Drew at his side, Ian strolled about the crowded room, occasionally greeting Drew's friends and acquaintances. Between-times, Drew would incline his head and whisper: "Now, that one is an ardent loyalist who defends King George to the high heavens. But that one there—Mr. Thomas Jefferson—is known to harbor patriotic sentiments. The gentleman by the window, Mr. Patrick Henry, is quite rabid on the subject of independence. 'Tis not decided yet who will be representing Virginia at the Continental Congress scheduled to convene in Philadelphia in early September. Not *everyone* favors independence, but Mr. Henry most definitely does. I have heard him advocate dissolving our English government and forming a new nation made up of the thirteen colonies."

"And no one accuses him of treason?" Ian had not realized things had gone this far. The king would consider the mere voicing of such sentiments as just cause for war. The thought turned Ian's stomach. A bunch of disorganized zealots could never hope to defend themselves against the most powerful military and naval force on the face of the earth.

"Oh, some might consider him a traitor—people like the McCallisters perhaps. Your hosts hate the king's taxes as much as anyone but will defend his *right* to tax us until we have all been bled dry as a bone, themselves included."

"This Patrick Henry . . ." Ian nodded toward the intense, energetic-looking man engaged in vigorous debate with two other guests. "Is he a planter, then?"

"No, a barrister—and a very successful one. Worked his way up from poverty, they say. Tries hundreds of cases in a year's time and wins most of them. A very persuasive speaker, from all accounts."

"I should like to hear him sometime." Ian greatly admired fiery speakers though he himself favored diplomacy in controversial situations.

"Look over there! That is Colonel Washington from Mount Vernon," Drew murmured behind his hand.

Ian turned to see a tall, ruddy-faced gentleman with an aristocratic countenance and a demeanor of authority that would have made him notable in any company.

"He is very well respected, a member of the House of Burgesses," Drew continued. "He proposed making the first of this month a day of fasting and prayer in hopes of preserving our liberty while avoiding the evils of civil war. When the British closed Boston Harbor to punish the perpetrators of the Boston Tea Party, they won many supporters for American independency. Virginia has already sent thousands of bushels of corn and wheat to Boston to keep the inhabitants from starving as a result of General

Gage's enforcement of the royal edict. Much of that aid came from people in this very room. . . . Colonel Washington is now drawing up a set of resolutions for the citizens of Fairfax County to further resist Parliament's attack on Massachusetts, while Thomas Jefferson is writing a pamphlet summarizing the rights of British America. Rebellion is in the air, my lord . . . Ian."

Just as he had feared, Ian thought. "And you, Drew? Where do you stand on the issue?"

"Oh, I dread the thought of confrontation, but if it comes to war, I will be forced to fight on the side of liberty."

Ian suppressed a sigh and mentally added him to the list of traitors he must send to the king.

"Excuse me a moment, will you, Ian? . . . I see someone I have been waiting to catch alone all evening. Over by the window . . . the young woman in white." Drew's face was radiant.

"Go right ahead. Do not think you must keep me company all evening."

"Oh, but I want to! I mean I feel privileged. I just need to tell her something, and I will return directly."

Ian envied the young man his eagerness to pursue the girl. He wished he could feel the same toward Elizabeth. The girl in white looked so young . . . so innocent. Boring actually. She had no fire—but then, neither did Elizabeth.

As Ian downed the last of his cider, he suddenly spotted another young woman standing in the doorway. *This* woman was riveting. Inhaling sharply, he choked on the fiery mouthful, then coughed so hard that his eyes began to water. It was several moments before he could catch a normal breath. By then, the girl had disappeared, presumably withdrawing into the adjacent room. Ian wondered if he had truly seen her or only conjured her in his imagination.

She had been dressed all in green, he recalled, with green feathers protruding from an elaborate wig. Even in this gathering of resplendent females, her vivid green eyes, rosy cheeks, and saucy air of mischief had made her stand out from the rest. Small, slender, and graceful, she had possessed an almost ethereal beauty, the effect of which left him feeling as if Thor had kicked him in the stomach.

Such an instantaneous physical response to a woman had never happened to him before. Ian was both embarrassed and disgusted with himself. After all, he was betrothed to another female whose considerable charms he had already sampled. Why should a momentary glimpse of a total stranger exert such a powerful effect on him?

"Are you all right?" Drew anxiously inquired, appearing suddenly at his elbow. "You look pale, my lord. That cider must have gone down the wrong way. Do you need something else to drink—plain water, perhaps?"

"No . . . no, I am fine. Did you mark a young woman who stood in the doorway of this room a few moments ago? She presented a most amazing appearance. So vibrant. So incredibly alive. The most exquisite woman I have ever laid eyes upon."

Drew's jaw dropped, and Ian suddenly realized what he was saying and clamped his mouth shut.

"What color were her eyes?" Drew asked very seriously. "Not green, by chance, were they? I didn't see her myself. I was preoccupied with Sarah Gumble, the girl in white. But if the one you saw had eyes as green as new spring leaves—incredible eyes, really—it could only have been one person."

"She *did* have green eyes," Ian sheepishly admitted. "They matched her gown and the feathers in her wig. And she stepped so lightly one might almost think she was floating. I blinked—and choked—and she was gone. Now I wonder if I truly saw her."

"I am sure you did." Drew sounded glum. His face had lost its brimming good humor. "I know not if she is wearing green tonight, but in all other aspects, you have just described Miss Mercy Collier, the lady whose betrothal will be announced tonight."

"I see," said Ian, struggling to recover his composure. "The gentleman who won her heart is certainly a lucky fellow. For all I know she might be a harridan, but still, she possesses a rare beauty."

"That she is, my lord . . . a harridan *and* a beauty."

"A harridan? You cannot mean it. Why, she looked a bit saucy but not at all malicious. I thought she had an air of sweetness about her."

"Oh, she is sweet as vinegar! 'Tis obvious you have never tried to keep up with her on a foxhunt. *That* is why she is still unwed at the ripe old age of nine and ten."

"Because she prefers foxhunting to domesticity? I cannot think that so great a fault. She must have slaves and servants aplenty to do her bidding."

"Oh, she does indeed. 'Tis how she *uses* the foxhunt that humiliates the male species. Every time a man offers for her, she delays making a commitment until the next hunt season, then invites him to accompany her at the manor's annual foxhunt. Naturally, he desires to impress her with his riding skills, but Miss Mercy, whom we all call The Thoroughbred, for reasons which will be apparent once you make her acquaintance, somehow manages to lose the rest of us and take her would-be husband off on his own. . . . When they finally return, he has lost all desire to wed her."

"You cannot be serious."

"I am dreadfully serious," Drew insisted. "It happened to a friend of mine. When he returned, he refused to discuss the matter—only informed me there would be no marriage after all. He vowed he would not wed the vixen if she were the last female on earth."

"You must be joking. That mere sprig of a green-eyed girl could hardly have so much mettle as to scare off a man who was truly enamored of her."

"That is precisely what I am saying. She has *too* much mettle. 'Tis why they call her The Thoroughbred. Not all horses can be dominated, my lord. If you succeed in breaking them to saddle, they never *will* make trustworthy mounts. When you least expect it, they will dump you in the dust. Miss Mercy is exactly that sort, headstrong and opinionated as they come. There is no sweetness in her."

This last was related in a whisper. Even then, Drew glanced around nervously as if he expected the lady herself to be listening.

"You must introduce me to her," Ian demanded, struck

with an urgency he could neither suppress nor explain. "Point out to me the man she is going to marry. I would see for myself if he is worthy of her."

"Oh, Reggie Wharton is undoubtedly worthy. He has bundles of money. 'Tis said he made it all on trade, shipping goods back and forth to England. But some say he secretly dabbles in human flesh. Buys and sells workers for sugar plantations in the West Indies. This will be his second marriage. His first wife died of the coughing sickness, leaving no heirs. Being an older man—older than *you*, my lord—he is unlikely to allow Miss Mercy to run roughshod over him."

"Let us go and find her." Ian *had* to confront the young woman face to face. He could hardly wait to see how a second encounter would affect him.

"If you insist, Ian." Drew sounded reluctant.

"I do insist."

"My lord . . . wait a moment!"

Ian was already heading in the direction Mercy Collier had gone.

"I think you should be aware . . . that is, I must warn you . . . Mercy Collier has an uncanny ability to cause men to make fools of themselves."

Somehow, Ian cared not a whit.

CHAPTER TWO

Mercy was searching for her father, but as luck would have it, the first person who waylaid her was the last person she wanted to see: Reggie Wharton.

"There you are, my dear! I have been looking all over for you. Considering your reluctance to show your face this evening, one would almost think you were dreading your father's announcement about us."

Reggie's bold greeting took Mercy by surprise. She stopped in her tracks and studied him—heartily disliking what she saw. He was dressed from head to foot in a bilious shade of purple that made him look as old as her father and sallow-faced besides. It was unkind—and unfair—to judge people by appearances, but Mercy could not help feeling a strong aversion to Reggie. His attire was always impeccable and cut from the finest fabric, his wigs of enviable quality, and he could not be called ugly by any means, but his face and hands made her skin crawl whenever she thought of him touching or kissing her. His hands were too soft and white, his eyes too glittery. His nose was too hooked, his mouth too thin and cruel-looking. When he smiled, as he was doing now, he looked as if he had a problem with his bowels. The thought of marrying him made her shudder. She *had* to get out of this somehow!

"Is my father making some announcement?" She batted her lashes at him in a parody of innocence. "That would seem to be rushing things, would it not? You hardly know me, Mr. Wharton. And I do not really know you."

The grimace that passed for a smile deepened. "Surely you jest, my dear. You *know* I have spoken to your father. He gave me every reason to believe that you welcome the announcement he intends to make tonight."

"Perhaps you should have spoken to me *first*, Mr. Wharton. My opinion must surely count for something. Granted, you have money but no land, while we have land but little money. Monetary considerations aside, should not my *happiness* be important, too? And your own, as well?"

"Ah, but you *will* make me happy, my dear." He stepped closer to her, blocking out the faces of the surrounding guests. They were all trying to listen while appearing not to be doing so. "And I will endeavor to make *you* happy, too."

"That is what we must still determine, sir." Keeping her tone light and teasing, Mercy tapped him on his purple-clad chest with her fan. " 'Tis my hope that this evening will help us decide whether or not we can make each other happy."

His brows dipped in a frown and he rocked back on the heels of his silver-buckled shoes. "Exactly what do you demand of me? Shall I dance attendance on you, like so many of your previous suitors? Do not suggest I mount a horse, however, for riding is not my pleasure."

"For now, you may fetch us each a cup of punch," she answered. "And be sure to tell me if you spy my father near the punch bowl. I have been looking all over for him. He seems intent upon hiding *his* face, this evening."

"Stay right here, my dear. Punch I can manage."

"Oh, I am not planning on going anywhere." Mercy flipped open her fan and held it in front of the little drawstring bag dangling from her opposite wrist. The bag was jumping about as if it had a life of its own. Her little toad was apparently protesting both his confinement and his close proximity to the kerchief-wrapped ball of horse manure. No doubt he was longing for a refreshing plunge into a nice cool pond. But he would have to be patient. He had a job to do first, and only after he had completed his mission would she restore him to more congenial surroundings.

As Mercy stood smiling at guests who now felt free to approach her, she spotted a tall, broad-shouldered gentleman, a stranger she had never seen before. He was headed straight for her. For no reason she could name, her heart suddenly thumped against the walls of her chest. Her friend Caroline, a vision in blue silk, took her arm and whispered something, but Mercy had no idea what it was. The pounding in her breast spread rapidly to her ears, blocking out all other sounds. She could not glance away from the handsome, aristocratic face of the tall man advancing upon her.

His eyes were a crisp, clear blue, his nose straight and regal as a monarch's. The firm set of his jaw indicated a strength and determination many men seemed to lack in these days of elaborate powdered wigs and fanciful clothing.

She saw all this in a flash—noting that he was dressed in a more somber manner than the other male guests. His brocade frock coat was a restrained burgundy color and his waistcoat a soft butternut. His remarkably plain wig suggested that he wore it only out of deference to fashion but did not much care for curls or queues. She had the sudden intuition that he cared little for proprieties, either.

He has the bearing of a king in a roomful of commoners, she thought, and was sure he did exactly as he pleased in all circumstances. She could not imagine anyone telling *him* what to do or manipulating his affairs.

He walked right up to her, and she had to tilt back her head to look up at him. He reminded her of her father's friend Colonel Washington, only he was far more imposing!

Indeed, the stranger locked gazes with her in a most challenging manner, and for a moment, all they did was stand and stare at each other. They might have been alone in the room; Mercy could neither see past him nor hear anything being said around her.

A dreadful, horrid heat consumed her. For the first time in her life, she feared she might swoon and collapse in a puddle at a man's feet. His feet were clad in tall brown leather riding boots, she noticed. The boots had been polished to a high sheen, but were not entirely proper for a formal occasion where most of the men were wearing pumps with shiny buckles on them. Who *was* this man?

Wonder and curiosity filled her, increasing her light-headedness. Mercy fought to breathe deeply and maintain her composure. Perhaps, she thought ruefully, she ought to have eaten something before allowing Chloe to lace up her corset and stomacher. She had gone riding in the early morning, missed breakfast, and been too busy to think of eating for the remainder of the day.

Now, of course, it was too late to worry about the lack of nourishment. While she was struggling to regain control of her rioting emotions, a familiar figure pushed in front of the tall stranger.

"Miss Mercy, allow me to introduce a gentleman newly arrived from England," Drew Elliot announced. "I doubt you have had time to meet him yet."

"Mr. Elliot! How nice to see you again."

Until that moment, Mercy had not noticed Drew Elliot's absence from recent social occasions, but now she realized she had not seen him in a long time. She somehow managed to tear her gaze away from the stranger and felt instantly better for directing her attention to the young man who had changed little since she had last seen him many months ago. He still had a puppy-dog earnestness that greatly appealed to her, and she wished *he* had taken an interest in her rather than his close friend Mr. Lloyd. She still felt a lingering sense of guilt over *that* unfortunate incident.

"I have not met him yet, so you must of course introduce me, Mr. Elliot. I take it this gentleman is your guest?"

Mercy could not resist another glance into the stranger's clear blue eyes. He was still watching her as if he had already made her acquaintance and they had something special in common. Without saying a word, he seemed to be sending silent intimate messages. While she was accustomed to receiving admiring looks from men, Mercy could not recall being unnerved by them, and her cheeks burned as if they had suddenly burst into flame.

Mr. Elliot leaned forward and his voice dropped to a whisper. "He is a house guest of the McCallisters, Miss Mercy, but pray do not hold that against him. Before he arrived in Virginia, he had never met the McCallisters—and he knew nothing at all about Miss Prudence's refusal to join your industrious little women's group, the Daughters of Liberty."

Mercy instantly took offense. "I do not think of the Daughters of Liberty as a paltry 'little women's group,' Mr. Elliot. We, more than anyone, are proving to the British that we can very well do without them. As you may or may not have heard, we have been weaving our own cloth for some time now. Soon, we will never again have to rely on English textiles to clothe our backs, or yours either, for that matter. As for the McCallisters, my father graciously invited them here this evening, but my own preference is to ignore them. I find their loyalty to the king who has no respect for us quite tiresome. If *your* friend is also *their* friend, I cannot promise he will be a friend of mine."

"Mercy!" Caroline hissed in her ear. "I cannot believe you are being so rude to a total stranger."

Mercy could not believe it, either. Something about the man made her want to demonstrate that she was unimpressed by him. Perhaps it was because she was greatly impressed. Lifting her lashes, she gave him a long look.

"Forgive me for bluntly stating the truth, sir. I have no personal animosity toward you, but the McCallisters and I do not suit each other."

"You are entitled to choose your own friends, Miss Collier," the stranger said in a low, mellifluous voice that reminded her of being wrapped up in her best homespun cloak. "But at least give me the chance to make your acquaintance before you fetch the tar and feathers."

He had a very British accent. As soon as he opened his mouth, Mercy would have known at once that he was fresh from England. Those who had spent most of their lives in the colonies tended to sound "American." A New Englander spoke one way and a Southerner another, but this man spoke like a British lord, which was reason enough to despise him.

"What is your name, sir? I am, as you know already, Miss Mercy Collier. And you are . . . ?"

"Ian Montjoy," he said, inclining his head but not actually bowing to her.

"*Viscount* Montjoy," Mr. Elliot corrected. "He has come to Virginia to assess the potential for future investments."

"Oh! Are you interested in purchasing a healthy portion of rebellion, my lord? I assure you that we have a surfeit in America. Perhaps you would like to take some home with you to impress the king." Mercy knew she was being reckless as well as sarcastic, but she could not seem to help herself.

To her surprise, the viscount laughed. "I can see you have that commodity to spare, Miss Mercy. Is rebellion the main crop here at Collier Manor?"

"No, that would be tobacco," Mercy haughtily informed him. " 'Tis a pity, for I see nothing good about tobacco whereas rebellion has a definite appeal these days. Papa has been growing the noxious weed for a long time. Before the king decided to tax it so heavily, we did rather well in the tobacco business."

"On my way here this afternoon, I saw more than tobacco growing in your fields," Ian Montjoy noted. "You have wheat and corn also."

"Yes, we have all we need to be self-sufficient. But I would like to see us stop producing luxury items for British lords, so we can devote ourselves to growing more food for the local people."

"That sounds quite reasonable to me, Miss Collier. Your father does not agree?"

"Unfortunately not, my lord. Papa and I differ on many things—the management of Collier Manor being only one of them."

"I would not worry too much about that. If what I hear is true, you will soon have a husband to manage your future inheritance. Undoubtedly, your influence over *him* will be quite persuasive.''

''I intend it *shall* be . . . when I finally marry. Have you met my dear friend, Mrs. Darby?'' Intent on changing the subject of her possible nuptials, Mercy drew Caroline forward. Caroline had been hanging back and gazing at them with over-large eyes in a most awkward manner. ''Mr. Elliot, I am certain you and Caroline have met. Caroline, you remember Mr. Elliot. He was Mr. Lloyd's friend. We have not seen either of them in a long time.''

''I am delighted to renew your acquaintance, Mr. Elliot—and to meet a viscount, Lord Montjoy.'' Looking flustered, Caroline curtsyed. ''You must meet my husband. We, too, grow tobacco.''

''And do you, too, consider it a poor investment?''

''Well, it has been a better one in times past. You will have to discuss the matter with my husband, as my opinion on the subject hardly matters.''

''Of course it matters, Caroline!'' For years, Mercy had been trying to raise Caroline's self-esteem, without, apparently, much success. As long as her husband continued to lower it, poor Caroline would never learn to value her own opinion.

''The Darbys are in much the same position we are,'' Mercy hastened to explain. ''Rich in land, horses, slaves, and buildings. But struggling to remain solvent after years of being bled dry by a greedy monarch who cares nothing at all for his subjects.''

''Mercy!'' Caroline blushed to the roots of her powdered wig. ''This is hardly the time and place to voice such extreme sentiments.''

''I quite agree.'' Reggie Wharton reached around Mercy to hand her a punch cup. ''You must learn to curb your errant tongue, my dear, lest it one day get you in trouble. Ladies should not be discussing politics, anyway . . . but I suppose you were growing bored without me. Forgive me for taking so long to get back to you. I encountered quite a crush at the table and had to wait my turn at the punch bowl.''

"Mr. Wharton, sir!" Mr. Elliot cried. "Allow me to introduce Lord Montjoy."

"Montjoy?" Reggie's brows rose. "You are a guest of the McCallisters, are you not, your lordship? I saw Miss Prudence a few moments ago, and she mentioned you had accompanied them here tonight."

Mercy wished he had remained longer talking to Prudence. She wished he would spend the entire evening— and the rest of his life—with Prudence. The two deserved each other. They were a much better match than she herself and Reggie.

"Yes, I am their guest," Ian Montjoy responded. "We have mutual acquaintances in England, which is how I came to be staying with them."

Mutual acquaintances, Mercy thought, sipping her punch to hide her disgust. He was probably referring to Lord North, the king's prime minister. Prudence was always boasting that he was a relative—at least, she had done so before he acquired the same reputation as the king himself. If Ian Montjoy knew Lord North, he *must* be a rabid loyalist who had come to America to profit from the suffering of her beleaguered people. If things continued as they were, her own father would soon be reduced to selling property just to pay the king's exorbitant taxes . . . and vultures like Ian Montjoy would be standing in line to buy it.

Assess the potential for future investments—*rubbish!* He was here to rape the country.

"If you will excuse me, please, gentlemen!" she burst out. "I really need to find my father and . . . ah . . . see to the refreshments. This punch does not taste quite right. Do not drink it, Mr. Wharton." Mercy snatched the cup from his hand. "Follow me. I will fetch you another."

"Why, what is wrong with it?" Reggie protested. "It tastes perfectly fine to me. Besides, I should like to get to know Lord Montjoy better, and—"

"No, 'tis not right, I tell you! A new batch must be made at once. I will see to it and give you some of that." Holding the two cups in front of her, Mercy swept past Caroline, Reggie, Mr. Elliot, and the odious Ian Montjoy. She could not bear to remain in His Lordship's presence another moment, so much did he offend her sensibilities.

Normally, Mercy was able to make any guest feel welcome, even Prudence and her family. Only lately had it become intolerable to endure the company of potential enemies. The lines of battle were being drawn, making it impossible to ignore what was happening all over the colonies. A person was either unshakably loyal to England and the king, or eager to cast his lot with a new and as yet unformed nation that must break away from its origins and pursue its own destiny. No longer was it a matter of gray; it had become an issue of black and white.

Mercy knew which side *she* was on—and she was sure she knew where Ian Montjoy stood. Very soon now, everyone else attending these festivities would have to choose. In the meantime, she had business with a toad and a horse apple.

Watching Mercy Collier rudely desert them, Ian felt a pang of irritation mixed with admiration. The lady knew how to speak her mind—and how to let people know when she did not like them. The disdain of a beautiful woman might demoralize many men, but Ian found himself invigorated by it.

The more difficult and temperamental the horse, the more satisfying it was to convince the animal that it *wanted* to do his bidding. Mercy Collier was no easy conquest, yet he sensed that when she gave her heart, she would give it totally, holding nothing in reserve. Her vibrant beauty along with her elusiveness probably accounted for the covert glances even the married men sent her way.

It seemed to Ian that every male in the room and beyond—in the entire house—was acutely and physically aware of her. Nor could the women ignore her. All eyes followed her out of the chamber and marked the way Reggie Wharton followed so closely on her heels. Wharton appeared annoyed at her bossiness, but helpless to resist her commands. Ian suspected that if she had given *him* a command, he, too, would have followed her to hell and back, not just to the punch bowl.

Pity the poor man who finally weds her, he thought. Envy pierced him. Wedding and bedding such an exquisite creature would be a great adventure, indeed. He was sorry she was already taken—and he himself was committed to Elizabeth.

"Well, that was our Miss Mercy," Drew Elliot said with a wry shake of his head. "Do you not feel as if a storm has just swept through the room?"

"She has a good heart," Mrs. Darby began, rushing to her defense.

"Oh, I meant no criticism!" Drew assured her. "Indeed, I'm quite certain her heart is good. Strong, too. Well armored, one might say—impervious to assault by mere mortal man."

Caroline's husband joined her just then, and after another round of introductions, Ian excused himself and casually strolled into the next room, where a groaning table held various liquid refreshments and an array of dainties to tempt the appetite before the announcement of supper.

There, from the corner of his eye, he was able to watch his outspoken hostess supervise the emptying and refilling of the enormous silver punch bowl that dominated the table. Several regal-looking Negro servants bore numerous vessels to and from the punch bowl, until Miss Collier deemed the final concoction suitable for her guests' enjoyment. With a gay little flourish, amidst much laughter and merriment, she began filling cups and handing them around to the onlookers. So graceful and enchanting was she that Ian could not look away. He feared he was doomed to stare at her whenever the opportunity presented itself.

While she fussed with the punch cups, Reggie Wharton stood conversing with others but occasionally cast a possessive glance in Miss Collier's direction. Ian thought it a mark of how little she cared for the man that she served him *last,* after seeing to the needs of her other guests. Ian received a cup of punch from her hands before Reggie did. She did not look at him as she thrust the cup into

Ian's hands with enough force that the red-hued liquid slopped over onto his waistcoat and made a large stain, which she failed to notice.

When she finally did serve Reggie Wharton, it was in a strange, half-furtive manner. She dipped out a cupful of punch, turned away for a brief moment, and fumbled with the little drawstring bag at her wrist. Ian was watching closely but the punch bowl hid her motions, and he could not see what she was doing. When she turned back toward Reggie, her smile as she offered him the libation was as bright as the sun.

"Here you are, sir! See if you do not think this is much better than the last batch. I think you will agree I have greatly improved it."

"I suspect you went to a great deal of bother for nothing, my dear—such deplorable waste! I can see I will have to teach you to be more provident."

Wharton took the cup, saluted her with it, and raised it to his lips. No sooner had the vessel touched his mouth than he let loose a howl of outrage and held the cup at arm's length. Half its contents sloshed on the polished wood floor and everyone stared in horror.

"Why, Mr. Wharton!" Miss Collier exclaimed, her green eyes dancing. "Whatever is wrong, sir?"

"Wrong!" he bellowed. "Why, look for yourself! There's a . . . a digusting, loathsome *toad* in my punch. *Swimming* in it . . . and putting me at great risk for contracting some fatal fever!"

"What?" Miss Collier peered into his cup with a great show of surprise that Ian instantly knew was false. "Goodness, do you think he could really be diseased? He looks quite healthy to me, sir. What do *you* think, Mr. Jefferson?" she asked the nearest bystander, the patrician-looking pamphlet writer Drew had earlier pointed out to Ian.

The gleam of amusement in Miss Collier's eyes suggested that she was not in the least as shocked as she should have been. Her lips curved in a charming half-smile that made Ian want to laugh out loud and share in the joke. Thomas Jefferson also seemed to be trying hard not to laugh.

"He appears to be a healthy specimen of toad-dom to me, Miss Mercy."

Wharton was not in the least amused. He looked ready to kill someone. "Will someone please explain how this toad got in my cup?" he demanded, red-faced and fuming.

"Dear me, I cannot explain it," Mercy demurred apologetically. "He must have hopped though the open window and headed straight for the punch bowl, thinking it a fine spot to refresh himself. I never noticed him when I dipped him out. Shall I fetch you another cup? I hope he did not . . . you know . . . relieve himself in the punch."

The men broke into guffaws, and laughter erupted among the ladies, though several peered suspiciously into their own cups. *She is really quite outrageous,* Ian thought, trying without success to keep a straight face.

Wharton only turned a deeper shade of red—a color that clashed woefully with his purple frock coat. "If this is meant to be an insult . . ." he sputtered. "Where is your father? I would know the meaning of this little incident, and I would know it now."

Ian could hardly believe the man was making so much of a harmless prank; did he have no sense of humor? If it had happened to *him,* he would have plucked the toad out of his cup and as calmly as possible dropped it down the front of Miss Collier's décolletage—by accident, of course.

"Here, here. . . . What is the cause of all this commotion? Has something dire happened?" A rotund man with a red face and a belly to match pushed his way into the midst of the trouble. "Mercy? . . . What is going on here?"

"A toad!" Reggie Wharton bellowed like a wounded bull. "I found a toad in my punch. Do you mean to insult me, sir?"

At that moment, the toad made a frantic leap for freedom. Three ladies screamed and jumped backwards, but the toad only landed on the floor, where he sat for a moment, looking stunned, before hopping across the crowded room in the direction of the open window. The crowd parted to let him pass, and an elderly female in a bright yellow gown put a hand to her head as if she were swooning, and fell backwards into the arms of a startled gentleman.

A man Ian did not recognize whipped out a pistol from beneath his frock coat and shouted: "Stand back, everyone! I shall dispatch the little bugger."

Acting instinctively, Ian launched himself. "Put that away!" he roared, grabbing the weapon. "Do not be a fool. Someone will get hurt if you fire in here."

"He is escaping!" the man cried, lunging to retrieve his pistol.

" 'Tis only a toad—not a thief or murderer." Ian had to wrestle with the fellow to keep him from reclaiming the pistol. Only the timely assistance of Thomas Jefferson and Colonel Washington enabled him to hang onto the thing. "Calm yourself, sir, and I will give you back your weapon, but only if you promise not to discharge it in here."

"He is right, Benjamin," Colonel Washington said, apparently acquainted with the owner of the pistol. "Someone will get hurt if you persist in this folly."

"Millicent has lost her wig!" someone cried, and the center of the fracas shifted to the fallen woman in yellow who had indeed lost her wig. The huge mass of powdered hair had toppled off her head and rolled sideways, revealing a slicked-down wad of dirty-looking gray hair in its woefully natural state.

Forgetting all about their voluminous skirts, several women bent over the unfortunate Millicent, and Ian was treated to a shocking view of feminine pulchritude which drew gasps and muffled laughter all around him.

"Ladies, look to your comportment!" shouted the rotund little man with the scarlet waistcoat.

More tumult ensued before order was restored, the women righted themselves, and Millicent regained both consciousness and her lost wig. By then, the toad had disappeared completely. During all this, Miss Collier was biting down hard enough on her lower lip to draw blood from the tender tissue.

Reggie Wharton still looked furious. "Collier, I demand to know the meaning of this incident. How and why did a toad get into my punch? Am I the victim of some monstrous plot between you and your daughter to make me look ridiculous?''

Ian thought he was doing well enough on his own to make himself look ridiculous; he needed no help from anyone else.

"Of course not, my good man!" barked Miss Collier's sire. "Do you take me for a charlatan? We have an agreement, you and I. My land and my daughter for your—"

"Dinner!" Miss Collier announced. "I believe what we all need now is dinner served straightaway. Do you not agree, Papa? A lovely meal will soothe our ravaged nerves. Mr. Wharton, will you escort me? Cook has prepared a veritable feast for the senses. Wait until you taste the soup. 'Tis filled with the most savory ingredients.''

"We have not settled the matter of the toad!"

"But I have already *told* you. He was an uninvited guest. Forget about the punch. I will instruct the servants to pour it all out. Would you prefer hard cider? We will have wine with dinner. It came all the way from France.''

In the wake of her solicitude, which Ian did not for a moment believe was genuine, Wharton finally succumbed. "Oh, all right! . . . What sort of soup did you say we were having?'' he demanded in a petulant fashion.

" 'Tis a very special blend of delectable meats and root vegetables. You will love it, Mr. Wharton. . . . Will he not, Papa? 'Tis your own favorite. My dear departed mother cherished this receipt, and I myself supervised the making of the soup.''

"Indeed,'' Reggie Wharton said, flaring his nostrils as if he could already smell it. "I vow, you are making my mouth water.''

"Come along, all of you,'' Miss Collier urged. "I promise you a meal to remember.''

Following the crowd, Ian thought about what she had just said. He could not have said why, but he had a sudden premonition that it *would* be a meal to remember. Miss Collier was planning some surprise. He wondered that no one but himself could see it. She had deliberately put the toad in Mr. Wharton's punch cup, and he would wager his much loved stallion that she intended further deviltry at dinner.

Her father and Mr. Wharton had apparently reached an agreement about her future without consulting her, and she was piqued. More than piqued, she was determined to change things.

Ian laughed softly to himself. He had not been so amused in a long time. What would she come up with next? . . . Would it be enough to discourage her suitor? Wharton did not look like the type to give up easily, especially when an estate like Collier Manor was involved.

The thought was sobering. In all probability, Miss Collier would only succeed in destroying her own chances for marital happiness. If Wharton were at all determined, he would ignore his future wife's mischief and bide his time until he gained control of her inheritance and could exercise complete authority over her. He had plenty of time to exact vengeance.

Ian could recall several instances where mean-spirited men had insisted on buying beautiful, free-spirited horses. They had then devoted themselves to eradicating the very qualities which had attracted them in the first place. Inevitably, they turned the engaging creatures into submissive brow-beaten hacks too beaten-down and brokenhearted to warrant any man's envy and attention.

Reggie Wharton struck him as that sort of man, and Ian suddenly had no stomach for dinner. He had no desire to witness Miss Collier's doomed efforts to spare herself from an abysmal mismatch. What was her father thinking? Why would he give his only child to Reggie Wharton, a man twice his daughter's age who obviously had nothing in common with her?

Money. It was certainly because of money. Reggie had it, and Collier Manor needed it.

As the guests seated themselves at the longest table he had ever seen, Ian studied Mercy Collier's father, Daniel. Despite his round face and figure and his florid coloring, accentuated by the garish garments he had chosen to wear this night, the man did not look well. All his movements were slow and stiff. He tried to hide the fact, but his hands shook.

He fears dying before he can get her safely wed.

The grim suspicion added a new dimension to an evening already spoiled. Ian sighed. He would try his best to remain a disinterested observer. Unfortunately, he was already interested. Far more than he wanted to be. Or *ought* to be. Whatever happened, he could take no part in it. Miss Collier would have to look after herself.

CHAPTER THREE

"This soup is everything you claimed it to be," Reggie Wharton murmured, leaning across the table toward her. He kept his voice low enough to avoid interrupting the flow of conversation around them. "It is delicious, my dear."

"I'm so glad you like it," Mercy responded, trying not to feel guilty. "Have you guessed the secret ingredient?"

"Not yet, but I still have almost the entire bowl left, including this large round thing here. Whatever can it be, I wonder?"

A donation from Liberty. Look a little closer and you will figure it out, Mr. Wharton. Do look before you bite into it.

Mercy was surprised by her own tendency toward remorsefulness. At the last moment, she had almost *not* slipped the horse apple into the bowl of soup she had insisted upon personally serving Reggie Wharton. However, she had only to recall the statements he had been making to her father only a few moments ago to be reminded of why she was resorting to such drastic measures.

First, he had disparaged horses, calling them "absurd

creatures with puny minds but useful bodies—rather like women in that regard."

Then he had ridiculed patriots, referring to them as "illiterate malcontents who will bring ruin upon themselves and America if they ever have a chance to make the decisions in this country." This despite the fact that he very well knew that most of the people in the room considered themselves patriots.

Finally, he had dubbed King George III as "our beloved misunderstood monarch who only has our best interests at heart."

His comments had caused a ripple of indignation up and down the long table, at which point Mercy had suggested they cease discussing politics for the duration of the evening.

"Excellent idea," Colonel Washington had agreed, while his plump, pert wife Martha, whom he called Patcy, nodded and smiled in relief. The colonel's face was a rosy color, indicative of deep emotion, but for the sake of politeness, he was obviously restraining himself.

Even the fiery Patrick Henry seemed determined to avoid arguments at the dinner table, though he had been holding forth with great exuberance before they sat down.

Mercy was disappointed that her own father had not taken exception to Reggie's views, but tonight he seemed more distracted than usual. Ephraim McCallister, meanwhile, was at this very moment agreeing with Reggie, pointing out that the rabble-rousers in Boston deserved to be punished for refusing to bow to the king's authority.

"We cannot support anarchy and the breaking of the law!" he insisted, pounding his fist down with enough force to rattle the silverware.

With a weary sigh, her father finally roused himself and set down his spoon. "As long as we get no trouble here in Virginia, I shall stand by the king, Ephraim. But if matters ever get to the point where George sends his lobsterbacks against me and mine, look out! I will be the first to take up arms against them."

Heads nodded around the table, including Colonel Washington's whose face had gone from rose to red. Before anyone could say anything more, Lord Montjoy inquired in a casual drawl: "When does foxhunting season begin around here? I am curious to know the proper manner of dress for pursuing the sport in Virginia. I may need to have something made if I am to accept all your kind invitations."

The abrupt change of subject raised a few eyebrows, but Martha Washington eagerly responded.

"Oh, it will not be cold enough to hunt until November, my lord. Before that, everyone will be too busy with the harvest anyway. As for the manner of dress, I would think you might wear whatever is acceptable for a hunt in England."

"You *have* hunted in England certainly," John Willardson, their closest neighbor, interjected.

"Oh, a bit," Ian Montjoy conceded.

His modest tone annoyed Mercy. Anyone could see it was false. As a viscount, Ian Montjoy had very likely been Master of the Hunt, as her own father had once been and several other men—including Colonel Washington—still were. He had probably kept his own hounds, and knew exactly what manner of dress would be appropriate for the hunt field anywhere in the world. Still, she had to admire how easily he was deflecting a potentially disastrous dispute among the guests.

"Do tell me about your American customs," he now said, as if he were the greenest novice at the sport.

What a sham you are! Mercy thought, her annoyance growing. By now, everyone at the table knew he was a viscount newly arrived from England. One would expect him to defend the king and the aristocracy, yet here he was, prattling about foxhunting customs.

As several people eagerly embraced the subject, Mercy sat and fumed. Not even counting Lord Montjoy, she had plenty to fume about. Surely her father must see that a match between her and Reggie would be a great mistake! If she were foolish enough to actually marry the man, they would spend all their time arguing . . . or did Papa expect her to somehow keep her mouth closed for the rest of her life and never utter a word of protest no matter *what* outrageous things her husband said or did?

She was heartsick—not merely over the situation with Reggie but because of her deteriorating relationship with her father. Lately, the rift between them had been widening. Gone were the days when Papa doted upon her, granting her every whim and delighting in her every accomplishment. Once, they had shared everything and spent hours on horseback together, riding around the estate, supervising the daily activities of the workers, debating the best way to do things . . .

But one day Papa had gotten an odd look on his face, lost consciousness, and toppled off his stallion, Rubric. After that, he had never been the same. The doctors said he had a weak heart. They bled him, dosed him with physics, and cautioned him not to overdo. . . . Now, he sat indoors most of the day and brooded alone in his study.

Mercy saw him only at the dinner hour, and then he spoke little except to berate her for not yet having married. He wanted grandchildren before he died. Insisted that it was her duty to marry as she could not possibly manage Collier Manor on her own. Ignored the fact that she had been managing it quite well for years, albeit with his indulgent supervision. Apparently, he regretted ever having encouraged her to develop her mind and now wished that she would behave more like . . . Prudence McCallister!

In sharp contrast to herself, Prudence enjoyed womanly tasks, clung to hearth and home, and behaved as if men were the only members of the human race to be granted intelligence and the right to manage their own affairs. Prudence *always* did as she was told. She *rejoiced* in her conformity to parental expectations, letting everyone know that *she*—Prudence McCallister—epitomized filial virtue . . . except that *she* wasn't married, either. Only one man had ever offered for her, but since he had no money, her father had not approved of the alliance. Thereafter Miss Prudence had professed herself delighted to remain unwed.

In the midst of these grim thoughts, Mercy watched Reggie Wharton scoop the horse apple onto his spoon and balance it in front of him so he could bite into it. Just as he raised the spoon to his mouth, her conscience got the best of her.

"Mr. Wharton, stop!" She half-rose from her chair. "You do not want to eat that. It might make you ill."

"*Ill?*" His brows shot up. "Why should it make me ill?"

He probed the horse apple with one long finger, then gingerly leaned down and sniffed it. Comprehension suddenly lit his eyes. Still, he did not seem to believe what his senses were telling him. He looked up and down the table, searching the crockery of the other guests. No one else had anything in their bowls resembling the firm round ball teetering precariously on his spoon. The guests sat frozen in place, watching in stunned amazement.

Reggie's glance came back to Mercy, and this time a spark of fury flared in his eyes. "If this is what I think it is . . ." he began.

"It is," she said. "I put it purposely in your soup to let you know exactly what I think of your offer of marriage. We will never suit, you see. You and my father made this agreement without consulting me or taking my feelings into account. The toad was my idea, too. I freely admit it. I was willing to try anything to make you change your mind about marrying me."

"Well, you have succeeded. I *have* changed my mind." In a quick twist of his wrist, Reggie flung the horse apple across the table at her. Mercy instinctively ducked and had to grab her wig lest it fall in the soup tureen. The turd splattered on the wall behind her and scattered in bits on the floor.

There were several loud gasps, punctuated by her father's wounded roar. "*Mercy!* In God's name, girl, you have gone too bloody damn far this time!"

Reggie's face was the color of his coat as he pushed back from the table and rose to his feet. "This finishes it, Collier. Our deal is off. I wouldn't wed your impossible daughter if you offered me an estate twice the size of Collier Manor. She just tried to *poison* me!"

"No, no—it was but a prank!" her father pleaded, rising also. "My daughter has a rare and ofttimes twisted sense of humor. After you are wed, you have only to forbid her to play any more—''

"There will be no wedding! Did you not hear what I just said? She is a scheming, devious . . . *patriot.* That is what she is! I doubt not that if I *did* wed her, she would be holding meetings to encourage rebellion right behind my back. You have raised her with far too much leniency. What you should have done was whip her senseless years ago when you might still have achieved some good by it.''

"Whip my own daughter?" Her father drew himself up to his full height. "Do you take her for a horse or a beast of burden? Whip her I shall *not,* sir! Nor would I lay a whip on anything of value I owned—human or animal. Depart this house and never again show your face here. You are no longer welcome. Nor is anyone else who maligns my daughter *or* her efforts to free us from the yoke of England.''

"Oh, Papa!" Mercy wanted to cheer and hug him at the same time. "I knew you were a patriot at heart—and that you must soon see that Reggie and I have nothing in common.''

"You and your daughter are fools, sir, and vile traitors to the crown!" Reggie hollered. "I am delighted to take my leave of you both.''

As he stalked from the house, shouting for his horse, her father turned his ire on her. "What you say may be true, Mercy, but 'tis still a wicked, heartless thing you have done this night. You have shamed both me and Mr. Wharton in front of the finest families in Virginia. Ladies and gentlemen . . .'' he turned to their guests, most of whom were watching in open-mouthed embarrassment. "I beg your pardon, but suddenly I have lost my appetite. I feel unwell. Stay and finish your meal. But please excuse me as I must go lie down. In solitude, I will ask myself what I have done to deserve such a difficult, disobedient daughter.''

Mercy was stung to the quick. "Papa!"

A quick glance at their guests revealed an avid determination to avoid catching her eye. Even Colonel Washington —who had clearly been angered by Reggie's comments— appeared absorbed by the centerpiece of fruit and flowers, as was his wife. Only Lord Montjoy dared to look directly at her. His expression was thoughtful as his gaze met hers.

Then—incredibly—he smiled and *winked*.

She had been ready to dissolve into tears but suddenly rallied. The incident *had* been funny. Funny and most effective. If she lived to be a hundred years old, she would never forget the look on Mr. Wharton's face when he realized he had been about to bite into a ball of horse manure.

However, she had never meant to shame her father and make him regret having her as his only child! She had never meant to do that at all. Only Ian Montjoy—of all people—seemed able to see that. Even Caroline refused to look at her.

"Forgive me, Papa." Summoning all her courage, she managed to keep her voice from wavering.

He spoke not a word. Walking like an old, old man, he ignored her apology and shuffled from the room.

"Forgive me, all of you!" she begged. "I regret having disturbed your dinner. I should never have forced you to witness this unfortunate display of my wickedness. But please do stay and finish the excellent meal Cook has prepared. I'm going to make certain Papa is resting comfortably. After that, I will rejoin you for the remainder of the evening. I intended it shall be far more pleasant than the portion you have thus far endured."

"No need for you t' leave your guests, Miss Mercy," Chloe said from the doorway. "I can look after your Pa. He doan wanna see you right now, anyway."

"Thank you, Chloe. Perhaps you are right. I will remain and give Papa's anger a chance to cool."

"Well, *really* . . ." Prudence McCallister huffed into the awkward silence.

Mercy's attention—along with everyone else's—fastened on the young woman who sat between her stern-faced parents. She wore pink—a girlish, unbecoming hue for one of her maturity and pale coloring.

"Prudence, did you wish to say something?" Mercy refused to be intimidated by a guest in her own home.

"I only wish to know if you poisoned *our* food as well.

Will we all become ill for eating the soup or drinking the punch? I confess to feeling queasy already."

"No, of course not. The only soup or punch I tampered with was Mr. Wharton's."

"It makes me ill to think of it—poor Mr. Wharton! Someone should check to see if he is all right. On his way home he may fall off his horse and . . ."

Ephraim McCallister suddenly stood. "Prudence knows whereof she speaks. Someone should check on Mr. Wharton. We will leave at once and do so on our way home. I have had enough of being insulted for one evening."

"Insulted?" Mercy echoed. "How have *you* been insulted?"

"*You,* Miss Collier. You are an insult to all of us. You and your Daughters of Liberty. We should have known better than to come here this evening—or to bring Lord Montjoy. My lord, I apologize for exposing you to this rebellious riffraff. We will seek out Mr. Wharton whose attitudes are far more compatible to our own. And we will rejoice with him that he is well rid of a young woman who would only have brought him misery, as she has done her own father. Anyone else who feels as we do is welcome to join us at *my* estate. . . . Lord Montjoy, are you coming?"

Lord Montjoy had not moved a muscle. Nor had he blinked an eye. "I will join you later, Ephraim," he replied in an even tone. It was impossible to tell if he agreed with Ephraim or simply refused to be controlled by him. "I still have business to discuss with Mr. Elliot. Go ahead. I will be along when I am ready."

"*I* will go with you, McCallister," said Angus Croughton, a man Mercy had long suspected of being a loyalist.

"So will I," another voice chimed in, this one from a "fence straddler."

"Well, I intend to remain right here," said Patrick Henry. "And if several other prominent Virginians I could name had been able to make it tonight, you can be certain *they* would remain also. *You* are staying, are you not, Colonel Washington?"

Colonel Washington nodded. "I see no reason to remove myself from this house."

"I am staying, too," Thomas Jefferson added. "In truth, I see more reason to remain than to depart."

Oh, dear! Mercy thought. *It was turning into a split between patriots and loyalists, after all.*

She had never meant for *this* to happen.

"I should like more soup," Caroline blurted, sounding quite determined.

"Caroline!" Her husband looked aghast at the notion.

"Well, I am still hungry," she explained, darting a quick sympathetic glance at Mercy. "Besides, Mr. Wharton only got what he deserved."

"Caroline, be quiet! What has gotten into you?" her husband demanded.

"Nothing has gotten into me, William," she calmly countered. "I would simply like to have more soup."

"So would I!" Arabella Lee piped up. She was one of the most enthusiastic supporters of the Daughters of Liberty. She lifted her bowl and held it out to Mercy. "Fill it up, Mercy dear, only refrain from putting anything too exotic in it, will you? I have never tasted barn dainties before, but I fear they will not agree with my stomach."

Laughter exploded around the table. Mercy herself could not suppress a giggle.

"We are getting out of here *now!*" Ephraim McCallister shouted.

He swept out of the room with his wife, daughter, and all his supporters in tow.

"Good-bye!" Arabella called out. "And good riddance," she added in a loud whisper. More laughter ensued.

"Thank you all for standing by me," Mercy sighed, soup ladle in hand. "I am truly grateful, my friends."

"No need to thank me," Ian Montjoy protested. "I did nothing of note."

You stayed, Mercy thought, although she was not at all sure what his staying meant.

Probably nothing.

A British lord could not possibly side with a bunch of patriots, could he? . . . So why had he stayed? And what was the meaning of the smile and the wink he had given her?

*   *   *

"Good-bye, Miss Collier," Lord Montjoy said, bowing slightly. "Thank you for a most diverting evening."

"Are you and Mr. Elliot certain you don't wish to spend the night?" Mercy inquired, as was only proper. " 'Tis a long ride back to the McCallisters, and the hour is late. Several of our other guests have decided to remain."

"Oh, we have already had a couple of offers from your nearest neighbors," Drew Elliot assured her. "We need not impose upon *you*, Miss Mercy."

"You will be staying with one of them?" She wondered which one it might be.

"*I* will not," Ian Montjoy answered. "A long ride is good for clearing the head. Besides, the moon is exceptionally bright tonight and dawn cannot be far off."

"Be careful of ruts in the road," she warned. "One must always keep a sharp watch when riding at night."

"My stallion is sure-footed. I am not worried," Lord Montjoy said. "I am glad I rode instead of joining the McCallisters in their carriage. Otherwise, I would have been forced to depart when they did. Then I would have missed the chance to become acquainted with so many fine people."

"Ephraim will be angry you stayed." Mercy could think of nothing else to say. She had avoided speaking to Lord Montjoy for almost the entire time he had been there. However, she had been acutely aware of where he was at every moment and to whom he had been speaking. He had spent a long time in conversation with Colonel Washington and Thomas Jefferson—had even sought out Patrick Henry.

He had made an obvious effort to get to know all of these important people, and she could not help wondering about his motives. She still did not trust him. He could be as friendly as he wished to her friends, but when all was said and done, he was still a British lord and a guest of the McCallisters. He undoubtedly had family and friends in England, all of whom were loyal to George III.

"If Ephraim is distressed by my behavior this evening,

he will have to deal with it," Lord Montjoy answered. "If he is too distressed, I will look for other quarters."

"Oh, you should have no lack of invitations, Ian!" Mr. Elliot exclaimed. "As I keep telling you, Virginia is known for its hospitality. Were my own circumstances not so modest at the moment, you could stay with me, but—"

"I am not looking for new quarters yet, my friend. Come, 'tis time we depart. Miss Collier looks weary."

Weary, she thought, hoping she did not have bags as big as anvils under her eyes. For once in her life, she wished she were stunningly beautiful—the sort of woman to make a man like Ian Montjoy fall hopelessly in love with her. Then she could disappoint him, as she had so many others! Men were only interested in her land, anyway. The certainty of a large inheritance was what drew them to her, not her physical beauty and certainly not her active mind, which many considered a serious flaw in a woman.

Ian Montjoy started to turn away, but Mr. Elliot seemed reluctant to leave. "Miss Mercy, will we be seeing you at the Willardsons in two weeks' time?"

"The Willardsons?" Mercy dimly recalled accepting an invitation to the Willardsons for a summer party in early July, two weeks away. "Why, yes, I suppose you will—that is, if both of you will be attending."

"I would not miss it for the world," Mr. Elliot enthused. "Mr. Willardson has challenged His Lordship to a race involving his stallion, Thor, and Mr. Willardson's stallion, Old Pig Eye."

"Really!" Mercy decided she did not want to miss it for the world, either. Despite his homely name and appearance, Old Pig Eye was an extremely fast horse. It would be a pleasure to watch him beat Ian Montjoy's horse and teach him a lesson about underestimating Virginians. In addition to foxhunting, horse racing was another favorite local sport, one which had been curtailed lately due to recent political events.

"We cannot spend *all* our time planning how to break away from England," Mr. Elliot defended. "Life must still go on, eh?"

"Indeed, it must, sir," Mercy said. "I will look forward to watching you race, my lord."

His Lordship's eyes gleamed with amusement. "I will look forward to watching you watch me race."

He had known she was watching him all evening! Had she been that obvious?

"Well, perhaps I will be too busy gossiping with the ladies to find time to watch you," she coldly informed him.

His smile only broadened, and Mr. Elliot was quick to protest. "Why, Miss Mercy, everyone knows what an avid horsewoman you are. You never spend time with the ladies when there is a horse race or a foxhunt under way. You are right out there with all the gentlemen, either participating or placing your own bets."

"This time I will bet on Old Pig Eye," she retorted.

Both men laughed. "Not me," said Mr. Elliot. "I have seen His Lordship's stallion, Thor, and I am convinced he is the better horse."

"You are entitled to your own opinion, Mr. Elliot. But do remember how deceiving looks can be."

As she said the words, Mercy decided to keep a close watch on Ian Montjoy at any social occasions they mutually attended. Let him think she was personally interested in him if he was arrogant enough to do so! She intended to discover what he was up to—why he had not departed with the McCallisters. Could he possibly be spying on the planters? Determining who was still loyal to the crown and who was not?

Many people privately supported rebellion but feared the consequences of openly challenging England. Tobacco planters, in particular, had to be careful. They would have no market for their goods if they became too vocal in support of independence. In the event of full-scale war, Bostonians and other city folk had far less to lose than wealthy Virginians.

Yes, she would keep an eye on Ian Montjoy and not allow herself to be charmed by his easy smile, diplomatic ways, and certainly not by his knowing blue eyes or handsome appearance. The man had a long way to go to win *her* friendship.

"Until we meet again, gentlemen." She smiled politely but kept her tone chilly.

Ian Montjoy grinned. "Until we meet again, Miss Collier."

After the two men had departed, Mercy bade farewell to other guests who were leaving, saw to the comfort of those who were staying, and then went to check on her father. A single beeswax taper burned in his chamber, illuminating the large bedstead on which he lay, dressed in his nightshirt and cap, his eyes closed and his breathing deep and slumberous.

She was happy to find him resting peacefully and not sitting in his chair, staring into space and looking forlorn. Quickly, she went to the bedside table to remove the taper in its engraved pewter holder. No sooner had she lifted it when her father opened his eyes and turned his head to look at her.

"Papa?" She paused, candle in hand. "Are you feeling better?"

"I am feeling miserable," he responded. "And 'tis all your fault. . . . Who will have you now, Mercy? I will go to my grave without seeing you safely wed or knowing if I shall have descendants."

"Papa, I am so sorry!" Mercy replaced the candle on the table and sat down beside him on the edge of the bed. "I never meant to hurt or disappoint you. 'Tis just that I could not abide marrying Mr. Wharton, and I knew you would never listen to me if I tried to dissuade you from pursuing this union. I had to *show* you how unsuitable he was!"

"That you did—*show* me," he sighed, but the corners of his mouth turned up a little. "The man is a pompous ass. The matter with the toad was bad enough, but I will not soon forget the look on his face when he discovered that *thing* you put in his soup."

Mercy was trying to look repentant, but she could not suppress a smile. " 'Twas evil of me, I know. But I didn't let him actually bite into it. At the last moment, I lost my nerve."

"After reviewing the matter, I think maybe you *should*

have let him bite into it. What he had to say beforehand
did not much impress me. I had not realized he was so
attached to the monarchy. Why, if that viscount—what's
his name again?—had not changed the subject, we might
have had a brawl on our hands at the dinner table."

"Ian. Ian Montjoy," Mercy said, feeling a quiver of
excitement and pleasure at the mere mention of his name.

"Montjoy, eh? If I ever see the man again, I shall have
to thank him for keeping the situation in hand. He kept
that hothead Benjamin from shooting off his pistol, too,
did he not? His Lordship could have sided with Wharton,
you know—and stirred things up royally. McCallister alone
was a disaster, but if a viscount had joined in defending
King George and belittling most of our neighbors, you can
be certain we would have come to blows."

"Yet I wonder how he *really* feels," Mercy murmured.

"Who—Montjoy? I should imagine he supports the
king, but at least he had the good manners to keep from
insulting my guests. Which is more than I can say for
Wharton or McCallister. I am done with 'em, Mercy. Hope
to God I have seen the last of 'em."

"Papa, you were going to *marry* me to Reggie Wharton,"
Mercy gently reminded him. "Now, do you not think you
should forgive me for doing all I could to expose the man's
true character?"

"Humph!" her father groused, reaching out to take her
hand. "I just want what is best for you, my girl. Nothing
more, nothing less. Marriage is what is best for you. I hate
to say it—dread seeing it come—but we could well go to
war with George's lobsterbacks. If we do, you need a husband to protect and defend you. To decide what is best
for Collier Manor and all our people here. I cannot do it
anymore. And you cannot do it, either."

"Papa, I—" she began.

"No, Mercy. I have been wrong all these years. I see it
clearly now. I never should have led you to believe you
were equal to a man when it comes to decisions about the
estate. Can you hold off a bunch of soldiers if they suddenly
show up at the door with muskets and order you to hand
over the house to serve as military headquarters?"

"Well, perhaps not, but neither could—"

"Well, nothing! You would not stand a chance . . . and 'tis coming to that, Mercy. I can see it plain as your doubting face. You are a woman. You should have little ones clinging to your skirts by now. Domestic matters should occupy all your time—not politics. If there is war, it will be a man's war, which is only as it should be."

"Nonsense!" Mercy erupted. "Women will be involved as well. We are already involved. The Daughters of Liberty have no less of a responsibility to our future than the Sons of Liberty."

"I am too tired to argue any more tonight. You need a husband, Mercy, and if it is not going to be Reggie Wharton, you had better find someone more to your liking. You have rejected every single man who has expressed an interest in you—rejected them and driven them off. Now, who is it going to be?"

"I do not know, Papa. All the best men seem to be taken."

She thought of Colonel Washington, who was far older than she and devoted to his dear Patcy besides. *He* was the sort of man who attracted her—someone with solid values and an idealism she could share. A man she could respect. Someone whose integrity, strength, and honor were easily recognized.

Colonel Washington had proven himself to be a leader among men—but he was already taken, and she could think of no one else who stirred her soul . . . except Ian Montjoy. Quickly, she corrected herself. He seemed to have the capacity to stir her *body*, not her soul. She felt contempt for him rather than respect. Indeed, she could not understand why she had thought of him at all in the context of a husband. She certainly would not think of him again. She hoped never to see him again. Perhaps she would not attend the Willardsons' summer party after all.

"So when is our next chance?" Papa suddenly demanded.

"Chance?" Mercy echoed.

"To get out in society! To look over the crop."

"The crop—"

"The crop of young men! Bloody damn, Mercy, you

must look over the crop and make your choice *this summer,* or I swear I will cut you out of my will entirely. Collier Manor will not be yours after all.''

"Papa, are you threatening to disinherit me if I fail to marry? ... And do stop swearing. It shows a want of culture.''

"Bloody damn right I am, girl! The place will be sold at auction and the proceeds given to the Sons of Liberty— or the poor folks in Boston. Maybe that viscount fellow will want to buy it. I heard someone say he was looking for a good investment. Not that Collier Manor will be all that good if things continue to go the way they are. He probably has money to wait out the hard times—and influence back home in England to ensure that his tobacco brings a good price.''

"Papa, you would *not!*''

"Oh, yes, I would, Mercy. I have always dreamed of my descendants running Collier Manor. But if I am never to *have* descendants, my wealth should go to a good cause.''

Mercy leapt to her feet. "I cannot believe you have so little regard for your own daughter that you would deprive her of the only home she has ever known. Would you turn me out to starve then?''

"No," he said, gazing at her stubbornly. "I will provide enough money for you to live in town—Williamsburg perhaps, or wherever else you choose. But you will not get Collier Manor, which needs a *man's* hand to keep it running properly.''

"I suppose you would take Liberty from me, too!" she flung at him.

"Now, there is an idea, Daughter. *First,* I will sell your favorite horse. And if that fails to work, *then* I will rewrite my will to have Collier Manor auctioned off instead of being passed on to you.''

"I never thought you could be so cruel, Papa.''

"I never thought I would *have* to be so cruel, Mercy. You have driven me to it. A dying man has no choice but to issue ultimatums.''

"You are not dying!"

He expelled a long sigh and suddenly looked woefully tired. "So when is the next chance?" he repeated.

"Two weeks!" she shouted. "At the Willardsons'. There is to be a race."

"A race! How perfect for our purposes. Every eligible man in Virginia should be there. *Horsemen*, Mercy. A horseman should look better to you than a tradesman. Pick out the best of the lot. And pick out a patriot, not a loyalist. If we must be one or the other, we are going to be patriots."

"Oh, Papa. You think this is all so simple, so easy. But we are talking about my future happiness."

"That is my main concern—your happiness. . . . Will Lord Montjoy be there?"

"Yes!" Mercy snapped, frowning. "He is taking part in the race. But you cannot consider *him*. He has just come from England."

"That means nothing. Some people leave England because they can no longer *endure* the king."

"He is a viscount!"

"I will make it a point to speak to him and determine where he stands. Did he mention if he was married?"

"I never pursued the matter. I had no interest." In point of fact, she had been very interested but would not permit herself to wonder about it.

"Then I will pursue it. I rather liked the fellow."

"Well, I despised him!"

"You like Reggie Wharton better?"

"Oh, good night, Papa! I will leave you to your plotting."

Her father chuckled. "Good night, Mercy. Be sure and wear something pretty to the Willardsons', eh?"

Mercy refused to answer. Taking the candle with her, she left him alone in the dark.

CHAPTER FOUR

The man and the horse were beautiful together. Mercy hated to admit it, but Ian Montjoy and his stallion, Thor, seemed created especially for each other. The horse was a sleek bay with a white stripe down his face and a black mane, tail, and stockings. His proud carriage complemented an obviously fiery disposition, yet he responded to his master's slightest commands as though born to do so.

The horse alone would have caught Mercy's eye; horse and man together made her heart pound so loudly that she feared the whole assembly would hear it. Fortunately, no one was even looking at *her*. Lord Montjoy and his mount held everyone's attention, for Thor had just done the impossible: beaten Old Pig Eye so soundly that he would probably never want to race again.

Now, as Ian Montjoy rode up to the crowd on the sweeping front lawn of the Willardsons' estate, he was grinning from ear to ear. Mercy inwardly cursed him for being so stunning. He wore no wig today and had tied his long dark hair into a club at the back of his neck. Both his hair and the stallion's shining coat caught the rays of bright sunshine and reflected a rich mahogany color.

His garments—snug-fitting butter-colored breeches, high brown boots, and a white shirt—were the simplest of any man's in attendance, yet he managed to outshine them all. His broad shoulders, narrow flat waist, slim hips, and muscular thighs had women noticeably sighing; Mercy was pleased with herself that she could look at him and admire his beauty without being moved in the slightest.

His stallion pranced and snorted as people rushed to surround him and offer their congratulations. Ian Montjoy never moved in the saddle. All his movements were fluid, graceful, and in total harmony with his horse. He was a master horseman, but he could still be unseated by the unexpected, and her mind raced with ideas of exactly how to achieve that. If he were still around when the fall hunt season arrived, she knew a few tricks to teach him humility!

Then she remembered Mr. Lloyd and mentally chided herself for making plans she had no intention of keeping. She did not want Ian Montjoy to attend the annual Collier Manor hunt. She wanted him to disappear forever. One thing America did not need was another English aristocrat intent on making a profit and taking it back to England.

To Mercy's consternation, Lord Montjoy graciously accepted all the adulation heaped upon him and rode right through the crowd to get to her and Papa, who was standing beside her and merrily applauding.

"Forgive me for winning, Miss Collier, but I do hate to lose," the man had the gall to announce. "From your expression, 'tis apparent you bet a good deal of money on my rival this afternoon."

"You bet on Old Pig Eye?" her father exclaimed. "Why, how could you, Mercy, once you had set eyes on *this* horse? Lord Montjoy's stallion is obviously the superior animal."

"I was counting on Old Pig Eye to do what he has so often done in the past—make his challengers complacent. Then he calmly and soundly beats them," Mercy responded as politely as her churning feelings would allow. "But do not worry, Papa. If you bet on Thor, and I bet on Old Pig Eye, we should still come out ahead, since you usually bet more than I do."

"But I was counting on *huge* winnings!" her father wailed.

Lord Montjoy laughed and shook his head. "Perhaps you should have consulted with your daughter ahead of time, Mr. Collier."

"Daniel," Papa corrected. "Call me, Daniel . . . Ian. I feel as if we are old friends by now. Do get off that horse and allow me to thank you properly for what you did at my house the last time we met."

Oh, no! Mercy thought. *Papa was determined to befriend this aristocrat—and after that, to marry her off to him!*

"I would prefer cooling out my horse first," Lord Montjoy answered. "But I would be pleased to join you later for the refreshments we have been promised. My man, Hiram, is somewhere around here. Once I have walked Thor out a bit, I will hand him over to Hiram and come join you."

"You need not rush, Lord Montjoy," Mercy could not resist saying.

He turned a blinding smile on her. "Oh, but I do," he responded. "I have been hoping for a chance to converse with your father. I had no time to really get to know him the last time we met."

Why should you wish to know him? Mercy frowned at the notion.

"I like you better when you smile, Miss Collier . . ." was his parting comment. "And I like your *natural* hair much better than a wig."

With another of his brilliant smiles, he cantered off, leaving Mercy to gawk after him. She had to force herself to refrain from patting her reddish-gold curls. Since today was informal—and also blisteringly hot—she had refused to don a powdered wig and suffer wearing it all day. Her gown was a cool, summery affair with yards of cream-colored lace and her hair a mass of artfully arranged ringlets it had taken Chloe two hours of labor to achieve before the sun rose.

That he had noticed—and commented upon it—gave her a warm, melting feeling. Unless she had simply had too much sun.

"Papa, let us seek the shade beneath those trees over

there, shall we? A picnic lunch was a marvelous idea. The Willardsons are fortunate to have all these trees so near the house, where they can set up tables outside to accommodate their guests."

"Escaping this sun would suit me," her father muttered. "My brains are roasting beneath this wig. Good, I see an empty chair. I am going to claim it. Keep an eye out for one for yourself. . . . Have you noticed there are no loyalists here? None of them attended. I suppose we accomplished that, did we not, girl? We have divided our friends and neighbors."

"Lord Montjoy attended," she disputed. "You do not count *him* a patriot, do you? The man has not been here all that long, Papa. Do watch what you say to him."

"Watch what I say? . . . I will say what I bloody well please, girl, and damn the consequences. I am not ashamed of who or what I am."

"Of course you are not. Nor should you be. I meant only that we would be wise to be careful these days. We must question Lord Montjoy's motives. He is still living with the McCallisters, I hear. So why did he alone of all the loyalists attend?"

"Because of the race, that is why! Too bad Colonel Washington and several other confirmed patriots could not make it. Guess they are all too busy with government business to attend summer frivolities. I am surprised the Willardsons even went ahead with this. Why, if it had not been for the race, we might have all stayed home today."

"Lord knows there is enough work to be done," Mercy sighed. "I myself should be home making preserves right now."

"Humph! You do not make preserves anyway. Our people do. And so long as we have all those mouths to feed, their owners might as well earn their keep."

"Papa, I supervise our people! The work does not get done without me. Here is the chair—sit down for a while. Perhaps the sun *has* roasted your brains. I am going over to talk to Caroline and the other ladies. . . . Just remember. Guard your tongue around Lord Montjoy."

"I have never guarded my tongue in my life. How am I supposed to start now?"

"By keeping your lips together. Try it. It works wonders."

Mercy left him sitting beneath a large willow tree and made the rounds of her friends, sharing gossip and laughter, teasing and being teased about the outcome of the race and her lack of good judgment in choosing Old Pig Eye. Even Emma Willardson had been tempted to place a bet on Thor once she had seen him—though most of the ladies agreed that Thor's rider was responsible for the race's outcome. Ian Montjoy's name was on every woman's lips. As Mercy had suspected, he had conquered more than his fair share of feminine hearts.

Could *no* one see what she did—that the man was a threat to them? Every single female at the party—with the exception of herself—was steadfastly ignoring the subject of politics. Not one of them seemed anxious to discover where Lord Montjoy stood on the issue of independence. Normally, that was the first thing everyone wanted to know about a newcomer. However, when it came to the handsome viscount, the women were apparently willing to overlook his preferences if only he would smile at them!

Which he did, frequently, when he returned to the crowd without his splendid horse. He mingled among her friends and neighbors as if he had known them forever. Mercy avoided him—until he headed for her father. Then she hurried over to make certain Papa remembered to be discreet.

As she came up to them, her heart sank, for Papa was once again effusively thanking Lord Montjoy for preventing bloodshed at their dinner table.

"So how are you getting along with Ephraim, Phoebe, and Prudence?" Papa demanded. "Are they treating you well? If not, come stay with us. We have plenty of room."

Mercy choked, caught her breath, and blurted: "I am sure the McCallisters are excellent hosts, Papa—especially to a viscount."

"As a matter of fact," Lord Montjoy said thoughtfully, "our relationship has been strained since your party. . . . Mr. Wharton has been a regular visitor at the McCallisters since that night, and we can find little to discuss—or rather, to agree upon.''

"You do not say!" Papa exclaimed. "Wharton and the McCallisters—birds of a feather flocking together, eh? 'Tis one of our colonial sayings, Ian. I think Mr. Franklin—Ben Franklin—wrote it, or maybe it was someone else. I cannot remember. But it certainly applies here, does it not?''

"It would seem to, Daniel. Mr. Wharton and the McCallisters have much in common.''

"And *you* do not?" Mercy snapped. "How can that be, Lord Montjoy?''

He glanced at her in surprise. "What are you implying, Miss Collier? That I have abominable manners—or am I offensive in some other way? I cannot seem to entice a smile from you. Whenever I try, you only scowl all the harder. You must dislike—or disapprove of—me intensely. I am not sure which.''

"Both, my lord.''

"Mercy! How dare you be rude to a man who has been nothing but kind and helpful to us!''

"I am sorry, Papa, but I cannot help it. By his own admission, Lord Montjoy has come to the colonies looking for investments. I assume that means he wishes to profit from our difficulties—exploit us in some way. Of course, he will be charming while he does it, so none of us take exception to what he is doing. But 'tis hardly different from what the king and other English aristocrats have been doing to us for a good long time.''

"Point conceded, Daughter. So what do you have to say to *that*, Montjoy?''

"Every bird seeks to feather its own nest, Daniel.'' Lord Montjoy's blue eyes shot sparks as he looked directly at Mercy. "As far as I know, that is no crime—or if it is, you and your daughter must be held guilty of it, too. You own slaves, do you not? I suspect you work them to your benefit. You probably also take advantage of any opportunity that presents itself to make a profit. That is all I am seeking to do—make an honest profit. If someone wishes to sell good land, I will buy it. That hardly means I should be held responsible for the circumstances that forced them to sell in the first place.''

"Well spoken!" Papa clapped his hands together.

"I do not think it so well spoken," Mercy protested. "You, sir, are a symbol of all I have come to loathe. Like most English aristocrats, you care nothing for the people who live here. Your own personal gain is foremost in your mind. Once you have taken what you wish from us, you will return to England and forget you ever knew us."

"Bloody damn! 'Tis far too harsh a judgment to apply to a man you barely know, Mercy."

"I know him well enough, Papa ... Do I not, Lord Montjoy? Is that not your plan—to depart our shores once you have robbed us of a portion of the wealth we have gained through our blood, sweat, and tears?"

She avoided all mention of slavery; *that* issue cut too deeply. She did *not* condone the institution and would abolish it tomorrow if she could. Let Lord Montjoy believe what he wished; he probably had slaves or bondsmen of his own. If he *did* purchase land in Virginia, how else did he intend to profit from it if not by employing an overseer and slave labor?

"I have not come here to rob anyone," he responded, his blue eyes crackling. "If I buy land, I intend to pay gold for it. If I need laborers, I will hire them and offer a just wage. When I do return to England, I will probably become an advocate on your behalf before Parliament and the king, telling them what I have found here—industrious, intelligent people who deserve more of a say in their own government."

"Marvelous!" her father crowed. "I like your attitude, Montjoy. But they will only laugh at you, you know—the way they have laughed at and mocked Ben Franklin. Parliament and the king refuse to listen to a word he has to say. For years, he has tried to tell them plenty."

"What, precisely, is your attitude toward the Coercive Acts, my lord?" Mercy demanded.

"The Coercive Acts?" His eyes searched her face. "I am not certain which acts you mean—the king's or the colonists'."

"The king's, of course! First, there was the Boston Port

Act which closed the harbor in Boston to all shipping until the tea ruined during the Boston Tea Party was paid for in pounds sterling—including the duty on it. Next came the act for regulating the government of Massachusetts Bay and forbidding town meetings without the governor's approval. That was followed by the Administration of Justice Act which allows any British soldier or official who commits a crime in America to be tried in England, where he cannot be touched by those he has wronged." Mercy paused for breath. "Those royal edicts, sir, are known as the Coercive Acts. They also authorized regiments of British soldiers to be dispatched to Boston and Royal Army officers to be quartered in the homes of private citizens. What do you think of all *that,* my lord?"

Now his true colors would be revealed.

Mercy could see that her questions disturbed Lord Montjoy. Her blood quickened in anticipation of his reply.

"I fear I have not your intimate knowledge of political matters, Miss Collier. I am still making up my mind on where I stand on these issues. However, I have no doubt you know exactly where you stand, and I respect you for it."

"You have not made up your mind?" Mercy mocked.

"Leave him be, Mercy. He is entitled to think things over, especially when he has not been here long yet. Why, those of us who have lived here all our lives are still wrestling with doubt and conflicting loyalties. Indeed, some of us still hope to avoid war if we can."

"Were I a man, I would be *eager* to take up arms in defense of liberty," Mercy retorted. " 'Tis insufferable what has been done to us."

"You do not appear to have suffered greatly." Lord Montjoy bestowed a meaningful glance at their congenial surroundings. "I am happy to see you are still able to enjoy horse races and summer parties—and that I may enjoy them, too, while I am visiting your fair country."

He had her there, and Mercy knew it. In vain, she searched for a blistering reply and was disgusted she could not immediately think of one.

"Girl, 'tis too hot to argue," her father said. "Leave the poor man alone. Find a chair and join me, Ian. I know of some land that might interest you. I would much rather talk about land deals than politics."

"What land, Papa? I know of no land for sale among our neighbors."

"Ah, well, Mercy . . ." He sighed in a condescending fashion. "Land is not a topic of interest to most females. Now, if we were talking about the circumference of a woman's skirts and how many yards of fabric are needed to accommodate the current fashion . . ."

"The topic of land is of interest to *me*, Papa, and you very well know it."

"Nonetheless, we wish to have a *men's* conversation, Daughter. Do allow us that courtesy. Run along, if you will, and fetch us each a cup of punch."

"*Punch*, Papa? You trust me to bring you and Lord Montjoy a cup of punch?"

"Only if you promise not to put any toads in it." Ian Montjoy grinned, apparently enjoying the way her father insisted on treating her like a child or some brainless ninny.

"If I bring you each a cup of punch, you may be certain it will contain something surprising," she threatened.

"Then forget the punch." Papa waved his hand dismissively. "Go find your friend Caroline. Lord Montjoy and I wish to talk business."

"Papa, you had better not—"

Her father gave her a long, quelling look. She knew it well. It was the expression he always wore when he had made up his mind to something and would not be budged. She just wished he would not resort to such tactics in front of Ian Montjoy. It was embarrassing; all she could do, it seemed, was make a fool of herself in front of the man.

"I am certain you will do as you wish no matter what I think," she finished lamely.

"Precisely," he answered.

Glaring at him, she retreated and joined her friends, but kept an eye on both of them for the remainder of the afternoon. Lord Montjoy and her father spent most of it together. From time to time, other men joined them, including Drew Elliot. Mr. Elliot was in hot pursuit of Sarah Gumble, a shy young woman who in the past had rarely mustered the courage to speak to Mercy, much less a man. When Elliot wasn't chasing after her, he drifted in and out of the group of men who pulled up chairs to sit with her father and Lord Montjoy and talk horses, land deals, or whatever it was that men talked about when left to their own devices.

Mercy longed to join the group and discover what held their interest. Lord Montjoy would certainly suspect her of eavesdropping if she got too close. So she kept her distance, but their laughter carried to her, and when they grew serious, she became even more intrigued.

It was so unfair.

Why should men have all the interesting conversations while women were doomed to trivialities? All Caroline wanted to talk about was the exorbitant price of toilet water, wig powder, and other English luxuries. The other women wanted to talk about the men—especially the handsome, exciting Lord Montjoy. During the course of the long afternoon, Mercy discovered that he was as yet unmarried but betrothed to a woman in England.

So much for Papa's aspirations.

Not that she would have been interested, anyway. She was not—now more than ever. Lord Montjoy had refused to commit himself. Had avoided telling her where he stood. Yet here he was, ingratiating himself with all her friends and neighbors, and even her own father.

Why?

He ought to be off socializing with the McCallisters, the Croughtons, and others of their ilk. Rebecca Brandenbush had reported that the Croughtons were also entertaining today. On her way over to the Willardsons', she and her husband had gone right by the Croughtons' and seen carriages lined up in the drive. They had recognized the equipages of several prominent loyalists. Lord Montjoy belonged with them—*not* with the patriots.

When it came time to leave, Lord Montjoy accompanied her father to the carriage where Mercy sat waiting and tapping her foot in impatience. It was dusk and would soon be dark, but old Moses, their driver, had forgotten to bring the lanterns.

"I will see you next week then," Papa said to Montjoy. "Sometime on Wednesday."

"Look for me early afternoon," Lord Montjoy responded. "It will take at least that long for me to ride over from the McCallisters'."

"You should plan to spend the night. Otherwise, we will be too rushed."

"Excellent. Thank you. Do you mind if I bring my man, Hiram? He goes most places with me to look after Thor, who can be a menace around strangers. Besides, Hiram would hate being left behind at the McCallisters'. He will be happy to bed down in the stable."

"Naturally, you may bring him. No need to ask. He is always welcome—as are you, Ian. I look forward to Wednesday."

"Good day to you, Miss Collier." Lord Montjoy nodded to Mercy. "It was diverting to see you again. . . . Until Wednesday, Daniel."

Mercy could contain herself only until they reached the end of the Willardsons' drive, where it joined the main road. "Papa, why did you invite Lord Montjoy to Collier Manor on Wednesday?"

"Because I felt like it. We have plans." He settled back against the leather seat, leaned his head against the upholstery, yawned, and closed his eyes. "Wake me when we get home, will you?"

"Papa, *what* plans? I think I have a right to know. Will he be staying for the evening meal?"

"Mercy, you just heard me invite him to spend the night. Of course he will be dining with us. Make certain the meal is a nice one—and be sure to dress for it. And smile. You know how to be a good hostess when you want to be."

"That is the point! I no more wish to be a good hostess to Lord Montjoy than I would relish entertaining a serpent. I do not *want* him at Collier Manor. Why is he coming?"

"That is *my* business, Daughter. If I can get a leg over a horse again, I intend to ride out with him."

"But—you have not mounted a horse in over a year! Why would you ride out with him?"

"To show him the estate, of course—particularly that nice bottomland down by the creek."

"Why would you want to show him—Papa, no! You *cannot* be thinking of selling that land to Ian Montjoy!"

"Why not? We are not doing anything with it at the moment. I have let it lie fallow for years, and 'tis time to think of planting it again—or selling it."

"Not to Lord Montjoy! Papa, you *would not.*"

"Yes, I would." He opened his eyes and looked at her in the fading light. "We need the money, Mercy."

"Papa, we cannot need the money that badly! . . . And why to Lord Montjoy, of all people?"

"Because he is the only one I know with enough money to buy it . . . except for Reggie Wharton. If you were marrying Reggie, I would not need to sell the land at all. Collier Manor would be secure. As it is, we are *not* secure—not in the least, my stubborn, wayward daughter."

Mercy clamped her mouth shut. Papa was right. By refusing to marry Reggie, she had put Collier Manor in a precarious position. She knew better than anyone how difficult it was to meet all their needs on the funds available. She kept the books, carefully listing every item bought or sold. Right this minute, they had more needs than they had money to cover them. The roof leaked on the house, various outbuildings required repair, and she had been promising the slaves to build several more huts to accommodate their growing numbers as children grew up, married, and began to have children of their own.

Chloe had been reminding her for months that a new hut was urgently needed for a couple who had jumped over the broomstick together after it was discovered that the bride was expecting a child. The babe was due in a couple of months, and she still had not done anything.

Feeling suddenly overwhelmed, Mercy sat back and stared into the gathering darkness. To sell a single acre of her beloved Collier Manor would be like chopping off a finger; to sell it to an English viscount would be cutting out her heart. But Papa would do whatever he had to do; he always had and always would. He had not blinked an eye when he had had to shoot his favorite hunter—a horse he himself had bred, raised, and trained. The horse had broken its leg jumping a stone wall, and Papa had dusted off his hunt coat after the fall and demanded his gun.

Mercy had bawled like a baby, but Papa had been dry-eyed and determined. "Cannot be helped, girl," he had said. "Best to do it quickly and put the poor creature out of his misery."

Yes, Papa would sell land to King George III if he thought it would save the rest of Collier Manor ... but to Lord Montjoy! The bottomland along the creek was practically on top of them. And it was rich good land—*too* good for the likes of Ian Montjoy. She wished the man would go home to England and leave them all alone. Then she could cease worrying about his motives and not have to feel guilty about finding him so attractive. She should have made a nuisance of herself that afternoon. And never left Papa alone with him. Should have used the opportunity to get to know him better so she could expose him for being a ... a what?

An Englishman and a viscount? He had made no attempt to hide the fact. A confidant of the king? He was only a viscount, not a duke or an earl. A loyalist? He was very good at hiding his sympathies and ingratiating himself with both sides.

How perfectly frustrating! She knew nothing about the man except that she did not trust him. And that he excelled at making new friends, including her own father. Perhaps, when he came on Wednesday, she might try being extra charming to him and thereby discover his true intentions. She would smile, laugh, and talk with him ... even flirt a little.

She knew how to flirt. At least she thought she did. Other women did it all the time. She would practice in front of a mirror. Chloe could help her.... No, forget Chloe. Chloe could not be trusted either.

Well, that was exactly what she was going to do. Before she was finished, she would know all there was to know about Ian Montjoy. If he intended anything wicked, she would expose him to all her friends and neighbors. He was up to no good. Why, every time she saw him, the fine hairs prickled on the back of her neck!

All the way home, she made plans.

CHAPTER FIVE

"Will ye be makin' your first report back t' the king soon, me lord?" Hiram asked as they turned the horses into the long drive leading to Collier Manor.

"I suppose I must," Ian muttered. "But I am not looking forward to it."

"I canna say I am lookin' forward t' the long ride t' Boston, either. Wait 'til the weather cools. I will not mind so much then. Virginia is a lovely place but too hot in the summer for me own tastes."

"Every climate but the cold, dank one your mother favored is too hot for your tastes. I am growing accustomed to it," Ian answered. "At least, the horses seem to have adjusted. After this long ride, you would think Thor would be short of energy, but he is suffering no lack that I can see."

The stallion shied at a butterfly sailing past his nose, and Ian shook his head at the horse's antics. "See what I mean? . . . I hope Daniel Collier is serious about selling me land," he continued. "If he is, I could have it planted by next year. He would have to provide the labor, too, of course. We have much to discuss."

"Are ye thinking of plantin' tobacco, me lord?" Hiram nodded toward the field on their left where a sea of swaying green leaves emitted an earthy, rich odor.

"No, I prefer wheat or corn—grain crops that can be

sold locally. I want nothing that needs to be shipped to England to bring a good profit. Shipping may not be possible, anyway—not if war breaks out."

"Then ye expect it will come t' war."

"There are many more patriots than loyalists, my friend. The McCallisters are the minority. Even I find myself taking the opposite side. It is happening so often now I am beginning to feel guilty."

Hiram released a long, low whistle. "No wonder ye dread makin' your first report back t' the king. Ye might have t' put your own name on the list."

"Ah, but I know how to hold my tongue, Hiram, while these Virginia planters say what they think, regardless of consequences. . . . I have been too long among titled aristocrats who weigh their words carefully, particularly if they think the king might hear of them. The outspokenness of the planters is refreshing and gives me all the more reason to like them."

"Well, the common folk are different here, too, me lord. They consider themselves the equal of anyone. In England, a man measures himself by the title he serves. Here, he looks to what he can achieve on his own without serving a title."

"Giving you ideas, is it?"

From beneath his battered three-cornered hat, Hiram slanted him an offended look. "No, me lord. But I can see the attraction of it for others. If the Americans do gain their independence, what's to prevent the lowliest people of *this* continent from rebellin' against their lords and masters?"

"You mean slaves?"

Hiram nodded. "Were I a slave, I would find meself rebellin'."

"You are probably right, Hiram. The slaves will be next. I have never approved of the institution, but I understand why plantations like this one are less than eager to abolish the practice. Still, it will cause no end of trouble if the Virginia planters support the rebellion yet refuse to grant freedom to their own workers."

"The Colliers tend toward rebellion, do they not, me lord?"

Ian sighed. "The daughter especially. She can scarcely endure *my* presence, so resentful is she of the English aristocracy."

"And what do ye think of *her?*"

"What?"

The question caught Ian off guard. He had been trying not to think of Mercy Collier. Not while he was awake, anyway. He had already dreamed of her twice. In his dreams, she had been naked—gloriously naked—with her red-gold hair tumbling down around her shoulders and her manner as welcoming as Elizabeth's.

The thought of seeing her again—even fully clothed— made his blood race.

"What do ye think of the lass?" Hiram repeated. "Will ye be puttin' females on your list for the king—or only the males? From what I hear, if Miss Collier wore britches, she would be first in line t' volunteer t' fight English soldiers."

"No doubt she would, but no . . . I will list only the men. The king has never seriously considered the contribution women might make. He speaks only of men—and he already has some notion of those he can trust and those he cannot. My mission is to verify his notions and supply specifics. But you already know that."

"I'm thinkin' that packet will be mighty heavy when I finally ride to Boston. I might need to take Thor just to be certain I can make it there and back."

"If you need a better horse, I will see you get one," Ian promised. "Ah, we are here now. Enough talk of lists for the king. Today, we are here to talk business."

"Good luck, me lord. I hope ye get everything ye's come for and then some."

Ian thought of Miss Mercy Collier and resolved he would not leave until he had won a smile from her—a single, genuine smile that came from the heart.

"His Lordship has arrived!" Chloe peered around the door to Mercy's bedchamber and flashed a huge grin. "Oh, you look fine, girl! I'm glad to see you finally makin' the effort t' charm a man."

A bundle of energy packaged in a plain dark gown, white apron, and turban, Chloe hurried into the room and gave Mercy a pat on the cheek. "Green is your color, girl, even if it is only homespun. Them white roses in your hair is pure inspiration. They go with the white trim on your gown—and now with this fan. I found a white one among your Mama's old things." She thrust the fan into Mercy's hand. "Lord Montjoy may be comin' t' see *land*, but keepin' his mind off you will be his biggest problem."

"This is *not* what you think, Chloe, so stop grinning. Lord Montjoy holds no interest for me. I have already told you: I am only going to be nice to him so I can discover what wickedness he is planning."

"How can you be sure His Lordship is plannin' wickedness?"

"Stop calling him His Lordship. He is only a viscount. One only refers to an earl or a marquis as Your Lord*ship* or His Lord*ship*, though it is perfectly proper to say *my* lord or *his* lord, without the *ship* on the end of it. I never can keep it all straight. That is another good reason for breaking free of England. All these distinctions about titles are ridiculous."

"You ignorin' my question, girl. How do you know he is plannin' wickedness?"

"Because he is staying with the McCallisters! And he plans on returning to England once he has figured out how to take advantage of us. My greatest fear is that he intends to tell that odious Lord North—or the king himself—what is happening here. We will all be condemned as traitors. The McCallisters already consider us such."

"If it's gonna come t' war anyway, what Lord Montjoy tells the king will hardly make a difference, will it?"

"I plan to *expose* him, Chloe, and prevent him from using us. . . . Do you know what they do to informers in Boston? Tar and feather them! They do *not* sell land to them or welcome them into their homes. I must keep Papa from making a mistake he will only regret, especially when it comes time to sell our tobacco crop to England."

"Would you really want to see Lord Montjoy tarred and feathered, jus' 'cause he's a friend of the king?"

"Well, I hope to see him run out of Virginia! He does not belong here. Let him return to his precious England. Selling land to him would be like welcoming a fox into the henhouse. Today, I will prove that to Papa. I do not plan to *attack* Lord Montjoy—only to charm him into saying something that reveals his true intentions. By tomorrow, Papa will order him to leave, just as he did Reggie Wharton."

"Lord Montjoy is no Reggie Wharton, girl." Chloe rolled her eyes. "Even *I* can see that."

"Which is why I am handling him differently. I have given a great deal of thought to this, Chloe. I know what I am doing."

Indeed, she had done little *except* think about Lord Montjoy, but she was not about to tell Chloe that.

"Then you had better start doin it, girl, 'cause the viscount has done arrived, and your Pa has sent me to find you."

"Of course, I would be delighted to show Lord Montjoy that parcel of land down by the creek." Mercy uttered the lie with a smile as false as the words themselves. She was anything *but* delighted.

"I would do it myself if I did not feel so poorly this afternoon," her father said. "You know I was intending to ride out with him, but in this heat . . . I cannot do it. We could take the riding chair, I suppose, but even that seems beyond me today."

"You must not distress yourself, Papa. Lord Montjoy and I will take the riding chair. I will handle the lines myself. Chloe, go tell Moses to hitch Liberty to the riding chair, will you? We can go all over in it, but I will not have to change into a riding habit—a welcome thought in this heat."

"It would indeed be a shame for you to change your attire, Miss Collier," Ian Montjoy said as Chloe hurried off to do her bidding. "You look quite fetching in it."

"So you like my gown?" The opportunity to boast was irresistible. "Our Daughters of Liberty wove the fabric for it and even the white trim. It was one of our first successful garments—made entirely without any help from England."

"That must be why it is so charming," he gallantly responded, his wry smile the only hint of sarcasm.

Mercy cast another sidelong glance at him. He was dressed much as he had been the last time she had seen him—discreetly, in well-tailored riding clothes that fit like a second skin. She was beginning to think he slept in his high brown boots. They, too, seemed molded to him. With effort, she tore her gaze away from him.

"Go and rest awhile, Papa," she urged her father. "Lord Montjoy and I will spend the remainder of the afternoon together—viewing the estate. You can join us for the evening meal. Cook has promised it will be quite special."

"Thank you, Daughter. I am delighted to have your cooperation in this matter. . . . She has been most gracious since she joined us here in the library, eh, Ian?"

"Oh, yes. . . . She has been exceedingly gracious." Ian Montjoy slanted Mercy an amused, knowing look, as if he wondered why she had not slit his throat yet.

He was not at all deceived by her efforts to show him her best side. He seemed to see right through her. Well, she had all afternoon to pierce *his* armor . . . and when she did it, he would never realize what was happening until it was too late.

"Are you hungry or thirsty, Lord Montjoy?" she inquired solicitously. "I will have Cook prepare a basket for us. 'Tis a long time till the evening meal. When we get to the creek, we can stop in the shade and refresh ourselves."

"How kind of you to think of my needs, Miss Collier." He gave her a little bow. "Please do not bother yourself on my account. I am sure I can last until evening."

"Oh, 'tis no bother at all! Come along, Papa. . . . We will leave the viscount to amuse himself for a few moments while I consult Cook and check on the riding chair."

As Mercy took her father's arm to escort him from the room, he waved his hand at all the rare books he had assembled over the years. "Make yourself at home, Ian. To an educated man such as yourself, my books may seem modest, but to me, they are treasures. I am pleased to share them with you."

"Thank you, Daniel. I will enjoy exploring your library

while I await your daughter's return. A man is never lonely when surrounded by books.''

"You see?" Papa hissed to her as soon as they had left the library. "He loves books! 'Tis a good sign.''

"The devil himself probably loves books," Mercy retorted. "For your sake, I will continue to be nice to him, Papa, but I still do not trust him one bit.''

"Not for my sake—for *yours!* He is handsome, charming, polite, and he loves books. He is also an excellent horseman. What more could you want, Mercy?''

Picking up her skirts, Mercy prepared to mount the staircase. "I want you to stop matchmaking. I said I will show him the bottomland, and I am doing my best to be polite. More you cannot ask of me, Papa. Lord Montjoy is no more a suitable husband for me than Reggie was. Indeed, he is *less* suitable.''

"Not in my opinion. He *likes* you, girl. He finds you attractive. I can tell by the way he looks at you.''

"Nonsense." Mercy paused halfway up the wide wooden staircase. "If you are going to talk foolishness, this is as far as I go with you. Besides, I must see Cook. Cease your plotting, Papa. Where Lord Montjoy is concerned, this afternoon is all I can promise you.''

"He is a virile young stallion, Mercy. You are a prime young mare. Give him a chance, girl.''

"He is already betrothed!''

"But she is in England . . . and he sympathizes with our cause. I can tell he does.''

"You can tell nothing of the sort! You hardly know the man, so stop defending him—and pushing him at me. An English viscount would be my *last* choice for a husband.''

"Maybe I will sell him Collier Manor, not just the bottomland," her father grumbled, puffing as he continued up the stairs. "While I am at it, I will ask him if he has any use for a good swift mare to breed to his magnificent stallion.''

"Papa, stop bullying me! If you continue, I will refuse to show him the bottomland, after all.''

"Oh, all right . . . but mind you put nothing strange in that basket you are taking with you. Do I have your word on it?'' Several steps above her now, Papa turned and glared. "Well, Mercy?"

"Yes, you have my word! Now, go and rest. You look pale this afternoon. I do not understand it; your skin is normally ruddy."

" 'Tis this abominable heat! Makes it hard to breathe. A little climb up a staircase, and I am as winded as an old nag whose foxhunting days are far behind him."

"Rest, Papa. I will see you at dinner. By then, it will be cooler."

Suppressing a sigh of worry, Mercy turned, descended the staircase, and headed for the outdoor kitchen where she knew Cook could be found at this time of day. After a brief conversation with the large, jovial slave woman who ruled the kitchen, she started for the stable. Halfway there, she spied Moses hitching Liberty to the riding chair.

Sudden misgivings swept her. The riding chair was a high, two-wheeled cart with a padded seat and curved backrest, also padded and covered with brown leather. It was ideal for her purposes, except for one thing: One person could sit comfortably; two were crowded. A large man like Ian Montjoy would take up more than his fair share of space. She would be squashed into the seat beside him, much too close to his big body for her peace of mind. . . . But it was too late now to make other arrangements; Moses had Liberty ready to go.

As she watched, he climbed into the high seat, picked up the lines, and clucked to the mare. Liberty set off at a brisk trot for the winding drive in front of the house. There was no way out of it now; she was committed. . . . Why had she not remembered how small the seat was?

Because she did not normally mind sharing it with another person. Nor had she wanted to change into her plain dull riding habit.

Ian Montjoy was a bad influence on her. The thought of sitting pressed to his side for several hours caused her to feel suddenly faint. She must stop this at once! How could she let him do this to her? She must regain control of herself.

But it was several long moments before she was able to

summon enough courage to return to the house, pick up the basket of food and drink, and invite him out to the riding chair for what she feared was going to be the longest afternoon of her life.

And it was. From the moment he climbed into the riding chair ahead of her, making it creak under his weight, then offered her his strong, warm hand to help her up beside him, Mercy had the sense of living in a dream . . . a hot, breathless dream where her body tingled in forbidden places, and a restlessness both frightening and intriguing consumed her.

They sat shoulder to shoulder, hip to hip, and knee to knee. At every little bump or jolt, they were thrown against each other. Lord Montjoy had to rest his arm along the curve of the backrest to make enough room for both of them. That meant his arm was actually around her waist, a position far too intimate for their short acquaintance.

She had sat in this very cart next to any number of individuals and never even *noticed* the close quarters. Now, she could think of little else. Her neck got a crick in it from turning her head to catch his expression, and she usually only saw his profile anyway—a profile that was much too handsome. Her intense physical awareness of him blunted her mental awareness, so that for the first full hour she was with him she had no idea what they talked about . . . except that they were inconsequential things, surely.

The hot weather. How tobacco was grown, cured, and prepared for market. How many acres belonged to Collier Manor. The number of slaves required to operate it. How many horses, cattle, ducks, geese, chickens, milk cows, hogs, and other creatures lived there. What type of songbirds nested on the estate. How long it had taken her father to build Collier Manor to its present size.

Mercy knew she was talking endlessly—blathering away like some foolish young miss the first time a gentleman noticed her. *He* was asking all the questions and revealing almost *nothing* about himself. All she could discover was that he had an inquiring mind and was well acquainted with the doings of a large estate.

She talked all the way to the creek, pausing only to give Liberty a command now and then, or to soothe her when she took exception to the occasional odd rustling sound in the brush off to the side of the worn track that went all the way around the estate.

By the time she arrived at the creek, Mercy was giddy and out of breath—as if she had run all the way beside the horse. She told Liberty to Whoa! and sat still for a moment, struggling to breathe normally. Except for the twittering of birds in the green tangle of tree limbs over-head, and the murmur of the creek tumbling over stones in the shallows, there was suddenly no sound. In the awkward silence, Mercy succumbed to acute mortification. She had talked too much, and her heart was beating too loudly.

It must be the heat, she told herself. It was so very hot. But she knew it was not the heat at all. It was Ian Mont-joy . . . sitting too close. So close she could smell the soap he had used to bathe himself. And she could smell *him,* the man himself. An odor redolent of leather, horse, and sweat. No man had ever made her feel this light-headed and uncom-fortable—could he hear her heart thundering?

When he suddenly spoke, she almost jumped off the seat and could not at first make sense of the words. He had to repeat them.

" 'Tis apparent you love this land and are loath to part with a single blade of grass on it. Is that not true?" he asked—twice now.

"Collier Manor is my home," she answered. "And my inheritance, unless my father decides otherwise."

What had made her say that?

She realized she had taken him the long way to get to the creek and the bottomland along it. Pride had driven her to show him the tobacco and grain fields, the meadows and pastures, the neat stone fences, the flower and herb gardens, the many useful buildings, the wild spots and the tame ones, saving the best for last—the bubbling creek shaded by a score or more of trees and bushes that flowered in season and made the bottomland the most secluded, private spot on the whole estate.

"I cannot believe your father would ever disown you." Lord Montjoy seemed in no hurry to take his arm away from the backrest curving around her. In sharp contrast to her own churning feelings, he looked relaxed and at ease with his surroundings. "He has no son, and you are his only child."

Mercy bit her lip, preventing herself from blurting her father's threats and why he was making them.

"Yes," she finally said. "One day, what you have seen this afternoon will all be mine. That makes me vulnerable to men who covet what my father has." She turned slightly to look him full in the face. "If you were not betrothed to another woman, you could have this bottomland and more simply by marrying me, Lord Montjoy. As it is, I oppose selling so much as a bucket of dirt to you or anyone else."

She forgot about being charming and learning more about *him*. Her natural honesty asserted itself, and she spoke her mind. "I have worked as hard as my father to make this a prosperous plantation where our people— even our slaves—can be happy. But because I am a woman, I have no say in what becomes of it. I have no rights. If Papa wishes to sell land to you, he will. If he wishes to auction off the land and the house and give the proceeds to the Sons of Liberty, I cannot stop him. I am only a woman. . . . So have a good look around, Lord Montjoy. If the land along this part of the creek suits you, make an offer. Papa may accept it, and the land will be yours."

To her great embarrassment, tears pricked her eyelids. To weep in front of this man would be humiliating! All her plans to flatter and flirt with him, to draw him out, collapsed around her. Handing him the lines, she quickly climbed down from the cart and fumbled beneath the seat for the basket.

"Would you like some hard cider now? Cook packed a small jug for us. I have bread and cheese, dried apple tarts, and—"

"Miss Collier, wait." Leaning over the backrest, he grabbed her hand.

She raised her head to look at him, frowning through her tears. "Before you decide on the land, you should know that the mosquitoes are quite bad here at certain times of the year—after heavy rains especially. And sometimes the creek floods. When it does, it may destroy whatever you have planted. The ground is usually too wet to plant until late into the growing season, and—"

"*Miss Collier.* Be still a moment and listen to me." His eyes were so blue it hurt to gaze into them, so she looked at the white cloth spilling from the neckline of his billowing shirt.

"I am listening," she whispered.

"I only want to say . . . the right man will eventually come along for you. When he does, he will want you for yourself, not for your land. He will value your opinions and consult you when he makes decisions regarding your inheritance. You have only to be patient, and—"

"How *dare* you presume to advise me about my personal affairs!" She snatched her hand from his. "I did not ask for your advice. You barely know me, and I do not know you at all."

"I know you," he calmly countered. "I have been listening to you all afternoon. And before that, whenever I had the opportunity, I made it my business to observe your behavior. Aside from my own observations, I have heard the gossip."

"Gossip! . . . Exactly what have you heard?"

"That you are temperamental . . . not easily managed. You know your own mind and seek to go your own way. They call you The Thoroughbred, you know—"

"No, I did not know!"

"Well, now you do. However, I am disinclined to believe gossip, Miss Collier. I prefer to draw my own conclusions about people."

"And what have you concluded?" She stood staring at him, one hand on top of the basket, the other clenched tightly into a fist at her side. She could hardly breathe. Their conversation astounded her. She could not understand how it had become so personal . . . and disturbing. She had meant to expose *him* today; more likely he would expose *her*.

"I have concluded you are a very loyal person, and that you—"

"I am no loyalist!"

"I am not referring to your political beliefs. I mean you are loyal to the people you love and the land that bred you. You are also opinionated and unafraid to express your opinions. You believe in fighting to obtain what you want— and for what you think is right. You are honest and forthright ... except when you try to be devious. Even then, your honesty bursts forth like a wellspring. You are also mischievous ... intelligent ... industrious ... and a leader. Of women, if not of men. But I believe you could lead men—or at least a *man*—with little effort or prompting. You are incredibly beautiful—an enchanting temptress with your flashing green eyes, red-gold ringlets, and slender proportions. But you are far too wary and suspicious to let any man get close to you. If one tries, you have a trunkful of tricks to discourage him. What I want to know is: What will you be like when you finally surrender your heart—when you choose to give your love to a man who loves you in return?"

Mercy had no answers to such a question. It was far too impertinent. Besides, she did not know the answer. She had never yet given her heart into anyone's keeping. How could she? Too much else was at stake.

"You will never discover what I am like when I give my heart to a man, my lord. For one thing, I have no intention of becoming any man's slave. A friend or a partner, perhaps—*that* I could manage, but only with a special sort of man. One who will never seek to dominate or control me. When I marry, it will be for friendship—not for love. I must be able to *trust* the gentleman."

"You do not trust any man, do you?" He cocked his head, studying her. "What has happened to make you so suspicious of my gender?"

"A long succession of men who only wanted my inheritance. Men who cultivated friendship with my father but forgot to make friends with me. Men who feared that I might outshine them and demanded that I behave in a certain way. Men who could not deal with the fact that I am a competent horsewoman and an excellent manager of people and resources. Men who wanted only to compete with me and *win. That* is what has happened to make me so suspicious and mistrustful of your gender."

"You have no desire for the joys of the marriage bed? . . . Or even for children?"

"My desires or lack of them are not your concern."

"I am making them my concern."

"I refuse to share them with you."

"Ah, Miss Collier. . . . Is it not possible for us to be friends, at least? You intend to share the contents of that basket with me. Why not share the contents of your mind as well? You have just condemned half the human race for failing to be interested in the real you. *I* am interested, yet you rebuff my attempts to learn anything about you. Why is that, Miss Collier?"

"You above all men I have no reason to trust!" She spun on her heel and walked toward the shelter of the trees, then turned back to face him. "Why have you come here, Lord Montjoy? . . . Was it only to buy land—or was it to spy on us? . . . Did you hope we would share our plans with you—give you information to take back to the king?"

Something flickered in his face, increasing her certainty that he was hiding something. "Do you *have* plans for the rebellion?" he drawled. "I am aware of popular sentiment, which favors independency, but I had not thought anyone had gone so far as to make actual plans yet."

"If we did, I would never tell you—no more than I would reveal my innermost dreams and desires to a man betrothed to another woman. Have you no sense of honor, my lord? Considering your status on the marriage market, we should not even be having this conversation."

His jaw reddened, and he finally removed his arm from the back of the cart. "You are mistaken, Miss Collier. I have always been—and will always be—a man of honor. I pride myself on my honor."

"You English always do. You boast of liberty, too. The king himself writes essays about liberty being the pride and glory of Britain. But freedom as you define it is not meant for the common man—or woman—but only for the aristocracy. I could never bare my soul to you, my lord . . . nor offer my friendship. You must first prove yourself to me. I had intended to be nice to you for my father's sake this afternoon, but I find I cannot do it. Perhaps we should just return to the house.''

"All right,'' he answered. "Come get in. Will you drive or shall I?''

"She is *my* mare—for the time being, at least. No one rides or drives her but me.''

He held out the lines to her and silently waited while she climbed back into the cart. But as she took the lines from his hand, he suddenly slid one arm around her waist, cupped her face in his hand, and pressed his mouth to hers.

Stunned, Mercy could not move. Nor had she had time to take up the whip which she had put in the whip holder before climbing down from the cart. She could only sit there and allow him to kiss her, which he did with great expertise. His lips allowed no resistance. Firm and warm, they met hers with a purpose that made her head spin. She had never been kissed so determinedly—but without any hint of violence.

He simply kissed her as if it were his right to do so, and he expected her to acknowledge it. When done, he leaned back and gazed down into her eyes.

"Had I no honor, Miss Collier, I would cease talking to you and simply ravish you on the spot. That is my desire at this moment—to remove that pretty green gown, let down your red-gold hair, and teach you what it means for a man and woman to know each other. I should like to be your lover as well as your friend—but honor prevents me from pursuing ravishment or marriage. Another woman awaits me in England, so however much I might like it here—however much I might come to appreciate your American notions of liberty—I must keep to my word and honor my responsibilities and previous commitments. . . . Forgive me for taking liberties with you. I trust you will understand my own private spark of rebellion. . . . You above all women should be able to understand.''

The amazing thing was *she did*. She could muster no

indignation. In this, at least, he had been honest with her. *He lusted after her.* How could she be angry or self-righteous when she wanted *him* in the same way?

His kiss had been far from unpleasant. She half-wished he would kiss her again. But as he turned away from her and put his arm back up on the backrest, common sense returned in abundance.

"We will pretend that nothing happened out here, my lord." Taking the lines in one hand, she reached for the whip. "I showed you the bottomland and almost all of the estate. We were not hungry so we returned without sampling the contents of the basket. . . . Think no more of that kiss. *I* have forgotten it. You succumbed to a momentary weakness, and I did not fight you as I should have. We will speak no more of it."

"What a cool head you have!" He burst out laughing. "Miss Collier, you quite astonish me. Have you no wish to slap my face—or tell your father?"

"Papa would be delighted. Believe me, he is the last person I would tell. As for slapping your face, I am saving that for any future occasions when you might try to kiss me without my consent."

"Perhaps I shall *have* your consent."

"No," she denied with a shake of her head. "I, too, have honor. Even if I welcomed your kisses—which I do not—I would not consent so long as I knew you were pledged to another woman."

"Again I apologize," he said after a moment. "I am embarrassed, Miss Collier. I do not normally succumb to wayward impulses. At least I try not to do so."

"Apology accepted, Lord Montjoy." She snapped the whip so that Liberty could hear it. "Home, my girl! Take us home before anything else happens."

With Lord Montjoy, she was afraid something might.

CHAPTER SIX

To Mercy's immense relief, her father was feeling much better that evening, and she did not have to bear the whole burden of making conversation with Lord Montjoy through dinner. Papa talked enough for all of them—directing his comments and observations to their guest, so that Mercy was able to withdraw into herself and concentrate on hiding her thoughts and emotions.

That proved difficult enough beneath Lord Montjoy's scrutiny; he watched her almost the entire time with a hooded, half-amused expression that suggested he knew exactly how uncomfortable he made her feel and that he *enjoyed* having this power over her. Papa seemed oblivious to their silent battle and blithely repeated half the information Mercy had already given the viscount about the workings of Collier Manor.

She suspected he was preparing for the time when they would retire to the library for an after-dinner brandy and the serious business of negotiating a price on the bottomland by the creek. Mercy could hardly wait until the meal's end, for then her responsibilities would be over. She would not have to see Lord Montjoy again before he departed, though she realized that if he bought the land, he would have to visit a few more times to make arrangements for its use. But perhaps he would send his man, Hiram, to take care of things while he himself made plans for his return to England or his pursuit of additional investments. If she were fortunate, she would never have to be alone with him again—or even *see* him.

At last, her father pushed back from the table and motioned for Lord Montjoy to join him in a glass of ". . . the last good imported brandy I have left. And possibly the last bottle I shall see in my lifetime. I fear I shall have to start making my own from now on."

"I take it you consider war to be imminent," Lord Montjoy said, rising also. "Not in the near future, I hope."

As usual, he was drawing her father out, encouraging him to reveal his opinions while his own remained closely guarded. By now, Mercy knew his habits.

"Oh, I do not look for any mass outbreak of hostilities before next year at the earliest," Papa continued. "First, we must wait to see what the Continental Congress will do. As our leaders go, so shall the people go. Whether or not the leaders can agree among themselves on a proper course of action, I cannot say, but while we are waiting, life must continue. For myself, I am eager for the summer's heat to pass, and the hunting season to arrive. You do plan to attend our annual foxhunt, do you not?"

Mercy wished her father had not mentioned the event. Given the precarious political situation, it was entirely possible it would not take place this year. "I am sure Lord Montjoy will be gone by then, Papa. His business here in America should be finished long before November. If war becomes imminent, he will have even more reason to make a rapid departure."

"I have no plans to return to England before November," Lord Montjoy calmly disputed. "If I am invited, I shall be pleased to attend the Collier Manor hunt."

"Of course, you are invited!" In his enthusiasm, her father almost knocked a chair over. "You must plan to stay with us for at least a couple of weeks. We hold our main event near the middle of the month, but if the weather is right, we often have smaller hunts just for our immediate neighbors—or they hold their own hunts. 'Tis a grand time, I can tell you. . . . Tell him he must stay with us for the month of November, Mercy. That way he will be right here in the thick of things and not have to go riding back and forth to the McCallisters'.''

"I may not be staying with the McCallisters much longer," Lord Montjoy said. "If I move elsewhere, I will let you know where I am."

"I am surprised you have been with them this long," her father snorted. "As I have said before, you are welcome here. We have plenty of room."

"You have already been more than kind. I have no wish to inconvenience you further." He cast a sideways glance at Mercy.

"It would be no inconvenience at all," Papa insisted. "Would it, Mercy?"

"If you gentlemen intend to retire to the library, I will say good night to both of you," Mercy responded, ignoring the question. "When you are ready, one of the servants will show you to your bedchamber, Lord Montjoy."

Lord Montjoy gave her a courtly bow. "Thank you, Miss Collier—my gratitude also for a lovely afternoon. Your daughter is a wonderful hostess, Daniel. She could not have been more gracious and accommodating today. It was kind of her to sacrifice so much time on my behalf when I am sure she had other things she could have been doing."

Papa beamed in her direction. "Mercy manages to keep herself perpetually occupied, but she can be good company when she makes herself available. I am delighted *you* were delighted."

"Too much delight endangers one's health," Mercy muttered. "Good night, gentlemen."

She fled the room but not fast enough to be spared Lord Montjoy's laughter and parting comment. "What a pert tongue your daughter has, Daniel! 'Tis an evening's entertainment matching wits with her."

"I am glad you think so, Ian. Most people find her intimidating," her father answered. "Come along now to the library."

*   *   *

By midafternoon of the next day, Lord Montjoy had departed. An hour later, Mercy learned that her father had reached an agreement with him on the sale of the bottomland near the creek. The terms included the use of labor to clear a portion of the land and prepare it for planting by the following spring.

In his secretive manner, Lord Montjoy had failed to reveal *what* he intended to plant or how long he planned to remain in the area overseeing the project before returning to England. Papa refused to tell her what price they had agreed upon or exactly how much land was involved.

"This is business between *men,*" he informed her as they sat together in the library. "There is no need for you to know everything. I am sure you will only be critical, anyway, especially when I tell you I sold him not only the bottomland but the big upper field that slopes down to the creek on the west side."

"What? . . . You sold him that, too? Papa, how could you? Does he get the corn planted on it as well? He had better not. We need it to see ourselves and our stock through the winter. . . . I had hoped to sell the excess to bring a bit of cash before the new year."

She stabbed a needle into a piece of embroidery she always worked on when she wished to look busy but was actually engaged in thought and did not wish to be bothered. She had been working on it for years without ever finishing it. Whenever she got close to the end, she simply ripped out the stitches and started over. Papa never seemed to catch on to the ploy; he was always too pleased to see her doing something "feminine" to question why the work was never finished.

"Do you think me witless?" he complained from the depths of the big chair where he was supposedly recovering from the fatigue of entertaining. "The crop will be ours. And next year I intend to plant corn on a piece of tobacco land I have been letting lie fallow. Have you not been urging me to do that for months?"

"Yes, but—"

"But nothing! You are never satisfied, Mercy. I thought you would be glad Ian finally talked me into it. He is most persuasive. I like his ideas on several other things as well."

"*His* ideas! Papa, what about *my* ideas?" Mercy laid aside her embroidery and stood up in agitation. "Why do *any* ideas sound better coming from *him* than they do from me? I know Collier Manor better than anyone; he has only an afternoon's acquaintance with the estate."

"You are wrong, Mercy. He is very knowledgeable and has a good deal of experience in managing large estates. . . . Oh, and I talked him into staying with us for half of October as well as all of November. He wants to personally oversee the clearing of that overgrown section of the bottomland . . . and to put up a small cabin overlooking the creek, something with a paddock and a shelter for horses."

"A viscount will be staying in a *cabin* when he comes to check on his investment?"

"He says he will . . . but of course, we can never allow *that*. His man, Hiram, can stay there—or whoever else he decides to send, but when he comes, he must stay here. . . . Smile, Daughter! We came out well in this deal. He did not try to cheat or insult me. There is something to be said for dealing with the aristocracy; when they want something, they are willing to pay a fair price for it."

"Papa! You cannot truly believe that. They will cheat you as soon as look at you. Indeed, they will cheat you worse than most men."

"Not Lord Montjoy. I am pleased with the arrangement. We will be seeing him often, so keep his chamber ready. I told him to stop any time he wishes. I expect he will soon leave the McCallisters, anyway. When he does, I intend he should stay with us."

"He can live somewhere else but not here!"

Her father gave her a hard look. "Be nice to him, Mercy. He has money and no fear of spending it. Even if he were poor, he is a fine gentleman, and I am glad to do business with him."

"You know nothing at all about him or his *real* reasons for being here!"

"Trust me to know more of men than *you* do, Daughter."

That was the problem: Mercy did *not* trust him, but there was nothing she could do about it.

Mercy managed to avoid seeing Lord Montjoy again for the remainder of the summer. The combination of the heat, which was worse than usual this year, and the unsettled political climate served to discourage the normal round of social occasions. In early August, she learned that Colonel Washington had been selected by the Virginia House of Burgesses to be a delegate to the Continental Congress in Philadelphia in September. So had Patrick Henry. Thomas Jefferson failed to make the list, but the Burgesses had ordered a printing of his fiery pamphlet *A Summary View of the Rights of British America,* and everyone was talking about it.

They were also gossiping about a letter Colonel Washington had received from Bryan Fairfax, brother of George Fairfax, Colonel Washington's neighbor at Belvoir. Citing right and wrong on both sides, Bryan was demanding a respectful, even conciliatory, approach to Parliament and the king. At Mercy's Daughters of Liberty meetings, the women scoffed at this notion and bitterly criticized prominent loyalists such as the McCallisters.

"I hear Prudence and Reggie Wharton are planning their nuptials—or close to it," Caroline told them all one week in late August as they sat sewing around a huge table in the parlor of Collier Manor. "Lord Montjoy is no longer living with them, but I have not heard where he has gone. Does anyone know?. . . . Do you, Mercy?"

Mercy bent over her needlework—this time a section of quilt the women were making to be sent to aid the embattled citizens of Boston. "Why would you suppose *I* should know?" she asked peevishly. "I am hardly privy to Lord Montjoy's personal affairs."

"But he has bought land from your father, has he not?"

another woman demanded. "I heard he was going to clear and plant it."

"That much is true," Mercy said. "Now you know as much as I do about him. I have not seen him since he concluded the arrangement with my father."

"If we go to war with England, what will Lord Montjoy do, I wonder?" asked a third woman—tiny, pert Anne Marie Bointon.

"What will *any* of us do if we go to war with England?" gray-haired Eunice Galvin replied. "We shall have to deal with it. I wish *I* were a delegate to the Continental Congress. I would give them all the woman's point of view: Get it over quickly and spill as little blood as possible— particularly blood from the men in *my* family."

Mercy sought to steer the topic away from Ian Montjoy. "We must pray they reach agreement in the Congress."

"They never will," Caroline asserted. "The colonies are all too different. What does a Quaker from Pennsylvania or a New England Yankee have in common with a Virginian—or a South Carolinian? All they will do is argue and very likely settle nothing. Instead of sending this quilt to Boston, we should keep it for our own militia. Regardless of the course of action the other colonies decide to take, Virginia will fight for freedom."

"We must not be selfish," Eunice disputed. "Bostonians need all we can give them."

"Do you approve of your father selling land to an English lord?" Emma Leeds suddenly asked Mercy. She was a spare, thin woman with small dark eyes that seemed to see everything and disapprove of most of it.

Glancing up from her work, Mercy locked eyes with her. "I had no part in my father's decision. He did what he thought was best."

"It would be difficult to say no to such a handsome, charming man, Emma," Anne Marie pointed out. "Besides, Lord Montjoy may decide to remain here in Virginia. He would not be the first Englishman to lose his heart to this region."

"Has he mentioned he was staying?" Emma retorted. "No matter how handsome he is, I would never trust him.

He must have plenty of high-placed relatives and his own big estate in England. What does he need with a bit of *our* land? Your father should never have sold to him, Mercy— and you can tell him I said so."

"I already have, Emma. Your sentiments echo my own." Mercy set down her section of quilting. "Does anyone care for refreshments? Cook baked a delightful cake this morning."

"I admit I am hungry," Anne Marie replied. "But tell me, Mercy. Do you not agree he is a most attractive man? And he will be so close to you! How can you avoid him if he *does* decide to stay here?"

"I shall worry about it if and when it happens," Mercy said. "I am certain it will not."

"If he plans on leaving, he had better leave soon, or he might not be able to leave at all. If war breaks out . . ."

Mercy stopped listening. She had no interest in Lord Montjoy's plans. And she did not want to see him again.

But as she served refreshments, she could not help wondering: Where was he staying now, what was he doing, and why had he not yet left? *Would* she see him again? . . . And if she did, what would she say to him?

My dear Lord Montjoy. I cannot seem to forget that kiss you stole from me. I wake up at night thinking about it. I recall every tiny detail . . . the way I felt, the way you held me, the scent of your hair, skin, and clothing. All day long I try not to think of you, and I think of you anyway. . . . When I sleep, I dream of you kissing me—and indeed doing much more to me than kissing.

Her cheeks flushed at the memory of what had happened in her dreams—or *almost* happened. Since she had never actually *been* with a man, she had trouble imagining the act itself. But everything leading up to it—or what she suspected led up to it—she could imagine in vivid, excruciating detail: exchanging kisses and intimate caresses . . . *seeing* his splendid body . . . *feeling* his hard contours pressed against her own softer ones.

She ate a piece of cake and tried not to think about him, but as usual, it was hopeless . . . and then Chloe suddenly appeared at her elbow and motioned her outside the room. There, she whispered an urgent message: "Lord

Montjoy is out in the front hallway askin' to see your Papa. What should I tell him?''

"Tell him Papa is resting, and he must come back at another time! We had no word he was coming."

"I cannot tell him that, girl! He is all dusty and sweaty. Looks like he's come a long way. I could take him into the library and give him something t' eat and drink."

"Do that, Chloe. I will see if Papa feels up to visiting with him. *I* cannot do so. I am busy here. . . . And do be careful no one sees him, or it will cause no end of gossip and speculation."

"You should at least come out and greet him, girl. That would be the polite thing t' do."

"I am not greeting him! I told you; I am busy here."

Chloe shrugged her shoulders and rolled her eyes, then turned and departed as quickly and unobtrusively as she had first appeared.

"Is something wrong, Mercy?" Caroline asked when Mercy rejoined the group at the table.

"Oh, no!" she denied with a bright smile. "Just a . . . a small problem in the kitchen."

Caroline narrowed her eyes at Mercy. "Goodness! You are all pink-cheeked and excited. Your eyes are sparkling. Truly, one would think you had just met the man of your dreams."

Mercy gulped and bent her head low over her sewing. "What a ridiculous thing to say! You know how I feel about men, Caroline. I want as little as possible to do with the annoying species."

"Why, good afternoon, ladies!" drawled a familiar male voice.

Every head in the room whipped around to face the open doorway. Eyes widened, and mouths dropped open. Mercy herself almost fainted. There stood Ian Montjoy in his overly snug breeches, white shirt, brown brocade vest, and brown boots. He swept off his three-cornered hat and flashed them all a devastating grin, as if he had just come in from a ride and was delighted to see them all there in *his* parlor.

"I trust I am not interrupting anything, but when I heard

voices I had to come see for myself what was happening. . . . Good afternoon, Miss Collier.'' His glance swept over her as if taking in every detail of her hair and clothing. ''You are looking well today—lovely as a rose in full bloom. But then you always look lovely. Forgive me for bothering you. Go back to your sewing, ladies. I just wanted to say hello.''

Behind him, Chloe shrugged her shoulders at Mercy. Mercy could have wrung her neck. What was she going to say to these women—how was she to explain Lord Montjoy's presence and her own reluctance to acknowledge it earlier? They would think she was trying to hide something. Even if she claimed that his appearance was a complete surprise, everyone would suspect she was lying. Servants *always* announced the appearance of unexpected guests— and indeed, Chloe *had* come to fetch her.

With a wave of his sun-bronzed hand, Lord Montjoy proceeded on his way to the library.

For several moments, no one spoke. Then Caroline said: ''A problem in the kitchen, Mercy? Whenever a man sets foot inside a kitchen, 'tis bound to cause a problem. However, this one seems able to cause a problem no matter where he sets down his elegantly booted foot.''

Several ladies tittered, their eyes bright with speculation. Some frowned with suspicion and disapproval, as if she had done something wrong.

''His appearance is as great a shock to me as it is you,'' Mercy tried to explain, but she could tell no one believed her. ''Please continue without me. I must see if my father is well enough to greet visitors. He usually rests in the afternoons during the worst heat of the day. Neither of us anticipated Lord Montjoy's visit, but I am sure the viscount has come to see Papa. The two have become good friends.''

No one said a word. Their silence was more telling than words might have been. Most of the ladies were smug and smiling, but Emma Leeds looked scandalized. Arabella Lee, the mistress of the pungent comment, finally broke the silence.

''You must not keep a viscount waiting, Mercy. Fetch your father, or better yet—entertain him yourself. If such a handsome lord ever came calling at *my* house, I would change into my best gown and wig faster than you can sing 'Yankee Doodle Dandy.' "

"There is no need for her to change her gown or put on a wig," Caroline observed with raised eyebrows. "As I have already mentioned, I have never seen Mercy look so glowing."

Oh, do be quiet, Caroline! For a timid woman, Caroline could be quite forward—especially away from her husband.

Mercy quickly rose. "Excuse me please, everyone. I will return shortly."

"Take your time, dear!" Arabella Lee urged. "Do not worry about us. We are almost finished here, and we can see ourselves out, can we not, ladies? If we wish to be home before dark, we must leave soon anyway."

"I trust you will all return next week at the same time," Mercy said on her way out of the room.

"My dear, you could not keep us away if you barred the door," Arabella sang out, laughing. "Mind you, we shall expect a complete report on the viscount's visit!"

"Tell him I will be down momentarily." Papa sat up and swung his legs over the side of the bed, then groaned and began to pant in his excitement. "This bloody damn heat! I can scarcely breathe, and my heart is pounding."

"Take your time, Papa. There is no need to rush."

"Go down and keep him company while I dress," he instructed. "Send Caleb—my lazy manservant—to me. I need his help."

" 'Tis unnecessary to make some grand effort, Papa. Lord Montjoy is only in his riding clothes. He is *always* in his riding clothes. *He* takes no pains with his appearance."

Nor does he need to. He is beautiful no matter how he dresses. Mercy's own heart was pounding, but she could not blame it on the heat or a weak heart.

"Invite him to stay over tonight. Have you done that yet?" Papa barked.

"Perhaps he has no wish to stay over. I have had little time to converse with him, Papa. There is a Daughters of

Liberty meeting under way downstairs. We are working on a quilt."

"Send them all home, Mercy. You will see them next week anyway. You must entertain Lord Montjoy now. I have been wondering why he has not been back to visit us since we made our deal on the land. You said nothing to insult him, did you?" Breathing hard, her father sat on the edge of the bed in his nightshirt and glared at her.

"How could I insult him when I have not seen him? I have no time for him now, Papa. I must hurry back to my ladies."

"Forget your ladies. They will understand that a viscount deserves your attention."

"He does not *deserve* my attention! . . . But all right. I will go and tell him you are coming shortly. Then Chloe can see to his needs."

"Chloe! *You* stay and talk to him until I get down there."

"Oh, Papa! You are making too much of a simple visit. If Lord Montjoy expects us to drop everything and attend to him, he should have had the courtesy to let us know he was coming."

"That is not always possible, Daughter, and you know it. Go now, and send Caleb to me."

Mercy sighed. "I am going."

A short while later, she stood on the threshold of the library. She dreaded coming face to face with Lord Montjoy again. Taking a deep breath, she smoothed back her hair and stepped inside the room.

Lord Montjoy stood by her father's desk, thumbing through a rare copy of Thomas Jefferson's newly printed *A Summary View of the Rights of British America.* How Papa had managed to obtain it so quickly still astounded Mercy. Keeping quiet, she helplessly admired Lord Montjoy's broad shoulders and trim waist. Not yet noticing her, he frowned, his lips moving ever so slightly as he read. He appeared deep in thought.

Mercy could not resist the opportunity to catch him unaware, before he had time to fashion an evasive answer. "Well, do you agree with Mr. Jefferson or not?"

He glanced up in surprise and smiled at her. "How do you know which part I am reading?"

"It makes no difference which part. *Every* part would displease the King of England."

His smile broadened. "Probably, but it would displease him only because it was written by someone here in America, not because of the sentiments themselves. Most Englishmen, the king included, consider themselves champions of liberty."

"I believe we have had this conversation already," Mercy said. "And we settled nothing."

He replaced the pamphlet on the desk. "How true—unfortunately. You still look at me as if you hate me and I am your enemy."

In the awkward silence that followed, he strolled over to her and stood looking down at her, so close that she inadvertently backed up a step.

"You have done nothing to prove that you are *not* my enemy," she ventured.

"Nor nothing to prove that I am. . . . Give me a smile, Mercy. I have ridden all this way to see you. Can you not spare a smile for me?"

"You have ridden here to see *me?* . . . Or to see my father and your land? No work has been started on it yet. Papa thought you would want to be here to supervise the matter."

"I have been busy," he replied. "Among other things, I bought a piece of land from your neighbor. It abuts the bottomland I bought from your father."

Mercy gaped at him. "Mr. Willardson sold land to you? No one mentioned that bit of news to me."

"No one knows about it yet. Mr. Willardson owed me a large sum of money when Old Pig Eye lost that race to Thor, my stallion. He was more than happy to give up a portion of land and come out ahead in the deal than to pay what he owed me and suffer a great loss."

"And all that has taken six weeks of your time?"

"Has it been six weeks since I saw you last, Miss Collier? . . . You must have missed me to have been counting

the days. I confess I have missed you. I have an absurd
attachment to your scowl."

"What else have you been doing?" she demanded. "I
hear you are no longer living with the McCallisters."

"You have heard correctly. I have taken a room at
Chinn's Crossroads."

Mercy's heart sank. Papa would never stand for that.
The tavern was a popular meeting place for the colonists
and planters, but hardly suitable lodgings for a viscount.
It would be much better if he were staying with another
family, preferably a patriotic one.

"What finally drove you to leave the McCallisters?"

"I grew weary of hearing them criticize their former
friends."

"Do they criticize us much?"

"You in particular. I assure you they find nothing good
to say about *you.*"

Mercy lifted her chin a notch higher. "That bothers me
not at all, for I find nothing good to say about them."

"Yes, but it does no good to nurture resentment and ill
will toward others. Such feelings—if allowed to go
unchecked—can only hurt those who harbor them, not
those toward whom they are directed."

Mercy conceded he was right. However, she still could
not find it in her heart to overlook the fact that he was a
British lord here to take advantage of them and succeeding
very well at it. "Why have you come, Lord Montjoy? Papa
will be glad to see you, but I am not."

"I am sorry to hear that," he answered, moving closer
still. "Since the last time I saw you—and kissed you—I
have found myself thinking of you much too often. I came
to oversee the work on my land and cabin, but also because
I wanted to see *you* again—and discover whether or not
you still have the same effect on me."

Mercy backed up another step and bumped into a chair.
"What effect? I have no idea what you are talking about."

"Yes, you do," he gently chided. "If you truly have no
idea what I mean, why is your color so high and your eyes
so vivid a green?"

"It must be the heat."

"Undoubtedly—the heat between *us.*" He slid an arm about her waist and hauled her tight against his hard body. "I keep telling myself I do not want to do this—reminding myself of how honorable I am. But somehow, whenever I am near you, my damn honor deserts me."

"Lord Montjoy!" Mercy gasped. "Release me this instant."

"Only if you can assure me that you do not feel the same way I do." He pressed his lips to her temple. "God have mercy on me. You even *smell* delicious. Exactly as I have been remembering."

Mercy was too busy inhaling *his* scent to explain that it was probably only the rose water Chloe made for her that so attracted him. Enthralled by his nearness and the temptation of the moment, she swayed against him, closed her eyes, and simply reveled in his presence. The man himself was much better than any dream, and she *was* shamelessly glad to see him again. He was so much taller, stronger, and more handsome than she remembered.

He has spent time recently in the sun. His face and hands are darker, and he smells of leather and the sun-warmed earth. If he kisses me again, I shall swoon and puddle at his feet. Why does he have this effect on me?

"Where is that rogue and rascal who talked me out of my best bottomland and then did not return to do a thing with it?"

Papa's voice in the hall outside the library brought Mercy to her senses. She leapt back from Lord Montjoy as if his touch had scalded her. He merely grinned and turned toward the doorway.

"In here, Daniel—alone with your daughter and trying to convince her that I am not a rogue and rascal, after all."

Yes, you are. You are the worst rogue and rascal I have ever met.

CHAPTER SEVEN

Lord Montjoy remained with them for five days but was so busy down at the creek that Mercy found it easy to avoid him—except at the evening meal. True to his character, Papa provided the conversation, while Lord Montjoy seemed to be concentrating on long, intimate glances. Mercy could scarcely eat in the combustible atmosphere of the dining room; the very air threatened to burst into flame.

She tried without success to avoid his smoky blue-eyed gaze. Whenever she did cross glances with him, he gave her a lazy, provocative smile that raised the fine hairs on the back of her neck. The evening meal was a perfect opportunity for exposing his true intentions, but when he looked at her like that, she could not think, let alone plot his downfall in her father's—or anyone else's—opinion. Meanwhile, Papa appeared more and more delighted by him and open to his suggestions.

Mercy interrupted a discussion on the merits of planting wheat over oats and made a suggestion her father had many times rejected in the past. When Lord Montjoy supported *her* opinion that wheat was a better investment, Papa readily agreed! . . . But only because Lord Montjoy was making the same points *she* had been making for months.

It left her feeling both frustrated and amazed.

As she had anticipated, Papa insisted that Lord Montjoy send his man, Hiram, to collect all his belongings from the tavern at Chinn's Crossroads and bring them to Collier Manor. When His Lordship pointed out that he had additional business with the Willardsons as well as several other families—business that would keep him away from the estate until well into the fall—Papa refused to be dissuaded.

"You will stay with us whenever you are not occupied elsewhere, and that is that," he announced. "I shall hear no more about it."

"I think your daughter might have an opinion on whether or not I should stay here," Lord Montjoy drawled in his infuriatingly arrogant fashion.

"Mercy has no complaint, do you, Daughter? She knows who rules here. A man should never allow a woman to have opinions, anyway—except about minor matters. If he is always consulting a female before he makes a decision, she will *develop* opinions when and where he least wants or expects them. I have learned that lesson the hard way— by treating Mercy as if she were a son. If I had not made so many mistakes, she would have been married long ago. Instead, she is headed for lonely spinsterhood, and I shall go to my grave without heirs to inherit my kingdom."

"Papa, *please . . .*"

Her father had made no mention lately of marriage; for him to bring up the thorny issue now—in front of Lord Montjoy—was mortifying.

" 'Tis hardly your fault—or your daughter's—that she has not wed, Daniel," Lord Montjoy said. "Few men are worthy of such a prize. You must be patient and seek only the best. Sadly, the best are not always easy to find."

"If you two have finished discussing me as if I were a mare in need of breeding, I will excuse myself and take my leave of you." Mercy pushed back from the table. "Good night, Papa . . . Lord Montjoy."

Papa took one look at her and turned to his guest with

a puzzled expression. "What have we said to make her so angry? . . . You see? Women are impossible. I believe you just paid her a compliment, and one would think she had been insulted."

Mercy departed without waiting to hear his answer, and the next morning, Lord Montjoy was gone. Telling herself she hoped she never saw him again, Mercy plunged into her daily labors with a vengeance. Political matters took much of her attention, though she still found it difficult to avoid thinking—and dreaming—about him.

The Continental Congress met in September, but reports were discouraging. The forty-five delegates from twelve colonies—Georgia lacked representation—could agree on little. Not even Patrick Henry's eloquence could convince those who wanted reconciliation with England to abandon their position. Mr. Henry led the firebrands, while others rallied around John Jay, an argumentative young lawyer from New York who strongly disagreed with dissolving the present government.

Rumors of war breaking out in Boston set Mercy and her ladies to frantically sewing for the local militia. Several days later, they learned there had only been a standoff between some militiamen and General Gage's troops who had seized a cache of gunpowder. The incident failed to unite the delegates. Then they received word of the Suffolk Resolves. Calling England "the parricide which points the dagger to our bosoms," Massachusetts declared its compact with George III to be null and void, denounced the Coercive Acts, and called for an immediate cessation of all trade with England, Ireland, and the West Indies. The delegates from Massachusetts urged all Americans to arm themselves and organize their militias.

When Mercy heard that Colonel Washington had joined the firebrands in approving the Suffolk Resolves and ordering them to be printed in all the newspapers, she was certain war would soon follow. But after forbidding all imports from England after December and all exports after the fall of 1775, the Congress adjourned until the following spring, and the delegates returned home. The distant date

for exports was adopted precisely so Virginia could sell its
tobacco crop.

This year's crop—an excellent yield—consumed a great
deal of everyone's time, including Mercy's. After ripening
in early September, the plants had to be cut and the leaves
cured in special barns. Then they were stemmed and
packed into hogsheads for shipment to England and Scot-
land. It was late October before the work neared comple-
tion, and in all that time, Mercy neither saw nor heard
anything from Lord Montjoy.

Though she would not admit it, even to herself, his
absence disappointed her. She also mourned the abrupt
loss of momentum toward independency. Hoping for a bit
of excitement, Mercy persuaded her father to allow the
Collier Manor Hunt to proceed as planned. He was happy
to go ahead with it to alleviate his own boredom and inactiv-
ity due to declining health. The weather had cooled, but
he continued to have occasional difficulty with his breathing. His spirits soared at the prospect of filling the house
with people and activity. His only dictate to Mercy was "to
be sure and invite all the eligible bachelors before they go
off to war next year."

He remained serious about his intention to see her
wed—now before the new year, since summer had passed
without any action in that regard. None of Mercy's arguments could convince him to stop hounding her.

"I have not much time left!" he thundered one afternoon in the library just before guests were due to arrive
for the hunt. "Can you not see that? I should like to have
your future settled before I die."

His declaration tore at her heart, but Mercy stood her
ground. "You must cease thinking such morbid thoughts,
Papa. Your physician claims you can live many more years
yet, provided you maintain a cheerful disposition and do
not overexert yourself."

"Bah! What does *he* know? He is a bloody damn fool
who can prescribe nothing better than inhaling steam to
improve my breathing when it grows labored. This is no
disease of the lungs, but a sign of the heart growing weaker.
A man knows when he is nearing the end."

"If you are indeed nearing the end, we should call off the hunt and start planning your funeral instead."

"We bloody well will *not* call off the hunt! . . . Have you heard from Lord Montjoy? Is he coming? I wish the man would end his betrothal to that female in England. He would be perfect for you. I could die happy knowing you were wed to *him.*"

"Papa, stop this at once! By now Lord Montjoy may have returned to England. If he is still here and war breaks out, he will probably be fighting on the side of the British. The authorities will rush to commission him as a high-ranking officer."

Her father took a long drink of the tea made from rose hips they were drinking these days instead of real tea. "Did you send someone to remind him of the hunt? Perhaps he has forgotten about it."

"He *knows* when it is, Papa. The weather alone would remind him it is hunt season."

"Tell Old Moses to drive down to Chinn's Crossroads and fetch him."

"Papa, I am *not* marrying Lord Montjoy! You must abandon this notion. He is not a patriot, nor is he free to marry. I promise, however, to look closely at every other unmarried male who attends the hunt and shows an interest in me."

"Now listen to me, Daughter. I forbid you to take anyone on that track through the woods that you so enjoy. Stay with the others—and try not to outshine them jumping obstacles that most riders of any sense would avoid."

"You are asking me to fall off my horse in order to impress any possible suitors with my helplessness and ineptitude on the field?"

"No, of course not! You know what I mean. When you ride circles around a man, you cut his pride to shreds. If he is still drawn to you, he will never get up enough nerve to ask you to marry him. You have played that game for too many years, Mercy. Behave yourself. That is all I ask."

"All right, I promise not to discourage any potential suitors by riding circles around them or inviting them to accompany me alone into the woods. This year, I shall be as foolish and inept as Prudence always was—squealing in terror whenever my horse startles at a tiny sound."

"I did not say you had to behave like a goose," Papa grumbled.

Caleb—Papa's manservant who doubled as a butler whenever they had guests—suddenly appeared in the doorway. "The guests are arriving, sir. Will you come and greet them?"

"Naturally! Who is here, Caleb?"

"We got a crowd, sir. A big crowd of people."

Mercy's heart raced at the prospect of seeing Lord Montjoy again—if he were among them. When she discovered he was not, disappointment flooded her. Suddenly, she could summon no enthusiasm for what was normally the happiest time of year for her. In the "crowd" were several eligible young men, but Mercy knew she could not bear it if any of them showed an interest in her. Only one man interested *her*—and *he* had not yet arrived.

He came the next morning, in company with Drew Elliot.

"Am I here in time?" he demanded of her father. "Or has the hunt been held without me?"

"We were delaying it just for you!" Papa roared. "Tomorrow is the day. With this nip in the air, the scent should be good for the hounds. 'Tis grand to see you again, Ian . . . you, too, Elliot."

Lord Montjoy gave Mercy a long, heated glance which she studiously ignored, but later that night, she was inspired to stitch a saucy-looking new feather into her hunt cap. She also added a green velvet ribbon all the way around the hem of her sensible gray riding habit. Sewing by candlelight until her eyesight blurred, she stayed up half the night doing it and managed to convince herself it was to dazzle the eligible young men in attendance and had nothing to do with Ian Montjoy. Over and over she reminded herself that Lord Montjoy already belonged to another woman.

The morning dawned gray and rainy, with a mist rising from muted fields and woods. The night's downpour had stripped away the bright-colored leaves, leaving behind only a few dull gold ones. The cold and damp ensured that the fox's scent would remain close to the ground, easy for the hounds to find. Swept with excitement, Mercy dressed hurriedly and joined the throng of guests already milling about the stable. Few had taken time to eat; feasting would come after the day's sport.

In his youth, her father had kept his own hounds. When hunting became impossible for him, he had sold the entire pack to their neighbor Mr. Willardson. In the absence of Colonel Washington who had sent his regrets, Mr. Willardson had agreed to serve as Master of the Hunt today. He had brought his huntsman, an indentured servant named Jarrod, to control the hounds, and to supervise two whippers-in.

The field master had come down with a wretched cough, and everyone had decided that Mercy should manage the riders and signal them where to go, for she best knew the estate and surrounding lands. She relished the appointment, for she could now assume complete authority over men as well as women, and no one would dare question her decisions. No one was even supposed to speak to her without permission or distract her in any way from her duties. The safety of horses and riders depended upon her.

"Do not look so pleased with yourself, Mercy," Arabella Lee said to her from the back of her sturdy cob. "We all agreed that allowing you to be field master is an excellent way to ensure no repeat performance of last year's debacle with Mr. Lloyd."

"You need not worry, Arabella," Mercy pertly responded. "I promised Papa to lead no suitors into the woods today. If I decide to go myself to enjoy the jumps, I shall simply motion the rest of you to go around."

"Good! You may be certain none of us will follow, anyway. We all value our hides too much. If the fox runs headlong into the woods, you should simply wait and let the hounds, the huntsman, and the whippers-in do their jobs and flush him out into the open again."

"Thank you for your good advice, Arabella. Perhaps this year I shall follow it."

But as Mercy mounted Liberty and caught sight of Lord

Montjoy astride Thor, she reconsidered. Perfectly attired in somber-colored riding attire, jaunty three-cornered hat, crisp white stock, and shining boots, Lord Montjoy handled the eager stallion with ease. Thor pranced and reared in his excitement, but the viscount only laughed and patted his neck encouragingly.

"Patience, my friend. Soon we will be off," he soothed the big horse.

Anyone could see that this was not the horse's or the rider's first hunt. . . . How she would enjoy challenging both horse and rider with a wild dash through the woods and over the obstacles that had so sorely tested poor Oliver Lloyd's skills! . . . But she had promised: no suitors in the woods.

Lord Montjoy is not a suitor, a little voice reminded her.

Mercy fastened upon that thought as the entire field of riders rode away from the stable area and fanned out behind the pack of hounds headed out to a promising covert. At first, it was slow going. Everyone kept to a walk and remained silent so as not to distract the hounds.

While the English-bred black-and-tan hounds cast about, searching for scent, Lord Montjoy rode close to Mercy and inquired in a low voice: "Why do they not draw that patch of woods down there, instead of this field? There is bound to be a fox or two in those woods."

"Mr. Willardson and his huntsman, Jarrod, know what they are about, Lord Montjoy. Do be quiet. You should not be speaking to me."

"You are too beautiful to ignore," he answered, his blue eyes shining like twin beacons in the dull gray morning light. "Believe me, I have been trying to ignore you, but you manage to creep into my thoughts anyway."

She wanted to ask him why—if he thought of her so much—he had remained so long away from Collier Manor, but she held her tongue. However he was spending his time, he apparently had no inclination to share the information with her or anyone else. Besides, she had not missed him—much.

"Go back with the others," she hissed. "I am the field master. I have responsibilities."

"Yes, and one of them is to look after the riders. *I* am a rider. You must make certain I come to no harm."

"I cannot entirely prevent mishaps, though of course I shall try. Stay with the others, follow my signals, and you will be fine, Lord Montjoy. Just remember not to get between the huntsman and his hounds."

He smiled at that, though he ought to have been insulted to be lectured like a beginner. "I know the rules," he drawled, grinning now.

"No, you do not, or you would not have approached me. Neither do you know the land. This field contains one of our best coverts. The hounds will soon find a fox. Give them a few moments more, and—"

Just as she said it, a young bitch gave tongue. Several other hounds immediately confirmed her find. The effect was spine-tingling—all the more so when Jarrod blew a series of short, sharp blasts on his hunting horn, calling the pack together to follow the line of scent.

Mercy leaned forward in her saddle and scanned the terrain, searching for a wave of tail or parting of wheat stubble to indicate which way the fox had gone. Sir Fox might decide to go to ground, lead the hounds on a chase through familiar surroundings, or set off for some distant refuge.

Mercy believed she knew this fellow. He had been drawn last year but never caught. Cunning and fast, he had eluded them by plunging into the woods. Because of the dangerous terrain and close quarters, the field master had sent everyone around, following Arabella's advice. It was the prudent thing to do. Only she and Mr. Lloyd had ridden through the woods. But then, she had never been prudent. . . . What would Lord Montjoy do? she wondered.

A moment later, one of the whippers-in on the far side of the covert raised his cap to indicate a sighting of Sir Fox, as the wily creature was often called. The whipper-in cantered his horse a short distance and gave the high-pitched, thrilling gone-away call that everyone had been eagerly awaiting. The fox was running!

Jarrod reached the spot before anyone else, raised his

horn, and issued a series of long and short blasts that
brought all the hounds together streaking after the fox.

Mercy kept the riders in place until she was certain the
fox was well started. She did not want to overrun him,
especially if he doubled back or made a sharp turn, as
many did early in the chase. She must allow the hounds
and the fox to establish a good line of chase, and then
must choose a route to ensure that she and the other riders
could safely follow on horseback. Foxes were notorious for
picking the roughest terrain in the hopes that the hounds
might lose their scent. Whatever happened, Mercy's job
was to lead the other riders across country in the same
general direction while avoiding ground that might prove
injurious to horses.

The countryside around Collier Manor abounded in
woodchuck holes and other refuges for foxes. Sometimes
the hounds dug the fox out, but usually a fox headed for
open country before becoming exhausted and going to
ground. Often there was no kill at the end of a run; the
fox simply disappeared. But while he was running, there
was great sport to be had in pursuing him.

After a long, breathless pause, Mercy succumbed to the
thrill of the chase. With a joyous cry, she gave Liberty her
head, and they streaked after the hounds now baying in
the distance. Lord Montjoy stayed at her side, checking
his stallion just enough to keep from passing her—an
unpardonable sin in hunting etiquette. The field followed,
strung out behind him.

She glanced at him in annoyance and saw that he was
grinning widely, enjoying the pounding gallop as much as
she was. She pointed Liberty at a low stone wall and soared
over, while Thor kept pace right next to her. Into the creek
they splashed, crossing at a shallow spot which afforded
little danger to less confident riders. Up a small hillside
they raced—following the call of the hounds. Down the
other side and over another low wall.

Liberty's hoofbeats pounded in Mercy's ears. Wind and
rain battered her face. She felt like shouting or singing
with the sheer exhilaration of speed and excitement. Lord
Montjoy rode on her left. Another horse pulled close on

her right. She saw that it was George Wadsworth, one of
the eligible young men who had been trying to catch her
attention. The contrast between him and Lord Montjoy
was inescapable.

George's hands pumped up and down. His ankles
banged his horse's sides. His knees bounced. But he was
grinning at her, apparently trying to get her attention.

"This is graaand sport, eh, Miss Collier?" A thin line of
spittle streamed down his chin.

Mercy gave Liberty a nudge, and the mare lengthened
her strides, leaving George far behind. For Thor, it was no
effort at all to keep up. They jumped two more stone walls
and recrossed the creek when the fox made a wide arc
and attempted to head back toward familiar terrain. Ahead
of her, Jarrod, the whippers-in, and John Willardson split
to go around the patch of woods in two directions while
the hounds plunged bravely into it. Mercy circled and
slowed to a trot to wait for the other riders.

As the rest of the field closed on her, she motioned
for them to go around the woods, following either Mr.
Willardson or the huntsman and whippers-in. Checking
their horses, the riders split into two groups. Only Lord
Montjoy remained beside her.

"Go around!" she hollered at him. "I will meet you on
the other side."

He shook his head. "I prefer to follow you!" he hollered
back at her.

"No, you must not. I am going into the woods after the
hounds."

"Is there something I should fear in the woods?" he
asked, blue eyes twinkling.

"Yes, 'tis very dangerous. The footing is uncertain—
even more so because of this rain—the jumps more difficult than any we have taken yet, and—"

"Lead the way, Miss Collier! If you can make it, so can
I."

"You will regret it!" she warned again.

"Whatever happens, I will not hold *you* responsible,"
he responded.

All right then. Follow me, and we shall finally discover what you are made of, Lord Montjoy.

Casting caution aside, Mercy urged her mare into a flat-out gallop and headed for the twisting, turning, narrow track through the woods. Liberty's long red mane whipped back into her face as she ducked to avoid low-hanging tree branches. She could hardly see the first jump—the huge fallen log, but she knew where it was and so did Liberty. They soared over together, and Mercy listened intently to hear if Thor had made it. She dared not turn back to look. She needed all her concentration to prepare for the remaining obstacles.

The only sound behind her was the thud of hoofbeats— close enough to let her know Lord Montjoy was right behind her. She wove through the trees at an even greater speed than normal and found herself jumping the stream long before she anticipated it. A newly fallen tree offered an unexpected challenge that almost proved disastrous. Liberty saw it before she did and jumped without signal or preparation.

Mercy tried not to jerk on Liberty's mouth as they landed and dodged the boulders strewn across the track. Approaching the ravine, she assessed the jumble of logs to determine if there were any surprises. She saw nothing out of the ordinary until she was airborne; suddenly there was a two-wheeled cart where no cart had ever been before! Piled high with newly chopped firewood, it loomed right in front of her. Mercy had no time to pull up or even to think about it. All she could do was urge Liberty forward.

Caught by surprise, the mare barely had time to lift her front legs over the odd-shaped obstacle. When she came down, she clipped the top wood with her hind feet, dislodging the entire pile and sending it tumbling.

Mercy knew at once that she had left a dangerous situation for the rider behind her. She could hear logs rolling in every direction as they tumbled; the cart itself must have tipped over, spilling its contents.

" 'Ware cart!" she screamed over her shoulder and prayed Lord Montjoy would hear the warning and pull up.

Reaching a clear spot, Mercy whirled Liberty around

just in time to witness Thor gather up his gleaming bay body, tuck his front legs, and arc over the whole mess as if it presented no problem whatsoever. Glued to the saddle, Lord Montjoy followed the stallion's movements—indeed *urged* him over the obstacle—in so flawless a form that Mercy could only gasp in admiration. His technique was perfection.

When horse and man came down, the stallion's right hoof struck a fat wet log and set it rolling. The motion flipped both of them head over heels. Mercy screamed . . . and screamed again as the horse landed heavily on his back and flailed his legs in the air for a moment. As she watched in horror, he rolled over and shakily regained his feet. Beneath him in the crushed leaves, Lord Montjoy lay still and unmoving.

"Lord Montjoy . . . Ian!"

Scrambling down from her horse, Mercy raced toward him.

Ian was sure he was dead. Except he hurt too much to be dead—and he kept hearing voices. He could not seem to open his eyes or move any part of his body. He found it difficult to breathe. Even harder to think. He could not remember what he had been doing before this happened to him. All he was able to do was lie there and listen as voices rose and fell around him—voices he struggled to recognize.

"Will he live? Bloody heaven! How could this have happened? You promised me to take no one into the woods with you!"

"Stop shouting, Daniel. Mercy feels badly enough as it is. Look at her. She is as gray as the morning. Have you sent for the physician yet?"

This was a woman's voice, only faintly familiar.

"Of course I have! But will he get here in time to save him? Arabella, 'tis up to you. *Do* something, damn it."

"I am doing my best. Neither his legs nor arms seem to be broken. We must remove his garments. Mercy, can you

help me? Pull yourself together, girl. Where is your cook?
Is she not experienced in dealing with injuries?"

"Nothing like this," Mercy answered. Ian would know
her voice anywhere. "Oh, Arabella! I have done it this
time! The horse landed on him when he fell. I am sure
of it. No one could survive such a terrible battering."

"He is pale and unconscious, but still breathing, my
dear. Come and help me get his clothes off so we can
better examine him."

"Right here in the parlor?" Daniel thundered. "Should
he not be moved upstairs to a bedchamber first?"

"This is no time for modesty, Daniel. Keep everyone out
in the hallway. Goodness, where is his manservant? We
need some help here."

"Caleb, come assist us!" Mercy called out. "Chloe, you
come, too. I trust your judgment more than Cook's."

A moment of silence followed while Ian felt himself
being lifted, handled, and probed. Every movement
brought a new surge of pain. He sought to protest, but
cobwebs clogged his brain and mouth, rendering speech
impossible. *Just breathe,* he told himself. *Try to keep breathing.
Let them do what they will.*

When they moved him, the pain in his chest sharpened,
and a groan escaped him.

"Lord Montjoy, I am so sorry!" Mercy wailed. "I never
meant for this to happen. That cart ought not to have
been there—"

"Forget the cart! If *you* had not taken him into the woods
with you—" Daniel roared.

"You are right, Papa. 'Tis all my fault. No one is to blame
but me."

*Nonsense. I insisted on accompanying you. You tried to warn
me, but I refused to listen.*

"If he dies because of this, I should be taken out and
shot," Mercy earnestly continued. "I will never ride a horse
or hunt again. . . . Lord Montjoy rode so splendidly. He
was magnificent. You should have seen him, Papa."

"I will shoot you myself! If he dies, you *should* be shot."

"Stop it, both of you. . . . Save your threats for later. We
must tend him now as best we can. He is bruised from

head to foot; *that* much is certain. And look here! . . . His chest. His ribs must be broken. If we are not careful, one of them could pierce his lung."

"What should we do?" Mercy implored. "I wonder he can even breathe like this."

Ian moved his lips—tried to tell them precisely where it hurt. The effort was futile. Cobwebs lay so heavily upon him he could scarcely move. Behind the cobwebs, he sensed a wall of blackness. The blackness beckoned, promising relief from the pain. With as deep a sigh as he could muster, he allowed himself to sink into it, surrendering all thought and feeling.

CHAPTER EIGHT

"Lord Montjoy, are you awake? I have brought your supper."

Supper. Was it time to eat again already? What day was it? . . . Hard to remember, when the days all seemed to run together. Today was the third—no, the fourth—day after his accident. Four days ago Thor had somersaulted and fallen on top of him. Somehow he had survived, sustaining only three broken ribs, a badly sprained wrist, and, of course, more bruises than he could count—plus whatever made his head ache so terribly day and night.

Ian opened his eyes. His one joy in life—his one respite from constant pain these days—was watching Mercy Collier flash her beautiful guilt-tinged smile. It almost made his agony worth it, though he still felt humiliated that she should see him like this. He knew how bad he looked; she had brought him a hand-mirror the previous day when he had insisted upon trying to shave his own chin, an endeavor at which he had not entirely succeeded. The shock of viewing his face—still puffy, swollen, and discolored—had made him want to bawl like a baby. He would not have recognized his own features had he met himself on a street in Williamsburg.

He supposed he should be grateful that he and Thor were still alive. Mercy had assured him that the stallion bore no visible injuries. The rain-softened ground had saved them both. He had not, apparently, borne the full brunt of the horse's weight—just enough to break his ribs and leave him bruised and battered. It was a miracle actually.

Struggling to keep that in mind, Ian ignored the pounding in his head and did his best to return Mercy's smile. Busy rattling crockery on the tray she had set down on a nearby table, Mercy suddenly paused and leveled her green-eyed gaze upon him. The full magnitude of her smile hit him like a physical blow: She was so damned beautiful! So full of life and energy. Just looking at her made him feel breathless.

He knew that her smile derived from a firmly rooted belief that the accident was all her fault, but Ian still relished it. Eventually, she would realize that nothing had changed between them. He was still a viscount with ties to England, and she was still a Daughter of Liberty determined to break away from the Mother Country. Indeed, he was everything she accused him of being . . . but for the moment, none of that mattered. She obviously intended to heal him first and resume hating him later. He was shamelessly grateful for her change of heart, temporary though it might be.

"Are you hungry?" She held up a bowl of something that wafted steam in a thin, rising curl. "I do hope so. There is enough food here to last any normal man a week. Cook believes that proper nourishment will cure any illness or injury. We will begin with chicken broth and progress to the entire bird, adding root vegetables and a freshly baked corn pudding along the way."

"Sit first and talk to me," he begged. "Tell me how you have spent your day."

"Oh, it was quite tedious, I assure you, dominated by domestic chores I have been neglecting." Spoon and bowl in hand, she perched on the edge of the bed beside him. "Our guests have all departed. The last one left this morning. We had piles of laundry to wash, and . . ."

While she talked, he concentrated on studying her face and hair. A fire crackled in the grate of the bedchamber, and its glow imparted a rosiness to her delicate features and a sheen to her red-gold hair. Her gown was a simple affair, plain as the feathers of a sparrow, but she needed no silks or laces to set off her glorious coloring. He wished he dared pull her down and kiss her—but if he did, he risked having hot broth spilled on him. Even worse, her smile would almost certainly vanish.

"Open your mouth," she instructed, pausing in her recitation of the day's events.

"I can feed myself." Gritting his teeth against the pain, he struggled to sit up.

"Must we fight about this every time I bring you a meal?"

"I am no invalid. Give me that spoon."

"No." She shook her head and held the utensil out of his reach. "You are not to exert yourself. Your wits could be addled by moving about too soon after your injury. I warned you about that yesterday when—"

"Nonsense. I am perfectly fine," he lied, feeling dizzy and nauseated.

"No, you are not. Among other things, you have sustained a severe blow to the head. You must lie still and recover your strength. Your head must still be hurting. If not, why are you grimacing like that?"

He had not been aware he was grimacing. He forced a smile. "Because I am weary of lying here like a corpse. 'Tis past time I start to do for myself."

"Not yet," she insisted. "Tomorrow, if you are very good and eat all your supper, perhaps I shall allow you to be carried to a chair in front of the fire."

"Carried! *I* will allow no such thing. Nor can you force me to remain in this bed. Tomorrow I will walk to a chair unaided."

For all his brave words, Ian doubted he could do it today. The pain from his broken ribs and bruised body was bearable, but the pounding in his head frightened him. He must have struck his head on a rock or a log. Another frightening thing was the way he could fall asleep

without any warning. He would just suddenly doze off—
right in the middle of a thought!

"Open your mouth, please. Be civil, Lord Montjoy, and
do as I say." The spoon hovered near his mouth again.

His perversity and irritation deepened. He hated being
helpless—especially in front of *this* particular woman. Yesterday, when she had summoned the servant she called
Caleb to finish the job of shaving him, he had not minded
so much being waited upon hand and foot. It was only
when *she* ministered to him that he found his limitations
almost unbearable.

"Where *is* my worthless servant, Hiram? Has he returned
from Williamsburg yet?"

Hiram had been nowhere around when he was injured,
he recalled. He had sent him to Williamsburg—not with
letters to the king, as he should have done by now, but to
take care of some legal matters related to his land pur-
chases.

"Hiram is downstairs having his own supper. He returned about noon today and sat with you all afternoon
while you slept. Would you prefer he come and assist you
instead of me? I am sure he would like to see you now that
you are awake." She lowered the spoon and the bowl and
cocked her head, studying him.

"Yes—no! . . . That is—he needs a respite from his journey. So let him be." He did not want to drive her away;
he only wanted her to stop waiting on him like a servant,
reminding him that he was less than a full, whole man.

"Then you will allow me to feed you with no more
argument?"

He considered his options. "Yes, but only if you smile
at me again."

She smiled. He opened his mouth. She spooned broth
into it. He obediently swallowed. Soon the bowl was empty.
She replaced the bowl and spoon on the tray, but before
she could reach for the plate of food, he caught her hand.

"Mercy, wait."

She paused and gazed at him questioningly.

"You are feeding my body, but my spirit—my soul—
needs nourishment, too."

"What do you mean?" A small frown wrinkled her brow.

"I am battered and broken," he whispered. "Nourish me, my sweet Mercy."

"Lord Montjoy," she began, her voice suddenly tremulous and uncertain.

"Ian . . ."

"Ian . . ." she repeated.

"A kiss," he implored. "A tiny innocent kiss to heal my injuries."

" 'Tis another who should be kissing you . . ." The protest sounded half-hearted, but she voiced it nonetheless.

"She is far away across the sea. Have mercy—Mercy."

For a long moment, she said nothing, but only watched him with shadowed eyes. Then she lowered her lips to his and did as he asked, giving him a soft, reluctant kiss that nonetheless awoke a storm of feeling in him.

He greedily inhaled her scent, which was clean and hinted of roses. Warmth and happiness flooded him. Even the pain in his head receded. At the same time, another part of him stirred to life. Yearning flooded him. He wanted to make love to her—fast and furiously, throwing caution and restraint to the four winds. . . . Unfortunately, weakness glued him to the bed. While he wrestled with his ungovernable desires, she calmly reached for his plate of food.

"Breast or thigh meat, Lord Montjoy . . . Ian? Which do you prefer?"

"You can ask me that with a straight face?" he growled, wondering if she was mocking him.

She bestowed another magnificent smile on him. "While you are convalescing, you must strive to think more lofty thoughts, my lord. You have just narrowly avoided meeting your Maker; one would expect you to be more mindful of mending your ways. I meant nothing personal by the question; perhaps I should have inquired whether you prefer light meat or dark? I suppose *some* men might misinterpret that, too, if they wished."

"I prefer delicate fair skin with a charming tendency to go rosy at odd moments, red-gold ringlets, and eyes that can turn pure green without warning," he bluntly informed her.

Her eyes turned green now. "And what color of eyes and hair has your betrothed back in England?"

"I cannot remember," he answered honestly. "As God is my witness, those details have escaped my mind."

"You would do well to remember that God *is* witnessing all your transgressions, my lord. . . . Forget the meat. Here is a bite of corn pudding. 'Tis plain, simple, and tasty. I can think of no associations it might have to remind you of anything wayward or naughty."

"Ah, Mercy . . . what am I to do with myself? Food itself does not whet my appetite. Helpless as I am to explain the how or why of it, *you* do."

"That is most unfortunate, my lord, for I do not return your feelings." She blushed as she said it and would not meet his gaze.

"You refuse to acknowledge having any feelings for me, is that it? You refuse to see me as a man and prefer to keep your distance because of *who* and *what* I am."

She raised her eyes. "I could never love a man who belonged to another woman. Nor could I love one who did not believe in freedom."

"*I* believe in freedom," he protested, ignoring her first objection. "Why do you doubt me when I say that?"

"Freedom for everyone? . . . Or only for members of the aristocracy," she challenged.

"Freedom for everyone," he insisted. "Even for slaves."

Her color deepened. "The slaves in this house are not mine to free or I would have done so already."

"Then forgive me for being unfair to you. . . . Tell me more about your beliefs, Mercy. Tell me about your Daughters of Liberty—and the Sons of Liberty, too. Tell me what has brought you—and so many others—to this bitter parting from the land that bred your ancestors."

"You already know the history of our discontent."

"Yes, but I want to hear it from *you*. I want to view it through *your* eyes."

She stared at him with consternation in her remarkable

eyes. "Can I trust you, my lord—Ian? . . . Or must I fear that whatever I say might one day be used against me?"

"You can trust me," he promised and meant it. He had yet to post a single letter containing the information the king desired. At least a half dozen times he had written such a letter—and torn it up. While at Chinn's Crossroads, he had even received a pointed inquiry from a high-placed British official, asking if he had any "news" to be sent home. It was a less than subtle way of reminding him of his duty. Hiram should have taken a letter with him to Williamsburg—or even gone directly to New York. Now, of course, he could use his "accident" as an excuse for being so tardy in writing his sovereign . . . but no matter what Mercy told him, he would keep it to himself. He really did want to understand her better and would use none of what she said to condemn either her or anyone she might mention.

"When you return home, you will forget all about us," she murmured, still looking doubtful. "While you are here, 'tis easy to sympathize with our plight. But once you are among your own kind—"

"Do you honestly believe I could ever forget *you?*" he interrupted. "That would be impossible. Would I forget how you have fed me, bathed me, and seen to all my needs while I could not do so for myself?"

"Caleb has bathed the more . . . ah . . . intimate parts of you," she disputed. "You would not even allow me to shave your chin."

"I was afraid to trust you so close to my neck with a blade in your hand."

"With good reason!" she exclaimed and laughed. Then, sobering, she looked down at the plate of food in her hand and set it on the table. Sighing, she gazed at him, and he knew she was about to impart something private and of great importance to her.

"For me, this fascination for freedom started when I was a young girl. I found a baby squirrel too small and helpless to survive on its own. So I put it in a cage. I fed it nuts and fruits—whatever I thought it might eat. It ate everything I gave it and grew very fast. I tried to make a pet of it but it got to be a nuisance, always getting into things and destroying them whenever I let it run loose in the house."

"So what happened? I can guess from your expression that something unpleasant occurred."

She nodded. "More and more, I had to keep it confined. And the more I kept it locked up, the wilder and nastier and more destructive it became. I myself grew afraid of it; it would bite even me when it could. Finally, Chloe persuaded me that making it live a life of *my* choosing—not its own—was being cruel. I expected my little squirrel, whom I called Red Tail, to be grateful for all I had given it, but instead, it wanted only its freedom. So one day, I had Moses harness a little driving pony we had then, and we took the squirrel in its cage and drove it far away from here to a deep woods where I let it go."

She paused and smiled at him. "I wept when I did it and immediately tried to call him back. But Red Tail seized the opportunity and quickly disappeared. I never saw him again. Later that night, I told Papa what I had done. I was still unhappy—even angry. I knew I had done the right thing, but I was hurt that my squirrel had not loved me the way I loved him."

"And what did your Papa tell you?"

"He said: 'The nature of all living things is to crave freedom, Mercy. Put yourself in the place of the squirrel, and you will understand why he ran away.' "

"And did you?" Ian watched the play of expression on her face and glimpsed the child still inside the woman. . . . What a handful she must have been! And what a delight.

"Oh, yes. Shortly after that, I began to beg Papa to release all the slaves and let them go free. However, he failed to see the connection between slaves and squirrels— or refused to acknowledge it. When I grew up and began to understand that a faraway king was trying to control us and take our wealth, I became a Daughter of Liberty, and . . . well . . . you can guess the rest."

"Indeed, I can . . . and I myself can closely identify with your squirrel. This bed is fast becoming a cage to me. No matter how well you treat me while I am in it, I long for my freedom."

"Then you know how we colonists feel," she whispered, gazing at him intently, ". . . being forced to obey the dictates of a capricious and distant master."

"Yes," he said. "I do."

The irony of it was that he did. But could he ever explain it to the king? George III would no more listen to him than Mercy's own father had accepted her arguments regarding slaves. When a man's financial interests were threatened, he tended to think that his own cherished values ought not to apply to *him*.

"Come, you must eat now," Mercy chided. "Your supper grows cold."

"Having no desire to appear ungrateful like your squirrel, I will obey and try very hard not to bite you while you feed me."

"Thank you," she answered. "However, when you are finally healed and set free, I still expect you to run far away—back to England, in fact."

Ian wanted to deny it, but could not. What she said was true. One day, he must return to England, while Miss Mercy Collier remained here. He could always break his betrothal to Elizabeth, but there was no chance whatever that Mercy would wish to accompany him to his ancestral home and the life awaiting him across the sea.

By the new year, Ian was well on the road to recovery. Mercy could see it in the spring of his step and the ease with which he took a deep breath and did not have to wince while he did so. He still tired easily and occasionally suffered from headaches, but he was able to participate in the modest festivities to welcome the new year of 1775.

He made no mention of returning to the tavern to live and seemed more than content to spend long hours in her father's library during the cold, dull days of January. When he felt up to it, Papa often joined him there, and they debated a multitude of topics. But often, her father refused to dress and come downstairs, which left Mercy feeling obliged to entertain Ian . . . not that entertaining him was a chore.

Rather, it was the most exciting and challenging time of her day. She strove to remain aloof and suppress her blossoming attraction to him, but instead found herself wanting to spend every moment of every day with him— matching wits, discussing the doings of the estate, and bemoaning the icy weather which discouraged outdoor pursuits and visiting neighbors. As much as she did not want to rely on Ian for brightening her days, that was exactly what he did, *both* for her and her father.

During the latter part of January, her father had a particularly bad spell, and Ian took to spending part of the day upstairs in his cozy chamber—encouraging the older man to at least get out of bed, take a chair by the fire, and engage in a game of cribbage. Sometimes Mercy joined them—but not too often, no matter how much she was tempted. She could bear only so many of Ian's piercing glances and remarks that were both innocent-sounding and suggestive.

In desperation, fearing the consequences of too much togetherness, she finally ordered Chloe to be present for all occasions when she could not avoid spending time alone with Ian. Thereafter, Chloe was always there, patiently mending in a corner or performing some chore in the same room.

Of course, Ian noticed and lost no opportunity to joke about it. "Is someone important coming to visit in the morning, Chloe? What pressing task must you accomplish this evening that cannot possibly wait until tomorrow?" he teased on a frosty evening in late February. "You must be weary. You ought to retire for the night."

"Got to polish the brass on this lamp, Your Lordship," Chloe replied. "Got too much else to do tomorrow."

By now, they had the shiniest brass in all of Virginia. With an exaggerated sigh, Ian went back to his book, and another evening passed without incident.

As the days warmed, spring tasks occupied much of Mercy's time, and she saw less and less of their house guest. He, too, spent the major part of each day outdoors— usually down at the stables with Hiram and Moses or overseeing activities that were normally her father's responsibility.

No one mentioned his leaving; Mercy assumed he would remain in residence at least through the spring planting. This year it would include that portion of his land which had been cleared last fall. She was therefore much surprised on a warm April afternoon to see him and Hiram mounted, preparing to depart somewhere, and apparently coming to say good-bye to her.

She was out in the herb garden, cleaning the rows of newly sprouted weeds, when he called her name. She looked up, noticed the stuffed saddlebags and Moses in the small dog cart loaded down with Lord Montjoy's belongings, and guessed that he was moving out.

Hurt welled up in her; why had he not said anything about his impending departure?

Wiping her hands on her apron, she rose from her hands and knees. "Ian? . . . Where are you going?"

Detaching himself from the others, he rode closer and smiled down at her. "I think I have presumed upon your hospitality too long, Mercy. Now that warm weather is here, I must go to Williamsburg and arrange for construction materials for the cabin I wish to build on my own land. I intend to purchase what I need and see it transported safely back here. In the meantime, my things can be kept at Chinn's Crossroads, where I will be staying until the cabin is completed."

"Have you spoken to Papa about this? He will never allow you to live in a tiny cabin without any comforts or amenities. Why should you stay at Chinn's Crossroads during the building of the cabin, anyway? He will not allow that, either."

" 'Tis not for either of you to allow or disallow. I must do what I came here for. Your father is sleeping at the moment, so I cannot tell him my plans. I am counting on you to inform him."

"How very ungracious of you! He will be livid when he hears of this. How can you do this to him?"

"Mercy, 'tis time for me to go."

"Why?" she shouted. "Have you not been comfortable

here? Have we not seen to your every need? Have we not
fed and amused you and restored you to blooming good
health?''

"Yes," he said, nodding. "And that is precisely why I
must go."

"I do not understand—"

"Yes, you do." He gave her a long, searching look.
"Think about it, and you will understand why I must go.
Would you force me to say it in front of Hiram and these
others?''

He motioned to Chloe and several other slave women
working in nearby flower beds. Everyone was intently occupied—behaving as if they could not hear a word being
said—but Mercy knew they could probably hear everything.

"This is ridiculous!" Lowering her voice, she added:
"Nothing has happened in all these months. Why should
anything suddenly happen now?''

"It is to keep something from happening that I am
going. I have cherished these past several months, but they
have sorely tested my honor. I cannot continue this way."

"Ian . . .'' she began and stopped, uncertain what she
meant to say. There was so much between them left unsaid
and no way of saying it.

He was right. It was time for him to go. Winter had given
them a period of calm before the storm—but they both
knew the storm was coming. They stood on opposite sides
of an issue they could scarcely continue to ignore. Even
as they spoke, Virginia was busily arming itself—the result
of a vote taken by the House of Burgesses. Had the threat
of war not been hanging over their heads, he was still
betrothed to another woman . . . and still a viscount whose
loyalties belonged to England. What sort of future could
they ever have together?

It was best to end their relationship now. It could not
be called a relationship anyway, consisting as it did of no
more than a few longing glances and a stolen kiss here
and there. She had spent the entire winter making certain
there was nothing further between them. If he stayed . . .

"Farewell to you then," she managed to get out. "I wish you Godspeed and a safe journey."

She bent to her task, ripping up a perfectly good plant in her haste to appear unaffected by his departure.

"Mercy," he said softly.

She refused to look at him.

"Thank you for everything," he persisted. "Especially for constantly reminding me to hold fast to my sorely tested honor."

His damnable honor. It was as much a thorn in *her* side as it was in his. For once in her life, she wished she had no loyalties or responsibilities. She wished she possessed all the wiles necessary to tempt Ian to stray from the path of righteousness. Her own feelings urged her to run to him, drag him down off his horse, topple him to the ground, and roll over and over with him in the tender green grass. She wanted to wrap her arms around him and never let him go—consequences be damned! She wanted *his* passion to finally and irrevocably overwhelm all of her own objections.

"Tell your father I shall miss our discussions and arguments," he calmly continued. "When I am settled in my own quarters—humble though they may be—I hope he will come and visit me."

"He will not!" she spat, ripping up another hapless plant in the hot rush of anger. "He would not be comfortable in a rude cabin. Besides, the effort of getting there would be too much for him."

"Nonsense. It would do him good to get out of the house. He must fight infirmity, or it will soon become a habit with him."

"You should tell him that yourself," she snapped.

"When next I see him, I will."

"And when will *that* be?" She raised her head to glare at him.

"I cannot say," he answered without rancor. "When I get back from Williamsburg, I will stop by the house."

"How kind of you," she hissed. "Do not be surprised if I have no time to greet you. Spring is our busiest time. I am rarely sitting in the house awaiting callers."

"I never imagined you *would* be sitting in the house awaiting callers, especially when that caller is me."

"Oh, good-bye! Get you gone, my lord. Lengthy leave-takings only bore me."

"You do not look bored; you look furious. For the life of me, I cannot comprehend why."

"Just . . . just *because!*" she shrieked, at a loss to explain it even to herself.

She spun away from him and tramped through the herb bed, crushing tender new growth as she went. He said nothing further, and she refused to look back at him until she was certain he had ridden away. She could hear the rumble of the wheels on the departing pony cart, crushing the fine stone on the drive leading away from the house . . . crushing her heart . . .

When she finally did muster the courage to look at him again, all she could see in the distance was his elegant figure blending easily with his impressive bay horse.

"Girl, you are one foolish, stubborn female," a voice murmured at her side.

Mercy snapped her head around to confront Chloe, who was watching her with knowing eyes.

"How can you let him ride away like that?" Chloe demanded with a shake of her white turban.

"What do you mean? . . . What are you saying?"

"I mean that if you want him, you have t' fight for him—give him a reason for *stayin'*. Anybody with half a mind can see the two of you was meant for each other."

"I do *not* want him! We have nothin' in common! I am *delighted* he is finally leaving here!"

"If you say so, girl . . ." Chloe sniffed. "Seems to me you got *pridefulness* in common, if nothing else. I never in my life saw two more prideful, stubborn people—both denyin' to themselves and everybody else what's as plain as your red hair in a roomful of ladies all wearin' their best white wigs."

"I have not the least notion what you are talking about!"

"This is the *one*, Miss Mercy Collier—the one you been waiting for all your sad, lonely, miserable life. If you let him get away just 'cause you are too prideful and stubborn to go after him and make him yours . . ."

"How dare you say such things to me! You have no idea what—"

"What's keepin' you apart? Oh, yes, I do. It's your own blind foolishness. If you want him bad enough, you could have him. What has he got in England that he cannot have here? If he was so happy bein' a viscount in England, he never would have come here in the first place. . . . And if he was so eager to get home again, he would be leavin' for England today, instead of Williamsburg. Open your eyes, girl. He is ripe for the pluckin' . . ."

"Mind your own affairs, Chloe!"

"You *are* my affair, girl. Much as if I birthed you myself. Lud a' mercy! Who else is gonna tell you these things if'n I keep my mouth shut?"

Who else indeed? Mercy wondered, all her anger suddenly draining away.

Chloe's attention shifted to the herb bed. "My, my . . . jus' look what you been doin' here. Why did you tear up this pennyroyal?"

Mercy glanced down in surprise; she had no idea why she had torn up the pennyroyal.

CHAPTER NINE

Less than two weeks after Ian arrived in Williamsburg, alarming news reached the pretty, charming town where spring was in full flower: The British Army had attacked at Lexington and Concord. The colonies were now at war.

Even before he knew all the details, Ian ignored the ensuing clamor in the streets, sent Hiram out to gather the particulars, and set himself down alone with pen and paper in the room he had taken at a local tavern. Not wanting to create a stir by his presence, he had avoided seeing anyone he knew—had not stopped by the Governor's Palace or the General Court, both of which were beehives of activity these days and would be even more so now.

Feeling clearheaded for the first time in months, he set himself to writing two letters. The first was to his king, telling him that with the outbreak of war, he now found it impossible to "straddle the fence" regarding his own political beliefs. The king's policies and actions were insupportable; much as he regretted having to go against him, he could not continue to act as his spy.

The second letter he addressed to Elizabeth, his betrothed. In it, he informed her as gently as possible that he wished to sever their relationship because he was hopelessly in love with another woman. After writing the words, he paused and stared down at them. He could summon almost no guilt about the king, but Elizabeth was another matter.

Even though he had not known her long before asking her to marry him, he had still proposed—and worse, it now seemed, he had bedded her. Both had happened quite suddenly and unexpectedly. They had been introduced by mutual friends who had been trying to marry him off for years. Elizabeth was pretty and charming, and in a rare moment of impulse, he had asked himself, "Why not marry the girl?"

It was time for him to marry—*past* time, according to friends and relatives who worried that he was not doing his part to preserve the family name. So he had asked her, she had accepted, and he had allowed himself to be swept up in a whirlwind of social activities, which normally he shunned. Having a beautiful young woman at his side and imagining the envy of other men had amused and entertained him—but as for Elizabeth herself?

He realized now that he hardly knew her!

She was blond and blue-eyed; he remembered that much. And she had an annoying, high-pitched laugh. Her political beliefs, what she thought about all day, what moved her to tears or laughter were total mysteries. He was sure he was equally as mysterious to her and hoped she would be relieved, not disappointed, that he had changed his mind about wedding her. Perhaps she, too, had found someone else . . . or perhaps not.

He deeply regretted that on the night before he sailed for the colonies, he had not been more careful. She had clung to him and wept on his chest, declaring herself bereft at his parting. One thing had led to another, and before he knew it—without any planning or conscious seduction on his part—he had wound up in bed with her. He blamed himself, not her. She was young and innocent. As the older and presumably wiser partner, he should have known better.

Afterwards, he had begged her forgiveness for allowing

things to get out of hand. To his great surprise and relief, she had not been nearly as upset as he had expected. "At least now I know you will come back to me," she had said, almost preening.

Therein lay the source of his guilt. "Of course I will," he had blithely assured her. "We are betrothed. Besides, who would ever want to stay in the colonies?"

They had laughed together over the sheer ridiculousness of the idea that he could ever want another life besides the one he had always known in England.

Such arrogance! Only his ignorance exceeded it. From the moment he had set foot on her shores, America had been a humbling revelation—a place like nothing he could have pictured beforehand and nothing at all like England. He could see it now so clearly: Hundreds of rules and conventions bound the Mother Country, stifling rich and poor alike. Centuries of tradition doomed people to live and die playing the same roles their ancestors had played.

In sharp contrast, America was fresh, new, and ripe with possibilities. Even without money, title, or an inheritance, a man could build something new, wonderful, and uniquely his own. He could go as far and fast as his time, talent, and appetite for hard work allowed. He could take pride in the labor of his own hands and not judge himself or others by the mere accident of birth into the right or wrong family.

Best of all, America had Mercy Collier.

Ian had never expected to fall in love with the spirited rebel. Yet, looking back on their entire relationship, he realized he had fallen in love with her the first time he had laid eyes on her. Just as America was everything England was not, Mercy was everything Elizabeth was not. Mercy had goals, beliefs, and plans. . . . She had purpose, passions, and deep commitments—the very things Ian had always considered lacking in himself.

True, he had responsibilities . . . but he did not have a passionate belief in his own government or way of living. He could think of nothing in England for which he would willingly sacrifice his life or his fortune, as so many of the colonists were preparing to do. Looking back on his past, he could see that his life up until now had been empty and meaningless. It had even been boring.

Fortunately, he did not have to reside in England in order to meet his responsibilities there. His estate practically ran itself, just as it had done when his parents were still alive. Being an only child, he had no siblings, nieces, or nephews to tug at his heart. The relatives he did have spent their lives meeting meaningless social obligations, overspent their resources, and regularly prevailed upon him to assist them in "keeping up appearances."

He had long ago wearied of the entire lot but continued to subsidize them because they were family. That could be done as well here as in England. Indeed, if he stayed here and continued to invest wisely and manage prudently, he could build a fortune here—war or no war. Even more exciting, he could help lay the cornerstone for a new way of government—one that treated its citizens more fairly.

With Mercy at his side, there would be no stopping him!

But he was getting ahead of himself. It might never happen. First, he would have to prove himself to her— convince her that he had come to share her hopes and dreams for America. She had said she could never love a man who did not believe in freedom. He would help fight for freedom—offer his services to the leaders of the budding republic, bear arms against his own countrymen, do whatever was necessary to secure America's future.

As soon as Hiram returned, he would entrust his letters to his old friend and tell him what he meant to do. Then he would return to Collier Manor long enough to tell Mercy . . . if she would even believe him. He feared she might not. He would beg her to wait for him . . . give him a chance to prove his newfound loyalties.

Ian paused over his letter to the king. He wondered if he should be so quick to denounce his sovereign on paper. There might be some advantages in maintaining the appearance of loyalty to the crown. He had been a spy for George III; he could just as easily be a spy for the opposite side.

Taking another sheet of paper, Ian started again, striving

for ambiguity. He rewrote the letter twice more before he was satisfied. By then, Hiram had returned.

"Me lord, I got all the news t' be had for the moment. Are ye ready for it?" Hiram twisted his hat in his hands, as excited as Ian had ever seen him. " 'Tis a great thing they are about now in the colonies, me lord. Makes me sorry t' be on the wrong side of the issue."

"Why must we remain on the wrong side, Hiram?" Ian set down his pen and leaned back in his chair. His old friend's sentiments were hardly surprising. Hiram had apparently come to the same conclusion: Freedom was a thing worth fighting for. "I am ready to change my allegiances. Are you?"

Hiram blinked and stared at him. "Ye are not suggestin' . . . that is, ye canna be thinkin' treason, are ye, me lord?"

"If I am, will you stand with me?"

Hiram paused only a moment before answering. "Have I ever stood elsewhere, me lord? I have always been loyal t' Lord Montjoy first, me mother's Highlands second, and England a distant third."

"Yes, but I have never asked you to make such a choice before. This may mean we can never return to England. If the crown wins the war, it may mean we will hang."

"Then I will stand—or swing—beside ye as the case may be," Hiram declared, his eyes glowing. "I bear no love for the aristocracy—exceptin' only yer fine self, me lord. 'Tis ye who have the most t' lose here."

"I am prepared to take my losses—and regain my soul in the bargain, Hiram. My soul and my self-respect. I sold both to a greedy, stubborn monarch for whom I have no love or liking. 'Tis time to remedy all that."

A sly smile lit Hiram's grizzled features. "Would a certain young lass have aught to do with your decision, me lord?"

"Possibly," Ian conceded. "I hope I would have made this decision even without her. She adds—shall we say— an extra spice to this stew of rebellion."

Hiram grinned. "I thought as much. Well, let us hope the dish rests well on our stomachs, me lord. This notion of freedom is a great grand thing, but I fear it will not go down easy for any of us."

" 'Tis fight or starve, Hiram. Now that I have tasted freedom, 'tis the only dish I crave."

"Hah! I meself have no more appetite for servin' the king and his puppets."

Smiling, Ian gestured toward the letters. "I finally have some mail to be sent home to England, Hiram. See to it, will you? You may have to travel clear to Boston to find a ship headed back in that direction."

"I will do so with pleasure, me lord. And where will I find ye when I return from this mission?"

"At Collier Manor—at least until I decide where to go from there to take part in this war. Where else, Hiram?"

"Where else indeed, me lord?" Hiram winked and nodded in undisguised approval. "I will seek ye there."

Mercy was busily adjusting the long pendulum and driving weights on a tall "coffin" clock, which had stood in the entry hall for years, when Chloe came to tell her that she was urgently needed down at the stable.

"Why?" she demanded, her mind totally occupied by the difficulties of getting the clock to work properly. "Tell Moses to handle whatever the problem is. As you can see, my time this afternoon is already claimed. This clock has long been in error, and Papa becomes quite distressed whenever he looks at it—and no wonder. It was made by Benjamin Bagnall, the same gentleman who made the tower clock for the city of Boston."

"Lud a' mercy, girl!" Chloe exclaimed. "Why you prattlin' on about clocks when Lord Montjoy has done arrived and is down at the stable unsaddlin' his horse?"

"Lord Montjoy? Lord Montjoy is here? . . . Goodness, I thought he would be on a ship headed for England by now!" Stopping what she was doing, Mercy picked up her skirts and raced for the door. "I am going to the stable, Chloe. Let no one so much as breathe on those pendulums, and do not touch them yourself."

"Why would *I* touch 'em?" Chloe sounded much aggrieved. "Clocks are a pure nuisance, far as I can see."

Mercy fairly flew out of the house and into the gold and green afternoon. She could not believe that Ian had returned to Collier Manor. With tempers running so hot these days and everyone rushing to prepare for further clashes with General Gage's redcoats, he *should* have left for England by now! He was too closely identified with the aristocracy, too newly arrived from the Mother Country. If she herself could not trust him, how could anyone else? All the known loyalists such as the McCallisters were hiding their faces, and some were even fleeing the area. Why had he come back? Surely, he did not intend to calmly pursue his plans while war exploded all around them!

Rushing into the darkened interior of the stable, she almost knocked Ian down.

"Ian!" she gasped. "What are you doing here?"

His response was to gather her into his arms and plant an impassioned kiss on her open mouth. For a moment, she resisted. Then, abandoning all pretense, she returned his embrace and freely kissed him back.

The unexpected intimacy reverberated through her body like lightning felling an oak tree. Sagging weakly against him, she struggled to regain her composure. "I thought you would be long gone by now. You ought not to be here. Anyone could see you and take issue with who and what you are. You risk your life riding so freely across the countryside. . . . Where is Hiram? He should be with you. Have you come all the way from Williamsburg alone?"

"So many questions," he murmured against her hair. "Hush a moment. Just let me hold you, and I will answer everything."

"But the servants—"

"Have had the good sense to quietly disappear. Look around you, Mercy. There is no one here but us."

Mercy peered into the depths of the stable and saw only the horses sticking their heads out of their boxes in hopes of being fed. Thor—in his customary box on the right-hand side of the aisle—nickered softly at her, then plunged his head out of sight. He apparently had food while the others did not. Her mare, Liberty—at the other end of the aisle on the left—kicked the back of her box in annoyance, then pricked her ears expectantly in Mercy's direction.

"You are right," she sighed. "We are alone. So let us talk here."

She grabbed his hand and pulled him over to an empty box where a large mound of straw was stored for use as bedding. Spreading her skirts, she plopped down in the straw and indicated the spot beside her with a nod of her head.

"I wonder if this is a good idea," Ian murmured with a wry grin as he settled himself beside her. "All I can think about is bending you back in the straw, not talking to you."

"You will talk," she said firmly. "I am unbendable."

So he began talking, while she hung on his every word and devoured the sight of him. He was even more handsome than she remembered and seemed younger. The careworn, guarded look had left his face, which now glowed with enthusiasm. He wore plain, somber traveling clothes and his customary riding boots but had removed his hat. His natural hair lay dark and curling against his collar, making her wish she dared run her fingers through it. But even as she watched him intently, he watched her—his vivid blue eyes studying her face.

What he had to say took her breath away every bit as much as his kiss had done. He admitted he was a spy, just as she had always suspected. He made no excuses or apologies, but simply stated the truth . . . then went on to describe his change of heart and growing awareness that he could not continue serving the king in this or any other fashion.

To her great amazement, he claimed he now planned to stay in America and build a new life for himself—and to fight for America's independence. Now that blood had been spilled, there could be no turning back from war. The king would never stand for this rebellion. George III demanded subjugation. Ian had lived directly under his rule for a long time—certainly long enough to know that compromise and conciliation were concepts beyond the king's understanding.

Pausing for breath, Ian raised Mercy's hand to his lips and pressed a kiss on her fingertips. "Mercy, I realize I have no right to mention this, especially after all I have just told you. You must hate me for my duplicity and for all the harm I could have done to you and others. But—"

"Yes," she interrupted. "I *could* hate you for that. But first, I must know something. *Did* you send information about us to the king? If so, whose names were on your list? Mine and my father's surely, but who else did you report as traitors?"

"No one," Ian said, gazing steadily into her eyes. "A dozen times, I sat down to write that letter. A dozen times, I found excuses for *not* writing. At first, it was because I did not want to name anyone unfairly, without sufficient proof. Then, as I began to sympathize with the rebels instead of with the loyalists like the McCallisters, I delayed doing my duty. I put it off for as long as I could."

"And now that war is imminent, have you yet written to him?" She could not explain why his answer mattered so much, but it did. Even more important was whether or not he had written to his betrothed—and what he had told her.

He nodded. "Yes, I have, but I was not completely honest with him. I said only that I could send no names at present, as the entire continent is in a state of rebellion. I led him to believe that I fear for my life and purposely left my intentions ambiguous. I did this because there may be some advantage in the king not knowing precisely where I stand."

"Advantage?" Mercy sucked in a deep breath. "What do you mean?"

"I intend to bear arms against my own countrymen, sweet. I am committed to the fight. But there may be a better use for me. I must wait until a leader emerges from your rabble-rousers—and then I will go to him and offer my services as a spy for the American side."

"The Continental Congress is meeting shortly—the tenth of May," Mercy breathlessly informed him. "All of the delegates are expected to attend to decide on a course of action in light of this atrocity by the British. Colonel

Washington has already left for Philadelphia. I am told he wore his buff-and-blue Virginia military uniform to convey the message that Virginia, at least, is ready to fight.''

Suddenly inspired, she gripped Ian's hand. "You should go to Philadelphia, Ian, and tell Colonel Washington what you have just told me! He will know best how to advise you on the sort of role you might play. The knowledge of the king's efforts to discover who our leaders are will be of great interest to him, I am certain.''

Ian cocked his head, considering. "That sounds like a reasonable plan. But before I go, I must know where I stand with you, Mercy. Is there the slightest chance—''

"Yes,'' she replied without hesitation. "But what about your betrothed back in England? What have you done— or do you intend to do—about her?''

Ian grinned. "I am coming to that, sweet. 'Twas next on my list of things to tell you. I wrote to her, too, advising her of my change of heart in the matter of wedding her.''

"What did you say, exactly?'' Mercy shamelessly pressed, wanting—*needing*—to hear the words for herself.

"I said I could not possibly marry her because my affections have been claimed by another. Whether or not this *other* returns my devotion remains to be seen, but the fact is I will wed no one but her. If she refuses me, I never *will* wed, regardless of my lack of heirs.''

"Oh, Ian!'' Mercy released her breath in an explosive gasp. Tears gathered in her eyes.

"Am I to assume you might possibly consent to wed me and bear my children—if God sends us any—when this is all over?''

"Yes!'' she cried and threw herself at him, toppling him backward in the straw.

He burst out laughing and pulled her down on top of him. " 'Tis glad I am you are such a shy, retiring miss,'' he teased.

"I will show you how shy and retiring I can be,'' she vowed, wrapping her arms around his neck and bending to kiss him with all the fervor she had thus far been denying herself.

It was a kiss to rival all kisses—a kiss such as she had

never given anyone, a kiss only Ian could claim . . . as
the man she loved, the man she adored, the man whose
children she would one day bear. . . . It was a kiss to indicate
all she was feeling and *allowing* herself to feel for the first
time in her life.

"My God . . ." he breathed when they both finally sur-
faced for air. "If you keep kissing me like that, you risk
losing your virginity here and now. . . . I have no appetite
for tumbling you in the straw like some common strumpet,
Mercy Collier. You are to be my wife."

"Your partner, your helpmate, your lover, your best
friend . . ." she clarified, not about to let him up yet. "You
must realize what you are getting into, Ian, when you ask
me to wed you. I am not like other women—"

"How *well* I know that! You forget that I have had ample
opportunity to make your acquaintance, dearest. I am well
aware that wedding you is likely to be a grand adventure—
war or no war. But are you sure in your heart that you can
be satisfied with my own humble self? I can hardly be
considered a viscount any longer—especially when all my
resources are back in England. If the king demands my
return, and I refuse to obey, he is likely to turn everything
over to—"

"Hush!" she pleaded, not wanting to spoil the moment
with worries about the future. She clapped her hand over
his mouth to stop any further discussion of the matter. "I
would wed you even if you had nothing but the clothes
on your back, Ian Montjoy. Your resources or lack of them
mean nothing to me. *I* have enough for both of us."

The sudden darkening of his face told her he did not
much appreciate that sentiment.

"Let us be clear about one thing, sweet. I am not marrying you to get my hands on Collier Manor."

"Nevertheless, it will be yours, Ian—rather, *ours*—"

"I intend to build my *own* empire, Mercy. You have had
enough suitors in the past who wanted only your inheritance. I could not be content simply running this estate—
grand though it is. My own estate in England is equal to
it, if not grander. I have less land than your father, but
more buildings and animals. It makes a good income—

most of which goes to maintain my household and keep up appearances, both for myself and a small horde of needy relatives. What I have lacked—until now—is the chance to start from the beginning, to prove to myself that on my own I can survive and prosper, creating something of worth and beauty. America has given me this opportunity, and I am vastly excited by the prospect. Here, I can help to create a new government that deals fairly with all classes of people. . . . Here, I can test myself as a man seeking the same wealth and success I once enjoyed in England. All I have now was handed down to me, but *here,* I must earn it."

"Oh, dear!" Mercy pouted, thrusting out her bottom lip in an effort to lighten the moment. "Does this mean I will have to live in a small, rude cabin and bear our children on a heap of straw?"

His face softened. "If I asked it of you, would you?"

"Not unless you asked me very, very nicely," she retorted, walking her fingers up his chest to his chin. For this man she would live anywhere, suffer any hardship, and still count herself the most fortunate of women.

He grabbed her finger with his mouth and gently suckled it, then pulled her down again for another long kiss. When this one ended, leaving them both breathless, he whispered: "I will not ask you to live in a cabin, sweet. I just want you to understand—"

"I do, Ian," she hastened to assure him. "You would not be the man I have come to love if you *were* marrying me for my inheritance. Nonetheless, you must accept that I have it. It must not become an issue between us simply because of your pride."

"I trust I shall be too busy to be prideful, my love. First, we have a war to win, and then—"

She snapped upright. "Let us go tell my father! He will be overjoyed you have asked me to marry you, and I have accepted."

"Wait a moment." He caught her hand. "Let us not be too hasty. I came here for only one reason—to tell you all I have just revealed and to ask you to wait for me until I return, which will not be until this is all over."

"Over? Do you mean this conflict with the British?"

He nodded and rose slowly to his feet. "Yes, my sweet. I like your suggestion that I should go to Philadelphia and consult with Colonel Washington. The more I think on it, the more positive I am that he will want to use me to spy on the British. And if I am to spy on the British, no one must suspect that my affections belong to a prominent Daughter of Liberty. Otherwise, I might be suspected of harboring divided loyalties."

Mercy instantly understood that they must keep their newfound love a secret. Nevertheless, she could not imagine keeping it a secret from her own father. Rising also, she laid her hand on his arm. "Papa would not tell anyone—" she began and stopped, not at all certain he could or would keep it a secret.

"Does your father know I am here, Mercy?" Ian's brow furrowed in thought.

"No, I doubt it. This is the time of day when he usually naps. Chloe came to fetch me. But I am certain by now that the slaves and servants all know you have come—"

"Then we must give them something to talk about. Something to remember if anyone should ever question them about my visit. They must not see us kissing farewell or gazing forlornly into each other's eyes. Nor must they hear of our plans."

Mercy gaped at him, her mind grappling with what he was suggesting. He had become a master of deceit, apparently, while deviousness was strange to her own nature. Yet she knew he was right; his usefulness to the American cause might well be destroyed if anyone knew of their love for each other or their plans for the future. . . . He would be so good—so adept—at spying on the British! After all, he had succeeded in winning her heart all the while she herself had suspected him of spying for the king.

Shaking the straw from her skirts, she began to holler at him. "So why did you come back, you rogue—you loyalist dog? Was it only to gloat over the spilling of American blood?"

At first, he looked dumbfounded, but then a slow smile lit his face. "I came back to try and talk some sense into you!" he shouted back at her. "You must cease your traitorous activities at once, or I will be forced to go directly to the king's authorities and tell them what you and your lady friends have been doing behind closed doors."

"What is the good of even talking to you?" she screamed. "I knew what you were the first day I met you. How could I have let myself hope that a viscount might admit to the error of British ways?"

"How could *I* have allowed myself to hope that a spoiled little colonial rebel would learn to think for herself?"

"You never should have returned here!"

"I regret I did! I only wanted to warn you—because of all you did for me after my accident—that you had best choose the right side."

"I *have* chosen the right side!"

They stood grinning at each other, delighted by their own inventiveness.

"Do you think anyone heard us?" Mercy whispered.

"Your father probably heard us. If he has not, someone will undoubtedly tell him."

Mercy preened a bit. "I can scream quite effectively, can I not? But, Ian . . ." Despair suddenly flooded her. "How will I ever say good-bye to you, now? How can I be sure I will even see you again?"

He tugged her into his embrace and held her so tightly she feared her ribs might snap. "I will come to you again as soon as I can, my love. If ever I am in this area, I will seek you under cover of darkness. Have no fear of the future, Mercy. We fight on the side of the angels. 'Tis clear we must win."

"I have no doubt we will win, Ian! But I fear for your safety." Her blood chilled as she thought of all that could happen to him. "I wish you did not need to go so soon."

She clung to him and molded her body to his, desperately memorizing the feel and the scent of him.

He rested his chin on her head. "The sooner I go, love, the sooner I can return. I only hope your Continental Congress does not back down now or attempt to placate the king instead of fighting back. That would be disastrous. They must waste no time in debate, either. If they mean to go to war against England, they have much to do. I have thought long and hard on it and have a long list of suggestions."

"Give your advice to Colonel Washington. He is not as long-winded as some of the delegates, but his opinion is deeply respected. He will value what you have to say and will see that others hear your ideas, without the necessity of your speaking out in public. . . . Oh, but I shall miss you so!"

"I have to go, Mercy," Ian whispered. "I must resaddle Thor and gallop away from here, like a huntsman on the heels of a fox."

"Yes," she agreed, nodding through her tears. "I will help you saddle him. Then I will walk slowly back to the house, my shoulders sagging, my eyes red from weeping. If anyone asks about you, I will call you the worst sort of swine. No one will suspect that we are pledged to one another . . . and no one will have to lie if ever they are asked about you and me. They will think we parted enemies, not lovers . . ."

He hugged her more tightly to him. "I only wish I had the time to love you," he murmured. "I have dreamed of loving you—taking down your hair . . ." His voice caught on a groan. "Removing all your garments. . . . But I guess loving you will have to wait," he murmured softly and regretfully, drawing back from her.

She would have willingly lain down in the straw with him that very moment—but they could not risk it.

"Good-bye, my sweet Mercy." He brushed his lips across her forehead. "Wait for me and think of me each morn and night—as I will be thinking of you the first thing when I awaken and the last thing before I sleep at night."

"I will," she answered, missing him already. "I am yours, Ian, and you are mine. I promise to wait for you forever if need be."

She trembled with the need to hold him again, but he stepped quickly away from her and headed for Thor's box to saddle the stallion. She watched with love and fear warring in her heart. . . . What if he never *did* return to her? What if this conflict with England took his life?

CHAPTER TEN

From the moment Ian departed, Mercy began to mark the passage of time by the events that kept him away from her. The Continental Congress proved disappointing because it did not immediately adopt a resolution for war and independence. The delegates spent weeks debating the issue. Not until June 14, eight weeks after the bloodshed at Lexington, did they even decide to appoint a general of the Continental Army.

Most of them wanted a New Englander, but after a night of heavy politicking, the Congress charged Colonel Washington with the responsibility of upholding the American cause, defined as "the maintenance and preservation of American liberty."

The colonel reportedly responded: "With the utmost sincerity I do not think myself equal to the command I am honored with."

Mercy could only wonder if Ian had spoken to him yet or if Washington—like many of the delegates—still hoped that the British Parliament and George III would mend their ways. After the mid-June Battle of Bunker Hill— actually a place called Breed's Hill on the Charlestown peninsula in Massachusetts—she was certain everyone would finally "see the light." Both sides suffered heavy casualties, and to Mercy it seemed eminently clear not only that conciliation was impossible but that the war could drag on for months, not days.

The battle decided nothing, except that both sides conceived a new respect for the power of the opposing side. Boston was said to be overrun by bleeding British soldiers, but most of Mercy's acquaintances considered the conflict a defeat for the Americans.

Near the end of June, the Continental Congress adopted an Olive Branch Petition to George III. Men of vision such as Benjamin Franklin bitterly opposed it, but it passed anyway. Then, in the latter part of July, Mr. Franklin tried to get the Congress to adopt a Declaration of Independence and a document he called the Articles of Confederation and Perpetual Union.

Only Thomas Jefferson enthusiastically endorsed his plan; the rest of the Congress soundly rejected it. Their refusal to accept reality dismayed and angered Mercy. As she had feared, the King of England arrogantly refused to consider the Olive Branch Petition. In late August, he issued a Proclamation of Rebellion and appointed Lord George Germain to take charge of the war effort. Germain had advocated the use of force against America from the very beginning of the quarrel.

Meanwhile, in anticipation of the next clash with the British Army stationed in Boston, Colonel Washington struggled to organize, train, and equip the fledgling Continental Army, while Mercy herself spent her entire summer and all the early days of autumn preparing Collier Manor for war. She had no illusions that the estate might escape unscathed. She knew she had to plan for the worst. She stockpiled and hid food, clothing, and blankets, oversaw the butchering, smoking, and salting of various meats, and buried family treasures to keep the lobsterbacks from finding them if they ever came to Virginia.

She also helped organized a massive effort to gather supplies for the army. Washington had already sent emissaries to Virginia to recruit volunteers and locate powder for American guns. Mercy knew that much more would be needed. But no matter how tired she was when she finally fell into bed at night, she never failed to think of Ian, say a prayer for him, and send her love winging through the darkness to shelter him.

One night in November, she retired to her quarters with a sense of weariness heightened by a pervasive sadness she could not explain. She almost never permitted herself to think sad thoughts or dwell on the possibility of defeat, but tonight she could not seem to help herself.

As she sat on a stool and brushed out her hair by the light of a single candle, she blamed her melancholia on the fact that this year there had not yet been nor would there be any foxhunting. It might be years before anyone could spare the time or the horses to pursue the sport again.

She had already sent all of the estate's serviceable horses—with the exception of Liberty and several animals needed for transportation and farmwork—to Colonel Washington in the company of a band of backwoods Virginia enlistees led by one Daniel Morgan, a big, brash, ex-wagonmaster with an enormous grudge against the British.

Mercy did not regret the sacrifice, but she sorely missed riding to the hounds this season. Then, too, there was her father's deteriorating condition. More and more now, he refused to leave his bedchamber—or even his bed. Some days he did not recognize her or the servants and slaves who had waited upon him all his life. When she tried to talk to him, he spoke nonsense or was living in the past. None of the remedies suggested by the physicians she had consulted were working. He was slipping away from her—day by day drawing closer to the grave. Even on his good days, he no longer badgered her to marry and produce some heirs.

These things were reason enough for a bit of sadness and despair, she told herself, drawing the brush slowly through her hair until it crackled with energy and life. But the real reason for her sadness was a longing to hear from Ian. No battles were being fought now; both the Continental and British Armies had postponed any further fighting

until next spring. . . . Why had Ian not contacted her and
at least let her know where he was?

Their love was too new and untried to allow for such
long separations. What if time and distance had made him
decide he did not really love her and want to marry her?
Absence had cooled his ardor for his betrothed in England;
might it not cool his ardor for *her?*

Sensing someone behind her, Mercy drew her wrapper
more closely around her chilled body and half turned on
her little stool. "Chloe?"

Only Chloe would dare disturb her after she had retired
for the night. But it was not Chloe who stood in the shadows
of the doorway to her chamber. She started and gasped
his name. "Ian!"

Stepping quickly inside her room, he held a finger to
his lips in warning and closed the door behind him. Mercy
overturned the stool in her haste to get to him. She flew
into his arms. His beard-roughened jaw abraded her cheek,
and she greedily inhaled the scent of leather, horse, and
cold November night. She reveled in the earthy odors and
the feel of his strong, hard body against her own.

"Oh, Ian, where have you been all this time? I have been
so worried and filled with dread and doubt."

"Hush," he soothed. "I am here now, and I can stay
until dawn. We have all night to talk, my love. . . . For now,
just let me hold you."

"Holding each other is not enough!" she whispered
after a moment in his embrace. "I cannot get close enough
to assuage my hunger for you. Even kissing you is not
enough," she said, and kissed him anyway—long and pas-
sionately.

While they kissed, he held her tightly against him, but
soon his hands began to explore her body—touching,
caressing, eagerly discovering that she wore little to impede
his explorations.

"Oh, God," he breathed, pausing between kisses and
caresses. "I know not if I can stand this, Mercy. I am a
mere mortal man, not a stone statue."

"Nor am I fashioned of marble, incapable of feeling.
Ian, I have missed you so much . . . I *want* you so much.

Wait a moment . . ." She broke away from him just long enough to extinguish the candle, plunging the room into darkness.

As Mercy's eyes adjusted, she saw that a full harvest moon lit the night outside, and its silvery light filtered through the glass-paned window. Taking Ian's hand, she pulled him toward the moonlit bed.

"No, Mercy . . ." he protested. "I did not come here to do *this.*"

"*Yes,* Ian," she corrected. "I shall not let you leave here until you make me your woman."

"I want you for my wife! Not my strumpet."

"All the more reason to seal the bargain with the sharing of our bodies, dearest. Please, Ian. . . . I promise you I will not be sorry come morning."

Still he resisted, refusing to follow her toward the bed. "If anyone finds out about tonight, your reputation will be ruined."

"Do you think I care? If I should conceive a child this night, I will tell everyone I am secretly wed, but because of the war we have chosen not to reveal ourselves until we can live openly together."

"No one will believe such a lie!"

"The Collier name and influence will persuade them to believe it. If they do not, I still do not care." She had to release his hand to shrug off her wrapper, but quickly seized it again. "Ian, come to my bed. Stay with me tonight. Give me memories to sustain me when you are not at my side. If the struggle for independence should claim your life, I could never forgive myself if we denied ourselves these few hours of intimacy and pleasure."

"Mercy, I have so much to tell you . . ."

"Later, my heart. There will be time enough later." She pulled him down on the bed, and Ian growled deep in his throat and rolled over on top of her.

"You win, vixen. I must do as you bid."

"I intended to win," she said, laughing softly, her lips against his mouth. "We thoroughbreds always win."

He stilled her speech with another kiss that made the bed sway madly in the silvery gloom. After that, she was lost—rendered a mindless creature obeying instincts that before tonight she had not known she had. Impeding garments disappeared as if by sorcery. Her lack of shyness would have been shocking to her if she had had time to think about it.

But Mercy attacked lovemaking the same way she did foxhunting—with wholehearted joy and enthusiasm, holding nothing back. Indeed, she sensed that in lovemaking, as in foxhunting, one must risk all in order to gain all. Timidity and shyness would avail her nothing. . . . Yet she was wise enough to let Ian be the huntsman, showing her the way . . . and show her he did.

He taught her how to kiss with an open mouth and mating tongues—then taught her uses for her tongue she had never imagined. He kissed her in places she had never associated with kissing, and she was an eager student, stunned by the delight of her lessons. She learned what *he* enjoyed, as well as what *she* enjoyed, and the knowledge gave her confidence, a sense of power, and an overwhelming tenderness toward him.

He was man needing woman, and she was woman needing man. Somehow their needs complemented each other and gifted both of them with intense pleasure. Their joining, when it happened, caused pain *and* pleasure. Tears spilled down her cheeks even as her cry of wonder sounded loud in her own ears. Ian stilled it with a soul-shattering kiss that soothed the pain and stoked her inner fires almost beyond bearing. . . . How could she want more when she had already experienced so much?

She arched her body against him and strained upwards. "Yes," he urged. "That's it, my love. Come with me. Soar with me."

He sounded like a rider urging his mount over an impossibly high obstacle. Years of riding Liberty, becoming one with her, *trusting* her, yielding to her power and strength, gave Mercy the knowledge of what to do. She yielded, trusted, and let herself go . . .

Rapture! It engulfed her. Above her, Ian stiffened and pumped his seed into her. His life-giving force flooded her, and the moment branded itself into her soul as one of the most exquisite and perfect moments of her life.

Like a gem strung onto a necklace of moments that she would treasure and remember for all of her life, it joined other perfect moments that defined who she was, Mercy Collier of Collier Manor: her first ride . . . first horse . . . first jump . . . first foxhunt . . . flying through the woods on a crimson-gold day, bending low over Liberty's neck, knowing herself to be gloriously alive and at one with the universe . . . her first kiss . . . first ball gown . . . the first time she had looked into a man's eyes and sensed her own power and promise . . .

Tonight, she had fulfilled that promise.

Now she belonged to Ian and he to her, and nothing—*nothing!*—would ever sever the bond they had forged this night.

"I love you, Ian," she whispered into the crook of his neck.

"God help me, I love *you*, Mercy." He raised himself on one elbow to gaze down into her face, his face just visible in the wash of moonlight illuminating the room. "This was like nothing I have ever experienced before. I swear to you, my love, it was all new, wonderful, and beyond any past experience—"

"Tell me not about your past experiences, Ian," she gently chided. "That is hardly what a woman in my position wishes to hear just now."

"I know! I did not mean—" He laughed ruefully. "Ah, God, I am undone, my sweet. I know not what I am saying. I only meant to tell you that had I loved a hundred women before, none could compare to you. None could move me as you have done tonight. I am your slave . . . I am your bondsman. I grovel at your small, perfect feet."

His words fed her starving heart. He was meat and drink to her. He was sun and air. All she would ever want from life was this man beside her, galloping their horses through wood and field, leaping stone walls, sharing all they encountered . . . laughing, loving, teasing, arguing. . . . She asked nothing more of God than to give her this man and long life to enjoy him.

"And *have* you bedded a hundred women, Ian Montjoy?" She could not resist pricking him. "Am I simply the last in a long line of mares this great stallion has serviced?"

It was too dark to see if he reddened, but he had the good grace to drop his head and peer at her through his absurdly thick lashes. "When a man has drunk champagne, he forgets sour ale," he countered. "And he vows to drink *only* champagne from that moment on—even if he finds himself dying of thirst."

She laughed. "You plan to be intoxicated all your life, then?"

"Yes!" He pressed her down against the pillows once more. "You have spoiled me for all else, my sweet. It would be like trading Thor for a plow horse."

"Ah, I see. . . . Now that you have ridden me, you plan to keep me. I am pleased to hear it, for I have no intention of letting *you* go, either."

They smiled at each other in the dim light, and Mercy wallowed in the sensation that her heart had floated up to the moon in the sky outside. "Now get up and tell me all your news, Ian. Where have you been all this time? Why did you not come here or send word before now? You are long overdue for an ear-boxing."

"Forgive me, my sweet." He nuzzled her cheek. "I have been with the general."

"The general? Oh, you mean Colonel Washington. I am not yet accustomed to his new title, I fear."

"I know. 'Tis hard to remember, and he makes it no easier because he gives himself no airs. Never was a more humble man thrust into a position of leadership. Yet never did a leader show more promise. You should have seen him as I last saw him, before Hiram and I departed to come here."

"Hiram? Hiram is here, too?"

"He and the horses are camped out in the woods, awaiting my return. Let me finish my story, love. I know you will find it amusing. It had been snowing, and—"

"Snowing!"

"Yes, love. New England gets snow a bit earlier than Virginia, it seems. Anyway, a snowball fight broke out between the men from the Marblehead regiment and a bunch of unruly enlistees led by one Daniel Morgan."

"Oh, I am so glad to hear that he got there safely with the horses I sent with him!"

Ian frowned. "I know nothing about the horses. *This* Morgan is a big, brash fellow who brought a thousand men—some from Virginia, others from Pennsylvania. They are wonderful marksmen but completely undisciplined and always causing some trouble or other—like this snowball fight."

"Forgive me for interrupting so often. Tell me about the snowball fight, and I promise to be still and listen."

"Well, it got so unruly that the colonel of the Marblehead regiment sent to Washington's headquarters for assistance. The general and I were conferring together, but he immediately ran out of his tent, mounted his horse, and galloped off in the direction of the fray. In order to follow him, I first had to fetch Thor from my quarters. I might not have gone at all, except I wanted to see what Washington intended to do about the matter—especially since he had gone by himself. I arrived just in time to witness him jumping his horse over a ridiculously high fence and landing right in the midst of the brawl. He set his mount down on its haunches, reached down and grabbed two men by the back of their shirts, lifted them off the ground, and roared commands at the rest. The fight stopped in a heartbeat, so astonished were the soldiers to see him. I doubt not that his perfect horsemanship also had a quelling effect. They stood and gaped at him as if he were a god, not a human."

"So you believe good horsemanship to be a prerequisite of leadership. Now that you mention it, I can see how important it would be in enabling a man to function effectively as a soldier. . . . Why, if he could not ride at all, he could scarcely go where he was needed in battle. Moreover, his inferiors might think him weak and inept. 'Tis glad I am that riding to the hounds taught him something so helpful to his present position."

"You may be sure it did. His soldiers cannot stop talking about the incident. It has given them inspiration and con-

fidence—and that is all to the good, considering that the
enlistments of many of the men expire on the first of
January. He is now frantically trying to persuade them to
stay for the winter, rather than go home to their hearth
fires.''

"If he needs men so badly, how came he to let you go,
my dearest?'' Mercy idly caressed Ian's jawline with her
fingertips as he lay on his side facing her.

"He gave me leave to disappear for a short while before
I offer my services to the British.''

"Then he *does* intend to use you as a spy.''

Ian nodded. "From here, I go to Boston to ingratiate
myself with the British leaders there. I will tell them I am
loath to give up my title and have decided to fight on the
side of reason and righteousness.''

"But it will be so dangerous if your true sentiments
should be discovered!'' Mercy could not suppress a shiver
of apprehension.

"I will not be found out, Mercy. I am far too clever for
that—I hope. Indeed, I will finally furnish a list to the
British officials, if not to the king himself, naming all those
who consider themselves patriots fighting for the American
cause. It cannot hurt them now, for they are already well
identified. But it will prove my good intentions. I will publish my own proclamations, write inflammatory arguments,
do whatever I can to assist the British in their efforts to
trounce the colonists. Soon you will be hearing terrible
things about the infamous Lord Montjoy. . . . Do you think
you can bear it, my love, and restrain yourself from
defending me? In truth, it will help my cause enormously
if you vilify me as much as possible.''

"Oh, Ian! I know not if I can do that. Everyone will
suspect I am lying anyway. Whenever I say your name, my
love for you will shine from my eyes.''

He leaned over and kissed first one eye then the other.
"You must do it for me, love—and tell no one the truth.
The better you can lie about me, the safer I will be. Rumors
spread faster than you can imagine. If I am hated throughout Virginia, Boston will surely hear of it, and no loyalist
will dare question my loyalty. That is what I want—to be

hated by the Americans. 'Tis the only way I can gain the confidence of the British authorities enough to be entrusted with all their plans.''

"Cannot someone else take these risks?'' Mercy shamelessly begged. As committed as she was to the cause of freedom, she still hated to see the man she loved embark on such a dangerous course.

"Others are taking these risks already. Since July, Washington has had spies gathering information. Few will be able to do it as well as I can. The fact that I am a viscount not long in this country—and have worked for the king—will give me entrance where others may be denied.''

"But you never did work for the king! You never sent him the lists he demanded.''

"No one knows that but you, me, and Hiram. As I just said, I *will* send him a list now—to cover myself on the issue. If you like, I will even mention your father and you.''

"Do mention us, Ian. I would be proud to be named on such a list. You are right; it no longer matters if the king knows about us or not. We will not back down from this struggle nor change our minds. 'Tis far too late for that, anyway. Why, our most prominent loyalists—people like the McCallisters and Reggie Wharton—have all fled. The McCallisters, I believe, went to Canada where they have relatives. The others have simply disappeared—slipped away while they still could and went to join friends or relatives who share their views.''

"I cannot say I blame them. Almost everyone has chosen sides and banded together with like-minded acquaintances. When I leave here, Mercy, we shall not see each other again until this is over.''

"You cannot come to me again under cover of darkness? Ian, if ever you are within a day's ride from here, you *must* come!''

"No, my love.'' He gently kissed away her protests. "I cannot risk it. Once I am known as a rabid loyalist working to stamp out the rebels, my life will be forfeit. Hotheads like your Daniel Morgan will come looking for *my* head, hoping to make an example of me . . .''

"Yes, 'tis true!'' she conceded. Quickly she muffled her

anguish with a sheet pressed to her mouth. "You will be like a fox with a pack of hounds on your heels. I know my own people. Any man with a gun in his hand will shoot you and count himself a hero for doing so!"

She pulled him over on top of her. "But I have you now, Ian. For tonight, you are mine. Unless you have other important news to impart, let us waste no more time talking when we could be loving instead."

"Nothing else is more important than what I have already told you," he murmured, bending to kiss her. "Loving you but once tonight would be a waste of a rare and precious opportunity."

She wrapped her arms around him and surrendered once more to their mutual passion . . . and so the night passed. Too soon came the hour of his leave-taking. Exhausted, she had fallen asleep but awoke as soon as he rose from the bed. The pale light in the room told her the hour; they had tarried longer than he had planned.

"Be still," he whispered, tugging on clothes and boots. "Stay here. I can find my own way out. I may have to dodge your servants."

"Perhaps I should come with you. If anyone sees you—"

"Trust me to be careful, my love. I got in unnoticed. I will get out unnoticed. 'Tis good practice for my mission in Boston."

"Sneaking in and out of a lady's bedchamber will be part of your mission?" she demanded, sitting upright and clutching the bedclothes to her naked breasts.

He grinned at her. "Did anyone ever tell you how lovely you are with your hair all tousled and your mouth swollen from kisses?"

She narrowed her eyes at him. "You had better kiss me one last time before you go or I swear I will follow you naked from my bedchamber and damn the consequences."

Laughing softly, he returned for the kiss but did not linger long in her arms. Sobering, he gazed down at her. "Farewell, my sweet. Stay as beautiful as you are until I come back to you. Stay safe. Stay well. . . . God! I am missing you already."

She grasped his hand and squeezed it hard. "Worry not about me; 'tis *you* who must stay safe and well. God go with you, Ian."

He kissed her once, quick and hard. Then he hurried to the door, opened it, and slipped out of her room, closing the door softly behind him. Mercy heard no cries of alarm or any other sounds to indicate that anyone had spotted him.

Finally, she lay back on the bed and stared up at the ceiling, praying as she had never prayed in her life. *Bring him back to me, God! Do not let me lose him now that I have just found him. Let this war be over soon and the colonists be victorious. Then bring him home to me . . .*

A disturbing thought occurred: If he succeeded in all he intended, how could he come home to her? No one would believe he had been fighting on the side of the Americans all along. . . . He might be killed by her own people! Or driven from America's shores along with the rest of the loyalists.

She could not imagine her friends and neighbors welcoming back the McCallisters, much less Ian—especially not if this conflict proved to be as long and bloody as she feared it might. Why, the war might last for a whole year or two! Perhaps even more.

She shuddered at the thought and pulled the bedclothes up over her head. It was time to rise and greet the new day, but for once—just this once—she wanted to burrow into the warmth and comfort of her bed, savor her memories of the night just past, and avoid seeing anyone.

CHAPTER ELEVEN

"Come on, Papa, you must eat." Mercy tried to spoon some gruel into his mouth but he shook his head and kept his lips firmly closed.

"No sense eating, girl," he growled a moment later, sounding perfectly lucid. That was her only comfort; today he knew her and even seemed to remember some of the news she had shared with him when she thought he had no idea what she was saying.

"Where is that pamphlet by Thomas Paine?" he complained. "I would rather you put down that bowl of hog slop and read to me. I had much rather feed my mind than my body."

Mercy's exasperation warred with hope that his own common sense might reawaken if she read him a bit of the pamphlet called *Common Sense*. It had caused a sensation when it first appeared early in the year. Seventeen seventy-six was now three-quarters over and had already proved to be a year to remember, but for much of it, her father had been too ill to mark the important events or even be aware of them.

"All right," she agreed, setting down the bowl on his bedside table. "Let me fetch it for you."

"Oh, forget it." Papa wearily waved his hand. "Better you should send a copy to that fool, Lord Dunmore, our incomparable royal governor. *He* needs to read it—not me. Do you know he tried to stop the revolution here in Virginia by offering freedom to the slaves? Invited the whole lot of 'em to join His Majesty's troops in helping to put down the rebellion."

"Papa, that was over a year ago, and Dunmore has now left Virginia," Mercy gently informed him. "Besides, everyone knows that any slaves foolish enough to believe Lord Dunmore were headed for the sugar plantations in the West Indies."

"Humph! What about that Ethiopian Regiment? Did he not help to form that? Why, the damn fool fought his own friends and neighbors—drove more people to support independency than if he had joined the cause himself!"

"Papa, why are we discussing last year's news, when so many other things have happened since then to—"

"If I knew how to find Lord Fox, I would send Paine's pamphlet to *him*, too, along with my own defense of the sentiments expressed therein. I would just like to hear what he thinks about *my* arguments."

Mercy's heart stilled in her breast. She drew a deep breath. "Lord Fox? Who do you mean, Papa?"

The Sons and Daughters of Liberty had taken to calling Ian by the name of Lord Fox, but Papa had surely been too unaware of current events to have heard of the title now conferred on the man known far and wide for his inflammatory articles refuting Thomas Paine's pamphlet. When a bunch of irate patriots had gone after him near Boston, from which the British along with many of their supporters had retreated in March, he had led them on such a merry chase across the countryside that they had dubbed him Lord Fox. After that, he had taken refuge with General William Howe in New York, another loyalist stronghold.

Lord Fox—her own dear Ian!—was said to be Howe's closest military advisor and the inspiration behind the British victory at the Battle of Long Island in August. He might also be the man responsible for persuading Howe not to press his advantage following that disastrous rout; if the British *had* pursued the fleeing Americans, the war would be over by now, with England the victors.

Mercy assumed that Ian was still in New York, where the Continental Army also remained, regrouping and preparing for what was hoped would be the final, decisive battle yielding an American triumph.

"Lord Fox is Lord Montjoy, of course!" her father erupted. "I am talking about Lord Montjoy—the scoundrel! Do you think me witless, Daughter, that I know nothing of the latest news? I do read such issues of the *Virginia Gazette* as make their way to Collier Manor, you know."

"I know you *used* to read the *Gazette*, Papa, but lately I thought—"

"You thought I no longer have a brain just because my body refuses to function?"

"You must admit you have not been yourself lately," Mercy hedged. Indeed, this was the most energetic and lively he had been for months. For the first time in a long time, they were actually having a conversation. Now all she needed to do was steer it away from Ian.

"You do appear perfectly fine today, Papa," she continued. "You even have a spot of color in your cheeks this afternoon."

Actually, she marveled at the change in him. He had grown thin, pale, and bony—a mere shadow of his former self. But the light of his personality glowed at this moment with much of its old fire and vigor. Propped up on pillows, his wasted hands clutching at the coverlet and his nightcap slightly askew, Papa returned her scrutiny with all his customary belligerence.

"The corpse is not dead yet, girl. Today I feel a flush of strength such as I have not felt in an eon. Why, I may live another whole month yet—that is, if I can last the week. I should like to make it to foxhunting season, but I imagine that would be asking too much. God is just humoring me to let me live this long."

"Oh, Papa!" Mercy smiled at him through a sudden rush of tears. "I am so happy you are feeling better! But

if you want to see hunt season, you must start to eat more.
'Tis only mid-September.''

"Humph!" her father snorted. "Damn cold for September. Must be going to have a miserable winter this year.
Have those fools in the Congress got around to signing a
declaration of independence yet?"

"Yes, Papa. It happened in July. There were many cele-
brations. We celebrated here, but you slept through it.''

"Did I, now? I do not remember it, so I must have. . . .
I suppose there is no chance you have found a husband
yet, either. Maybe I slept through that, too.''

Mercy blushed and again thought of Ian. "I am still
unwed, Papa.''

He heaved a huge sigh. "I thought so. I really am going
to die without seeing you wed. Somehow, I had hoped . . .
well, never mind what I had hoped. He has gone off to be
Lord Fox now, fighting on the side of the British. Guess I
was wrong about him all along. I had this odd notion he
might become one of us—might want to stay in America
and build a new life for himself. Might even want to marry
my daughter.''

It was Mercy's turn to sigh. She wished she could tell
him the truth, but she had promised Ian to say nothing
to anyone, and thus far, she had kept that promise.

Watching her, her father suddenly chortled. "Hah! I
knew it. You have feelings for him, do you not, girl? I can
see by your face that you do.''

Mercy decided she might as well admit the obvious. "I
will grant you I *did,* Papa. But what is the use of discussing
him? He is long gone from Collier Manor.''

Too long gone, she thought, recalling their last sweet
encounter.

"No use at all discussing him," Papa agreed. "Except I
think of him quite often, and I have a pain in my heart
whenever I do. Of course, I often have pains in my heart.
'Tis the pains will kill me one day.''

"Not the pain over Ian surely!''

"Ian now, is it?" Her father darted her a shrewd glance.
"You were never that familiar before.''

Mercy could feel her blush deepening. Fearing to reveal herself further, she refused to look at her father.

"What? . . . Have you ceased condemning him? You were always quick enough to condemn him in the past, Daughter. Here he's turned out to be even worse than you thought. After living in our house and partaking of our hospitality, he took himself off to aid our enemies. No doubt he hopes to gain Collier Manor if the British manage to defeat us. That would explain why he is working so hard for the loyalists. The lands of all those who refuse to give their allegiance to the king will be granted to those who remained friends of the Crown."

"Ian would never . . . !" Mercy began and stopped.

"Would never what, Daughter? . . . Why would he *not*? Together with the land I have already sold him and the land he bought from our neighbors, the remainder of our estate would make him one of the biggest landowners in Virginia."

"I just know he would never do a thing to harm us, Papa. Can we not leave it at that?"

"No, we cannot. Why are you defending him, Mercy?"

"I am not defending him! He is indeed a scoundrel— the worst sort of villain."

"Hah!" her father said. "Your mouth says one thing, but your eyes say another. That makes me doubly angry. I wish I were strong enough to get out of this bed, seek him out among his British friends, and shoot him in his traitorous heart. 'Twould be a fitting reward for his wickedness."

This was more than Mercy could bear. "He is not wicked, Papa! Trust me when I tell you this. They may call him Lord Fox and speak his name with loathing, but he is not wicked. I assure you he is not!"

"This from my daughter who believes so fervently in liberty? . . . Has he compromised you, Mercy? I thought I need never worry about that happening while he lived among us. He was too much a man of honor and you a woman of conviction. I *wanted* it to happen, mind you, but I feared it never would. Then, when he betrayed our friendship and joined the other side, I was glad he had not claimed your affections. But now . . . by God, if the scoundrel touched you and then deserted you . . .''

To Mercy's horror, her father suddenly began struggling to get out of bed. Throwing off the coverlet, he rose shakily to his feet. "Tell Moses to saddle my horse! I will ride out after him. Clear to New York, if I must. But I will find him and demand satisfaction for the wrong he has done me and mine!''

"Papa!'' Only Mercy's quick assistance prevented the old man from toppling to the floor. "Papa, get back into bed. You are far too weak for such a strenuous endeavor. You have not been out of that bed for weeks.''

"Fury will make me strong enough. If he compromised you and left you with a broken heart, I will have my revenge! God will keep me alive until I can punish him for his callous use of you.''

"Papa, no! . . . It was not that way at all. You have made a mistake . . .''

Her father fell back on the bed, his bony knees creaking. "Then what way was it, Mercy? Tell me, or I will go to my grave hating him. Heaven shall be denied me, for I will still have murder in my heart.''

Mercy drew another deep breath. "Oh, all right. I will tell you, Papa—but only if you swear by all you deem holy never to repeat a word of this to anyone else. No one knows what I am about to reveal—''

"Hah! I bet Chloe knows. You keep no secrets from that one.''

"Yes, I do, Papa. Chloe may have her suspicions, but she has heard nothing from me.''

Mercy proceeded to tell him about Ian's true role in the revolution. She also told him about the nature of their relationship—leaving out only the details of their intimacy. Her father need not know *every*thing.

"What welcome news this is to me!'' the old man exclaimed when she had finished. His grin was the widest she had ever seen on his face. Then he narrowed his eyes at her and demanded: "Has he bedded you?''

"Papa, how can you ask that? Whether he has or not, 'tis none of your concern.''

"I am making it my concern! I hope he has, for I want grandchildren. Is there any chance at all there could be a babe on the way?"

"No, Papa," Mercy answered honestly. Since a week after Ian's departure, she had known she was not pregnant. If she *had* conceived, the babe would have been born by now, but her father seemed not to realize just how long it had been since Ian had set foot in Collier Manor. Indeed, no one knew about his *last* visit. "There is no chance whatever."

"This is a time of war," her father testily reminded her. "You should have let him bed you. No one would condemn you for consummating your union before the ceremony. After all, you are a Collier, and they would never dare censure a Collier."

Mercy recalled saying almost the very same thing to Ian. But she still did not want her father to know all that had passed between the two of them. Her bond with Ian was sacred and private. She considered herself married to him already, but not until she and Ian formally exchanged vows was she willing to admit to the full extent of their commitment—especially not to her nosy father.

"Papa, swear to me to keep this secret. Ian's life would be endangered if word got out that he is not as he portrays—a fervent loyalist with enormous influence on the British military authorities."

"I still have a portion of my intellect, girl. To whom would I gossip anyway? These days, I see no one but you and a few worthless servants. But think me not unhappy; now I can die content knowing that when the war is over, Ian will return and wed you as I dreamed he would. Too bad I shall not be here to witness the event for myself."

"Of course you will be here!" Mercy chided. "Considering how well you are doing today, we have every reason to anticipate your attendance at my wedding. This war cannot last forever. Another few months and it will all be behind us."

"You are too optimistic, girl. Neither side is willing to quit. It may be a long time before we—*you*—see the infamous Lord Fox again."

"All the more reason why you must keep up your strength. Are you ready to eat now? . . . Your soup has gone cold and must be reheated."

"Perhaps I could eat a few bites," her father conceded. "Do not bother reheating it. Cold or hot, it will still taste like hog slop."

"You are so difficult!" Mercy scolded. "What am I to do with you?"

"Enjoy me while you still have me, Daughter, for soon I will be gone."

"I do not believe it. You will live for years yet." Mercy picked up the bowl and spoon. "Now, be a good boy and open your mouth this time."

"If you insist," her father grumbled.

Elated by his capitulation, Mercy began spooning the broth into his wasted body.

The next morning, when she went to wake him and feed him his breakfast, she discovered that sometime during the night he had slipped away. Papa had not lived to see her wedding after all. Nor would he ever know his grandchildren or who won the war.

Bleak and grief-filled, foxhunting season came and went. There were no foxhunts anyway, and the war news remained disheartening. Mercy read every scrap of news that came her way—searching for word of Ian. Town criers delivered the most up-to-date news, and the *Virginia Gazette* followed up with detailed accounts of various events, along with the usual advertisements offering land for sale or seeking information about runaway slaves and strayed or stolen horses. The articles pertained to events that had happened a week or more in the past, but Mercy still devoured every word.

From the *Gazette,* she learned that General Washington was gaining no ground in winning the war. The Americans succeeded in setting New York, a bastion for loyalists, ablaze, but a month later the British drove them off Chatterton's Hill in New Jersey. Again, for reasons no one could explain, Howe pulled back his troops at a time when he could have annihilated the Continentals.

Mercy silently thanked Ian—she was sure he was responsible!—but everyone else roundly condemned him for the scandalous articles he continued to publish. His cryptic rhetoric kept the loyalists staunchly pitted against their own fellow countrymen—this despite the Continental Congress's decision to grant free land to any British deserters who chose to join the patriot cause.

The news of all the battles and skirmishes was disturbing enough, but Mercy also had to deal with the rumors that a man had been hung for spying on the British in New York. If it had been Ian, Mercy was certain the incident would have merited more notice, but for weeks afterward she suffered nightmares, dreaming of him swinging from a tree limb.

In late December, after a November retreat in which General Washington was forced to leave Fort Lee to the British, the general redeemed himself by crossing the ice-choked Delaware River and capturing 868 Hessians, the elite German troops imported to fight for the British. This was followed by another stunning victory on the first day of the New Year, 1777, when he defeated Cornwallis and took Princeton.

The British now controlled barely a fifth of New Jersey. The news lifted the flagging spirits of patriots all across Virginia. Hearing that Washington attributed much of his success to "spies and scouts" who had supplied him with maps of Princeton and its environs, Mercy conducted her own quiet celebration. She *knew* Ian had played some part in these victories, and she prayed he would remain safe in his precarious position. Washington's own troops openly lusted after his hide as hounds lust after a fox's.

The winter of '77 shut down the war. Washington quartered at Morristown, New Jersey, while Howe—and Ian—remained entrenched in the eastern part of that beleaguered state. The news now became so dull and boring that Mercy began tossing the weekly issues of the *Virginia Gazette* into a pile on the table in the front hallway, where they languished unread until she could find a moment to quickly peruse them.

It was late April before she finally sat down with the stack in the library. Considering that it was the planting season, she had much to do, but today it was raining, and besides, she had a Daughters of Liberty meeting—the first of the spring season—scheduled for later that afternoon. She wanted to catch up on the news her lady friends would all be discussing.

She began with the oldest of the issues, dated January 10, 1777. It contained another article by Thomas Paine, this one called "American Crisis," which opened with the stirring words:

> *These are the times that try men's souls. The summer soldier and the sunshine patriot will, in this crisis, shrink from the service of his country; but he that stands it now, deserves the love and thanks of man and woman.*

She thought of Ian and all those others who were risking their lives for the American cause, and her eyes misted over. What Paine said was certainly true:

> *Tyranny, like hell, is not easily conquered; yet we have this consolation with us, that the harder the conflict, the more glorious the triumph. What we obtain too cheap, we esteem too lightly—'Tis dearness only that gives every thing its value.*

If Ian ever did come home to her—whole, in one piece—she would consider herself the most fortunate of women and spend the rest of her life cherishing and enjoying their love.

She finished reading the article but due to the lateness of the hour only riffled through the remaining issues. There were the usual notices advertising stallions to whom one could breed one's best mares at so many shillings a leap or a set amount for the entire season. Thinking of Liberty, she quickly glanced down the names: Mercury, Tristram Shandy, Merry Tom, Sprightly, Bucephalus . . .

She was acquainted with most of them and considered them fine horses—but of course, she was saving Liberty for Thor, the only stallion truly worthy of her high-bred darling. Sighing, she was about to lay the stack of papers aside when a single line on the top one caught her eye:

New Jersey, April 14, 1777. A trial date has been set for Lord Fox, lately accused of being a spy for the American cause . . .

Mercy stopped breathing. The print swam before her eyes. For a moment, she feared she might faint. Then she inhaled deeply and forced herself to continue reading. The article noted that the man known to the Americans as "Lord Fox" was also known as Viscount Ian Montjoy. Despite all the articles he had written on his sovereign's behalf, he was accused of betraying his British masters. Those same masters now intended to try and hang him for treason. The trial was being delayed for six weeks so that an adequate investigation could be made into the matter of his having passed sensitive documents to known American sympathizers.

There were few details regarding time and place, except a notation that the trial would be held in New Jersey. Presumably, it would take place within the British encampment. The article concluded that Lord Fox had somehow trod upon the toes of his superiors and lost their support to the extent that they now wished to be rid of him.

It would appear Lord Fox has only reaped what he has sown. If they do hang him, those who love liberty must waste no tears. Rather, we should say, "He only got what he, deserved," regardless of which side he embraced at the end.

Mercy raced through the remaining papers, but this was the only article on the subject.

They were going to hang Ian.

The thought almost strangled her. She could hear herself gasping for breath—choking on the horror of it. Today was the twenty-eighth of April. The trial was set for six

weeks from April 14. Quickly she calculated the days and
wondered if she had time to stop it.

How could she possibly stop it?

What could she do? Was there even enough time to
concoct some plan to save him?

Jumping to her feet and scattering the papers on the
floor, Mercy began to pace the library. She was still pacing,
her mind in turmoil, when Chloe appeared at the door.

"Your lady friends have arrived . . . Lud a' mercy! What
is it, girl? I never seen you look so upset—not even when
your poor Papa up and died."

"Oh, Chloe! Come in and shut the door. I must share
this news or I will surely go mad. The most terrible thing
has happened!"

Half an hour later, Mercy was ready to greet her guests.
She was not only ready, she was eager, for she had a tiny
kernel of an idea—unintentionally sparked by Chloe. Not
that Chloe would actually approve of the scheme once she
heard it, but it was Chloe who had urged her to seek the
help of "her lady friends."

"They a wise bunch of females," Chloe had said, her
white turban bobbing. "They can help you decide what t'
do. Men always think women are only fit t' have babies,
sew, and put up food for the winter, but you been provin'
men wrong all your life, girl. So have some of your lady
friends, especially durin' this here war. While their menfolks are off fightin', the women are runnin' the farms
and plantations as if they was born to it. Without the wom-
enfolk, there would be nothin' for the menfolks t' come
home to when this war is finally over."

"We will not be seeking any advice from men on this
issue," Mercy had agreed. "Men would only let Ian hang.
But once the Daughters of Liberty in this county understand what Ian has been doing for them—"

Another half hour later, all thirteen of the women
attending the afternoon's meeting were in agreement:
Something must be done to save Lord Montjoy.

Moreover, they were willing to do whatever they could

to help. Only Emma Leeds, disapproving as always, dared question any part of Mercy's story.

"How do you know all these things about Lord Montjoy?" she demanded, fixing Mercy with her piercing gaze. Her knitting needles stilled, as indeed all of the women had stopped working since Mercy had begun explaining her dilemma. "You have not precisely revealed the extent of your relationship with the gentleman in question."

Caroline, ever defensive of Mercy, immediately spoke up. "That is none of our business, Emma. Mercy is entitled to her privacy."

"In a pig's eye she is! She has requested our assistance, and who knows what dangers we may encounter in rendering it? I foresee many risks involved in this effort to secure the viscount's freedom. So I want to know exactly how our Mercy feels about him."

As with her father, Mercy had avoided any mention of her feelings—had left out the details of her relationship with Ian. But these women—her dearest friends who had been helping one another, including *her*, through these trying times—deserved to know the truth. The truth could no longer hurt Ian anyway and might, in fact, save him.

"I love him," she said simply. "When this is all over, we plan to wed. He came to me in the dead of night at the very beginning of this adventure and warned me I would be hearing the worst about him. He said I must hold my tongue and agree with the condemnations, many of which were uttered by persons sitting in this very room. . . . Also, he spent the night with me," she added, lifting her chin and staring at the shocked faces of her avidly listening friends. "I care not who knows it. The bond between us has been sealed by the sharing of our bodies. So you see, my friends, I will do all in my power to save him, *with* your help or without it."

"Well, that is surely opening the horse's mouth and showing us all its teeth," Arabella Lee dryly commented. "Do we buy the horse or not, ladies? After such a romantic tale, I feel I must leap to save the lovers and spare our dear Mercy's reputation. She must wed the viscount at once, or custom dictates we may no longer speak to her. That would be most awkward, to say the least."

"I am with you, Mercy," Caroline said quietly. "Nor can my William possibly say nay to me. The last I heard, he was with General Washington, but that was months ago. Now, I have no idea whether he still lives or not."

"Of course he still lives! Never doubt it. Doubt is our greatest enemy. We are *all* with you, Mercy," Eunice Galvin assured her. Heads nodded all around the room. "The question remains, what can we *do?*"

"I have a plan," Mercy confided. "A very reckless and ill-advised one, but a plan nonetheless. It will mean we must travel—not all of us perhaps, but at least some of us—for I can scarcely go to New Jersey alone."

"Go to New Jersey!" Caroline exclaimed. "I very much feared you were going to suggest that!"

"First we must examine our wardrobes to ensure we have the proper attire."

"Whatever do you mean by proper attire, Mercy?" Eunice demanded. "And how are we to travel? You younger ladies can ride horses, but we older ones—"

"Can go in a wagon and sew as we travel," Mercy suggested. "We all must sew, for we will need new gowns in loyalist colors."

"Mercy, have you lost your wits? I would willingly wear red, white, and blue, the colors of our new nation, but I refuse to go anywhere attired in plain scarlet and white!" Anne Marie exclaimed.

"Then we will fashion gowns in patriotic colors with removable blue trim," Mercy suggested. "That way we can travel safely through our own territory as well as those lands controlled by the loyalists. When people see us, they will know at once where we stand. Now, let me share the rest of my plan with you, and you can all tell me what you think."

The remainder of the afternoon passed in vigorous discussion of Mercy's plans, with the end result that five women plus Mercy herself agreed to go to New Jersey to rescue Ian. The fact that none of them knew where in New Jersey to look for him did not deter them. There was only one major road to New Jersey, and Mercy intended to follow it for as long as possible. When they got there, they could surely find someone who knew about the judicial proceedings involving Lord Fox.

The fact that they would be traveling through a land at war merited much discussion. For a party of Virginia planters—all female—to travel unescorted across a country at war was the height of foolhardiness. . . . But these women were no "sunshine patriots," Mercy was gratified to discover. Some of them had already lost cousins, brothers, sons, fathers, or husbands. Some would undoubtedly lose more before the war ended. . . . *This* man they would save.

Besides, as Arabella Lee pointed out: "If women can be camp followers, as so many poorer woman are, I know not why *we* should not succeed. If anyone seeks to detain us, we will claim we are searching for our husbands."

"If I did not have a plantation to oversee, I would have gone to war with William!" Caroline declared. "That is all the camp followers are doing—following their husbands."

"Humph!" said Emma, who had surprised Mercy by volunteering to go. "I just hope we live long enough to put our plans into effect."

"We will live long enough," Mercy insisted. "Our cause is right and just, so God will protect us."

"Assuming God is a patriot," Anne Marie added, sounding worried.

"Nonsense!" Arabella Lee exclaimed. "How could He be otherwise?"

How indeed? Mercy thought.

She supposed they would soon find out.

CHAPTER TWELVE

The trial was not going well, but Ian had no idea how to make it go better. He had too many enemies—had been too close to General Howe. When Howe had listened to Ian and taken his advice over that of others, the others—dissenters all—had been furious. Now they had their chance at revenge. Discrediting and hanging him was what they wanted, and it appeared they were going to get it.

Gazing up at the rafters of the large barn where the trial was being held, Ian wondered if word of the proceedings had reached Mercy. She might not even hear about it until after he was dead. His only consolation was that Hiram had not been caught; after apprehending Ian, the British regulars had searched for his companion, but thus far in vain. Hiram would be looking for a way to free him, but there was little a single man could do against half the British Army.

He was too well guarded. At night he slept in a granary shed surrounded by a ring of soldiers. On the outskirts of a small, predominantly loyalist New Jersey town, the farm belonged to a prominent supporter of the king who had put it at General Howe's disposal. The general and his highest-ranking officers occupied the house, while the army camped around it and made use of the outbuildings.

General Howe had refused to attend the trial. His parting words to Ian had been: "If you are found innocent, this will not destroy our friendship, but if you are proved guilty, you may count on hanging immediately following the trial."

The trial bore little resemblance to any judicial proceedings or court-martial Ian had ever witnessed. In truth it was a farce. The jury, if it could be called that, was made up of British officers who had every reason to be envious of his position of influence. Amazingly enough, the magistrate was a minister, a friend of the family who owned the farm and therefore supposedly unbiased. Inasmuch as Ian was a civilian, although he functioned more like a high-ranking officer, General Howe had been uncertain how to handle the matter. Ian had half expected to be hung on the spot. If not for his friendship with General Howe, he would have been. Howe, at least, had questioned the evidence.

It consisted of his first letter to the king, the one in which he had sent no names, and his being caught in the wrong place at the wrong time on the very night when military secrets en route to the Americans had been intercepted. He had, in fact, passed the incriminating documents to the "pigeon" a scant hour earlier, but no one had actually seen him do it. The "pigeon" had been shot and killed by a British patrol when he refused to stop and be searched. Upon finding the documents on the dead man's person, the soldiers had speculated that whoever had given them to him might still be in the vicinity.

He and Hiram both had been in the vicinity. When hailed by the British, Ian had attempted to outrun them on Thor while Hiram took cover in a wood with his horse. The soldiers had not spotted Hiram, but Ian had unknowingly run headlong into another British patrol. There was nothing he could do at that point but pretend to be glad to see them—a ploy which had utterly failed.

No one believed his story that he had simply been passing through the area on his way to locate a competent farrier for his horse and had somehow gotten lost. None of Thor's shoes were loosened, and the stallion did not appear in immediate need of a farrier. But it was all Ian could think of to excuse his presence abroad in disputed territory so late at night.

He would never know the name of the "pigeon"—the man who had volunteered to carry the valuable information on troop strength and movements to General Washington. He had carried no identification—only the packet of papers Ian had given him. Like Nathan Hale, another unfortunate spy, the "pigeon" had stuffed the papers into his shoes, the first place the soldiers had looked.

"Lord Ian Montjoy!" the minister/magistrate suddenly called out, and Ian straightened his back and looked him in the eye. The worst thing about this trial was the three-legged stool they had given him to sit on; he found it difficult to keep an erect posture for hour after hour of meaningless testimony.

"Yes?" He cocked an eyebrow with the same bored indifference he had been cultivating since the trial's beginning two days previously.

"You will please stand, sir, if you wish to address this court!" the minister fumed, his face reddening. He was a pompous old fellow who had drawn out the proceedings for as long as possible—probably because he believed it enhanced his standing in the community.

Many of his congregation had turned out from the nearest town—women and children mostly, who seemed in awe of these lofty happenings. Ian slowly rose to his feet and flexed his manacled hands to ease the cramping in them.

"Lord Montjoy, you have heard the testimony of numerous persons regarding your character. Have you anything to respond at this time?"

"My character—or lack of one—should hardly be an issue, should it?" Ian calmly stated. "What matters most is the evidence against me—or lack of it."

"We have been trying to determine what manner of person you are, my lord, which indeed has a bearing on these proceedings."

In his black frock coat, the minister looked like a crow amidst the splendor of peacocks. The British officers were all attired in their familiar red coats with long narrow lapels, collars, and small round cuffs, worn over white waistcoats, breeches, and dress gaiters. Epaulettes had recently been introduced to the uniform of the British officer, but not all the officers yet sported them; most just wore a crimson sash around the waist and a gorget at the throat to distinguish themselves from the regulars.

Giving them all a long look, Ian felt shabby by comparison. He wore only a soiled white shirt, a dark vest and breeches, and his comfortable tall boots. They had confiscated his coat and weapons, along with his horse. Nothing incriminating had been found, of course, for he had already passed on the documents.

"If you wish to know what sort of person I am, why not save time by asking me?" he continued. "Your witnesses barely know me, while those who sit in judgment upon me"—he nodded toward the row of seated officers—"could be said to know me almost as well as I know myself. Indeed, I could name most of you. We have rubbed shoulders together at social gatherings and military meetings throughout this campaign. Some of you have been present at the same strategy sessions I have attended—meetings where General Howe has elicited my views prior to making his own decisions. When I have voiced my opinion, some of you have disagreed with me . . . and *that*, gentlemen, is why we are here, is it not? You see this as an opportunity to be rid of me once and for all."

"That is untrue!" Lieutenant Joseph Woolwich—a hook-nosed, pinch-faced young man—leapt to his feet.

Ian fastened his gaze upon the man appointed as prosecutor in these proceedings. Lieutenant Woolwich had gathered the witnesses and fueled the jealousy of his comrades in arms. He was an ambitious officer who had not yet risen as high as he hoped in the British Army. General Howe had several times bypassed his advice in favor of Ian's, and Woolwich, proud officer of the Fifth Regiment, known as the King's Own, clearly resented it.

"What is untrue, Lieutenant?" Ian drawled. "Defend

yourself from the charge, if you wish. I should not be the only one forced to defend myself in these proceedings."

"You seek to evade the issue here, sir! We have your letter to the king—right here it is." Snatching a paper from a barrel top, he stalked over to Ian and waved it in his face. "In it you declare your inability to continue with the mission the king himself assigned you."

"Does it say in that letter that I support independency?" Ian knew it did not. He had worked hard to word it so no conclusions about his beliefs could be drawn from it.

"No, but why would you excuse yourself from doing your duty if you did *not* support the rebels in their cause?"

"Because we went to war over the issue," Ian explained as if speaking to a dullard. "What need had the king of spies when he intended to destroy the rebels, anyway? Later, I did send a list of names to the king; apparently you never found *that* letter, or else you have decided not to produce it because it supports *my* case, not yours."

"I doubt there *was* a second letter. No one knows anything about it. As for your *first* letter, you could have continued spying for the king, but you did not wish to do so because your sympathies now belonged to the rebels. Even if you can explain away *this* letter, you cannot explain your presence abroad at a very late hour on the night we apprehended your partner."

"You have yet to prove he *was* my partner."

"And you have yet to produce the farrier you supposedly went to see. Your horse was neither lame nor shoeless nor in dire need of a trimming. If he was, you could have used General Howe's own farrier."

"I dislike how he trims my horse's feet," Ian drawled, staring down his accuser. "As for my intentions, Lieutenant, I suggest you read my most recent articles if you wonder where I stand on things."

"A ruse, my lord! You wrote those inflammatory articles as a ruse. So you could go about the business of passing sensitive information to the enemy without being suspect. But we have you now. Only a very few men are informed about the details of our troop deployment, yet the details were in that scoundrel's shoes! 'Twas information so fresh and accurate it could only have come from someone extremely close to General Howe himself, someone such as yourself, my lord, someone who curried favor with the general and enjoyed far greater freedom than my tightly disciplined colleagues. How else can you explain what you were doing on your horse—alone in hostile territory—in the dead of night?"

"I have already mentioned I had gotten lost," Ian said, knowing it was hopeless. Every single man who knew what Ian knew had an alibi—and witnesses, including General Howe himself. Only Ian had produced so lame an excuse. There was no farrier such as he claimed existed, a fact he had tried to explain by suggesting he may have gotten the name wrong.

"You—*Lord Fox*—were lost?" the lieutenant snarled, wrinkling his long, thin nose. "You lie, my lord. Even the name *Lord Fox* is part of your ruse to deceive us. We foolishly took you into our confidence—our henhouse, as it were—when what we should have done was require you to prove your allegiance before we ever dared trust you."

"You still have not proved that I have betrayed that trust," Ian insisted.

"I believe we have, sir. Even aside from your refusal to serve the crown and your presence in the vicinity where we caught that spy, we know you have purchased large tracts of land in the colonies—obviously with the intention of settling here when this is all over."

"That is not obvious at all, Lieutenant."

"To me, it is—as it must be to every other thinking individual. Why else did you remain here with the outbreak of war? Most men would have returned at once to safety in England."

"I thought I might be of use to the British cause," Ian shot back. "I dare say I *have* been of use. My writings have helped the loyalists retain their purpose and optimism— encouraging them to band together and offer their assistance to the British Army. As several witnesses have already testified, I myself am a frequent visitor at loyalist gatherings, and—"

"And the witnesses have all noted how little actual participation they have seen from you in loyalist activities. You are quick to wield your pen but slow to act, Lord Montjoy. Worse, you have insinuated yourself into positions you have not earned and set yourself up as an expert in military matters about which you know little or nothing. Had we not followed your advice on several occcasions, this war would already be over.... Bah! 'Tis time we call an end to this delay of justice and do our duty. The crown rests its case. Lord Ian Montjoy is guilty as charged and deserves to hang for the crime of treason!''

Heads nodded among the seated officers, and the minister intoned: ''The time has come, gentlemen. When your name is called out, please render your decision—guilty as charged, or not guilty.''

''Major Edmund Braithwaite!'' a stony-faced ensign announced.

''Guilty!'' the major responded.

''Captain Thomas Buckingham!''

''Guilty!'' came the reply.

''Subaltern Adam Fonsworthy!''

''Guilty!''

On and on it went: *Guilty. Guilty. Guilty.*

''Wait!'' a woman suddenly cried out.

All eyes, including Ian's, turned to the barn's entrance. There stood an amazing sight—a half-dozen bewigged women gowned in loyalist scarlet and white, and at their center—*Mercy!*

Ian was dumbfounded. The last person he expected to see at this moment was the woman who came striding down the center aisle of the barn. Even more astounding was her condition; her midriff bulged as if she might be compelled to lie down and give birth at any moment.

''There you are, Lord Montjoy—you unprincipled brute! How shocked you look to see me, as well you should. You thought I was long gone from here, did you not? Returned in shame to Virginia. We are a long way from where we began, certainly. And you have come to a fitting end. But before you dangle him from a tree, gentlemen, you must compel him to marry me and give this poor babe that I carry a name—and an inheritance to sustain us after he is dead.''

"J-Just a moment here!" the minister sputtered. "Who is this woman? . . . Identify yourself, madam, and tell us how you know the accused. You cannot simply enter here and interrupt these proceedings with your incredible demands! Ensign, fetch her a chair, will you? 'Tis a wonder she can even stand in her condition.''

There was a moment's pause while the chair was brought.

"Thank you," Mercy said to the young ensign as she heaved herself into the chair and modestly arranged her scarlet skirts about her.

Aghast at the risks she was taking, Ian could only stare. *What was she doing here? Why had she come, placing her life— and the lives of all her friends, most of whom he recognized—in such mortal danger?*

He did not have to wait long to find out.

"I am Miss Prudence McCallister," she announced. "And these women who have accompanied me here today are other loyalists from Virginia. Alas, we were forced to flee for our very lives when we made known our political sentiments! We have all been living quietly in the area, praying for General Howe to win a great victory so that we may return to our homes unmolested. However—"

"Get to the heart of the matter, Miss McCallister," the minister exhorted. "We are about to hang this man. Please tell us what you know about him and why you have come here."

"The reason for my presence here today should be obvious. Lord Ian Montjoy is the father of my child. You must not hang him until he weds me, or my poor babe will have no father to call his own. I myself will have no means of supporting him—or her, as the case may be."

"When and where did you first meet and . . . ah . . . become intimately acquainted with Lord Montjoy?"

"In Virginia." Mercy tucked a stray white curl back into her powdered wig and smiled innocently at everyone. "Lord Montjoy bought land from friends of my family's— the Colliers. He courted me, and we . . . ah . . . began a relationship. The war prevented us from marrying as we had planned. When Lord Montjoy came east, I followed—but he seemed less enamored of me here than he was in Virginia. . . . Why, these days he rarely comes to visit me, though I am carrying his child! Worse, he keeps delaying our nuptials. 'When the war is over,' he always says, but the war may go on forever, and—"

"Miss McCallister!" the minister interrupted. "If anyone would know, *you* would. Is Lord Montjoy loyal to the crown? Has he said anything to lead you to believe that his loyalties lie with—"

"Oh, he is absolutely loyal to the king!" Mercy exclaimed. "But too busy writing his pamphlets and articles to do his duty by me and his child. The last time we were together, he told me that all my begging was useless. He might never wed me—especially if England loses this war. If that should happen, he himself will forfeit his lands here and have to flee for his life. I asked him why he could not take me with him, and he answered that being colony-born and bred, I would never fit into his life in England. It would be best if I remained here—but I think he must have a wife in England, and *that* is why he refuses to take me there!"

"A wife in England!" the minister exclaimed.

A buzzing sound broke out among the officers. They exchanged glances and murmured among themselves.

"Lord Montjoy," Lieutenant Woolwich said. *"Do* you have a wife in England? Is that why you refuse to do right by this young woman?"

Ian could only guess at Mercy's intentions. She had come here to save him—that much was certain—but he feared saying the wrong thing and ruining her plan.

"I have no wife," he finally answered, "but I do have a betrothed, a very sweet—and wealthy—young woman. Taking this young lady back with me to England would be a great embarrassment. She would not fit into my life there, nor be easy to explain."

"You swine!" Mercy shouted. She made as if to rise from her chair, but her lady friends gathered around her and gently pushed her back down. As a single unit, they glared at Ian.

"Gentlemen!" Mercy implored. "Do you not see? Before you hang him, you must make him wed me. My child needs a name, and I need a way to support us both. Lord Montjoy has money. As his wife, I can petition his family. The property he owns here will belong to my child when he comes of age. You must not hang him until he weds me!"

"Miss McCallister, this is a . . . a most awkward situation," the minister said. "We already have enough votes to hang this man, but now *you* appear, claiming he is loyal to the crown. I myself hardly know what to believe anymore."

"Oh, I am certain he is loyal! 'Tis all he talks about . . . all he thinks about," Mercy sobbed. Tears streamed down her cheeks—further amazing Ian. He had no idea she was such an accomplished liar. "He no longer even visits me in the daylight, but only comes after dark. I believe he is ashamed to be seen with me. He has no intention of wedding me. Why, he was with *me* the very night you captured him! He spent the entire evening in my company, then said he must depart before daylight. That was the night I begged him to relent and marry me before the babe's arrival. When he refused and walked out on me, I became violently ill."

"She could barely eat or even rise from her bed!" one of the women—Ian recognized Caroline Darby—declared. "She gave up all hope, wept constantly, and wished she and her babe would die rather than continue living. It took some time to persuade her to come here and plead with you, gentlemen. If you are going to hang Lord Montjoy, compel him to accept his responsibilities first and wed this woman. In our opinion, he *deserves* to be hanged for what he has done to her."

"He was with *you* on the night he was caught abroad and accused of treason?" Lieutenant Woolwich demanded.

"Yes!" Mercy cried. "Has he not admitted it? Does he hate me so much, then? I cannot think why! I gave him *every*thing, gentlemen! Despite my condition, I pleasured him in ways I am ashamed to admit—"

"In ways you are ashamed to admit!" The minister's jaw dropped. Ian would have burst out laughing if the moment had not been so grave. He could sense the mood of the onlookers changing. Mercy had better be careful she did not go too far; they would hang him for what he had done to *her,* if not for treason.

"I do honestly care for this woman," he interrupted, suddenly inspired. "Enough so that I would never consent to see her dragged into these proceedings and forced to admit what she has just told you. I lied when I said I had gone to fetch a farrier that night. I did actually go to see *her* and did indeed tell her I could not marry her unless— and until—the British prove victorious. If victory is ours, I can remain here and wed her—live on the lands I have purchased. But in the event of defeat, I must return to England and face the woman I have deserted—the woman who still believes herself betrothed to me. I thought I could avoid hanging without revealing the truth; it appears I was wrong in that assumption. You now know everything, gentlemen. . . . However, considering your dislike of me, I doubt it will change your minds about your verdict."

"It does not change *my* mind," Lieutenant Woolwich snapped. "You are as despicable as ever I thought you were."

"The vote must be retaken," the minister protested. "This changes everything. You cannot hang a man for treason when we *know* where he was on the night in question."

"But what about *me?*" Mercy paused to blow her nose in a handkerchief. "What will become of me and my poor child?"

"If they *do* hang me, I will wed you and give our child a name first," Ian blurted. "You should have had more faith in me, sweetling. I never intended to leave you without a shilling to your name. Even if I had to return to England, I would have sent you money—"

" 'Tis not the same as wedding me!" Mercy laboriously rose to her feet. "Either wed me or shoot me, my lord, for I have no desire to *live* without you!"

She flung out her arms in a gesture of despair, then collapsed weeping in the arms of her lady friends.

"Miss McCallister, restrain yourself! Gentlemen, in light of these revelations, you *must* reconsider," the minister cried. "Ensign, call the roll!"

"Major Edmund Braithwaite!"

"Not guilty."

"Captain Thomas Buckingham!"

"Not guilty."

"Subaltern Adam Fonsworthy!"

"Not guilty of treason, but guilty of many other things."

Laughter broke out, and Ian cracked his own first smile in weeks. When the last man voted, he knew he was free. He held out his manacled hands to Lieutenant Woolwich, who was quivering with rage and thwarted purpose.

"If you would be so good as to remove these, Lieutenant, I should like to embrace the mother of my child."

"Not until you wed me!" Mercy shrieked at him. "There will be no more kisses or sweet caresses until you do right by me and our babe, Ian!"

At this, the officers guffawed, and one of them called out: "We will see him wed you at sword point if need be, Miss McCallister. While there is a minister so close at hand, he can delay no longer. We will not permit it."

" 'Tis glad I am to hear *that,"* Mercy huffed while Lieutenant Woolwich reluctantly motioned for a private to remove Ian's shackles.

"You may have escaped punishment *this* time," the young officer spat. "But I will be watching you as closely as your new bride. This is not the end of this, Lord Montjoy."

"I had not imagined it was," Ian responded, rubbing his chaffed wrists. "One has only to look at you to see your resentment. . . . Ah, Prudence. How about a hug, at least?"

He opened his arms to Mercy, and she waddled into them. Only as he clasped her to him and felt her unfamiliar contours did he ask himself if she really *was* expecting a child—*his* child. The idea set him frantically counting backward to ascertain if it were possible.

" 'Ware my pillows," she whispered into his ear as she hugged him.

The warning reassured him, although he had suddenly realized he could not have done this to her. They had been too long apart. Just then, the minister came up beside them.

"You heard the members of the jury. You must wed this woman immediately, my lord," he scolded. "Do allow me to offer my services."

"I accept them and gladly," Ian answered. "Would this evening be too soon to conduct the nuptials?"

He had no intention of allowing Mercy to leave without spending time alone with her. Now that he could continue his work, she must, of course, return to Virginia, but not before he had enjoyed at least a night or two in her company. He deserved *that* much for the risks he had taken—and so did she.

"This evening would be excellent," the minister said.

"Thank you," Ian answered. "You are a man of many talents."

He did not mean it as a compliment, but the minister took it as such. "I do my best to serve both God and my king," he responded. "This evening, then."

They were wed that night in the farmhouse in the presence of General Howe and most of the officers who had earlier that day condemned Ian to hang. Only Lieutenant Woolwich failed to attend the festivities. All the other officers seemed relieved at the outcome and glad to exchange civilities with him.

Mercy's Daughters of Liberty—as well as the few officers' wives who were present—had exhausted themselves making everything as festive as possible during a time of war. The house glowed with candlelight, and a modest feast had been laid out on a long table. A fifer provided music for the occasion, and Mercy came to Ian wearing her loyalist colors—as did her friends, who continued playing the role of ardent loyalists. To everyone they met, they explained how they had fled Virginia and come east to escape persecution by "those patriot vermin," as Arabella Lee referred to them.

After the brief ceremony, Ian and Mercy chatted with General Howe.

"I am delighted to meet the man about whom I have heard such high praise from my dearest husband," Mercy gushed, fluttering her lashes at the general.

Ian groaned inwardly at her boldness. She seemed not to realize how much danger still surrounded them. One improper word, and they could *all* be hanged.

"What a delightful creature you are, my dear! No wonder Ian kept your relationship a secret. He must have feared competition for your affections . . . eh, Ian?"

"That might have had something to do with it, General." Ian took Mercy's arm. "Are you hungry, Wife? You *must* be. I insist you take time to eat now."

"Oh, I am not hungry!" Mercy bubbled, missing the point entirely. "I love talking to General Howe! Pray do not tear me away from him just yet, Husband."

Ian emitted another silent groan. "Really, my dear, I must insist that you keep up your strength. Come along now and eat. We can return to the general later."

"Oh, all right! But only if you promise not to slip away as soon as I turn my back, General."

Mercy's eyes were dancing. *She* may have been enjoying herself, but *he* was not. This was no game they were playing; as soon as he decently could, he intended to slip away with her—*far* away. He could only hope that her lady friends were wiser than she was and would slip away also before one of them said something to give them all away.

Prior to his imprisonment, he had been living in a room in a tavern in the nearest town, but he doubted the tavern keeper had held it for him these last six weeks. He did not even know where Thor was or what had happened to his belongings. He had yet to discover where Mercy and her friends were staying, but the sooner they departed the area, the better. Every moment they remained made it more likely they would all be exposed.

"Eat something," Ian hissed in Mercy's ear as he steered her toward the heavy-laden table. "It will give you something to do with your mouth besides get yourself—and me—in more trouble."

"Do not walk so fast," Mercy hissed back. "A woman in my condition cannot run, you know."

"You may *have* to run before this night is over. I hope not, for I want to be alone with you before you go . . . but if you keep prattling on so freely, I may not have the chance."

"Why are you so angry?" she whispered. "Stop scowling. You should be happy. Our plan has worked beautifully. 'Tis a grand success. You must admit I am devilishly clever. And so are my ladies. I am so proud of them—and of myself as well."

"I am proud of you, too. I am also furious. You took too many risks in coming here."

Smiling, Mercy turned sideways to allow an officer holding a piled-high plate to pass. "If I had not come, you would be dangling from a tree limb by now," she murmured. "Pray do not forget it."

"How can I?" he responded. "I am forever in your debt."

"Exactly where I am pleased to have you," she teased, grinning up at him. "I never intend to let you forget this."

Ian was simultaneously exasperated, charmed, and amused. He did not know how much longer he could last without capturing her in his arms and kissing the stuffing right out of her—exposing her charade himself!

"Such a wonderful array of foods!" Mercy exclaimed, arriving at the table. She leaned over it as if to make her selections. "Oh, Ian! In this time when so many are in want, I feel guilty we can still enjoy such abundance."

Suddenly she looked up and gasped. "Oh, no!"

"What is it?" he demanded, moving closer.

Her eyes were huge. Her face had grown pale.

"Reggie. Reggie Wharton," she murmured. "You remember—the man I was supposed to marry. He is here and heading straight for us. Oh, my goodness, there is Prudence, too! I thought they had fled to Canada. What shall we do? They will recognize *all* of us!"

CHAPTER THIRTEEN

As Prudence's eyes widened in recognition, Mercy struggled to recall the plan she and her friends had discussed that afternoon—what they would do tonight if anything should go wrong at the nuptial festivities. In her shock at seeing two people she knew—who knew *her*—she had almost forgotten.

"We must get out of here—*fast,*" Ian snapped behind her.

"No! My friends—I cannot leave them here!" Mercy placed both hands on her stomach and screamed as loud as she could. "Oh, God! Someone fetch a midwife—the babe is coming!"

"What are you doing?" Ian seized her hand as if to drag her away.

There had been no opportunity to tell him about their plan in case anything went wrong tonight. As yet, they had not been alone together. At least, since he was holding her hand, he would not get lost in the commotion sure to follow. She knew he would be happy to discover that Hiram was somewhere outside, waiting with saddled horses—their very own Thor and Liberty. The team and wagon were also there, ready for the Daughters of Liberty to make a quick escape if the need arose. Now, the need had arisen.

"Trust me!" she implored, quickly leaning forward and blowing out the tapers illuminating the table.

In a matter of moments, the room—and the whole house—went dark. That was the plan: for each of her ladies to immediately extinguish all the candles and make a quick departure the moment she pretended to be going into labor.

"Hurry, Ian," she urged, half-dragging him through the darkness.

He responded by dragging *her*. Stumbling into people—colliding with them and pushing them aside—they raced for the front door of the house. All around them, men shouted and women screamed as if convinced they were under attack. Mercy could hear General Howe himself hollering for a light and ordering his men to arms.

Once outside, Mercy spotted her friends already scrambling into the wagon in the starlit night.

"Me lord, here!" Hiram called out to them. "I have got the horses. Ye need not worry about the rest of us. I will look after the lasses."

How fortunate that the women had discovered Hiram in the nearby town! He had recognized them before they noticed him, and he'd advised them to camp in a thickly wooded spot near the town. It had the advantage of being not too far from the farm but far enough from the town for them to avoid just such a chance meeting with anyone who might know them. Hiram and Arabella had put their heads together and devised the escape plan for tonight.

Hiking up her skirts, Mercy climbed aboard Liberty, while Ian did the same with Thor. Already men were pouring from the house and lights were flaring inside.

"We must rush home and save our children!" Arabella Lee—who was childless—cried out. "Soldier, get out of our way! Go catch the enemy who ruined this fine evening."

Startled, the bewildered man obeyed. Arabella then grabbed the lines of the horses hitched to the wagon while Caroline seized the whip and snapped it across the team's backs.

Ian spun Thor around and shouted to Mercy, "Follow me!"

She barely had time to hook one leg over the high pommel of her sidesaddle and find her stirrup with her free foot before they were off—galloping into the night and leaving the commotion behind them. She knew they would be followed; General Howe would quickly sort out what had happened.

What were Reggie and Prudence doing here, anyway? They were supposed to be in Canada—a popular refuge for displaced loyalists. Prudence must be Prudence *Wharton* now. Mercy devoutly wished she had picked another name for her disguise; Prudence would be livid to discover that her name had been borrowed for the patriot cause.

Mercy had no more time to worry about Prudence. Keeping up with Ian consumed her attention. As he entered a patch of woods, darkness swallowed them both. Mercy had to grapple with sudden terror. Galloping through an unknown woods at night was begging for disaster. Look what had happened to Ian in full daylight! Mercy shuddered and gripped her reins more tightly.

Liberty responded by shying at shadows and almost unseating her; the mare then redoubled her efforts to stay close to Thor. *Pretend it is just a foxhunt,* Mercy told herself—a hunt like a hundred others she had ridden over the years. Only this time, her life and Ian's were at stake, not the fox's.

As Liberty twisted and turned to avoid trees, Mercy prayed that the mare knew where they were going. She herself had lost track of all direction. She could not even see Ian on Thor up ahead.

They shot out of the woods, and a stone fence loomed in their path. Ian and Thor sailed over it, and Mercy did likewise—urging her mare onward as if they were indeed on a foxhunt. Ian headed up a rise, reached the top, skidded to a stop, and whirled about to look for her. For a moment, man and stallion stood silhouetted against the starlit sky. To Mercy, they embodied all beauty, strength, and power. A lump rose in her throat. *How could she ever bear to lose them?*

Ian silently motioned to her, turned the stallion, and continued their headlong flight. They rode without stopping for hours. Skirting farms and homesteads, jumping hedgerows and the occasional fence, dashing in and out of woodlands and across hay meadows, Mercy conceived an even greater sympathy for the fox in a foxhunt.

Her muscles ached from the chase, her lungs burned, and Liberty's sides were heaving like a bellows. But the mare had been bred to run, and she had great heart. She did not slow her pace until Mercy signaled her—and then she slowed down only because Thor was slowing in front of her, allowing her to catch up to him.

"Where are we?" Mercy saw no signs of human habitation. The land around them was hilly and covered with thick stands of timber, but there was enough treeless country to enable them to remain in the open.

"Damned if I know," Ian responded in a low, troubled voice. "We long ago left land familiar to me. We must keep going south—I hope this is south. Eventually, we should encounter something or someone."

"Washington's troops? Is he not in the area around Howe's encampment?"

"Yes, but I am not sure where. We need to find him before his men find us. The Continentals have a price on my head—because of my articles and my close association with Howe. Besides, with the way you are dressed—"

"Oh, do not worry about me! I have blue trim rolled up in my pack—or at least, I did. I can change from loyalist to patriot in the wink of an eye."

"Amazing," Ian said. "This whole day has been amazing. But we are a long way from safety yet, my love. We need to find a place to hide before daybreak comes."

"A place where we can rest," Mercy agreed, stifling a yawn. She was suddenly so tired she could barely remain upright in the saddle.

Peering at her in the darkness, Ian frowned. "You are exhausted. We should stop awhile."

"No, let us continue. I am fine. However, if we see an old shed or a barn—somewhere we can shelter for a short time . . ." She did not finish the sentence. It was too unlikely—and too dangerous.

"By morning, General Howe will have soldiers scouring the countryside for us," Ian told her. "He will stop at nothing to find us. We—you more than me—made fools of everyone tonight, and they will not forget it."

"As I said, let us continue. 'Tis fortunate the weather is fair and mild. If it were winter, I might be worried." She leaned across Liberty's neck to take Ian's hand and squeeze it. "We are together now. That is all that matters. They did not succeed in hanging you. Nor will they capture us. The hard part is over."

"Ever the optimist . . . eh, my sweet Mercy?" Ian tugged on her hand to pull her closer and give her a kiss. Afterwards, he drew back, grinning ruefully. She could just make out his features in the waning starlight. "This is not what I had in mind for our wedding night, Wife."

"Oh? What *did* you have in mind? . . . I mean, where did you intend we should stay?"

"I had not gotten that far," Ian sheepishly admitted. "I have been sleeping these past six weeks in a granary shed, but I was hoping to find something nicer for you tonight. Before that, I was staying in the town tavern—hardly a fit place for a night of passion, either."

"Well, I am happy to be in the saddle then," she lied, determined to deny her fatigue. "Once a foxhunter, always a foxhunter. We are *always* happiest when mounted on our horses, dashing wildly about the countryside."

"Come along then." He urged Thor into a trot. "Staying in one place too long makes my skin prickle."

"Mine, too," Mercy admitted, keeping pace with him. "I just hope my ladies and Hiram got away safely. I cannot help worrying about them."

"General Howe and his officers do not know about Hiram. He took a job at the tavern where I was staying, but we pretended to be unacquainted with one another. As for your ladies, the general will be much less concerned about catching *them* than you and me. Besides, I am sure you planned some tale they could tell to explain *their* part in all of this."

"Oh, we did plan for that possibility! But Prudence's appearance changes everything. She knows all of us too well and despises us. I fear she would do anything to see us imprisoned—or even hanged."

"There is no use worrying about it," Ian gently chided her. "The British Army does not hang women—as far as I know. Besides, the ladies have Hiram to help them. We are the main quarry. If we fail to escape, all your efforts—and theirs—will have been in vain."

"I know. 'Tis why we must not fail."

They rode through the night in ever deepening darkness. Not long after their brief rest, the stars disappeared behind a heavy bank of clouds. A chill wind began to blow, and towards morning, rain fell—gently at first, then with astonishing forcefulness.

They sheltered beneath some trees, but it was no use. In a matter of moments, they were soaked to the skin.

"Wait here," Ian told her. "I thought I saw a farm up ahead. I want to see if we can stop there."

"The inhabitants may shoot you on sight! No, Ian—you must not go alone. With me along, they are far less likely to—"

"I do not intend to ride up to their door and drag them out of their beds, my love. I am interested only in their barn if they have one. If we stay out in this rain much longer, you will take a chill."

"A little rain will not hurt me," she protested, but she was already chilled to the bone and weak with hunger and fatigue. The day's events had not allowed for a meal. She wished she had eaten before spotting Reggie and Prudence.

"I will return shortly. Venture nowhere without me."

Where would she venture?

"Be sure you come back for me," she mumbled through chattering teeth.

"You know I will. Do you want to dismount first? On foot you could get further back under the trees."

She shook her head. "I think not. Liberty and I will wait right here for you." If she did dismount, she doubted she could summon the strength to remount. "Hurry back."

He nodded and was gone. Liberty whinnied forlornly when Thor disappeared into the rain. Fortunately, it thundered at the same moment, drowning out the mare's protest.

"Courage, my girl. Your stalwart hero will return for you," Mercy consoled both the mare and herself.

They waited—shivering and miserable—for what seemed like an hour but was probably only a few minutes. Liberty signaled Thor's—and Ian's—return with an approving snort.

"There is a barn with three empty boxes and only one old plow horse in it," Ian informed her excitedly. " 'Tis not close to the house, so I think we can risk it. We will stay only until first light and be on our way before the household awakens."

"Is there feed for the horses?" Mercy asked breathlessly. As usual, she was more concerned for them than for herself and Ian. The horses needed rest and nourishment more than *they* did.

"Yes," Ian said. "I am loath to take it without asking, but this is an unusual circumstance."

"I imagine the owners are accustomed to having things taken without permission," Mercy responded. "They are caught between two needy armies. At home, I myself must watch ceaselessly to avoid having my stock and food supplies stolen when I am not looking."

They were soon snug in the little barn—the two horses in the boxes with a bit of loose hay to keep them happy— and Mercy and Ian bedded down on a pile of straw in the third box. Thanks to the foresight of Hiram and Arabella Lee, they had been able to exchange their wet garments for dry ones and even had a blanket to share. A few items of necessity had been rolled in oiled cloth and lashed securely to the backs of their saddles.

Ian wrapped his arms around Mercy and shared the warmth of his body with her as they snuggled together beneath the blanket. To Mercy, it was pure delight to be so close, warm, and dry with the man she loved. It had been so long since they had been alone together!

Unfortunately, she could not keep her eyes open. She wanted to cuddle with him, kiss and caress him—spend time talking and savoring his company—but sleep claimed her almost the moment she relaxed in his embrace. She knew nothing else until . . .

"Blessed bones of my ancestors! What is *this*?"

One moment Mercy was deeply asleep and the next she was sitting bolt upright—with Ian trying to shield her by putting his own body between her and the intruder.

An old woman in a ruffled cap and clean white apron stood blocking the entrance of the box stall. It was fully light and very warm; a stray sunbeam pointed a long finger of light through a hole in the roof over the barn aisle. Dust motes danced in it.

"What are the two of you doing in my barn?" she demanded, brandishing a pitchfork in their direction. "You had better not be thinking of stealing my plow horse; he is all I have left. The Tories—damn their hides!—have taken everything else. My hogs and chickens . . . my milk cow and my riding horse . . ."

She is a patriot. Thank God!

"We are not planning to steal anything," Ian spoke up. "Last night we got caught in the storm, so we sheltered in your barn to escape it."

The old woman held the pitchfork in front of her—ready to use if needed. "Where are you from and where are you going?"

Her gaze strayed to Mercy's discarded scarlet and white gown, crumpled in the straw a short distance away. Mercy could almost see the workings of the woman's mind as she puzzled over the situation. "You are Tories, too, are you not?"

"No, we are not," Mercy denied before Ian could get a word out. "We are running from the British Army. They were going to hang my husband—the man you see here before you—but I managed to free him first."

Ian gave her a quelling glance, warning her she was revealing too much. But Mercy's instincts told her she could trust this woman; they *had* to trust her. What other choice did they have?

"That gown—a costly one it is, too—is done up in loyal- ist colors," the woman said. "My own husband is off fight-

ing with the British. He is faithful to the crown. But me—
I favor independency. If you can explain these lobsterback
colors, I will take you into my house and feed you breakfast.
If not, I will chase you out of here ..." She lifted the
pitchfork. "The Tories took my husband and almost all
we own that was not nailed down. My two sons serve under
General Washington; they were born with *my* common
sense. So, if you hope to eat, you had better start
explaining."

Mercy could not resist sending Ian a look of triumph.
"I would be glad to explain ..."

An hour later, they sat down to a breakfast of day-old
bread, hot gruel, a tea made from herbs, and thick, juicy
slabs of a smoked ham the old woman had been saving
for some special occasion. She was now treating them like
treasured friends or family.

"My, that is some story you told," she said, beaming at
Mercy across her polished plank table. She pushed a pewter
plate laden with thick ham slices toward her. "Eat all you
want. I am pleased to share my best with you. Any woman
who would dare to do what you did deserves my best."

"Thank you," Mercy said, taking two slices. The aroma
was heavenly, and she was trembling from hunger. "However, you yourself are a woman to admire—making do
here all on your own, while being raided by both armies."

Deborah, as she had introduced herself, smiled broadly,
revealing a gap where a front tooth had once been. "Yes,
first came the British. Then came the Continentals. Took
everything of value. Both times, I managed to hide the
plow horse because I saw them coming. I took him down
yonder to a berry patch and tied him up among the bushes.
Wish I had found time to hide the milk cow, too—and
the chickens and hogs. I have a garden planted, though;
I can get along with that—providing no one tramples it.
But I will have no meat next winter."

Mercy chewed and swallowed each bite of ham as if it
were more precious than gold—which it was. She decided
not to take a third slice, though she was tempted. Ian, she
noticed, ate only *one*, though he had to be even hungrier

than she was. He ate quickly, saying nothing, and when he was finished, set down his utensils.

"Do you know where we can find General Washington's army?" he asked the old woman.

Her head bobbed. "They are not far from here—a two-or-three-hour ride at most. If you had kept going last night, you might have run into them. Go south when you leave— and a little west. You are bound to see 'em. Of course, they may have changed their location by now. 'Tis hard to say where they are at any given moment."

"I understand," Ian said. "We should leave at once then, before the British come looking for—"

A sudden loud banging on the door interrupted him. "Open in the name of His Majesty, King George the Third!" came a muffled but imperious voice.

Mercy's mind refused to function, but Ian half-rose from the table. "Have you any weapons?"

"Only the pitchfork—but I left it in the barn!" Deborah wailed. "I know! Get you both behind the door. While they are searching in the house, you can run to the barn. If they have horses, just be sure to take them with you."

"It might work," Ian whispered. " 'Tis our only chance." He glanced around the interior of the simple house, which had no other entrance and only small, modest windows. "I see no other means of escape."

"Open up!" The banging came again.

While Deborah hid the extra dishes—evidence of their meal—Mercy prayed that the soldiers had not yet checked the barn but had come first to the house. She hurried to the door with Ian and stood behind it while Deborah unlatched the barrier.

"What is all this fuss about?" the old woman demanded. "What do you want? You have already taken all I own; there is nothing more to take."

"*We* will be the judge of that!" an angry male voice responded. "Have you seen anyone on the road this morning, old woman? Has anyone stopped here?"

Road? Were they that close to a road? Mercy exchanged a questioning glance with Ian.

"Yes!" Deborah answered, shocking Mercy. "I saw a

man and a woman—one riding a bay and the other a
chestnut horse. The woman was wearing a scarlet and white
gown—quite unsuitable for traveling. They galloped right
past without stopping, headed straight down the road. If
it's them you want, you can catch them if you hurry."

"Follow the road!" the voice hollered, and Mercy could
hear the jingle of spurs and stamping of horses. "They
were last seen on the road!"

Does he think we are such fools as to travel on the road? Mercy
hoped he did. She held her breath and listened as the
soldiers departed. Leaving the door open, Deborah
stepped outside the house.

"Good riddance to you, you bleedin' cockroaches," she
spat under her breath but loud enough for Mercy and Ian
to hear. "How my husband could choose *your* side I will
never know. He never was the smartest of men."

When she returned inside, Ian thanked her for her hospitality and told Mercy to wait until he had safely reached
the barn before she joined him.

"Borrow Deborah's cap and walk like an old woman
when you come," he advised her. "Just in case someone
sees you. I will be saddling the horses."

" 'Tis not *me* I am worried about; 'tis *you*. Be careful,
Ian. Wait a bit before you go out—"

"I am Lord Fox, remember? I can surely make it down
to the barn without being seen." He gave her a wink and
grin. "There's no time to wait. When they fail to find us
on the road, they may return here."

"Your man is right, child," Deborah agreed. "If they
do come back, they will search the whole place. You must
be gone by then. Soon as you leave, I will take my old plow
horse down to the berry patch, for I have no wish to lose
him."

Without another word, Ian slipped out the front door,
dropped into a crouching position, and started for the
distant building. Mercy stood behind Deborah at the window and watched him for part of the way as he took advantage of whatever lay in his path to conceal himself while
en route to the barn. When he finally disappeared from

sight, Deborah snatched her cap from her head and handed it to Mercy.

"Do as he says, child, and you will be fine. Take my broom, too, and carry it as if you mean to do chores. I think he has made it by now; I have heard no shouts of alarm."

"Thank you for your help, Deborah. I wish you well. Perhaps one day, when this is all over, we will meet again."

" 'Tis unlikely, child. You are a long way from home, and I am an old woman. God be with you."

The old woman gave her a quick hug, then thrust a nearby broom into her hand. Mercy jammed the cap down on her red curls—her wet wig had come off somewhere out on the trail last night—and walked outside. There was no sign of the soldiers. Golden sunlight drenched the tender pinks and greens of the season, and she found it difficult to believe that a war was going on and her own life was still in danger.

Humming a nameless little tune, she strolled toward the barn. In its shadowy interior, she could see Ian hurriedly saddling Liberty. The mare was already bridled, and so was Thor. Reins knotted around his neck, he hung his head over the side of the box and tried to nose Liberty.

Just then there came a shout. Glancing over her shoulder, Mercy spotted ten or twelve mounted redcoats, riding hard for the farm across an open field. Dropping the broom, she picked up her skirts and raced for the barn. When she got there, Ian gave her a leg up into the saddle.

"Thor is not saddled yet!" she cried. "What shall we do?"

"Run!" Ian instructed her. "Run and lose them. You know all the tricks."

"But what about you?"

"I will be right behind you. We are mounted on the two fastest horses in Virginia. They will never catch us. Go ahead, and I will follow—riding bareback, if necessary."

"Oh, Ian! I am so afraid."

"*You*—The Thoroughbred—are afraid you cannot out-run a few soldiers?" Ian laughed. *He actually laughed.* "Just pretend they are suitors. You will leave them in the dust."

"You are right," she said, catching his enthusiasm. "Liberty and Thor can outrun anything on four legs."

She burst out of the barn at a full gallop, riding with the confidence gained from years of foxhunting. Glad of the daylight, she jumped the mare over a hedgerow and then a stone fence dividing a pasture. Liberty seemed to sense she was in the greatest race of her life and willingly gave her all.

Across the open country they flew. Mercy had no need to look back. The distant thunder of hoofbeats told her that Ian was gaining on her. She could hear other hoofbeats, too—not as close as Thor's—and she urged the mare to even greater speed. When she saw a patch of woods, she headed straight toward it—knowing that Liberty and Thor could weave in and out of the trees faster and more accurately than the mounts of the British soldiers. Their horses could never keep up with two champions . . . and they did not.

Mercy kept them all dodging trees and jumping fallen logs for the better part of an hour before she decided it was time to quit. Whatever hoofprints Liberty and Thor had left in the soft soil were impossibly mixed with those of the horses belonging to the soldiers; they would have a devilishly hard time sorting them out, if indeed they attempted to do so.

On her way out of the woods, she passed quite close to the soldiers. By now, they were walking their winded horses. Some had dismounted, and one man was bent over, examining his horse's hoof. The others all looked spent, angry, and frustrated. Peering through the tender green leaves, Mercy could see sweat running down their faces beneath their red-cockaded black hats. They were the sort known as Light Dragoons, or mounted soldiers—and very stylishly turned out, she thought. Nor were their horses as ill-bred as she had expected them to be.

Relieved to see the last of them, she fled the woods with Ian and Thor following close on her mare's heels.

"You are merciless!" Ian declared, riding up beside her. "Two of those poor fellows got dumped on their backsides, and at least one of their mounts has gone lame."

"You told me to pretend they were suitors," Mercy reminded him. "I just did what I normally do when I am followed by men who think they can ride but know not what they are doing."

"To think I married such a heartless wench! I actually vowed to spend the remainder of my life with you."

"A vow I will make certain you keep! . . . Where to now, oh doughty horseman? Since we have escaped our pursuers, you may take over the lead of this little party."

"South and a bit west," he said. "That is all the direction we have."

"Other than to find Washington's army before his men find us."

"Yes," Ian agreed, nodding. "I doubt I can survive two such exhilarating rides in one day."

"I sincerely hope we have no others. Liberty and Thor have given us their best. To demand more would ruin them."

Mercy leaned down and gave her mare a pat on the neck. Liberty snorted as if she knew her talents were under discussion. Thor, she noted, was covered with foamy white sweat. They must avoid meeting anyone, not only for their own sakes, but also for the sake of the horses. Without them, they could never have made it this far.

Horses were the unsung heroes of the war, she decided. If not for Thor and Liberty, where would she and Ian be right now—and many others, as well? Horses carried men into battle and brought home the wounded and the dead. They hauled cannon and pulled wagons filled with badly needed supplies. They carried messages and news of distant events from one colony to another. Without horses, there would be no war, much less a victory.

"Why are you so quiet all of a sudden?" Though they had left danger behind for now, Ian kept his voice low.

"I was merely thinking about our horses," Mercy told him. "How useful they are—how precious."

"Indeed. If I could not mount a horse, I would consider myself less than a man," he declared.

"Now, that seems to be going *too* far," Mercy protested.

"Ah, but 'tis true," he insisted. "Thor gives me strength

and speed I could never know otherwise—and he has taught me so much. Through him I have learned patience, tolerance, and how to deal with others. I am a better man because of my horse. If ever the day comes when men no longer keep horses, the world will be a colder, harsher place."

"I agree. But to some men, a horse is nothing but a beast of burden, one they will abuse whenever the notion takes them."

"That is the first lesson of keeping horses: An abused animal will never give you his best, as Thor and Liberty have given us this day. A man's horse can tell you much about the man himself—what kind of person he is, or *she* is."

Yes, Mercy thought. *I know that—but what if something happens that you cannot ride or be near horses?*

She thought of Ian when he was injured in the riding accident. He had come close to being an invalid for the rest of his life! How would he have felt about that? How would he have coped with the situation?

It had not happened, fortunately, but Mercy suddenly had a hollow, frightened feeling. She loved horses as much as Ian. But she loved Ian more and hoped he felt the same way about her. . . . She wanted him to be content to spend the rest of their days happily together, with or without horses. In these precarious times, they must be prepared for anything . . . *anything*. Including the possibility that they could still lose each other.

This war was not over yet.

CHAPTER FOURTEEN

It was late afternoon by the time they found the Continental Army. Ian spotted a thin wisp of smoke on the horizon and speculated that it must be coming from an encampment—which it was. Demonstrating a care and cunning that astonished Mercy, he proceeded to lead them through a maze of guards and sentries who should have seen them but failed to do so—until he himself chose to make their presence known.

Mercy could only conclude that he had not earned the name Lord Fox without reason, and her admiration for his skills abounded. "One would almost think you were born an Indian instead of a viscount," she said after Ian had hailed a guard and demanded that he take them to General Washington's headquarters.

The guard now rode in front of them, leading them through tents, cook fires, picket lines, and camp followers. He had looked them over carefully first and apparently decided they were harmless since they bore no weapons of any kind. But he had peered at Ian and demanded: "Are you who I think you are, sir? If so, I should hold you at gunpoint."

"I have no idea who you think I am, so allow me to

enlighten you," Ian had responded. "I am Viscount Ian Montjoy, otherwise known as Lord Fox, and I have come here on a matter of grave importance to General Washington."

Considering that they had appeared out of nowhere and ridden right up to the man, he had not known what to think. So long as he took them to the general, Mercy did not care what he thought.

"I wish I were as good as an Indian," Ian now remarked. "I do the best I can. I have had to learn quickly. I have spent many a sleepless night planning my escapes through the countryside. Our old friend the fox taught me everything I know: how to make a sudden turn after a straight run and seek surfaces that will not hold a paw print or even a scent. If I can find a flock of sheep or a herd of cows or pigs, I always go through them, knowing they will wipe out my trail. Mostly, though, I try to think like a soldier and then do the exact opposite of what a soldier might expect."

They soon arrived at the general's headquarters, and the first person they encountered almost caused Mercy to tumble off her horse in surprise. Martha Washington, the general's wife, was just departing his large tent. Upon recognizing Mercy, she uttered a loud cry.

"Oh, my dear girl! Whatever are *you* doing here?"

" 'Tis a long story, I fear. While our husbands converse together, perhaps you and I can visit. I had no idea you had accompanied your husband to war."

"Husbands! Then you have finally married. I am so glad to hear it. As for myself, I came for a short visit and am about to return to Mount Vernon. I will be leaving tomorrow. Much has been happening, and I must depart while I can."

Mercy and Ian both dismounted, and Ian entered Washington's headquarters while Mercy accompanied the general's wife to a smaller tent some distance away. Their horses were led away by soldiers who promised to take good care of them.

Once inside the tent, Martha motioned for Mercy to take a seat on one of two plain wooden chairs drawn up to a round table surrounded by various trunks and chests in the process of being packed for a journey.

"Please excuse this untidy display. May I fetch you some refreshments?" she asked, as if they were in a parlor at Mount Vernon.

Mercy politely declined. She was far more interested in conversing with the woman than in eating or drinking. Pert, plump, and genteel as always, Martha joined her at the table. Mercy silently marveled at her dress and manner. She wore a blue gown topped with a white scarf tucked into the bodice. A delicate lace cap—not unlike Deborah's—covered her hair.

She was older than Mercy, and Mercy had always been in awe of her. But suddenly she felt quite comfortable in Martha's presence even though they still had little in common. The mother of two living children by a previous husband, Daniel Parke Custis, Martha had been one of the wealthiest widows in Virginia when she married the man then known as Colonel Washington. Now that Mercy was also married and their husbands were well acquainted, the gulf between them did not seem so wide.

"Please tell me why you are here, my dear—and all about your husband," Martha begged, seeming truly interested. "Not many women of our rank in society can be found in army encampments. I myself have suffered criticism for not supporting my husband better and coming more often. However, since I started making these journeys, the criticism has lessened. Still, I often wonder if people realize how difficult life can be for a woman in an army encampment. But I have been doing my best to ease my dear husband's burdens and keep him cheerful through these trying times."

"I am certain you keep him wonderfully cheerful," Mercy assured her. "Shame on anyone who criticizes you. Surely they must realize you have a plantation to run in your husband's absence."

"I hope history will realize it." Martha sighed. "But enough about me. I wish to hear about you now."

"All right then, let me tell you how I came to be here." They spent the remainder of the afternoon together. As darkness approached, Martha invited Mercy and Ian to share supper with them. Before the men arrived in the tent, the two women prepared a simple meal centered around a cured ham Martha had brought from home, along with some of the general's favorite relishes and jellies. By the time the men joined them, Mercy felt as if she and Martha had become dear friends. Martha had even arranged for her and Ian to have their own tent that night—a private place where they could finally enjoy being alone together.

The supper was most congenial, until Mercy suddenly lost her temper. "No, Ian!" she burst out. "I refuse to return to Virginia tomorrow with Mrs. Washington! I prefer to remain here with you. We have just been reunited, not to mention married, and I am not ready to leave yet!"

General Washington—ever the dignified gentleman in social situations—sat and stared at her as if she had suddenly bared her breasts or done something equally as shocking. Martha wrinkled her brow in distress while Ian's blue eyes darkened, hinting of anger and embarrassment. He obviously did not approve of her challenging him in front of his friend and leader.

"Mercy, dear—" Martha began.

Mercy rose from the table. "I am sorry. Forgive me, but this is between Ian and me. I am devastated that he wishes to be rid of me so quickly."

Ian had not put it that way, but that was how Mercy chose to interpret it. She had thought he would be delighted to have some time alone with her. Now, it seemed, he was satisfied with only a single night, a night already ruined by his insistence that she depart the very next morning.

Ian rose also and glowered at her across the table. "I am not eager to be rid of you, Mercy. But perhaps we should discuss this alone. If you and your wife will please excuse us, General, we will step outside to finish this discussion."

"Just a moment, Ian." General Washington tilted back his chair and regarded Mercy somberly. "My dear young woman, you do not understand what life is like here for camp followers."

"Camp followers!" Mercy did not at all consider herself a camp follower. The women who trailed the British and Continental armies had unsavory reputations—probably undeserved but unsavory nonetheless. "General, whatever else I may be, I am *not* a camp follower."

General Washington smiled at her reaction. "I beg to differ with you. While it is true that you would be the wife of an army officer—I have just persuaded your husband to accept an appointment—you would still be considered—"

"Ian has agreed to become one of your officers?" Mercy interrupted, as yet uninformed of Ian's plans or the content of his private discussions with the general.

"Yes, he has agreed to become one of my personal aides. I trust his judgment and look forward to having him at my side advising me, much as he once did with General Howe, except no one knew he was actually working for *me* at the time."

"Oh, yes!" Mercy exclaimed. "Ian can be most devious when he wants to be. 'Tis what he does best."

Ian's set jaw indicated his displeasure with her comments, but Mercy was too hurt to care. She had come all this way—had even saved his life!—and he wanted to send her back home as quickly as possible. Well, she had *earned* the right to be here, and it was time he realized it.

"My dear!" Martha interjected. "The camp followers live in a state of absolute wretchedness. There is little enough food to go around for the soldiers, let alone their wives. The women receive a half ration and their children only a quarter ration each, regardless of age or size."

"Why, that is terrible!" Mercy fumed.

"It is the best we can do." General Washington's tone was grim. "We are short of everything—not only food but gunpowder and musket balls. I am trying to make dedicated soldiers out of men with no weapons, clothing, horses, or training. I must somehow win this war with whatever supplies I can manage to obtain on my own. 'Tis a constant struggle. We need no more mouths to feed, even the mouths of women as courageous and beautiful as *you,* my dear."

His blunt speech put Mercy in her place. She would not

stay where she was unwelcome. Still, she could not forgive Ian for not taking her part and *wanting* her to stay. She glared at him across the table, and he glared back—apparently resenting her rebellious attitude.

"I really do not wish to leave here tomorrow and return to Virginia with you, Mrs. Washington, but it appears I have no choice in the matter. I *do* like to eat, and I have no wish to take food from men bearing arms for my sake," she managed to get out.

"Please refer to me as Martha, my dear—or even Patcy, as the general does. And please do not look so distressed! The lack of food is one reason why I myself do not stay long when I come," she said. "I bring provisions from home, naturally, and do all I can to help out while I am here, but I know I am a distraction for my husband."

"A delightful one," the general quickly defended, "whose help is invaluable. Patcy assists me with my correspondence and makes copies of important records," he proudly related. "She also mends and repairs my clothing. knits socks for the soldiers, and comforts those who are wounded or dying."

So could I do those things for Ian, Mercy thought. But she knew she could not go against General Washington. *This* would be her last night with her husband for the duration of the conflict—and she was too angry to even be civil to him, much less loving!

"The hour grows late, General," Ian said. "This is *your* last night with your wife, as it is mine with *my* wife. We will take our leave now and find a place to sleep."

"I have found you a tent!" Martha gleefully informed him. "Let me take you there at once."

She gave Mercy a hand lamp made of pewter, the sort that burned whale oil, another expensive commodity that must have come from home. This one was brighter than most, meaning it held sperm oil, which cost even more. Conscious of being indebted and disliking the feeling, Mercy took it reluctantly.

"I will see you tomorrow, Ian." General Washington bade them sleep well and immediately turned his attention to a sheaf of papers he had brought with him into the tent.

Ian responded with similar courtesies and followed Mercy outside. The tent Martha had found for them was not far away and stood off by itself. It was as private as anything to be had in the encampment.

"I am able to provide little else to make you comfortable except for some blankets," Martha apologized, stepping into the tent and illuminating its interior with her own hand lamp. "I hope this will do."

" 'Tis better than anything I have been sleeping in for some time," Ian noted approvingly. "Thank you."

Mercy added her own thanks, and quite suddenly she and Ian were alone. It was then Mercy realized just how small the tent was—barely big enough for the two of them to lie down on the blankets spread out at their feet. Two stools and a barrel served as a table and chairs. Back in the corner stood a chamber pot. Martha had thought of everything.

"Shall we?" Ian indicated the blankets with a nod. "Put out the lamp. We must get some sleep."

Get some sleep? she thought, seething inside.

"All right." She put out the lamp, set it on the barrel top, and knelt down on the blankets.

It was too dark to see anything, but she could hear Ian rummaging around, taking off his boots, and settling himself beside her. She wondered how she would ever get through the night. It was warm in the tent—and out of it, for that matter—but she felt a distinct chill in the air. The distance between her and Ian might have been as wide as the ocean for all the closeness she felt to him.

He was sending her away without protest or complaint. Even worse, he was furious that she had dared to protest!

When he said nothing and appeared content to lie there in the darkness, ignoring her, Mercy decided to lie down, too. But she allowed no part of herself to touch him. If this was the way he wanted it, so be it. Let *him* be the one to make the first move! . . . Or let him be damned.

"Mercy," he said softly.

She remained silent.

"Wife, I ache for you." It sounded like a plea, but she would not be swayed.

"I want your body soft and yielding against mine. Why do you deny me this comfort when tomorrow you must go? Surely there is enough misery and sadness in the world without two people who love each other creating more of it."

"You showed no sadness at my leaving in front of General Washington," she bitterly accused.

"I trusted you to see the sense of it," he answered with a sigh. "Instead, you behaved like a spoiled child."

She moved even further away from him, stopping only when she came to the edge of the blanket and cool grass met her questing hand.

"Which is precisely what you are doing *now*," he continued.

At that, she sat up. "Ian Montjoy! I am your wife, not a child. Spoiled or otherwise. How dare you treat me like one!"

He sighed again. "Mercy, I know you are disappointed that you cannot stay. I am, too, but—"

"Are you? This is the first I have heard of it."

"Is that what you want—to hear assurances that I care for you? Mercy . . ." He rolled onto his side to face her, but Mercy managed to keep enough distance between them so that he was still not touching her. "How can you doubt it? You are sunlight and air to me, my reason for living— for all the risks I take, for every breath I inhale. Without you, none of this matters. I would still fight for freedom— to overcome the king's tyranny—but if I do not have you, I will take no real joy in the outcome, assuming it is victory. I thought you felt the same. I thought we had come to share such a deep, lasting bond that even our thoughts were almost identical."

Identical? They were a long way from that felicitous state of being. His declarations were wondrous to Mercy's ears, but she still wanted more from him.

"Ian, I can ride as well as you. I am sure I can shoot as well also. I am able to manage a plantation with so many slaves and servants that I have lost track of their number. . . . Why am I not good enough to stay here with you and help to fight this battle? I could serve as well as any man—"

"My redheaded little warrior, 'tis just not done!" he said, chuckling. "I agree with you—you could do as well as any man. You lack neither the skills nor the courage—but who else could do as *you* do now? We men have our pride. Besides, we must have something left to come home to, and that is where a woman like you can best contribute. Go home and continue doing as you have always done. Keep Collier Manor productive. Get something started on the land I bought from your father. Otherwise we will have no food, livestock, or fine horses for the future—when this war is over."

"But I want to help with the *war* effort, too, Ian! . . . Wait, I know!" Mercy sat up in excitement. "General Washington said he lacks gunpowder and musket balls. I can do little about the gunpowder, but I have an idea for how we might make musket balls."

"How?" Ian groaned, flopping back on the blanket. "I long to make love to my wife, and all she can talk about is musket balls."

"If you do not have enough of them, you can never win this war, Ian," she pointed out in as reasonable a tone as she could manage. "I have a grand idea for obtaining them. I read in one of Papa's papers that the inhabitants of some town or other—I forget which one—pulled down a lead statue of Lord North, had it melted down, and made it into musket balls."

"Do you have any lead statues at Collier Manor? I do not recall seeing any," Ian said dryly.

"No, but we have pewter plates! So does nearly every other woman I know. We could collect them and have them melted down and poured into molds to make musket balls!"

"Only *you* would think of that. . . . Well, I have no objection. Who knows? It just might work."

"Of course it will work! Thus far, my lady friends and I have woven cloth to make garments for the soldiers, gathered food supplies, knitted socks, and sewn quilts, but this would be an *unusually* helpful activity for my Daughters of Liberty to undertake next, would it not?"

"Rescuing *me* was not enough excitement for you and your ladies?" Ian queried.

"There were a few exciting moments," Mercy agreed. "But I want to be a part of something that could mean the difference between winning and losing this war."

"Musket balls will do it. Go home and make musket balls then," Ian ordered. "But first, come here and let me love you. I am so badly in need of your loving, sweet Mercy."

"I am hardly sweet, and you know it." Mercy wondered why he even put up with her. She *was* different from most women. Not even her stalwart ladies would be willing to march into battle—would they? If it became a matter of necessity, as it had been with rescuing Ian . . .

"I disagree. I have always thought you the sweetest creature God ever created," he murmured, pulling her into his arms.

As their bodies met, Mercy made a startling discovery. "Ian! You are *naked!*"

Without a stitch of clothing to cover him, he had been lying there all this time arguing with her. If she had known *that* . . .

"Yes, and I want *you* naked, too. What is the sense of only one of us being bare as a newborn babe if the other is as snug inside her garments as a butterfly wrapped in a cocoon?"

"I am no butterfly," she began.

"Yes, you are," he insisted. "You are a beautiful butterfly anxious to break free of her cocoon and try her wings. Fly with me, little one. Come out of your wrappings and fly with me into the sun."

"Gracious! I had no idea I was married to a poet—"

"Not a poet . . . a frustrated lover who has been too long without his beloved."

As he bantered with her, his hands removed pieces of her clothing. Soon he ceased talking and began kissing her—giving her long, ardent kisses that made her heart sing and her flesh quiver. Within moments, she was naked, too, and he pressed her down onto the blanket and nuzzled and kissed her from mouth to toes, missing nothing in between.

He led her to intimacies Mercy had never imagined, and her own behavior was all the more shocking because their actions pleased and delighted her. She thought she must be wicked indeed for enjoying them so thoroughly—and Ian was even more wicked for having thought of them. Such wanton behavior could *not* be proper . . . but oh, how wonderful Ian made her feel!

Her breasts, belly, thighs—and all else—belonged to him and him only. Oh, yes, they were a part of *her,* but only Ian could make them so *alive.* His hands and mouth awoke the sinner in her—and then took her straight to paradise!

When at last he entered her, she could only arch her body against him and beg him to finish what he had started. She was ravenous for him and shameless in her need. He chose to prolong the moment—holding back when she wanted to be taken hard and fast.

"Ian, now!" she begged.

"Now?" he repeated, as if he knew not what she wanted.

She clawed his back with her nails and lifted herself to receive him more deeply. "Ian, please!" she half-sobbed, hardly caring if anyone heard her.

At last he began thrusting into her. She clenched her inner muscles around him and feared she might die of the pleasure as he gave her everything.

"Oh, my! . . . Oh, my!" she whimpered, but he stilled her cries with his kisses even as his body stiffened and shuddered.

It had been like flying into the sun, she thought mistily as she floated back down to earth again. Could any man love a woman as Ian had just loved her? . . . Oh, God, she loved him so much!

He moved to one side and she followed, loath to release him so soon. "Ian . . . Ian, promise me you will return to me!"

"How could I not, sweet?" He held her against him and stroked her hair with one hand. "I will come crawling on my hands and knees if I must—as would any man who had just been loved by a woman as I have been."

"I only responded to *your* lovemaking. You could melt a lead statue with your kisses. . . . There, you see?" She raised her head to look at him, though the darkness cloaked his features. "I should take you home with me to help make musket balls. That way you could still be useful while remaining safe."

"I doubt I could be inspired by a pewter plate," he drawled.

She laughed and hugged him, happier than she had ever been in her life. "Just be certain you come home to me, my Ian! I promise you that tonight will seem as nothing compared to what I will give you then."

"That promise will sustain me when I have nothing else to fill my heart or belly. Remembering you like this will give me the determination to win this war quickly so I can come home to you. Home is wherever *you* are, Mercy."

"I will be waiting for you," Mercy assured him. "Collier Manor, your land, your dreams . . . we will all be waiting."

"Hush," he said. "No more talking. For what little is left of this night, I want to spend it holding you, loving you . . ."

Brushing back tears, she cuddled close to him. He wrapped his arms around her, and she felt as if they were indeed one body and soul. If he survived this war, nothing would ever separate them again. She would permit no more separations.

Morning came too soon, as it always seemed to do when they had to part. General Washington sent for Ian early, giving them no choice but to say their farewells quickly.

"He could have waited until his wife and I had left!" Mercy fumed. "Why must he meet with you so soon?"

Fully dressed now and clean-shaven, Ian embraced her outside the tent where they had spent the night. "The general has received disturbing news, my love. It came yesterday, shortly before our arrival. He wants my advice on what we should do about it."

"What disturbing news?" Worry swept Mercy, reminding her that their brief idyll was truly over.

"General John Burgoyne, the British general who is presently in Canada, is said to be preparing for an invasion of the colonies from that quarter. He plans to travel down Lake Champlain and the Hudson River Valley to join General Howe in New York."

"How do you know this?"

"Weeks ago, I knew that General Howe was considering leaving New Jersey and heading toward New York. That was no secret to any of us close to him. But I did not know about General Burgoyne. One of Washington's other spies provided the information. I think their goal is to join forces to capture Philadelphia."

"How soon could that happen?" Mercy wanted to know everything. Once she was home again, she would have to rely on her regular sources, and the news would be old when it reached her.

"Not until late summer or early fall. Washington needs more men if he hopes to face such a large force and stand a chance of winning. . . . Make your bullets, Mercy. And encourage any man you meet to volunteer for the patriot cause."

"I will, Ian." She hugged him. "Be strong and do not forget how much I love you!"

They kissed one last time. Smiling, Ian pulled away from her. "After last night, I could never forget."

Winking at her, he grazed her chin with his knuckles. "No tears now. Instead, think of how it will be when next we meet. What we shared last night will be as nothing compared to our *next* meeting."

She nodded, refusing to weep in front of him. But as he walked away from her, heading for the general's tent, she had to turn aside and hide her face lest he glance back and spot her tears after all. She who had always been so contemptuous of weak women now found herself weeping at the least opportunity! That in itself was enough to make her weep.

An hour later, she left the encampment riding in the carriage which had brought Martha Washington to visit

and was now taking her back to Mount Vernon in Virginia.
Tied to the back end of the vehicle, Liberty plodded behind
them.

After a long but uneventful journey, Mercy was happy
to see Collier Manor again and bid farewell to Martha, who
refused to even step down from the carriage but wanted to
press onward to Mount Vernon in the hopes of reaching
it before nightfall.

"Have you heard anything from my lady friends—those
who accompanied me to New Jersey?" Mercy demanded
of Chloe the moment she saw her.

"No, girl, we done heard no word from anybody. But I
am sure glad to see *you*. Did you save him?"

Mercy nodded. "Saved him and married him. I will tell
you all about it later. First, I want a complete report of
everything that has happened in my absence."

"Married him!" Chloe shrieked. "Is it really true? You
been wedded and bedded?"

Her old friend abandoned all propriety and hugged her
so hard her ribs nearly cracked.

"Yes, yes!" Mercy laughed. "But there is no time for
celebration. We have too much to do."

"What we gotta do that cannot wait until you tell me all
about it?"

"Pewter plates. We must collect every single plate or
other pewter item we can spare. . . . We will need the help
of all my ladies. I just pray they make it home safely. I saw
no sign of them on our journey here. They should have
arrived home before I did," Mercy fretted. "Are you certain you have heard nothing from them?"

"How did you get separated from 'em in the first place?
And how did you join up with General Washington's
lady? . . . And what you gonna do with pewter plates? I
refuse to do a single thing—you can whip me if you want
to—until you answer my questions, girl."

"You have never been whipped in your entire life,"
Mercy reminded her. "Though maybe you should have
been. You are much too impertinent. All right," she

relented. "Guess I will have to tell you everything—and *then* we will collect the pewter."

"He is still alive?—Lord Montjoy, I mean. You can start with *that.*"

"He was when I left him," Mercy informed her. "And God willing, he will stay that way."

"Well, of course he will! Never you mind about the *bad* news I gotta tell you."

"Bad news? What bad news?" Mercy demanded.

Chloe's wide eyes and suddenly trembling mouth told her it was something serious. "Come sit down first, girl. I been dreadin' this moment—and I will dread it even more when Miss Caroline, your friend, shows up."

Caroline? It involved Caroline, who had gone with her to New Jersey and not yet returned?

Mercy's stomach churned with anxiety; bad news could mean only one thing.

CHAPTER FIFTEEN

William Darby, Caroline's husband, was dead. So was Drew Elliot, along with two other men of Mercy's acquaintance. During the women's absence, word had come and spread like a barn fire among the Virginia planters. The men had all died in late April in a battle with a British force at Ridgefield, Connecticut.

Mercy wept over Mr. Elliot, who had always seemed to be such a nice person. She had never really liked William, but she mourned him for Caroline's sake. When Caroline had agreed to go to New Jersey, she had known her husband would never approve—but she had gone anyway, leaving her home and family in the care of servants who were as close to her as Chloe was to Mercy. At least now, Caroline would never have to tell William about their "adventure."

That was scant consolation for Mercy now. She knew that Caroline would be devastated and could only hope she could find the right words to comfort her friend when the time came. Meanwhile, as she waited for the women's arrival, she started on her new project.

By the time the women finally made it back home to Virginia—in Hiram's watchful company—Mercy already had a wagonload of pewter gathered from her own cupboards and those of her nearest neighbors. Hiram brought his charges first to Collier Manor, almost as if he had known that Mercy would be there waiting for him.

"I thought it best to bring 'em here," he explained to her as she dashed out of the house to greet them.

"Oh, I am so glad you did! What delayed you for so long? I arrived four days ago."

"We stayed away from the main road and still had to dodge soldiers and hide from 'em in woods and creekbeds," Hiram explained. "I trust me lord is safe and sound somewhere."

"He is with General Washington," Mercy hurriedly explained. "But we can exchange tales later. Are you all safe, my dear good friends?"

She hurried to assist them in climbing down from the wagon.

"My bones ache from the relentless jolting," Arabella complained. "This is the last time I do something like this for you, Mercy. I always knew that getting you wed would require some effort, but this went too far. I am getting too old for such frolics."

Standing next to her, Caroline shook out her rumpled skirts. "William will be furious when he hears about this escapade. Perhaps I will wait a few years to tell him—until we are both so old and gray that he is unlikely to lose his temper over it."

Mercy's heart plummeted. "Caroline, dear, come into the house. I would like to see you alone for a moment."

Caroline lifted her head and stared at Mercy. The other women paused and exchanged glances. "Why?" Caroline demanded. "What has happened? . . . You have news of William. And it is not good news, is it?"

Mercy shook her head, her heart breaking for her friend. "No, dear, it is not."

Caroline's face crumpled. She lifted a clenched fist to her mouth, and tears welled in her eyes. "I had a feeling," she murmured. "I had this awful feeling I would never have to tell William about this adventure. . . . Oh, God!"

"Come into the house, all of you," Mercy urged. "Caroline, take my arm, dear."

But Caroline buried her face in her hands and leaned over the wagon wheel, her shoulders shaking as she sobbed helplessly. "Oh, William! I thought I was so brave going off to New Jersey to help rescue Lord Montjoy! Now I know I am not brave at all. How will we ever manage without you?"

"There, there, my dear," Arabella comforted her as the other women gathered around in silent sympathy. "We will stand by you. Be not ashamed to weep. We must all weep at one time or another, or else we should go mad."

Two days later, Hiram left to return to New Jersey in search of Ian. Mercy sent a letter with him, along with clothing, food, and whatever additional supplies could be packed on a spare horse. . . . Thus began the waiting for the next time she might see her own husband or possibly hear from him.

The day-to-day running of the estate, combined with her "project," kept her so busy that she was usually exhausted by the time she sought her bed at night. With her father gone and the market for tobacco now nonexistent, she was finally able to pursue her old dreams for the plantation. She derived great satisfaction from calling together all of Collier Manor's slaves and signing manumission papers for them. She offered them room and board if they continued working on the plantation. Some wanted wages, but Mercy could not promise to pay them anything until after the war ended—and maybe not immediately even then. Several of the men refused to remain, but almost everyone else was glad to be able to eat and have a roof over their heads in these uncertain times.

She planted wheat and oats on Ian's land, though it was too late in the season to expect a full harvest. In late July, a newly arrived French nobleman, the Marquis de Lafayette, was appointed a major general by the Continental Congress, and a young woman named Jane McCrea was murdered by Burgoyne's Indian allies, prompting a new wave of patriotism among the colonists, many of whom rushed to enlist in the Continental Army.

In September, at Brandywine Creek in Pennsylvania, General Howe's forces clashed with Washington's and drove them back toward Philadelphia. Next, they ambushed American troops at Paoli, Pennsylvania, and finally succeeded in capturing Philadelphia itself on September 26th. The Americans suffered another defeat early in October at Germantown, near Philadelphia.

Mercy fretted over these setbacks, but her spirits soared when the American General Horatio Gates overcame Burgoyne's forces at Saratoga. Ten days later, Burgoyne's entire army surrendered, prompting France to join the American cause.

In the middle of hunt season—another year in which no foxhunts were held—the Continental Congress approved Articles of Confederation for the United States of America and sent them to the states for ratification. The Continental Army went into winter quarters at Valley Forge, twenty-five miles northwest of Philadelphia, while the British remained entrenched in Philadelphia.

Now I will hear from Ian, Mercy thought, praying he had survived all these clashes. But the winter—an especially cold and harsh one—passed with agonizing slowness, and still she heard nothing. Not until the end of March did she receive word from him—a hastily written letter delivered by an exhausted, ill, battle-scarred soldier en route to his home in western Virginia.

Mercy attacked the poor fellow with questions, but he was unable to tell her much except that the winter at Valley Forge had been marked by mud, blizzards, epidemics of typhus and other diseases, along with an appalling lack of food, clothing, and medical supplies. Many of the soldiers had been forced to go barefoot, wrapping their feet in rags and leaving trails of bloody footprints in the snow.

Mercy insisted that the man eat and rest before he continued on his way. While Chloe took care of him, she retreated to the library to read her letter from Ian.

My dearest Mercy,

I would give anything to hold you right now—instead I must be content to write this as quickly as I can or it will not be finished in time for the departure of the soldier who will be bringing it to you.

Ian described some of the hardships in the encampment, but also mentioned the successes of a Prussian army officer who had come to Valley Forge to train the American troops and drill them in army discipline.

As bad as this winter has been—with deprivations you cannot even imagine—Baron von Steuben's efforts have given me hope that victory might still be within our grasp. Half-starved men clad in nothing but rags are learning how to march, fight, and follow orders with precision and enthusiasm—those who do not choose to desert, I should say. We started the winter with 11,000 troops here, but are losing men daily, not just to death or disease, but mainly to desertion. We are down to half our original number and with planting season upon us, I fear we will lose even more.

The remainder of his letter dealt with all the ways he was missing her and his hopes and prayers that she was safe and well, and still loved him—*as if she could ever stop!* He promised to write again in a few weeks when Martha Washington, who had been with them throughout the terrible winter, returned to Mount Vernon. He ended with words that dissolved on the page due to a blur of tears that suddenly marred her vision.

Until we meet again, my love, think of me often, as I do you—constantly. This winter whenever I was cold, hungry, or discouraged, I would close my eyes and imagine you galloping Liberty through the woods or across a wide meadow. I can picture your red hair streaming behind you, your cheeks as vivid a color as your hair, and your eyes sparkling with sun and laughter. . . . You and Liberty together I can never forget—two magnificent thoroughbreds so filled with life and beauty that your images are enough

to make my heart race and my palms grow sweaty, warming
me even now. One day, I will ride beside you again, my
love, filling my eyes and my heart with the wondrous sight
of you. Until then . . . I remain your ever faithful husband,

Ian

Mercy hugged the letter to her bosom and imagined—
just for a moment—that Ian was there with her, holding
her, hugging her, loving her as only he knew how to do.
Despite his promise to send a letter with Martha Washington, she knew it might be a long time before she heard
from him again. Travel was hazardous, and the mail, which
had been good before the war began, was now unreliable.

To help relieve her worry and fears, she resolved to keep
a diary—not of her own daily life, which she considered
unremarkable, but of war news. That very day, she began
noting dates of major events as she received them, which
was usually several weeks or even months after they had
occurred. The activity helped her to keep track of the gains
and losses, along with the events leading up to them.

If ever she wanted to explain this period of her life to
her children or grandchildren, she suspected she would
become confused and get it all wrong. There was simply
too much happening.

May 8, 1778: General Henry Clinton has replaced General
Howe—probably because Howe is not winning the war fast
enough to suit the British. (I received another letter from
my darling Ian! Again hastily written and containing little
war news I did not already know. The best part was that
he continues to miss me—but not half as much I miss him!
No one could miss another as much as I miss Ian.)

June 6, '78: A British peace commission has arrived in
Philadelphia—but the Congress will never accept their
terms. (I fear this war will go on forever, and I will grow
old apart from Ian!)

June 18, '78: Clinton has left Philadelphia and is
marching toward New York City! This means Washington
will be breaking camp and going to meet him. (Oh, Ian, be

*careful! If anything should happen to you, I could not bear
it!)*

*June 27–28: The American and British forces engaged
at Monmouth, but neither side could be declared the winner.
Charles Lee, one of Washington's generals, ordered a retreat.
(Martha has written that her husband will be furious over
Lee's cowardice. She has had no letters recently from her
husband either.) Meanwhile, only a half dozen of the colonies have signed the Articles of Confederation. (What is
wrong with them? Do people not realize that we must stand
united or we shall all be doomed?)*

*July 20: At last, some good news! George Rogers Clark
has captured a British fort at Vincennes, Indiana. (I wish
I understood better what is happening in the west where
Burgoyne's Indian allies have been wreaking havoc upon
the poor settlers in the wilderness. Why have the savages
chosen sides at all? Why do they not keep their noses out of
it? 'Tis said the British pay for all the American scalps the
Indians bring to them. God will one day punish them for
this wickedness!)*

In August, an outbreak of a mysterious fever kept Mercy
away from her diary. Even Chloe and Moses came down
with it. Two children and one old woman died, but the
remainder survived and were able to bring in the harvest.
Hunt season rolled around again, and after that, Christmas
and the New Year—a year Mercy hoped would bring an
end to the conflict.

With the arrival of cold weather, the war shifted to the
south. Savannah, Georgia, fell to the British in late December. In January, they took Augusta, but America now had
a warship donated by the French—the *Bonhomme Richard,*
captained by John Paul Jones.

Winter slid into spring, spring into summer, and summer
into fall. Winter came again—and the only news Mercy
had of Ian was that Washington's army was wintering in
Morristown, New Jersey. Her diary notations, when she
looked back over them for the year, were short and to the
point.

June 1, '79: British forces capture forts at Stoney Point and Ver Planck in New York. (Oh, Ian! Where were you when they fell? Where are you now?)

September–October, '79: Heavy casualties incurred by American forces attempting to take back Savannah. (Still no news from or about Ian.)

September 23, '79: The Bonhomme *captures the* Serapis! *I cannot believe an American warship has defeated a British one! (Ian, my love, how you must be rejoicing! I pray God you are rejoicing somewhere.)*

September 27, '79: Congress has appointed John Adams to negotiate peace with Britain. They have also named John Jay—former president of the Congress—as minister to Spain. (Ian, are you in a British prison? Is that why I have heard no word of you?)

May 12, 1780: Terrible news! American forces led by General Benjamin Lincoln have surrendered to the British at Charlestown, South Carolina. (Oh, my love, we are losing the war in the Southern colonies! If only you would find a way to write to me and let me know you are still alive. I have heard nothing from Martha Washington either, when I had so hoped she would bring me a letter from you when she returned to Mount Vernon after spending the winter with the general.)

The remainder of 1780 passed in a blur as war raged through the South and in New Jersey. First one side claimed victory, then the other. The news of Benedict Arnold's treachery rocked the colonies, including Virginia . . . and Mercy seriously began to consider the possibility that Ian was dead.

Why had she heard nothing from him?

And then came a letter from the headquarters of General Washington. A shivering, ill-clad soldier delivered it on the eve of the New Year of 1781. It had been almost three years since Mercy had last seen Ian and going on two years since she had received a letter from him. She had written to him many times, but had no way of knowing if he had ever received her letters. Probably not. They would have had to cross enemy lines to reach him.

She knew the letter was from General Washington as

soon as the soldier placed it in her hands. It said *G. Washington* in the corner. Trembling, terribly afraid of what the letter might contain, Mercy could only motion for Chloe to offer the soldier food and drink, while once again she retreated to the library to read her mail in private.

When she opened it, she discovered that it was actually from Martha, General Washington's wife.

> *My dear Mercy,*
> *We are entering upon what will surely be another harsh winter of deprivation for our brave men. I know from experience how difficult it is for those waiting at home for word of their loved ones. We must often go for long periods of time without knowing if our men are alive or dead. I know you must be imagining that your own dear Ian is still here with us at Morristown—thus my reason for writing.*

Mercy paused for a moment to gather her courage. Her hands were shaking so badly she could scarcely hold onto the letter. *If Ian was not at Morristown with General Washington, where was he?*

Recalling Caroline's reaction to news of her husband's death, she braced herself to discover the worst. Why else would Martha be writing except to soften the blow of bad news?

> *As you may or may not have heard, General Nathaniel Greene has replaced Horatio Gates as commander of the Patriot forces in the South. My own dear husband highly recommended him to Congress, and he is now in Charlotte, North Carolina, where we hope he will be able to inspire the militia there and drive the British out of the South altogether. My husband's second cousin, Colonel William Washington, is also in Charlotte, as is the Virginian, Daniel Morgan, and your own dear Ian.*

Mercy paused again. *At least Ian was not dead! He was in North Carolina.* Breathlessly, she continued reading.

*If these fine warriors should fail in their endeavors, I fear
we will lose not only the South but the entire war. So you
see how much trust my husband has placed in them! When
last I saw your husband, he was fit and eager to rescue the
South. I myself witnessed his departure on that big bay
stallion he rides. I thought then I must find a way to inform
you of what is happening. If anyone can keep Cornwallis
from conquering North Carolina, it is men such as your
courageous Ian who will do it.*

There was more, but Mercy knew she had read the most
important parts. The year 1781 was bound to be a crucial
one—perhaps the turning point of the war. This year, they
would either win or lose. The certainty of it vibrated in
her bones.

She wondered if the war would cease for the winter in the
South as it did in the colder regions. . . . No, she decided.
Otherwise, Ian and the others would have waited until
spring to travel. She just wished he would have found a
way to stop in Virginia on his way to North Carolina! He
must have had to travel through the region, but had probably had no time to stop, just as he had no time or opportunity to send letters.

She understood—but it was so dreadfully hard! She had
grown weary of the war and was desperate for it to be over.
All of her lady friends felt the same way. They were hardly
meeting anymore, and when they did, the mood was
gloomy. They had no more pewter to spare for bullets,
and everyone was too busy trying to survive, let alone keep
the Army going. Where would it all end? *When* would it
end?

This year, Mercy told herself. *This year will decide our fate.*

The first month of the new year brought heavy rains
and sleet, along with rumors of fighting in North Carolina
at a place called Cowpens, where local farmers pastured
cattle before driving them to market. Mercy could discover
few details of the engagement except that Daniel Morgan,
with Colonel Washington's help, had been victorious, lifting the spirits of patriots all across North Carolina—and,
of course, Virginia.

In early February, on a night when sleet rattled the
windowpanes, Chloe awakened Mercy in the wee hours of
the morning. Her eyes were huge and frightened, and she
clutched a blanket around her slender figure and held a
taper with trembling hands.

"Wake up, girl! Someone was bangin' on the front door
a few minutes ago. I *know* I heard sounds out there, but
they gone now, and I am sore afraid of who might still be
out there."

"Why, who do you imagine it might be—British soldiers?
Oh, my God, it *could* be! They might have come up from
North Carolina. Go quickly and rouse everyone down in
the slave quarters. Tell them to be ready to flee at once."

They still called the row of cabins where the workers
lived the "slave quarters." Mercy suddenly realized she
would have to begin calling it something else. Or maybe
not. If the British looted and burned Collier Manor, there
would be no need to call it anything; it would all be gone.

"Flee?" Chloe echoed. "Girl, how we gonna flee? Where
we gonna go in all this sleet? Our people will sicken and
die out in this bad weather. Better to throw ourselves on
the mercy of the soldiers and hope for the best."

"Do not be ridiculous!" Mercy snapped. "They will rape
and kill us all and burn the roof down over our heads. . . .
Did you not look out the window to see who was out there?
If not, *why* not? Maybe it is *not* the British, after all."

Chloe lowered her eyes and for once in her life looked
chagrined. "I was too afraid of what I might see. So I came
to fetch you straight away."

"I will pretend to be a loyalist, then. That is all I can
do. They may not believe me, especially since few loyalists
remain in these parts—or if they do remain, they are keeping their political beliefs to themselves."

Mercy scrambled into warmer garments for the room
was freezing. She tugged them on right over her night
clothes. Then she took the taper from Chloe's shaking
hands.

"Follow me. We will go together and investigate what
these strange noises might be."

"Oh, Lud a' mercy!" Chloe wailed. "They might kill us on sight."

"They are probably just cold and hungry," Mercy insisted. "We will feed and warm them, and send them on their way again. Show no fear, Chloe. An appearance of calm and helpfulness may be the only thing that saves us."

Her own knees were quaking, but Mercy was determined to be brave. She reminded herself that she had faced fearful situations before—and Ian must have faced hundreds of them by now. She must not shame him. Like Martha Washington, she must bravely endure whatever she found and strive to make the best of things.

She descended the staircase and walked sedately toward the front door. "Hurry! Light more tallow dips," she instructed Chloe who hovered behind her. Then she calmly opened the door.

The huddled figure of a man lay crumpled at her feet. Behind him was a horse, standing splay-legged, head drooping, icicles hanging from his mane and forelock. The animal trembled with exhaustion—*was that a wound on his side? Dear God, one leg was laid open to the bone!* It gleamed whitely in the flickering light.

"Chloe, take the taper!"

Mercy thrust the taper in the servant's direction and, heedless of the stinging sleet, dropped to her knees beside the man. Grasping his shoulder, she turned him over so she could see his face. His outer garments were stiff and sodden. Icicles clung to his beard and hair. She noted that he was bare-headed and . . . *Ian!* She was looking down at her own husband, who seemed more dead than alive.

An hour later they had him thawed out and in her father's bedchamber, where a fire glowed in the fireplace. Ian's teeth still chattered, and he showed no awareness of either her, Chloe, or his surroundings. Mercy had already stripped him naked, discovering terrible festering wounds as she did so. She needed to examine him more thoroughly and clean out his wounds as best she could until a physician could attend him—if there were any to be found.

She would have to wait until morning to send someone in search of one. As for poor Thor, all she had been able to do for the stallion was turn him over to Moses and hope the old man could save him. Both horse and rider were close to death. It seemed impossible they had actually made it to Collier Manor. How Ian could have ridden Thor, and the stallion could have carried him so far was a mystery—or a miracle. If she had not opened the door, neither would have survived the night.

Now, as she gently pulled back the covers to study her husband's thin, battered body, she could not conceal a gasp of mingled horror and shock. His wounds were much worse than she had at first thought. He had deep saber gashes in his right arm and thigh, a wound from a musket ball in his upper left arm, and he was black, blue, and yellow from neck to knees. But the thing that shocked her most deeply—and Chloe also—was the state of his "manly parts."

"Oh, my!" Chloe gasped when Mercy pulled the coverlet down to his ankles, and both women could see him clearly for the first time.

His manly parts were swollen, discolored, and misshapen, and Mercy quickly discovered why. High on his upper thigh—the one that bore no saber wound—was the clear imprint of a horseshoe. Ian must have fallen from his horse and been trampled—either by Thor or another animal.

"I know not what to do about *that*," she murmured, allowing his legs to remain bare but spreading the bed linens over the lower half of his torso for modesty's sake.

"He will never give you young'uns now," Chloe muttered. "Not after bein' injured like that. 'Tis the same as if he had been gelded."

"Do not say such a thing!" Mercy exploded. "He may hear you. Besides, I myself do not wish to hear it. He is alive. That is all that matters. The problem is how to keep him alive."

"Best face it, girl. We may not be able to save him." Ever blunt and honest, Chloe sadly shook her head. "He is too bad hurt. Just look at these deep cuts on him—and smell them. My Mama used to say that you can tell from a wound's stench if the victim is gonna survive or not.''

"I will not let him die! I saved him when he was thrown from his horse that time out in the woods, and I will save him now. If you cannot show more faith in me and the Almighty, you can leave, and I will do this alone," Mercy said.

"It will do you no good to get uppity with me, girl," Chloe scolded. "This is too big a job for you alone, and you know it. I am only warnin' you to prepare yourself. If he lasts 'til mornin', I will be greatly surprised."

To Mercy's own surprise, Ian *did* last until morning. He also began to show signs of regaining consciousness. They had cleaned and dressed his wounds, then piled quilts on top of him to keep him warm. The room was as hot as an oven from the fire Caleb was earnestly tending in the fireplace, but Ian kept shivering as if he would never be warm again.

As morning sunshine illuminated the frost-etched windowpanes, Ian became restless. Mercy had already offered him food and drink, but he had not yet opened his eyes or responded to anything she said to him.

"Ian, what is it?" she begged, sitting beside him on the bed and leaning close to his ear so he could hear her. "Are you in pain? Is that why you keep twitching and tossing your head from side to side?"

His only answer was a groan torn from deep inside him. "Ian, listen to me. You are safe at Collier Manor. You came home to me. Do you know where you are, my love—or are you dreaming?"

He flung his arms out wide and almost knocked her off the bed. Mercy grabbed his bandaged arm and looked at Chloe. Chloe shook her head and shrugged. Caleb watched with wide, worried eyes. None of them knew what to do. It was too icy and cold to think of sending for a physician, assuming they could even find one. They were on their own. Actually, it was all up to Mercy, and she dreaded making some grave mistake that might cost Ian his life.

Again leaning over him, she held his hand and gently stroked his brow with the other. "My dearest, you must wake up now and realize where you are. Open your eyes, my love, and you will see that you are here at Collier Manor, in my father's old bed. We put you here because we can keep it warmer than in my room."

Ian's gaze darted back and forth beneath his closed eyelids. The movement was so pronounced that Mercy was certain he could hear her. "Please try to wake up, Ian. You are alive. You are safe. You are home at long last."

Ian suddenly gripped her hand so hard that she winced. His eyelids fluttered open, and his blue eyes gazed up at the ceiling.

"Ian, look at me!" Joy filled her to overflowing. She had broken through his indifference; now he would fight to live.

His beautiful blue eyes sought her face but seemed to look right past her. "Mercy ..." His tone was so hoarse he did not sound like himself. "Mercy, I ... cannot ... see you."

"What do you mean, Ian? I am right here in front of you."

"Mercy ..." He sounded as if he were speaking to her from the depths of a grave. "Mercy, I am ... blind."

"No!" she cried. "No, you cannot be! How did you find your way home if you are blind?"

"Hiram ..." Ian mumbled. "Hiram brought me. Where is ... Hiram? He is ... hurt, too."

Hiram?

"Caleb, go and search the grounds! Chloe, help him. We saw no one else last night—no other horse. No other rider. Where could Hiram be?"

CHAPTER SIXTEEN

They found Hiram's body halfway down the hill from the house. His horse stood hidden from view in a copse of trees where he was hungrily stripping bark off the saplings. When the Scotsman failed to immediately rouse anyone by banging on the front door, he must have decided to ride down to the stable or the slave quarters. In the sleet and darkness, he had lost his way or become disoriented. The dismal weather—and his injuries—had gotten the best of him, but Mercy still blamed herself: *Why had she not realized that Ian could not have made it to Collier Manor on his own?*

Caleb and a couple of other servants carried Hiram's body into the house and laid him out on blankets on the library floor in front of the blazing fire. Caleb pronounced him "froze like a side of meat," but Mercy had to convince herself that he was truly dead.

Once she had examined him, she knew it was hopeless. A makeshift, blood-stained bandage around one leg could not be removed; it was stuck to the body. Ice encrusted Hiram's lashes, beard, and hair, but otherwise his face looked serene and peaceful—as if he had reached his goal of bringing his master home and therefore had died content. Mercy could only marvel at the effort the journey had cost both men. Their wounds were such that they ought not to have been traveling at all—yet they had come so far!

She instructed Caleb to see to the building of Hiram's coffin, and then, choking back tears, returned to Ian's bedside. That *he* still lived seemed even more of a miracle now, and she was doubly determined to keep him so. Hiram had made the ultimate sacrifice to bring her husband back to her. She did not care if Ian was blind, crippled, or unable to give her children; she cared only that he was alive.

Five days later—after a brief warm spell—they were finally able to bury Hiram. Until a grave could be dug, they had stored his coffin in the springhouse. Mercy called together every man, woman, and child on the plantation to witness his burial in the family cemetery a half hour's walk from the house. She read from the Bible and led the singing of hymns.

In the whipping wind, she stood still as a statue until the last shovelful of earth sealed the grave. In respect for Hiram's memory, she declared that the remainder of the day would be one of solemn tribute. No chores other than those necessary for survival were to be performed, and a respectful silence must be maintained.

The children were bug-eyed; even the grown-ups seemed impressed by the respect being accorded to a mere servant. But Hiram had been more than a servant, Mercy thought. He was the best of friends and a true hero, caring for his master to the end though he himself was gravely wounded.

Afterwards, she described the ceremony to Ian, who lay staring sightless at the ceiling, offering no comment. He was behaving as if he could not hear a word she was saying.

"Ian, you may be blind but you are not deaf. Can you not at least talk to me?" she implored.

Other than to ask about Hiram that first morning when he had awakened, Ian had said nothing to anyone. He simply lay in her father's big bed and allowed Mercy to minister to him. When she put a cup or a spoon to his lips, he opened his mouth and ate or drank, but other than that, appeared content to lie there unmoving.

She had yet to locate a doctor to come and examine him. The demands of the war had scattered the local physicians and taken them far away from this corner of Virginia. Fortunately, Ian's wounds looked no worse; however, they looked no better, either. She debated whether to try one or more of the usual remedies prescribed by doctors: bloodletting, blistering, the use of various emetics and/or cathartics. Chloe had thus far persuaded her against them, pointing out that Ian had already lost too much blood and furthermore was not eating enough to need a cathartic.

In any case, it would be a long time before Ian healed. Over and over, Mercy searched through her medicine chest, finding calomel, jalap, niter, Peruvian bark, and snakeroot—but nothing that might improve her husband's mental state.

The Ian she knew and loved had disappeared. In his place was this silent, taciturn man who took no interest in his surroundings. After almost killing himself to make it home to her, he appeared sorry he had made the effort.

"Dearest," she said, bending over him and stroking his now smooth-shaven jaw. "I understand that this has been terrible for you. The journey home must have been ghastly, and to lose Hiram when you got here was a great tragedy. I know you are often in pain, but can you not speak to me a little? I want to know what you are thinking and feeling . . ."

"Nothing," he said quite clearly. "I am thinking and feeling nothing."

"But . . . how can that be, my love? You do not sleep *all* the time. Your eyes are often open—indeed, more often open than closed."

"I sleep . . . little," he agreed. "But I do not think when I am awake. I . . . drift. My mind is empty."

Mercy's stomach muscles clenched in dread. She did not like what she was hearing. This was so unlike Ian, whose mind had always been so active. In the early days of their relationship, she had always wondered what he was thinking and plotting. She had never doubted he was plotting *some*thing.

"Ian, I will not push you yet—but the day is coming when you must do more than 'drift,'" she warned him. "You will have to get out of this bed and work your injured muscles. You must find your way around the house and the grounds outside. Papa had a gold-knobbed cane around here somewhere. I will find it for you."

"Why?" he asked, turning his face toward her—looking right at her but not *seeing* her. "Why should I ever get out of this bed again?"

"*Why?*" she echoed, astounded. "You ask me *why?*"

"If I lie here long enough, I will finally die," he said. "The part of me that is still living, that is. Half of me is dead already."

"Oh, Ian, no! You are still alive—very much alive, my love."

"No." He shook his head, his expression adamant. "I cannot see. I cannot move my leg—"

"*Which* leg? You never told me you could not move your leg!"

"My right one. It should be hurting like the very devil from all those cuts, but even after I was first wounded, it did not. It felt only . . . numb. Sometimes it tingles. But it does not hurt, and I can scarcely move it."

He grimaced a moment, as if trying. Mercy stared at the coverlet, hoping to see some movement. She saw none.

"There. You see?" Ian's tone was matter-of-fact. "I will never walk again."

"Yes, you will! I will *help* you walk again. Your leg must be used or indeed it *will* die! Once the cuts have healed, we will move it *for* you, until you can do it yourself."

The corners of his mouth curved slightly upwards—but only for a moment. "So *I* am to be your new cause, eh, Mercy? You think you can make me whole again. . . . Well, I think not. Will you exercise other parts of me as well?"

"What other parts?" she demanded, thinking he meant another limb. She was already planning to exercise *all* of his limbs for him. Indeed, she should have thought of it sooner.

"You *know* what other parts," he said. "You know how painful it is for me to . . . relieve myself."

She *did* know. He did not even want her in the room with him when he had to do it. He would always ask for Caleb to fetch him the chamber pot.

"You will heal there, too," she assured him. "Already the swelling has gone down, and you look . . . more normal."

"I will never be able to love you again, Mercy." His beautiful blue eyes held despair. "That is the greatest loss—the worst torment. I will never see—or love—my lovely wife again."

"It does not matter! Ian, it does *not.*" She grew frantic in her efforts to persuade him, touching his dear handsome face, plunging her fingers into his thick dark hair. "All that matters is that you are *alive,* and you came home to me. I know not how you managed it! But you did and I thank God for it."

"I do not thank Him," Ian said. "I curse Him. Him and Hiram both. I should have died at Cowpens. They should have let me die there."

Cowpens. This had happened to him at Cowpens. She had wanted to hear all about it—to learn all the horrid details. But not like this . . . not when he spoke with such bitterness and hopelessness.

"Hiram saved your life," she confirmed.

Ian nodded, his mouth a grim line.

"Tell me about it," she urged. "Tell me all you remember." She gently kneaded his upper arms and shoulders while she spoke. Beneath her hands, his flesh was stiff and unyielding.

"I was with Morgan. Daniel Morgan. We were six hundred Continentals—and about four hundred militia—against a far greater number of the enemy. Tarleton was on our tail."

"Tarleton?"

"Banastre Tarleton. He was leading the green-coated dragoons and the infantry of his British legion. Been terrorizing the South for almost a year. You have not heard of him?"

"Some news I get—not all," she told him. "Go on."

"He is a vindictive, coldhearted, ruthless bastard," Ian continued, without emotion. "He is also the best cavalryman on either side. You would admire his horsemanship, if nothing else."

You are wrong, Ian. I could not admire such a man for any reason. Indeed, I hate him for what he has done to you!

"He chased us into a woods—Cowpens, it is called," Ian continued. "We had no choice but to camp there. The men were exhausted but too afraid to sleep. Morgan spent half the night trying to lift their spirits for the coming fight. We were short on gunpowder and ball, but he told them if they could manage to load and fire three times, it would all be over. When you return to your homes, he promised them, how the old folks will bless you and the girls will kiss you."

Ian released a short, humorless laugh. "Such fools we all are! Men will do anything for a woman's kiss. The next day was proof of it. When Tarleton attacked, our troops were ready. They emptied saddles at a terrific rate. But three volleys was all our men could deliver. After that, they turned and ran. The cavalry pursued and cut them down with sabers. Young Colonel Washington—the general's cousin—appeared just in time to save the day. At least, it looked to me like he was saving it. By then, I myself was wounded and barely able to remain on Thor. I recall seeing British regulars tossing down their guns to surrender. Then a line of soldiers rushed me with bayonets. What happened next, I cannot tell you. When I regained consciousness, I was lying amidst bleeding, broken bodies from both sides. I managed to crawl to cover beneath some underbrush. There, I collapsed and lost consciousness again."

"Was that where Hiram found you?"

"I assume he did. The next time I awoke, I was slung across my saddle, my head dangling on one side and my legs on the other. I was in terrible pain—and cursing God for having saved me. I knew I was too badly hurt to recover; I wanted to die and be done with it."

"But Hiram would not let you die," Mercy supplied.

Ian shook his head. "When I began to curse him, too, he bashed me over the head with the butt of his musket to silence me so we could pass safely through enemy lines. After that, I gave up and let him take me wherever he wanted. . . . Later, I begged him not to bring me here. I did not want you to see me like this. He would not listen and brought me home anyway. So here I am, while he is dead and gone, now . . . the best friend I ever had."

Ian coughed and broke into harsh sobs. Mercy gathered him to her bosom and rocked him while he wept in her arms. She wept with him, hoping the tears would be healing for both of them, but Ian suddenly pushed her away.

"Leave me now," he ordered.

"Ian, please—"

"No—get out!" he shouted at her. "Just get the hell out of here!"

She jumped up and left him.

The next day, Mercy began her own campaign to restore Ian's health. Ignoring his protests, curses, cries of outrage, and general refusal to cooperate, she enlisted the aid of Chloe, Caleb, and another strong young former slave named Augustus to begin exercising the muscles of his arms and legs so they would not waste away. Chloe drew upon her ample store of slave lore mixed with superstition, and applied steaming poultices to his limbs, after which she and Mercy gently massaged him, taking care not to disturb his wounds but still working his muscles—while Ian mocked all they did. Chloe closed her eyes and chanted while she worked, seemingly oblivious to Ian's taunts, but they lacerated Mercy's heart and soul.

"Do you think this African sorcery and mumbo-jumbo will help?" he roared at them. "Why will you not let me lie here and die in peace? If you succeed in getting me on my feet again, I will still be blind and impotent. What kind of life is that for a man?"

Chloe responded by placing a steaming fragrant cloth over his face, covering even his mouth. Adding injury to insult, she had Caleb and Augustus hold him down while she flung off the blanket shielding his private parts and applied another hot poultice to his groin. Ian bucked and fought them. Mercy was about to intervene—until Chloe looked her right in the eye and said: "This will draw out the poison and bad humors the same as bleedin' him, but it not nearly so likely to kill him. It gonna help him heal, girl."

After ten days of such treatment, Mercy could see vast improvement. Ian was able to sit up and take his meals in a chair by the fire and could even put weight on his bad leg, and it would support him. He still could not walk unaided, but she knew that sensitivity was returning to the leg he had claimed was numb. When she accidentally spilled some soup on it, he hollered at her and jerked his leg away.

"Ian, your leg is getting better!" she crowed, delighted.

"A little," he admitted. "But I will never be the man I was before," he bitterly reminded her.

She wanted to tell him that he must find peace with the man he was now—the man she loved every bit as much as the old Ian—but it was still too soon. He refused to believe that life could get better.

In the second week of March, Moses came to Mercy with disappointing news: "I done the best I can t' save the master's fine horse," he said to Mercy, his round black face contorted with remorse. "But he never gonna be the horse he was, Miss Mercy."

"What do you mean, Moses? How bad is he?" She had not had time to go down to the stables recently and dreaded hearing that Thor was ruined . . . like his master.

"His injuries bad . . . real bad." Old Moses shook his grizzled gray head. "He not ever gonna jump fences or chase foxes again. He not gonna delight the eyes, neither."

"But surely he will be able to be ridden, at least!"

"Naw, Miss Mercy. I doan think so. How he done carried the master home I doan know. He all played out now. Lost his spirit, too. Doan even want to look at the mares. Be a mercy to shoot him and put him out of his misery. He not ever gonna be fit and strong again."

Mercy's heart sank. First Ian and now Thor! How could she ever tell Ian that she must put down his horse? It was all too much.

"I will come down and take a look at him, Moses. If he must be shot, 'tis I who must do it."

None of her former slaves had ever handled guns; Papa had always said it would be a big mistake to put guns in the hands of slaves. She looked in on Ian and found him sleeping—exhausted from his latest bout with Chloe, Caleb, and Augustus. Grabbing a shawl, she stepped out into a wild, windy day that hinted of rain and springtime. Indeed, daffodils were starting to bloom along the flagstone paths skirting the house.

Mercy greedily inhaled the earthy, warmish air. April would soon be upon them and with it another busy season for Collier Manor—and for the war. She had heard nothing of the war lately. Since Ian's arrival, time had ground to a halt. But events would soon be happening fast and furiously; of this she had no doubt.

She wondered if she ought to try and send word of Ian's whereabouts to General Washington. By now, Ian's name had probably been listed among those considered dead or missing. Martha Washington should soon be returning to Mount Vernon, so Mercy decided to wait and write *her* instead.

Entering the stable, she ignored Liberty's excited nicker of recognition and headed straight for Thor's box. As she peered inside, Moses came up beside her—just in time to hear her gasp of dismay.

"I done told you he was in bad shape, Miss Mercy," the old man said.

Mercy could only nod; she simply had not realized how badly the once magnificent stallion had been hurt. Barely healed cuts and gashes crisscrossed his rich brown coat. One side of his noble head looked as if it had been singed by fire. He had lost so much weight he hardly resembled his old self. Worst of all, she saw no hint of his former proud spirit and look-at-me attitude. The horse that stood before her now was as bruised, battered, and forlorn as his master.

"Is he lame?" she asked, remembering the gleam of white bone on his foreleg on the night Ian had come home.

She leaned over the side of the box to look down at his legs. New skin—puckered and ugly—had begun to hide the patch of exposed bone. Had muscles and tendons been injured? Perhaps not, since the horse had made it back to Virginia.

"Miss Mercy, this poor horse is so stiff, sore, and cut up he can hardly move at all. I hand-walk him a little up and down the aisle, but my guess is he never will be able to do any work. Jus' look at him. I think he done suffered enough."

Mercy was forced to agree. Thor's head hung down to his knees, and it was plain he had given up. Like his master, he had lost all joy in living and only wanted to escape the pain. She knew what she had to do.

"See if you can get him out in that field where we used to turn him out when Ian stayed with us before the war. I will do it there, Moses. We will bury him there. But first, I . . . I have to tell Ian. Thor is *his* horse, not mine. The final decision will be up to him, though I am sure I know what he will say."

"Do it!" Ian said from his bed. "Why do you even ask me? Just do it. His life is over. No one should force him to live when he no longer *wants* to or has a reason for his sorry existence. He is a horse, not a man."

His words were another condemnation of all their efforts to improve *his* lot. Ian could not accept his limitations. *She* could accept them, but he could not.

"I will be waiting to hear the pistol shot," he added. "I want to know his suffering has ended. You should have done it long before this, Mercy. What satisfaction do you derive from witnessing the misery of men and horses?"

"None," she answered. "I am trying to *heal* you, not force you to suffer. You still have a mind, Ian. You can still use it."

"How can I use it?" he muttered. "I might think of writing again, but I doubt anyone could read my scribbling since I can see nothing but shadows—and a little bit of light and dark."

"You can see shadows?" Hope flared in her breast. That

was more than he had confessed to being able to see when he first arrived.

"Sometimes. . . . Do not excite yourself. It means nothing, except that I may one day be able to tell day from night."

"But Ian, that is progress! I am delighted to hear it."

"Your delight comes too easily. 'Tis one of your more annoying traits. You must accept, as I do, that I am less than half the man you married."

"Perhaps you are right!" Mercy snapped, infuriated by his self-pity. "The man I married had more courage. He relished life and would never have willingly surrendered it and begged people to let him die."

"That is precisely what I have been telling you," Ian said, lying perfectly still and unmoving, his blue eyes focused on the ceiling. "*That* man is dead. When will you accept it, be merciful, and allow *this* one to slip away? After you shoot Thor, bring *me* the pistol, leave me alone with it, and—"

"*No!*" Mercy screamed at him. "I will not do it. I will *never* do it. How dare you suggest such a thing!"

"Mercy . . ." He turned his despair-ravaged face toward her in an impassioned plea. "Mercy, let me go. If I cannot be a true husband to you, I would not be a burden. It is pure torture for me to lie here day after day, unable to see you, hold you . . . make love to you, as I have dreamed of doing all the time we were apart . . ."

Leaning over him, she seized his hand. "Ian, you *can* still hold me, kiss me, comfort me! That is all I want or need—the rest I can do without."

He pushed her savagely away from him. "But *I* cannot do without it! I am no longer a man but a gelding—do not touch me! Stay away from me. Your nearness is a torture I cannot bear. Save your love for some other man. You deserve happiness and children—babes clinging to your skirts. I cannot give you that!"

"I want *you*, Ian—just you! It will be enough."

"No," he said, violently shaking his head. "No, it will not. Not for me. Not for you. Pity can never replace passion. I cannot bring myself to settle for that. I would rather die,

Mercy. When you are finished with Thor, bring me the pistol!''

"No, I told you! Never." She spun and started out of the room, then stopped on the threshold to look back at him. "Ian, you are breaking my heart—not with your impotence, your blindness, nor any of your other losses. You are breaking it with your hopelessness and your retreat from me. The man I love is in you somewhere. Come back to me, Ian . . . my dearest love, come back to me."

When he spoke, his tone never wavered. It remained distant and cold. "He is gone, Mercy. How many times must I tell you? He is dead and gone."

The stallion stood in the windswept field against a backdrop of gray storm clouds racing across the sky. Moses held the rope attached to Thor's halter, but stepped back from him so Mercy could take aim at the horse's head.

She raised her father's pistol and sighted down the barrel. Before squeezing the trigger, she tried to swallow the lump in her throat and blinked to clear the tears from her eyes. Thor chose that moment to raise his head and look off into the distance. His nostrils flared as he drank the wind and sought to decipher its contents.

In the adjoining field, Liberty had been turned out to take her exercise. Sighting him, the mare ran along the stone fence, whinnying and inviting the stallion to join her in a gallop along the fence line.

Excited by the coming storm, she raised her red tail like a flag, bucked and cavorted, all the while calling to Thor. The stallion's ears pricked. His nostrils flared even wider. Neck arched, eyes suddenly alight with interest, he took a single halting step in the mare's direction. Then he stopped, as if remembering all that had happened to him.

Go to her! Go, Thor! Mercy mentally urged him.

But Thor only stood watching, his interest ebbing moment by moment. He heaved a great sigh, and the noble head came down again.

Damn horse. Damn Ian.

Moses tugged on the lead rope to lift the stallion's head

again. Mercy aimed at the spot between his eyes. Thor
looked at her. His great brown eyes mournfully watched
her—watched and waited, as if he knew what was coming.

She could not do it. Not when he watched her with his
naked horse soul glimmering in his eyes. *He is pining for
his master,* she thought, the insight so startling that it
momentarily rocked her. Ian could not come to him now,
but one day he could. Blind or not, impotent or not, lame
or not, Ian could eventually come to him ... but Ian
wanted the stallion dead. Ian had *chosen* death for Thor,
and maybe Thor had chosen death for himself ... or maybe
not. He *had* shown that slight flicker of interest in life,
when he raised his head and watched Liberty.

Aiming the pistol into the sky, not at the stallion, Mercy
squeezed the trigger. The retort sent Liberty flying down
the fence line, but Thor barely quivered, so accustomed
was he to gunfire.

Moses raised his eyebrows in question.

"Put him in with Liberty," she instructed. "Or let Liberty
in with him. Today is not his day to die. Leave the two of
them alone together. Let us see if Liberty can accomplish
what *we* cannot—give Thor a reason to get well again."

"But, Miss Mercy—" Moses protested.

"I will hear no argument, Moses. If Thor wants to die,
he will manage it by himself. We do not need to help
him. ... The new grass is starting to come in now, and
they can drink from the creek. Put grain out for them
both, but otherwise leave them in God's hands."

"Miss Mercy, your own Pa would say to put this horse
out of his misery."

"I know, Moses. But I cannot do it today. Take off his
halter, and open the gate to the next field. Leave it open.
I can smell rain coming. Let Thor feel the rain and afterwards the sunshine. Let him be a horse again, not a servant
of mankind. He can choose to die—or to live, whichever
he prefers."

"Yes, Miss Mercy," Moses answered, nodding. "That
might be the best thing, after all. I sure can do no more
for him."

Holding the pistol at her side, Mercy began to walk toward the house.

I will not tell Ian, she thought. *Let him think Thor is dead. He will only be furious that I did not shoot him, just as he is furious that I refuse to allow him to die.*

She headed for the house with a renewed sense of purpose. Somehow, some way, she would teach Ian that life was precious no matter his limitations. She believed that with her whole being. It was even more precious when someone loved you, and you had someone to love in return.

CHAPTER SEVENTEEN

The arrival of spring brought a new crisis to Collier Manor: The war came to Virginia.

Post riders working in relays delivered the news across the state. Benedict Arnold, a traitor to the American cause and now a British brigadier, had sailed boldly up the James River to Richmond, routed the few militia who turned out to stop him, and sent Thomas Jefferson—now Virginia's governor—fleeing from Monticello into the countryside, along with his wife and children.

Arnold fired all the public buildings and tobacco warehouses, then pushed upriver to Westham, where he destroyed the foundry that made Virginia's muskets. All of this happened while General Washington was reportedly struggling to keep the Continental Army intact. Another harsh winter of scant rations and no pay had led to mutiny and mass desertions, just when dedicated and experienced soldiers were needed most.

Mercy hated to share such alarming news with Ian, yet she could hardly keep it from him; what if Arnold marched this far north? The Virginia militia would be helpless without an army at their backs and inspired leaders out in front. As fragmented as the militia was, the men might not turn out in time to defend their own farms, towns, and plantations. Virginia had no power to force the militia to turn out or even to muster them. Ever fearful of infringing on personal liberty, the Virginia House of Burgesses had never given itself the power.

It was an appalling state of affairs, and Mercy finally decided she *must* tell Ian before the redcoats came marching up the drive. Plans must be made to move him into hiding—and he must agree to cooperate—lest he be recognized and strung up from the nearest tree.

When she approached him, he was sitting by an open window in her father's bedchamber, where Caleb had placed him so he could feel the fresh breeze on his face and get a little sun in the bargain. His long dark hair was drawn back, plaited at the back of his neck and tied with a bit of black ribbon. He wore a white shirt, brown woolen waistcoat, breeches, and buckle shoes. Except for the shoes replacing his customary boots—and a few remaining bandages and the sling for his left arm—he looked almost normal. Only his distant expression suggested he was not yet himself.

Quickly and quietly, she shared the latest news. His reaction astounded her.

"Now you really must see the wisdom of giving me a pistol and leaving me alone with it," he drawled. "My presence here can only be a danger to you and everyone else at Collier Manor."

"Ian, I thought we had gotten past that." She strove to remain calm. "Lately you have been much less hostile than you were at first. I thought your improved mood was due to the progress you have been making. Why, you can almost walk now—"

"You mean with Caleb on one side and Augustus on the other. Oh, yes! That is *real* progress. I should definitely be able to defend Collier Manor by the time Benedict Arnold appears at the front door."

"I had in mind hiding you," she said, ignoring his sarcasm. "I could then pretend to be a loyalist who is glad to see the redcoats."

"Oh? Where do you plan to hide me—in your bed,

perhaps?" he mocked. "No one would think of looking for me there! Or how about under it? As useless as I am, I might as well cower under a bed. Cowering is all that is left to me."

"Stop it, Ian! Whining ill becomes you. You continue to thwart me at every turn. You do nothing to help yourself or adjust to your situation. I have come here to ask your advice. I want to know what I should do to prepare for attack, and all you can do is mock me. Stop thinking about yourself and consider what this means for the rest of us."

She was ashamed of herself as soon as she finished the tongue-lashing. To this point, she had avoided belittling or scolding Ian. Instead, she had tried to be patient and give him time to come to terms with the changes in his life. Now she *needed* him. He better than anyone could help her devise a plan for what to do if the British came. If she could not bluff them, she might have to fight them; she had to stop them somehow. Ian—the old Ian—would have known what to do.

For a long moment, neither spoke.

Then Ian heaved a deep sigh. "You are right, Mercy. If you will not accept the obvious solution to the problem created by my presence, I should be thinking of other ways to help you and help myself as well. If the British come to Collier Manor, sit me on a chair in the drive. Give me several loaded rifles or muskets. Then you and all the servants can run and hide. Knowing the British, they will march in formation right up the drive to the house. All I will have to do is fire in their general direction. I am bound to hit a few before they get me. *That* is how I want to die— as a man defending what is mine. Do me this one last favor, and I promise you I will never ask another—nor will I ever whine or complain again."

Mercy's vision blurred with tears. There was no reaching him! No scaling of the high wall that stood between them. No bridging of the chasm. He would not allow it.

"Your plan is unacceptable," she told him icily. "See if you can devise another. 'Tis obvious you need more time."

"A pistol, a musket, or a rifle, Mercy. That is all I need."

"God forgive you for despairing, Ian Montjoy!"

"God? Hah! ... What God? If there is one, He has abandoned me. Perhaps He has abandoned all of us, and America never will be free."

She could no longer bear his cynicism and fled the room. But later, the very next day, she noticed that Ian began taking more of an interest in his daily exercises with Caleb and Augustus. When normally they would have led him back to bed or to a chair, he insisted upon walking further. The next day, he amazed all of them by demanding a cane and trying to walk on his own. He managed four steps before he toppled, and they all rushed to his aid. By the following day, he was tap-tapping his way around the bedchamber. Grimacing whenever he misjudged a distance and jostled or bumped his wounded leg or arm, he doggedly persisted. Mercy watched in silent amazement and prayed he had undergone a change of heart as well as attitude.

"Caleb, come help me with my boots! I want to see if I can finally get them on again," he shouted a week later. "Damn your hide, where are you?"

Caleb had stepped out to fetch something, and Augustus was nowhere around, so Mercy gladly hurried to help him. As she knelt before him, he sat straight up in his chair, sniffed the air, and barked: "Where is Caleb? Get up off your knees, Mercy. Caleb can do this."

"How did you know it was me?" She sat back on her heels in front of him, his boot still in her hand.

"I can smell you," he said. "I would know your scent anywhere. It haunts my dreams at night."

Emotion clogged her throat. "It need not haunt you," she said softly as soon as she could speak. "You could start sleeping in my bed, or I in yours. We could sleep in each other's arms at night. No one is forcing us to sleep alone."

Tears glinted in his eyes, but all too quickly, his face hardened into the cynical mask she had grown to detest. "No, I could not endure that. I am sorry, but I could not."

"Ian, your wounds are healing! Your leg is improving each day. And ... and what about your eyesight?"

"There is improvement there, too," he admitted. "But nothing to crow about. I can tell light from dark, and sometimes I can see shapes and objects, but 'tis impossible to distinguish between them or identify them."

"There! You see?" she crowed. "If there is improvement in *these* things, perhaps—"

"There is no improvement elsewhere!" he spat. "Believe me when I tell you that. I remain . . . dead down there."

His bitterness devastated her far more than the possibility that he might remain impotent. "Does it still pain you when you relieve yourself?"

He shook his head adamantly. "I cannot talk about it, especially not with *you.*"

"But *why*, Ian? I am your wife, and—"

"Because you are my wife and I cannot love you as a husband should! Leave me a shred of pride, Mercy. We shall not speak of it again. And we shall not sleep together in the same bed—ever."

"Ian, I need you to hold me! To hug and kiss me. What could be the harm in that?"

"Because I cannot bear the feel and the scent of you, knowing I can never have you again! Mercy, stop torturing me!"

"But it is a torment to *me* that you will not let me touch you! Caleb and Augustus see to all your needs. Look! Even now, you flinch away from me." She reached for his hand, but he quickly jerked it away from her.

"Mercy, I am warning you! I will not stand for you to toy with me."

"Toy with you! Ian, I am desperate for your love. I am groveling for it. I am kneeling at your feet *begging* you to—"

"Get away!" He flung out his arm with such force that it sent her flying.

She struck her head on the table leg, and the resulting thump was both loud and painful.

"Mercy! Oh, God, what have I done?"

Heedless of his injuries, he launched himself off the chair in her direction. Banging his head, he groped for her, and when he found her, lifted her and clasped her to his chest. She could feel him shaking like a leaf in the wind.

"Are you all right? Did I hurt you? Mercy, I would sooner cut off my right arm than ever hurt you."

Do you not realize how much you hurt me every hour of every day? Do you not know how I die a little each time you push me away when I yearn to be close to you?

"Do not distress yourself. I am fine," she lied. Still, she took advantage of his concern by burrowing into his embrace as the feel of his arms around her was too heavenly to ignore.

Again he pushed her away—more gently this time.

"Mercy, forgive me, but I cannot give you what you need and want. I am half-blind, half-lame, and wholly impotent. To put that to the test—and confirm the truth of it— would destroy me. . . . God knows I am trying to get better. Have you not noticed how hard I have been trying lately?"

"Yes, my love, yes! I *have* noticed and silently rejoiced at your efforts."

He covered his eyes with his hand and sat on the floor beside her, his bad leg stretched out in front of him. "I feel as if I am trapped in darkness. There is no light any-where. There will *never* be light. You will not let me die, so I am trying to live—to regain some usefulness. You cannot ask more of me, Mercy. I have no more to give. I know not who I am anymore. Who is Ian Montjoy? . . . Tell me, if you can. *Who is he?* Some stranger I no longer recognize."

"You are . . . you will be . . ." She hesitated, lacking the answer to his disturbing questions. His whole life had changed. The rules had all changed. He was a man strug-gling to be reborn, one who doubted his own manhood and could no longer define it by old customs and habits. He only knew he hated his helplessness and dependence on others. He had yet to come to terms with it, and how could she blame him?

"You will always be the man I love," she finished lamely, knowing that her response would hardly comfort him or provide the answers he sought.

He laughed, a cold bitter laugh that cut her heart to shreds. "You mean the gelded stallion. All else I could tolerate with better grace, but not *that*. *That* is what I cannot bear."

"We will consult doctors," she suggested. "When the war ends, we will travel and find the best one."

"Doctors . . ." He shook his head. "You have more faith in them than I do. They are skilled only in the arts of butchery: trephining—removing disks of bone with their little round saws—amputating, and letting blood or blistering for every human ailment. I have seen enough of their handiwork to despise the lot of them. I am *glad* you could find no doctor to attend me, or I *would* be dead by now."

"Oh, Ian! You really do want to live, do you not?"

He sighed. "No—yes. Sometimes. There are moments when I cannot help myself, and I dream of being whole and strong again—riding Thor, making love to you . . . but Thor is dead now, and I cannot even defend you from attack by my enemies, much less bed you. Remembering all that, I again want to die. I am angry anew that I am still alive and helpless."

"Not so helpless as before, Ian. You are getting better. You will get better still. We will find a remedy for *all* your injuries."

He held up one hand. "Offer me no hope, Mercy. Give me no reasons to live. Just when I am learning to be content in my darkness, do not drag me toward the light. The light is too intense, too painful. Now I live for just one reason."

"What reason is that?"

"If the British should come here, I want to stand between you and them. That is all I ask of God. Let me shield you from them. If you will not give me a gun, put a saber in my hand and stand behind me. Let me die defending all I hold dear in this world."

It always came back to death—never life! He was obsessed with dying.

"Oh, Ian."

The British would cut him down in a heartbeat and get to her anyway. They would destroy Collier Manor, rape all the women, and enslave all the men. Burn the place to the ground probably . . . but why tell him what he already knew?

He simply wanted to die a hero—a man's dream, not a woman's. *She* wanted to live, and she wanted Ian to live along with her.

"If they come," he said. "Will you give me a saber?"

"Yes," she said. *But I will be standing behind you with a gun, and we shall both die heroes. No man but you shall ever touch me.*

The British did not come—at least not immediately. They spent the next month preparing for them, and Ian directed all their efforts. On the day after his conversation with her on the floor, he asked Mercy to gather together every living person on the plantation. Leaning heavily on her father's cane, he stood on the front lawn and asked for their help in defending Collier Manor.

At first, no one said anything, but then Moses stepped forward. "Master, we got no guns. Doan know how to use 'em if we had 'em. Be best if we all surrender. Otherwise they jus' kill us."

"They may kill you anyway," Ian brusquely informed him. "Surrender is no guarantee of survival. Mercy, is it possible to procure muskets, pistols, rifles, sabers, or any other weapons to give our people?"

Our people. At least he had progressed to calling them that.

She shook her head, then realized he could not see the gesture and was still waiting for her answer. "No, Ian. The British destroyed the foundry at Westham, remember? That would have been our best hope."

"What about sickles, scythes, and shovels?" he demanded.

"You want us to face an army with *farm* tools?" Mercy glanced around at the black faces—and a few white ones, too, indentured servants—who were watching Ian as if they thought he had lost his wits.

The blond-haired wife of the former tobacco overseer who had gone off to join the Continental Army—leaving her and two children behind—walked up to stand beside Moses. "We need militia to protect us!" she cried in a shrill voice, flapping her white apron in agitation. "We cannot be expected to protect ourselves. Except for a few good-for-nothing male slaves, we are mostly women and children here now, and—"

"There are no more slaves here at Collier Manor, Elsie," Mercy interrupted. Elsie was not a happy woman nor a pleasant one to have around, so Mercy kept her busy overseeing the chickens and weaving cloth in her own little house which was separate from the slave quarters. "We are all equals now and equally in danger," she added. "Perhaps we should give my husband a chance to explain himself before we offer criticism."

She glanced at Ian's face. The quiver of muscle in his clenched jaw indicated his anger; before the war, no servant or slave would have dared to question the judgment of a man of his class—however, she herself had just questioned him in front of them about the farm tools.

"Ian, tell us what you have in mind," she urged. "I am sure it is a fine plan."

"It is *not* a fine plan," he grimly disputed. "But in the absence of weapons, 'tis the best I can devise. I have in mind making a well-stocked refuge out of that patch of woods in which you once loved to lead your suitors on a merry chase."

"The woods where you were injured during the foxhunt."

"The very same," Ian informed her. " 'Tis the only place around here where we can all take cover and hide in the event of attack by British soldiers."

"But the soldiers would soon flush us out like we do the fox, and . . ." She halted in midsentence. "Tell us what else you intend."

"Traps," Ian said. "We must have traps everywhere, and only our people will know how to avoid them. Men on foot or on horseback will be unable to enter the woods from any direction without falling into concealed pits and injuring themselves on sharpened stakes, or stepping into nooses and finding themselves flying through the air to dangle by one leg from treetops, or . . . well, we must all use our imaginations to think of what else we might do to discourage them."

"This is startin' to sound like fun," Caleb boldly offered, exchanging glances with Augustus who stood nearby, ready to assist Ian if needed. "I bet we could think of other surprises for 'em, too—or *you* could, Augustus. You would be good at that sort of mischief."

Caleb was very dark, Augustus light—with skin the color of weak tea. Caleb had more muscle to him, but Augustus made up for a lack of brawn with brains. It was obvious that they had become friends while ministering to Ian. Fortunately, neither man thought less of him for his injuries and bad moods.

"I *would* be good," Augustus cheerfully agreed, flashing a white-toothed grin. "Is that why we need tools, Master Ian—to fashion traps?"

Ian nodded. "I applaud your nimble mind, Augustus. There is much work to be done. All of you must help. By the time we are finished, we will have a detailed plan for what every single person must do—and where they must go—the moment the British are spotted, or we hear they are on their way."

"It will never work!" Elsie snapped.

"Yes, it will!" Chloe snapped back. Rivalry had always simmered between the two women; Elsie resented the friendship between Mercy and Chloe, especially the fact that Chloe had more authority, even though she had once been a slave.

"Of course it will work," Mercy assured them by way of settling the matter. "Anyone who does not think so is forbidden to help—and will not be permitted to hide in the woods when the soldiers come. Indeed, they must leave here at once and seek protection on some other plantation."

She gazed pointedly at Elsie, and the woman lowered her eyes and held her tongue. Mercy took this to mean she intended to cooperate. "You may all disperse now and fetch the tools my husband suggested."

By the end of the month, they were as ready as they would ever be for the British to attack Collier Manor—

and Ian had recovered much of his self-esteem. He had worked tirelessly overseeing every detail of every trap, not *seeing* them, of course, but insisting on explanations for how they worked and making his own suggestions, which invariably improved on the original idea.

Mercy was delighted, all the more so because Ian's strength and endurance were slowing returning, offering hope that he might eventually make a full recovery. He would probably always have a limp and impaired vision, but at least he would not be confined to a bed or chair. She dared to hope that his physical improvement extended to *other* parts of his body, as she could no longer bear sleeping apart from him. Wanting only to be near him, she gathered her courage and visited his room one night, sliding into bed beside him as he slept.

He awoke in an instant.

"Mercy! What are you doing here? You must leave at once."

"I just want to be close to you, Ian." She snuggled up to him and draped one arm across his chest.

He picked it up and gave it back to her. "Mercy, I do not want you here. Please leave now."

She slid one leg across his legs. "Do not send me away, Ian."

"You are hurting my wounds," he ground out.

She pulled back her leg but refused to give up. With one hand, she lightly stroked his chest through the fabric of his nightshirt. He grabbed her hand and held it away from his body, his strength surprising.

"Mercy, I have no taste for this love play when it can lead nowhere except to disappointment."

"How do you know for certain that it will lead nowhere?" As if it had a will of its own, her hand resumed exploring.

"Go on then. Satisfy your curiosity. 'Tis apparent you care nothing for *my* feelings in the matter."

"I have feelings, too, Ian," she reminded him. "I only want to touch you—be close to you."

She leaned up on one elbow and pressed her lips to his mouth in a kiss. He remained as still and unyielding as a stone. His coldness pierced her heart like an arrow, but she refused to give up so easily. Next, she kissed his tightly closed eyes and his brow. After that, his cheekbones and chin—then the crook of his neck. She nibbled gently on his ear and kissed the ridge of his collarbone.

She kissed his wounded shoulder and, pulling up his nightshirt, moved her mouth across his chest. He inhaled sharply when she nuzzled his flat male nipple and traced the contours of his chest with her tongue.

"Mercy, stop," he groaned. "I beg of you."

"You told me I might satisfy my curiosity," she reminded him. "Can you honestly tell me you feel nothing when I do this to you?"

She took his nipple between her teeth and gently tugged on it. In response, he seized her hair and pulled her face up to his. "I want you, damn you! In my heart, in my mind, and yes—even in my flesh. But I cannot—"

"You *can*, Ian. How can you deny me without even trying? I will *help* you. Only tell me what to do."

"No! 'Tis futile—"

"Let me do what I will," she begged. "Let me lead the way, for once."

Her hand found his thigh and stroked it, then ventured closer to . . .

He grabbed her hand and held it still.

"Ian, let me touch you."

"No."

"Ian, let me try. Please, my darling . . ."

"All right, do it!"

She lowered her hand and explored the shape and feel of him. He was not as firm and large there as she remembered, but with a little encouragement . . .

"You are hurting me," he groaned, the words torn from him as if he were trying not to say them. "Mercy, the more I want you, the more I hurt!"

She jerked her hand away and flopped back on the bed. "Forgive me, Ian. I had no right to force this on you. 'Tis clear you are not ready."

He was silent a moment. "I will never be ready," he finally said. "It has been long enough. All my other injuries are healing, but every time I think of taking you . . . and I begin to ache for you . . . the pain begins.''

"Ian, I did not know!" She sat up, growing more disturbed by the moment. "Forgive me, my love. We will try again another time.''

"My pride would not survive another time. Believe me. If the time should ever come when I believe we can be one again, I will *tell* you, Mercy. I will join you in *your* bed and never again sleep apart from you.''

"Ian, can we not sleep together anyway? My bed is so lonely. I *hate* being so far from you.''

"Do you honestly believe you can lie down beside me and *not* cause this pain?" he asked. "There are days when I have only to look in your direction, and I suffer. My blindness is actually a blessing. I have only to imagine your smile or hear your laughter—even the sound of your voice—and my passion awakens. All too soon, the aching begins, and if I do not get away from you, it soon becomes unbearable.''

"All this time you have been suffering like this?" Mercy was aghast.

"Was I supposed to whine and complain about it?" he gently mocked. "My tongue is often sore from being bitten down upon to keep from mentioning it.''

She tossed back her hair and wrung her hands together. "Ian, I am so sorry. But I have been suffering, too. My own passions well up in me—and my need to be held. Then I grow angry with you for not satisfying the latter need, at least.''

"Come here," he said, reaching for her. "Let me hold you for a little while. Perhaps if I can train my mind not to dream of going further—''

"No." She rose to her feet. "I understand now, Ian. Before I did not. I thought you were only feeling sorry for yourself. I never realized you were truly hurting.''

"Oh, I do enough of that, too," he assured her with a wry chuckle that sounded like the old Ian. "That battle is not yet won. Being useful eases my despair, but at times, sorrow and fury still threaten to suffocate me. You see now why I still believe it would be best if I died.''

Mercy bit down on her tongue to keep from sobbing in front of him. She thought of all the times she had lost patience and grown annoyed with him. She had never fully realized the extent of his suffering. Now at last she understood why he always sent her away from him—why he was short-tempered in her presence and got along so much better with Caleb, Augustus, and even Chloe.

She had been thinking only of herself and her own needs, never imagining the cost to him. He had tried to tell her, but she had refused to listen. Not until she stole into his room while he was sleeping and *forced* the issue had he surrendered and revealed the truth.

"I still intend to keep you alive, Ian—but from now on, I will try harder not to . . . to inflict my presence on you."

In the darkness, she could barely see him, but she could hear his sigh. "My sweet Mercy, your presence has been my only reason for living. Otherwise I would never have accepted the first spoonful of broth you tried to pour down my throat. I cannot live without you—and I cannot live *with* you. What a sense of humor God must have!"

"Ian, that sounds like blasphemy."

"Then I am sorry for it. But one day I hope He will explain it all to me. I am at a loss to explain it for myself."

"Good night, Ian."

"Good night, Mercy."

Caught in the grip of her own despair, Mercy left his room and quietly closed the door.

CHAPTER EIGHTEEN

The war news grew ever more alarming. General Washington dispatched the Marquis de Lafayette and 1,200 regulars to Virginia to support the local militia in trying to hold off the British forces. Not long thereafter, Cornwallis marched up from the Carolinas, bringing the total of British soldiers to around 7,000 by Ian's estimate. Long before word reached them of Lafayette's retreat, he told Mercy that Lafayette would have no choice but to fall back in order to elude Cornwallis's grasp.

He accurately predicted the route Lafayette would take and what Cornwallis would do in response. At last she understood what had made Ian such a valuable advisor. Somehow he was able to take complex events and simplify them, viewing them almost dispassionately and then calculating how the participants would react. It was a gift she herself did not possess.

Without his help at Collier Manor, her plans for avoiding destruction would be haphazard at best. Ian thought of everything, assigning lookouts to keep watch for the enemy in all four directions. Over and over, he drilled everyone on what they must do if the enemy were spotted. Mercy herself grew tired of the continuous drilling; it interrupted

her daily activities as she tried to run the estate with an
eye toward feeding all the people and animals for whom
she was responsible.

Due to the difficulty of keeping track of what was happening around Virginia, she sought Ian's advice for setting up
a network of information so that important news could be
passed from one plantation to another. Collier Manor soon
became a rest stop for a system of relay riders carrying the
latest news from the home of one Daughter of Liberty to
the next.

The anxious women could now share facts, rumors, and
gossip just as they had always done. From Caroline, Mercy
learned that Banastre Tarleton, Ian's old nemesis, had
tried his hand at capturing Thomas Jefferson in early June.
Warned just in time by one of their own hard-riding relay
riders—a fellow named Jack Jouett—who beat Tarleton
to his quarry by a matter of a few hours, Jefferson escaped.

One of Tarleton's dragoons then shoved a pistol into
the chest of one of Jefferson's slaves and threatened to
shoot if the man did not tell where his master had gone.

The slave responded, "Fire away then."

The dragoon let him live, but Tarleton destroyed all of
Jefferson's corn and tobacco, burned all his barns, and
stole all his cattle, sheep, hogs, and horses. In a last act of
senseless vengeance, he slit the throats of horses too young
for service and destroyed all the fences on the plantation,
leaving it a wasteland.

Shortly thereafter, the Continental Congress invited Jefferson to participate in a mission to France where it was
hoped that a peace treaty might be negotiated. Mercy first
heard of this from Arabella, who had heard of it from
someone else. Mercy was much encouraged—not so Ian.

"Wait until you hear the terms of any such treaty," he
warned. "I promise you they will not be favorable. England
will never surrender America on paper or otherwise. Only
a resounding military defeat will force them from our
shores."

She prayed he was wrong, but the terms—when they
heard them—proved the truth of his deductions. The proposed settlement required both sides to agree to keep only

the territory their armies now controlled. Since the British controlled Virginia, along with the Carolinas, Georgia, and northern New York, Collier Manor would come under British rule. France was pushing for the settlement, and so were other European powers. The war itself appeared at a stalemate.

"Ian, what will they do? Tell me what you think," Mercy implored one night at supper. "What would be your advice to General Washington in light of all this?"

"Washington must push for a fight—a final decisive battle." Ian set down his fork. "He cannot do otherwise. If nothing has been decided by the end of this year, there will be mass desertions. Feeding and clothing the army through another winter will be impossible. I only wish I were there to argue when other men tell him differently."

"I wish you were there, too! Can you not go to him? I could take you—"

He cut her off before she could say another word. "The last thing he needs is another burden. My days of giving advice are over."

"Nonsense. Your mind is as sharp as ever! You give advice to *us;* why not to General Washington? I am sure he would welcome it, just as he did when you served under him."

Ian pushed back from the table and fumbled for his cane. " 'Tis all different now. I can find my way around here, but in a different setting—particularly a military encampment—I would be a hindrance, not a help."

"Not if *I* am there to assist you! We can take Caleb and Augustus with us. Our people can manage without us for—"

"Mercy, I said no! I cannot a ride a horse, and I will not be trundled around in a cart like some helpless child! How many times must you crush my pride and never realize you are doing so?"

That silenced her. Naturally, Ian—the consummate horseman—would resent going all that way in a riding chair or carriage, unable to elude pursuers as he had done with such great success as Lord Fox. How could she have forgotten that?

She fell to thinking about Thor: How was the stallion faring these days? She had been too busy to check on him. Moses had said nothing to her, so she assumed he was still alive, but she resolved to go down to the stable the very next day and see with her own eyes what had become of him. She could only hope he had made better progress than his master. Ian's continued bitterness remained a heartache and a trial, all the more so because her own need for closeness and intimacy bedeviled her daily.

Sometimes she thought she would go mad from it. He was not her brother; he was her *husband*. She longed to be treated like a wife, not a sister. He had always been her friend, but the character of their friendship had changed. She could no longer share everything with him. Some topics—like his impotence—they dared not discuss. She frequently found herself avoiding other topics that might inadvertently upset him. . . . How dare he accuse her of heedlessly crushing his pride, when she took such pains to avoid doing exactly that?

The next morning, before Ian arose, Mercy walked down to the stable. Moses was nowhere about, so she headed for the field where she had last seen Thor. From the house, she could glimpse the stallion from a second-floor window, but she wanted to view him up close.

Entering the field by the gate, she picked up her skirts and trudged up a rise toward a few scattered trees. From there it was easy to spot Thor and Liberty. The two horses grazed side by side in the field spread out below her. Liberty spotted Mercy first. She raised her head and nickered at Mercy. The mare had grown fat on the summer grasses, and her chestnut coat gleamed in the sunlight. However, her long mane and tail were tangled and full of snarls. Moses had left the two horses strictly alone—apparently not even grooming them.

Thor had fattened also. The stallion finally looked up, saw her, and moved away, his movements stiff and labored. But at least he was moving! She could detect only a hint of a limp in his injured foreleg. Like Liberty, his mane, tail, and coat were unkempt but far from dull or unhealthy. Nor were his scars glaringly apparent. His appearance would always be marred, but his cuts and burns had all healed. Only the side of his face remained disfigured.

Mercy hugged herself in delight. A single question danced in her mind: Had Thor managed to breed Liberty? It would be months before she could tell for certain. Watching the stallion retreat from her, taking Liberty with him, Mercy decided it was time to bring the two horses back into the stable and see if Thor could ever be used again.

By the time she returned to the stable, Moses was there to greet her. She gave him orders to fetch Thor and Liberty and begin hand-walking the stallion again.

"In a week or two, I will come down and see if he can bear weight on his back—but you must not tell my husband what I am doing! No one is to mention this to him. He thinks Thor is dead, and I do not know how he will react to the idea that the stallion is still alive, especially if he is no longer good for anything."

"I be glad you did not shoot him that day, Miss Mercy," old Moses said. "At first, I thought he would never make it. Every mornin' I went out in the field expectin' t' see the worst. But Liberty would not give up on him. Since the day she ran inta the field to join him, she's kept him company and been so gentle around him, you would think he was her foal. Whenever he lies down, she nips at him t' get him on his feet again, and lately she's been runnin' circles around him tryin' t' get him ta play."

"Does he respond?" Mercy had always enjoyed watching Liberty cavort in a big field. The high-spirited mare relished bucking, galloping, and rolling—especially when turned out with companions. Even the laziest old plow horses could not resist playing with her.

"Naw, not much—but he tries. Sometimes he breaks into a little trot, but I have yet t' see him go any faster."

That news did not bode well for his future.

"Oh." She concealed her disappointment with a shake of her unbound hair. "Well, I will check on him again next week. Perhaps some exercise in hand will help him— and maybe poultices on his injured muscles."

"I will do my best, Miss Mercy," Moses assured her. "If

Thor gets better, it gonna be a real boon to his master. Might encourage him t' try ridin' again.''

"Riding is not the *only* thing a man can do," Mercy tartly responded. "Ian has other talents—if he would but realize it and take pride in his accomplishments."

"For the master, ridin' a fine horse be everything," Moses sagely observed.

"True," Mercy conceded. "But Thor and Ian must learn *new* skills. If Thor can never be ridden, perhaps I can teach him to pull the riding chair."

"You gonna teach that proud, fiery stallion t' be a harness horse?" Moses was incredulous.

"I am not planning to hitch him to a plow, Moses. In time, I hope to use him for breeding. But I would also like him to be able to work in some manner. Papa always said that a stallion must earn his keep the same as any other horse or else he will soon adopt too high an opinion of himself and become unmanageable. Thor has surprised us by living this long, so he may surprise us by taking to a new occupation."

She wished she could say the same for Ian.

"Gonna be surprised if he likes it," Moses told her.

"If we get through the remainder of the summer without being attacked by the British, I will commence teaching Thor to drive in the fall. Get him ready, Moses—you know what to do."

Moses nodded. " 'Spect I do, Miss Mercy. Been doin' it for a long time. Gonna get young Henry t' help me, so's he can start learnin' and take over when I get too old t' do it anymore."

"Young Henry. You think he has the ability to work with horses?"

"Sure do. He follows me around all day, watchin' everything. I keep turnin' around and trippin' over him."

Mercy was heartened to hear that despite the war and the threat of danger, young people were learning the tasks of their elders, so there would be new workers to replace the old ones one day. An unexpectedly acute yearning for children swept over her; if she and Ian never had children, who would take over for *them*? What would be *their* contribution to the future?

Returning to the house, she found Ian already calling for another drill. "Where have you been?" he demanded, standing at the foot of the stairs with cane in hand. "I need a way to summon you when I need you. We must devise a system for alerting everyone to drop what they are doing and prepare for attack."

"How about a handbell?" she suggested, taking his hand to lead him into the library. "Years ago, Papa brought one back from a foundry in Philadelphia. He liked to use it at the table to call for the next course. I myself never liked the practice and put it away."

"A handbell would be perfect. Is it loud enough to call everyone together for a drill?"

"No, we must think of something else for calling together all our people."

"Yes, a bell might alert the British. We need some silent signal. How about a pennant that can be raised in the vicinity of the house? When everyone sees it, they will know to begin the maneuvers we have been practicing."

"Today I will make a pennant," Mercy promised. "What color would you prefer?"

"Red," Ian responded without hesitation. "As bright a red as you can manage. Red can be seen from far off, and if the British should spot it, they will think it means we are loyalists."

As usual, his mind ran far ahead of hers.

"Red it shall be," she answered. "Only how will *you* be able to see it?"

"I can see colors now," he said.

"Ian!" She flung her arms around his neck in a spontaneous hug. "Colors! Do you mean it? . . . What else can you see?"

"Everything is still a blur," he complained, not at all satisfied with his progress. "But now I can see color—the color of your hair, for example."

He picked up a length of her hair and rubbed it between his fingers. "Your beautiful, silken, red hair, Mercy. . . . I can almost see it—how I wish I could see your face in detail!"

"That time will come, Ian! I promise you it will!" She hugged him again, only to have him gently set her aside.

" 'Tis what I am afraid of," he said. "One day I may indeed be able to *see* what I can never have."

"Ian, you must keep hoping for the best!"

"No, love. Better to resign myself to the worst rather than pining for what will never again be mine."

It was the same old argument between them—the same gulf of opinion. Mercy could say nothing to convince him, but she resolved to prove to Ian that miracles were possible. She would start with Thor. If she could find a new purpose for Thor—a new reason for living—Ian himself might realize he could do the same.

It was worth a try; she simply could *not* allow him to settle for his limitations, believing them impossible to overcome.

"Will you grant me a kiss, my husband?" she shamelessly begged him. "Just this once—to celebrate the fact that you can see colors now."

He resolutely shook his head. "Go and make your pennant, Mercy. And put up your hair. When you wear it down like that, it reminds me too much of what you looked like when . . . when I could still do something about my feelings for you."

On those few occasions when they had been intimate, she had worn her hair down, naturally. She could recall the times as well as he. Now she often wore it down because she lacked the time to put it up. His request wounded her, but she would change his mind about her hair—and many other things. She would change it or die trying.

"All right," she sighed. "I am going. I will fetch the handbell and make a red pennant."

"And put up your hair," he reminded her.

"Yes," she agreed. "And put up my hair."

Ian could not sleep. It was a hot, humid night in late August—too hot to sleep but not too hot to think. His thoughts were, as usual, restless and unhappy. Try as he might, he could find no peace—no reprieve from the sense of helplessness and hopelessness that daily consumed him. How often he tried to shake it off!

But it would not go. Never had he known anything like it, but never had he faced such devastating personal challenges. Then there was the war and the knowledge that he could no longer play a meaningful part in it. The best he could hope for was that Collier Manor might be spared direct involvement. He no longer spoke about it to Mercy—for fear of distressing her—but he really did intend to die defending her if the British ever attacked the estate.

The idea gave him a reason for living.

In the stifling darkness of the bedchamber, he sat up and swung his legs carefully over the side of the bed. His bad leg throbbed with the effort, but he no longer paid any attention to pain. His days were marked by aches and pains. Far worse was his mental suffering.

Whenever he thought about Mercy, his anguish was fresh, new, and unbearable. Fortunately, he could always think about the war instead. It was *always* good for distraction; when it finally ended, he would need to find a new diversion—if he were still alive.

According to the latest news, Cornwallis had set up a base of operations in Yorktown, Virginia. Lafayette was God-knew-where at the moment, but had been joined by General Anthony Wayne and Baron von Steuben. The three were doing their best to combat British raiding across Virginia. Unfortunately, they were not strong enough to repulse the enemy altogether.

Washington *must* come to Virginia. The final, decisive battle must be fought here. Ian just wished he could discuss the situation with the general, but perhaps Washington already knew what he must do. The man was no fool; Ian had the utmost respect for him. If only the French would provide naval support off the coast of Virginia! Then the Continental Army might stand a chance. French ships could help transport American troops to Yorktown, saving them the time and effort of marching overland.

His mind buzzed with plans and ideas—but what good

were all his ideas if he had no way of promoting them or even suggesting them? He hated being so helpless! If only he could see properly—and *ride* . . . and had a fast horse like Thor!

There was Liberty, of course, but he could never take the mare and go alone, as he had once done as Lord Fox. Those days were over. Now he needed a cane just to navigate familiar surroundings. Without Hiram to carry messages back and forth to General Washington, he was stuck here in the darkness while war raged around him— stuck in this damnable bedchamber!—unable even to make love to his wife.

Bitterness welled up in him. Thoughts of death and escape beckoned. For Mercy's sake, he resisted them, but they taunted him anyway. Trapped as he was in a damaged body, he often felt he was holding onto sanity by the slenderest of threads.

Groping for his cane, he rose wearily to his feet and tapped his way to the open window. A light breeze cooled his overheated body. Finding the spot where he could best feel it, he stood gazing out into the darkness, wondering how long it would be until dawn. His window faced east, he recalled. Squinting and blinking, he searched for some hint of light along the horizon. . . . There *was* something— the glow of the coming sunrise?

He stared hard at it, trying to make sense of the blur. Light suddenly flared up, tinged with orange and red. *My God.* Something in the distance was burning. It had to be at John Willardson's place. Their nearest neighbor was an old man now, crippled by gout. He and his wife were rarely seen or heard from these days. Mercy spoke little of them. They were in dire trouble *now*—and their troubles might already be on the road, headed for Collier Manor.

"Mercy!" Ian shouted, wishing for once that she *did* sleep in his bedchamber. "Mercy, wake up! The British have fired the adjoining estate and like as not are headed this way!"

He hurried toward the door and in his haste collided with it, banging his nose and dropping his cane. There was no time to search for it. Yanking open the door, he rushed out into the hallway. Mercy's room was to the right—past the open stairway. Limping and cursing, Ian headed for it.

"Mercy! We must run up the pennant—damn it! No one will see it in the dark. Besides, they are all sleeping. What a fool I am! I should have thought of that sooner. . . . Who expected the British to attack at night? 'Tis more of a rustic American tactic than a proper English one. The handbell. . . . We could ring it in the slave quarters to awaken everyone."

He turned to go back into his room and fetch the handbell. He ought to have grabbed and rung it in the first place, he thought, instead of stumbling about in the dark. His need to awaken Mercy had robbed him of good sense— if it could be said he had any sense. He fancied himself a fine advisor, yet he had put everyone in danger by failing to consider the possibility that the British might attack in the middle of the night.

"Mercy, wake up!" he bellowed, his alarm mounting.

The hallway was black as tar. He could see nothing now. Yet he had to hurry—*hurry. Get the handbell.*

He groped along the wall, feeling for the doorway. It was not where he thought it should be. He swung around to head back toward Mercy's room. Surely she had heard him calling her!

"Ian? Ian, what is it?"

Oh, thank God!

"The British. They have attacked the Willardsons!"

He blundered in the direction of her voice—anxious to reach her, awaken all the servants, save the estate, get everyone safely into the woods. They would need torches so they could see where they were going and avoid the traps . . .

He took a huge step into nothingness. Then he was falling—hitting his arm and shoulder, smashing his head. Unable to stop himself, he went hurtling down the staircase. Unable to breathe or cry out, he banged and thumped all the way down. Something snapped in his bad leg. He could *hear* it—*feel* it. Pain exploded. *Oh, God, no—not now! This cannot be happening now!*

As his momentum picked up, he knew he had hurt himself badly. Had rendered himself useless. Now the marauding British would rape and kill Mercy before his very eyes. He could only hope he would break his neck before he finally stopped falling; it was a long staircase.

When he hit bottom, his head struck something hard and unyielding. Consciousness receded, not fast enough to suit him—or to spare him the full realization of his own carelessness and stupidity.

"Ian!" Mercy knew it was already too late. She had heard him fall. Each thump on the staircase echoed in her heart and soul.

It was suddenly breathlessly quiet. She could not hear him breathing. She stood at the top of the stairs in the utter blackness and could not catch her own breath. Her heart seemed to have stopped beating.

"Ian!" she repeated, saying his name softly this time and *willing* him to answer.

He made no sound. The urge to run to him bubbled up in her, but her arms and legs were like wooden posts. She tried to move her foot—to feel for the edge of the step. She fumbled for the banister to guide herself down. Her knees wobbled, and she had the sudden sickening fear that she, too, would tumble headfirst down the staircase.

She had to get hold of herself—for Ian's sake. For the sake of everyone else on the estate. . . . What had he said? Something about the Willardsons being under attack. How could he have known such a thing?

Light blossomed at the bottom of the steps. Chloe appeared, holding a tall candle in a brass holder. Quickly she set it down and bent over Ian's unmoving form. Mercy stared down at her servant's head, which blocked her view of Ian. Chloe wore no turban, and her long braided hair was completely gray—a fact which up until this moment Mercy had not realized. Somehow, when she was not looking, Chloe had gotten old.

Chloe looked up to see her standing there. "What are

you waitin' for, girl?'' she asked. ''His Lordship needs help.''

Somehow Mercy found the strength to descend the staircase. When she got to the bottom, she knelt beside Chloe to examine Ian. *He was so still!* His eyes and mouth were slightly open, but she could detect no signs of life.

Panic gripped her. ''Is he dead, Chloe?'' She leaned back, afraid to look too closely for fear of what she might see. ''Just tell me if he still lives or not. That is all I want to know.''

Chloe laid her head on Ian's chest. After listening a moment, she straightened. ''His heart is still beatin'. But 'tis certain he has gone and broke his leg—the one with all them sword cuts.''

She indicated Ian's oddly bent leg with a nod. Ian wore only a nightshirt, and the scars on the exposed limb were still reddish-colored and raw-looking. In addition to his broken leg, there was a gash on his temple—bleeding little but already beginning to swell.

''Summon Caleb and Augustus,'' Mercy said. ''We will need their help to get him back upstairs to bed—or into the woods.''

''The woods?'' Chloe frowned at Mercy. ''Why would you want t' take him there?''

''He said something about an attack. He was coming to get me.''

''He must have been dreamin','' Chloe scoffed. ''Or else we would be hearin' something.''

Both women paused and listened, straining to hear any strange sounds. There were none.

''We must go to the woods,'' Mercy insisted. ''Ian would not have been coming to get me without a very good reason.''

''If you say so.'' Chloe shrugged her shoulders. ''Maybe he jus' needed to be near you, and that's why he came searchin' for you in the dark.''

''No.'' Mercy's certainty deepened. ''That was not it at all. Ian has conquered any need he might once have felt for me. *I* am the needy one now.''

CHAPTER NINETEEN

They hid in the woods for hours, each person in his or her assigned spot, with the children divided among them. From time to time, Chloe made the rounds, warning everyone to stay still and quiet. Amazingly, even the children obeyed. They were afraid of Chloe's stern looks; she never did allow much nonsense and always made certain everyone obeyed Mercy's instructions.

Meanwhile, Mercy worked with Caleb and Augustus to fashion splints for Ian's broken leg. They managed to set it and fasten the splints in place without him regaining full consciousness. However, sweat poured down his face, and he grimaced in pain the entire time, which indicated that he could still feel what they were doing. When they finished and he was settled as comfortably as possible on a blanket and pillows, Mercy sat back on her heels with sweat pouring down her own face.

Heat and moisture thickened the air. Mosquitoes whined in the silence, and a gray/green stillness suffused the woods.

"Gonna rain," Caleb whispered, his black face slick and shiny from his exertions. "Wish it would."

"Well, I do not," Mercy retorted. "All we need now is rain. Ian will be lying here in the mud if it rains."

"How long we gotta stay here, Miss Mercy?" Augustus's brown face was solemn. He peered through the screen of brush concealing them from any soldiers clever enough to get past their traps. "You really think them British are comin'?"

"I know not what to think," she admitted. "My husband said they were. I myself would like to return to the house. It worries me that Ian has not awakened. I would like to get some brandy down him. It will help him wake up, and ease the pain when he does."

"Better he sleep, Miss Mercy," Caleb said. "He wake up when he ready."

"He hit his head so hard!" Mercy wailed, forgetting the need for quiet. "I heard it crack against the steps more than once as he went down. I just hope he will be all right."

Determined not to cry, she bit her lower lip.

"The master got a hard head," Caleb consoled her. "A little fall down the steps not gonna hurt it."

"That little fall broke his leg," Mercy bitterly reminded him.

"That's 'cause his leg was *already* hurt," Caleb patiently reasoned. "At least the bone not comin' through the skin. Folks can *die* from that. But a little bone break not gonna kill him."

"I hope you are right." She slapped at a mosquito biting her exposed neck. "Try to keep the mosquitoes off him, will you? I am going to go see if anyone is coming."

"Miss Mercy, you be sure and watch out for them traps!" Augustus warned.

"No need to worry; I know where everything is. We all do. Ian saw to that."

She left them and cautiously made her way through the woods toward a spot where she could see the house and a section of the road without being seen. The house looked undisturbed and the road empty. An unnatural quiet hung over the entire place. The only signs of life were the chickens pecking away in her herb garden. Someone had let them out of the hen yard with the idea of hiding them in the woods, but the chickens had gotten away from them.

In the distance, Liberty and Thor still grazed alone;

there had been no time to go out and catch them. Nor
had the milk cows been brought in from their field, or
the hogs rounded up and hidden. Darkness—and Ian's
injuries—had hampered the escape efforts. Getting *him* to
safety had been difficult enough, let alone all the animals.
When he awoke—*if* he awoke—he would be angry; his
plans called for hiding everything the British could possibly
steal.

She wondered if she ought to send someone out to get
the hogs and the chickens, or simply wait a few more hours
to see if the British were really coming. At this point, she
hardly cared what happened to the hogs and chickens. Ian
was her main concern. This accident would seriously delay
his recovery from his war wounds. She dreaded to think
of what it would do to his outlook. He faced many more
weeks of immobility and pain. It was enough to make her
weep, but she was too tired and frustrated even to cry.

*Where were the British? How long must she keep everyone in
hiding?*

She wanted Ian to wake up and tell her what to do now.
How ironic that he considered himself a useless burden
when *she* considered him her most trusted confidant!
Despite their communication problems, he could always
be relied upon to offer good advice in any situation. Even
on matters concerning the estate or problems with the
workers, she could always go to him, explain a problem,
and expect a well-considered response. Often she would
do as he suggested. When she did not, his suggestions
enlivened her own ideas, enabling her to come up with
something she might never have thought of without him.

An ominous rumble reminded her that rain was fast
approaching, and she must make some decision—to
return to shelter or stay out in the elements. As hot as it
was, the rain would feel refreshing at first, but later everyone would be uncomfortable. It could not be good for the
children and old people to be out in a downpour.

She started back through the woods—only to snag her
hem on a bramble. Tugging it free, she failed to watch
where she was stepping and set her foot down in the wrong
place. She knew what was coming as soon as she did it.

There was a great snapping sound, and she was yanked off
her feet by a snare closing around one ankle. Shrieking,
she flew through the air and slammed into a tree trunk.
The collision knocked the wind out of her. For a moment,
all she could see were red stars against a field of blackness.

There she hung—upside down, twisting, turning, and
flailing with her free foot. Then the heavens opened, and
the rain poured down.

It was an hour before they found her and figured out
how to rescue her in the noisy deluge.

"How is my husband?" she gasped after falling on her
head into a heap of branches Caleb had piled beneath
her to cushion her fall when young Henry climbed the
tree and cut the rope.

"He awake, Miss Mercy, and none too happy," Caleb
glumly informed her.

"I am relieved he is awake but sorry to hear of his
unhappiness. Does he think *my* life is a cause for envy?"
Mercy scrambled to her feet and stood a moment, dizzy
and swaying—wincing at the pain in her strained muscles.

"We was afraid t' tell him exactly what happened to you.
Anyway, he sent Augustus to spy on our neighbors' place
to see if the British have burned it to the ground yet. He
says we all gotta stay here in the woods until Augustus
comes back."

"We are *not* staying out here in the woods! British or
no British, we are seeking shelter. We will all contract lung
ailments if we remain here much longer—my husband
included. We will need the wagon to carry him back to
the house."

"Yes'm, Miss Mercy."

An hour after that, everyone was under a roof somewhere and changing out of sodden clothing. Mercy left
Ian to the ministrations of her servants while she quickly
donned dry garments. She wrung out her hair, hurriedly
plaited it, and pinned it up off her neck. Then she went
to Ian's bedchamber, where she knew he was awaiting her
with the biggest scowl she had ever seen on his face.

He had been scowling—and berating her—all the way
back to the house. "We must stay hidden until the danger
is past," he had growled at her between groans as the
wagon ride jostled his broken leg. "The British could be
here at any moment."

"If the British are out in this downpour, they are likely
drowned by now. As soon it quits raining, I will post sentries
until Augustus returns and we know what is happening. If
the British are in the area, we will run up the pennant and
return to the woods."

"If I could get out of this damn wagon I would!" Ian
had thundered in tune with the thunder. "We should have
stayed in the woods, I tell you!"

She had ignored him after that, and now she had to
face him again—face his renewed pain, frustration, and
helplessness. She was not looking forward to it. Entering
the room, she motioned for Caleb and Chloe to leave
and look after themselves. Then she gently shut the door
behind the two faithful servants and approached the bed.

Ian lay with his eyes closed, his features so drawn and
pale that she worried he was already coming down with a
lung ailment. She could not see his broken leg, for he was
covered to the chin with blankets. Even so, she detected
a shiver. He was chilled to the bone, but still determined
to stay out in the rain saving them all from the British!

Her heart contracted with love and exasperation for this
stubborn yet selfless man. Had he not been coming to get
her, he never would have fallen and broken his leg. She
still had no idea what had told him that their neighbors
were under attack.

Leaning over him, she lightly touched the large purple
swelling on his temple. A thin red line marked the gash
where it had been laid open by his fall down the steps.

He opened his eyes and gazed up at her, squinting
slightly in an effort to see her better.

" 'Tis me, Ian," she said. "Forgive me for defying your
wishes, but I had to get our people out of the rain. You
yourself may fall ill because of it. We could not stay out
there any longer."

"What good is my advice if you spurn it?" he growled. " 'Tis all I have left to give you, yet you esteem it not."

"You are wrong, Ian. I *do* esteem it." She sat down beside him on the bed. "But I may not always agree, and then I must do what I think is right."

"And I cannot stop you, can I? I am as helpless as a newborn babe. Nay, I am *more* helpless—and pathetic— for I am bigger. I could not even make my way down the hall to get you. . . . What good am I, Mercy? I cannot rescue you from harm, and you will not listen to me when I tell you what you must do!"

"Ian, what brought you out of your room in search of me? . . . I *did* follow your orders about going to the woods. But I never knew what happened to send us there. I *still* do not know."

"Fire," he said, passing a hand over his eyes. "I saw . . . flames. In the direction of the Willardsons. At first I thought it was the sunrise. But the light was too bright— too red. It could only have been fire . . . and why would there be fire unless there had been an attack?"

"So *that* is what alarmed you!"

He nodded. " 'Tis what I sent Augustus to check. If the British have laid waste to the Willardsons' estate, they are probably headed this way. We should be in the woods now—hiding according to plan."

"You will die if you go back out in the rain, my love, and our people will sicken. This is a cold, hard rain."

"Hah! It has been so hot lately I can scarcely breathe!"

"Are you hot now?" Mercy noted his chattering teeth.

"The fact that I am cold at this moment makes no difference," he answered. "If the British come, we will all die. They will shoot or bayonet me right here in this bed. Maybe they will make me watch what they do to *you* before they kill me. I will not be able to see it clearly, but I will certainly be able to hear your screams."

"Oh, Ian, you must stop dwelling on the worst that can happen!"

"I am only looking at reality, while you avoid it."

"Shall I drag you back out into the rain, then? Will that satisfy you? . . . Will you be happy to come down with congested lungs on top of everything else? Do you want others to be as sick and miserable as you are? ... If the British are spotted, I will run up the pennant. 'Tis the best I can do.''

"Who can see the pennant in a downpour or at night?" he grumbled. "That is another of my great mistakes. My foolish failures. I am of no use to anyone. God mocks me by keeping me alive.''

"Your traps work!" Mercy disputed. "They work marvelously well. I can attest to—"

"Get out, Mercy. Leave me alone. My leg hurts, and I am too weary to argue any longer.''

"Ian, please."

"Just get out, woman. Your pity is misplaced on a man who wants to die. I wish you would stop taking such good care of me. Were it not for you, my misery would have ended long ago.''

"Do not *say* that! Your leg may be broken, but it will soon heal.''

"Not soon enough to save my sanity. I cannot bear to be confined to this bed again! Once again I will have to learn how to walk and dress myself unaided. Who knows if it will even be possible? My leg muscles are already weakened. They will grow weaker still while the bone is healing.''

Mercy grabbed his hand and held it between her hands. "Ian, we will survive this! We will get you on your feet again as soon as possible. And I will send away for spectacles, in the hope they will help you to see better.''

He tugged on his hand to get her to release it. "Mercy, I want to die, not to see. You are wed to a coward. The thought of *living* ... struggling ... fighting to get well ... adjusting to my changed circumstances ... Mercy, I cannot *do* it.''

"But I will help you, Ian!"

He sighed—a long, deep sigh of sadness and regret. Then he closed his eyes and said nothing more. He simply retreated inside himself to that dark, frightening place where she could not follow.

Her heart shattered. For the first time in her life, she grappled with her own despair. Ian had succumbed to it;

why should she keep fighting? This constant battle seemed so pointless suddenly. Like the war, it had gone on too long, with no end in sight.

She had thought love could overcome anything. But she was wrong—so wrong! Love could not heal Ian or make him happy. It could not keep him safe. His body still lived, but his spirit was suffocating! She herself felt suffocated. Like Ian, she wished she could lie down on her bed and cease to exist. She longed for an end to all this suffering and futility.

Rising, she left Ian to his own miserable company, walked into her room, sat down on her bed, and stared at the wall. After a time, she lay down. She stared at the ceiling. She closed her eyes. She remembered Ian the way she had first seen him—looking so handsome, arrogant, impossibly confident and full of himself. Lord Ian Montjoy. A viscount. A splendid man in his prime.

How she had longed to see him brought low! ... and how low he had fallen. If not for her—if not for the dream of freedom she had awakened in him—he would be safe in England, living the life to which he had been born.

It was all her fault. Everything that had happened to him was her fault. She could see it plainly now—and she hated herself for it. She also hated him for being a mere mortal man, subject to flaws and imperfections, instead of being the perfect, uncomplaining hero she wanted him to be.

It was dark when Chloe finally awakened her. Augustus had returned. The Willardsons had not been attacked by the British, after all; their stable had burned down. Old Pig Eye, the stallion Ian had once raced and beaten, had been ailing. The slave assigned to look after the horse had fallen asleep, and his lantern somehow tipped over and started a fire. They had managed to get all the horses out—except for Old Pig Eye. The slave had died trying to save him. To make matters worse, the excitement had proved too much for John Willardson. Their old friend and neighbor had collapsed in the yard and was believed to be dying.

"That was the fire Ian saw," Mercy told Chloe. Sitting on the side of the bed, she ran her fingers through her tousled hair and wiped the sleep from her eyes. "He said he saw flames in the east, but I wondered if he had imagined them. With his eyesight so poor—"

" 'Tis a wonder he saw anything," Chloe agreed. "Poor Master Willardson. . . . Augustus forgot to ask the name of the slave who died. I wanted to box his ears for forgetting. Over the years, I have gotten to know most of the Willardsons' people."

"We could send him back tomorrow to find out," Mercy suggested.

"We could if there was not so much for him to do here. With Master Ian laid up again, he and Caleb gonna be busy."

"Oh, Chloe!" Mercy raised her fist to her mouth in anguish. "Do you think it is all worth it? This awful war may never end! It has caused so much loss and heartache. Life has sorrow enough without adding more burdens to it. Witness the Willardsons! Tragedy has just visited them— and *more* tragedy may be on the way. If the British should now appear . . . tell me it is all worth it, Chloe!"

Unable to stop herself, she started to weep.

"Mercy, child . . ." Chloe sat down next to Mercy on the rumpled bed. "How can you doubt it? You done had your share of sadness since the war started, but imagine what life would be like if you never had a choice about how you lived or died—if all your choices were made for you, subject to another person's whims. That is what this war is all about—your *freedom* to make your own mistakes and suffer whatever joys and sorrows come your way. Your freedom to love and be happy without havin' to ask somebody else's permission. Master Ian hates losin' his freedom so much that he claims he wants to die; that's what happens when people lose their freedom—or never had it in the first place. They plain give up. . . . Oh, yes, girl, this fight is worth it! You gave *us* our freedom, and one day all my people gonna be free, 'cause we gonna keep fightin' for freedom, too. You best not give up now, girl—not when

the end is in sight. You gotta keep goin'. Too many people
depend on you."

"If the end is in sight, I wish I could see it!" Mercy dried
her tears with the edge of her quilt.

"Quit your snifflin'. You is a Collier, and the Colliers
never bred no quitters. Your man is no quitter, either. You
just gotta show him the way. We all seen how he pushes
himself, grittin' his teeth against the pain. He gets riled
sometimes and a little mean, but he keeps tryin'. He looks
in your direction—*tries* to look at you—and we can all see
his love for you shinin' bright in his blind eyes. Only reason
he did not die long ago is *you,* girl. That man has gone
down to hell, but he keeps fightin' his way back up again,
so you gotta keep fightin', too."

"I will, Chloe, but 'tis so hard sometimes!" Mercy swallowed a sob.

Chloe gave her a quick hug. "You can do it. If anybody
can do it, *you* can. You always did have more gumption
than any ten women *I* know. You come into this world
hollerin', and you gonna be hollerin' when you go out of
it—fightin' every step of the way."

"*You* are the one with gumption, Chloe. You were born
a slave. I was born the pampered, spoiled daughter of a
wealthy plantation owner."

"Where you was born makes no difference, child. What
makes a difference is what you do with the life you got."

"Tomorrow we will send a wagonload of grain and supplies to the Willardsons," Mercy said, as her mind started
working again. "If their barn has burned down, they will
need all the help we can give them."

"You leave all that t' me. You jus' take care of Master
Ian. He needs you now more than ever."

"I wish I could send to Williamsburg for spectacles.
Spectacles might help him see better if we can find the
right pair. But searching for them will be impossible until
after the war ends—if it ever does. Right now they are
probably scarce, anyway."

"Then think of some other way to help him. Gotta get
him out of that room and that bed. He thinks of it as a

cage. The longer he's stuck there, the more unhappy he gonna be."

"I *have* thought of one thing I can do," Mercy said. "Tomorrow I will start."

Chloe raised her brows in question, but Mercy would say no more. Thor may not be ready to go back to work. The horse could be as difficult a case as his master. She would not know his limitations or capabilities until she started training him. Assuming he was able, by hunt season she could have him trained to pull the riding chair and be able to take Ian on long drives around the estate. When he saw how his horse had adapted . . .

She went to bed that night feeling much better. Working and planning was always better than moping and feeling sorry for oneself. Now all she had to do was find new work for Ian—something he could do without being able to walk or see.

"Ian, this is Rufus. He has come to teach you wood-cutting."

"Woodcutting!"

Ian's astonishment echoed her own doubts, but Mercy smiled brightly and refused to be deterred by his cynicism. "Yes, woodcutting. Rufus is a fine woodcutter. He has been doing it for years. Papa was always going to send him to Williamsburg to learn the art of cabinetmaking, but he never got around to doing so. Rufus has had to learn everything on his own. Do you recall seeing the mantel-piece in the library? Rufus carved the fruits and flowers on it. He cannot do much work anymore, for he suffers from rheumatism in his hands. But he can show you the skills he has mastered, and perhaps you will enjoy learning them while you are stuck in that chair."

Mercy got it out in a rush, for she knew how absurd it all sounded. Ian's expression only increased her anxiety. Grimacing as he jostled his outstretched leg, he sat up straighter in the chair before the window and shook his head.

"Mercy, you never cease to amaze. How am I to learn

the art of woodcutting when I can barely see your face—
or even my own hand?'' He held up his hand as if examining it. ''I know it is there, but 'tis still a blur. Are you eager
for me to lose a few fingers? I could no more carve a block
of wood than ride a horse right now. You have to see to
carve.''

''No, you do not. Tell him, Rufus.'' She motioned the
bent old man into the room. He was older even than
Moses—one of the oldest men on the plantation. He had
been there forever. His white hair, wrinkled black face,
and gnarled hands attested to his longevity.

Rufus shuffled part way into the room and stopped,
clearly discomfited by being in the master's own bedchamber.

''Once, when I was a little girl, I wandered into a slave
cabin and found Rufus carving a duck from a scrap of
wood. I asked him how he could see what he was doing
when it was so dark in the cabin. He said he did not *need*
to see; he could do it all by feel. Indeed, he could work
better by touching and feeling the wood than he ever could
by *seeing* it. So I thought—''

''You thought I could fill my empty, useless days with
woodcutting,'' Ian finished for her. His tone reeked of
sarcasm. ''If I cannot manage the estate or be a soldier . . .
a viscount . . . a lover . . . *a man* . . . I can always be a
woodcutter. Is that it?''

''You need not make it sound so *unworthy* an occupation.
Would you prefer sitting alone in that chair all day, staring
at nothing and growing meaner by the hour?''

Ian sighed. ''You know what I would prefer, Mercy.''

She *did* know; that was the problem. ''Give it a chance,
Ian. I meant no insult. 'Tis only to be a diversion until you
regain your feet—and your eyesight if I can ever locate a
pair of spectacles to help you see better.''

''Oh, I am certain there are spectacles *some*where to clear
up my vision—as certain as I am that I can now become
a *woodcutter* and do it all by feel.''

''Rufus says that each piece of wood will tell you what
it wants to be. He has brought a bucket of wood blocks

for you to examine—and tools. Today he will show you
how to hold the tools and listen to the wood."

"*Listen* to the wood?" Ian mocked. "I presume the wood
will speak to me."

"Rufus says it does. Will you allow him to sit with you
and keep you company? You can question him further if
you like."

Ian sighed again. "Do I have a choice? 'Tis not as though
I have anything better to do. Come here, Rufus. Fetch a
chair or a stool. Then you can tell me all about woodcutting."

"Yes, Master." Rufus fetched a nearby stool and sat down
next to Ian.

Mercy left them and headed for the stable. Today, while
Ian was occupied, she would begin working with Thor.

September passed in a flurry of harvest activity, uninter-
rupted by British attacks. All the fighting and battles stayed
east or south of Collier Manor. Some of the news encouraged Mercy, especially when the French fleet under the
command of Count de Grasse defeated the British naval
fleet in a battle on Chesapeake Bay.

However, this was followed by the news that Benedict
Arnold had looted and burned New London, Connecticut.
At almost the same time, American forces under General
Nathaniel Greene suffered defeat at a place called Eutaw
Springs in South Carolina.

"The French and American forces must join together
and lay siege to Yorktown," Ian told her one evening in
late September. " 'Tis the only chance we have to route
Cornwallis and win this war, once and for all."

Exhausted by the day's chores, which had included walking behind Thor all around the estate while he got used
to wearing his harness, Mercy sat mending a gown she
might once have tossed away in the days of luxury and
waste before the war. Laying the garment aside, she gave
Ian her full attention.

He sat across from her in his chair, where a table filled
with tools and wood shavings blocked her view of his bro-

ken leg. He had been working all evening on a small chunk of wood but had not yet offered to show her the results of his efforts. Until he offered, she was not about to ask. Rufus had advised her that it would be a long time before Ian could produce anything of use or beauty. The art of woodcutting could not be taught in the space of a few weeks.

"At least General Greene managed to push the British back toward Charlestown," she pointed out. "Even if he *was* defeated in the end."

"Greene is wasting his time in South Carolina," Ian scoffed. "He needs to come here to Virginia to help Washington."

Ian set down a tool. Wood curls drifted to the floor, where they joined a host of their scattered brethren. Woodcutting was a messy business, Mercy had discovered, and she wondered why she had not found some other task to offer her husband—something like mending, for instance. Threading a needle might be a problem for Ian, but at least mending was clean and tidy.

"How are you and Rufus getting along?" she asked in a burst of curiosity—and also because discussing the war never failed to disturb Ian and remind him of his supposed uselessness.

"Rufus and I?" Ian's blue-eyed gaze sought hers. "We are managing well, thank you. I cannot claim to be making great strides in woodcutting, but I am learning much about slavery."

"Slavery? Rufus is no longer a slave. I freed him and the others a long time ago."

"I know you did, but Rufus and I must discuss *some*thing all this time we have been spending together. Did you know that he has vivid memories of coming over to America on a slave ship with his mother?"

Mercy paused to think a moment. She really knew very little of Rufus's past. Like so many of her servants, Rufus had always just "been there." She had grown up in the midst of Collier Manor's people and taken them all for granted.

"No," she finally admitted. "What did he tell you?"

So Ian told her—about the terrible conditions aboard the ship, the wretched, meager food, cramped quarters, and the men chained belowdeck like animals. Some of the women, too, had endured such treatment, but Rufus's mother had fared better than most because she was young and pretty and had two small children—him and a babe in arms.

Unfortunately, neither his mother nor his little sister survived the journey, and Rufus found himself alone on the auction block—a child of no more than five or six—when the ship finally reached the colonies. Mercy's father then bought him in a lot with ten other slaves, most of them potential field workers.

Having never heard this tale before, Mercy listened in stunned silence. It was not hard to picture a grieving little boy all alone in a strange country without family, friends, or any idea of what was going to happen to him.

"How awful!" she murmured when Ian had finished.

"Yes." Ian stared toward the flames licking a log in the fireplace.

The nights had grown chill, and he was often cold when the sun went down, so Mercy pretended that *she* was cold and had a fire lit in his bedchamber.

"When I compare myself to Rufus, I realize I have led a very fortunate life," Ian said. "Even with my present limitations, I have suffered nothing like Rufus—or hundreds of other black-skinned men. Because I was born with white skin—and inherited a title—my life has been one of luxury and fighting off boredom, not struggling to survive and avoid a whipping or worse. Rufus humbles me. He makes me see how shallow my complaints really are—and how shameful it is that I have despaired, when I have *never* known the suffering he and so many others have experienced."

"Oh, my dearest!" Mercy leapt to her feet and went swiftly to her husband's side.

Succumbing to impulse, she clasped his head to her bosom. Instead of pushing her away, he wrapped his arms around her waist and hugged her—burying his face in the mound of her breasts.

"Mercy, can you ever forgive me for all my whining? For giving up on you and on God? I am so ashamed . . ."

"Ian, 'tis all right! Of course I forgive you. Do you think I myself have not wept in despair?"

He raised his head to peer up at her—squinting and furrowing his brow with the effort. *"You? You* have despaired?"

"Yes," she whispered. "I have despaired. I complained to Chloe about my lot, and she was kind enough to remind me that freedom is worth the sacrifices we have had to make. Those who have never *had* freedom recognize its value, Ian, but those of us who have lived lives of privilege seem to crumble when the time comes for sacrifice. I am as weak as you, Ian—and I have even less to complain about than you do."

"Hold me, Mercy," Ian softly begged. "Just this one time, hold me and let me cling to you. Thank you for all you have done for me—for all you have endured for my sake."

"Yes, my love, yes!" Mercy held him close to her and reveled in his embrace. But even as she did so, his words sounded a warning: *Just this one time.*

What about all the other times when she needed to be close to him? They had come this far—could they not go the rest of the way? Could they not resume being husband and wife—at least try to resume being husband and wife?

"Ian," she began after a moment.

"Hush," he pleaded, his mouth muffled against her bosom. "Let me have this moment, Mercy. After tonight, I can be strong again. I *will* be strong. I will accept what has happened to me and try to make the best of it."

"Ian, maybe you do not *need* to accept all of it—"

"Hush! Say no more. Offer me no more. Be content with this moment. 'Tis all we really have. *I* am content with it. We must both be content."

Yes, she thought. *Be content.*

Ian had come so far tonight . . . but she could not help wishing he might go farther still.

CHAPTER TWENTY

"Ian! Ian, the war is finally over!" Mercy took the steps two at a time and raced up them, her skirts flying. She dashed into Ian's bedchamber and skidded to a stop in front of his carving table. "Word just came by relay rider. The siege at Yorktown has ended; Cornwallis has surrendered. We have won the war!"

"When?" Ian demanded, his face radiating her excitement. "When did all of this happen?"

"On the nineteenth."

"Of this month—*October* nineteenth," he said as if he could not believe it and must repeat it several times to convince himself.

"Yes!" Mercy shrieked. "Less than a week ago. Oh, Ian, is it not wonderful?"

She spun around the room, so happy she was tripping over her own feet. Ian sat back in his chair—his wood-cutting forgotten. Beside him, Rufus was grinning from ear to ear.

"That wonderful news," the old man said, nodding to himself. "That good news indeed."

"Took them long enough," Ian said. "Almost two weeks. The siege should have settled things long before this. With the help of the French, we greatly outnumbered the British, but Cornwallis is stubborn. I give the man credit for that. If I had been there, I might have recommended—''

"Oh, Ian, if *you* had been there, the Americans would have won much sooner! I have no doubt of it. But at least we have won—we have finally won!"

She danced over to him and planted a kiss on his grinning mouth. He kissed her back—briefly, then pushed her away as he always did when she got too close for too long. Not that he was cold and hostile anymore—he was simply determined. He would not *allow* himself anything more than a brief hug or kiss. He would not risk failure, and until he was ready, she dare not push him and create embarrassment for both of them.

"Tell me the details," he ordered. "Everything you know."

"Well, there was a band there, and they played a tune called 'The World Turned Upside Down' while the British soldiers surrendered their muskets to the American and French troops," Mercy dutifully relayed.

"Now, *that* is an important piece of information," Ian drawled. "There, Rufus, you see? Ask a female about an event of major historical significance and you learn what music the band was playing."

"I found it noteworthy," Mercy defended. "And after that, they played 'Yankee Doodle' to mock the British for all the times they played that tune to mock *us* . . . . Oh, Ian, how soon will our lives return to normal, do you think?"

"Normal?" Ian echoed. "What do you consider normal?"

"I mean—when trade will resume and ships will be carrying goods back and forth, as they did before the war, and—"

"Trade! She is concerned about opportunities for trade!" Ian exclaimed. "Do you wish to purchase some fine lace, milady? Or how about tea? How long has it been since we last had real tea to drink?"

Actually, Mercy was thinking of how soon she might be able to obtain spectacles for Ian. They might not be available in Williamsburg or anywhere else in America. War

shortages included nearly everything, which meant she
would have to send away to England or France for them.
She was only thinking of *him*, yet he considered her frivo-
lous!

"I have more in mind than tea or lace," she primly
informed him. "Yorktown is not far from Williamsburg. I
imagine both places are short on every conceivable commodity. I cannot be the only one eager for trade to
resume."

"It takes only nine days for a frigate to make the run to
London," Ian reminded her. "As soon as word reaches
there that the war is over, the merchants will be delighted
to resume trading. However, we cannot discount the king's
reaction. George the Third may refuse to recognize that
the war is over and England has lost."

"That would be ridiculous!" Mercy exploded. "He will
have to recognize the truth. How can he not? Why, England
no longer has a single ally. Russia, Prussia, Sweden, Den-
mark have all formed a League of Armed Neutrality. *They*
will force the king to acknowledge our victory—or else
Parliament will."

"You do not know the king, my sweet—not as I do. Lord
North will try to persuade him to accept the inevitable, but
the king has been known to defy the House of Commons
without a single qualm. The king sees only what he wants
to see."

"Ian, we must write at once to General Washington and
tell him these things, so he can make them known to
Congress. Soon they will be selecting men to draft a peace
treaty with England. *You* should be one of those men; you
know the king so well. Others need to hear your view of
him. You have so much to offer—"

"I refuse to be dragged into the peace proceedings,
Mercy. I am unfit for travel. As flattering as I find your
insistence that my views are important, I myself do not
think I am the answer to all the nation's problems. . . .
Besides, how could I leave my woodcutting when I am just
beginning to make progress?"

He smiled at Rufus, who returned his smile with a broad
grin.

"You could travel by carriage." Mercy wished that Thor were ready for the task of pulling the carriage, which he was not. Nor would he be anytime soon. Teaching the stallion to drive was taking much longer than she had anticipated. Initially, he had resisted her. She had overcome his resistance with praise and handfuls of grain but still faced the challenge of his weakness and inexperience. Thor needed several more months of slow, quiet work before he could be considered fit and reliable as a driving horse. He would probably need even longer before he was fit enough to breed Liberty. She was now quite certain that Liberty had not yet been bred.

"I said no, Mercy. I am going nowhere. 'Tis enough of a challenge for me to leave this room and go downstairs for supper. I assure you I could never manage a long journey."

" 'Tis time we resume working your muscles," she said. "Your leg is healed enough now. Caleb and Augustus can help you as they did before you broke your leg."

"Caleb and Augustus have enough to do without additional burdens. Besides, it would be wasted effort. This leg"—he patted the appendage under discussion—"will never work properly. Fortunately, a woodcutter can do his work sitting down. Rufus and I have decided that the mantelpiece in this room should be done, since I spend so much time looking at it. After that, we—*he*—may redo the one in the library as he finds it crude by his present standards."

"I do not think it crude! 'Tis beautiful. However, I see no reason why you cannot pursue these objectives while *still* exercising your leg. You must not be satisfied with your current accomplishments to the extent that you progress no further."

Ian shook his head. "Make up your mind, Mercy. First you want me to make peace with my limitations, then you want me to keep fighting to overcome them. Now that I enjoy woodcutting, you insist I should be running the country. Am I never to know contentment in this house?"

"Caleb and Augustus will resume your exercises and

massages tomorrow morning," Mercy grimly announced. "After that, you may send for Rufus."

"Woman, you are a tyrant! Take care lest your subjects revolt against you," Ian warned.

She was happy to see the glint in his eye but dismayed by the hint of underlying resentment. Would she finally get him whole and well again—only to have him hate her for it? The thing that still stood between them—preventing a true union of minds, hearts, and bodies—was his impotence. If only she could find a way to discuss it . . . bring the problem out into the open . . . confront it and hopefully *resolve* the difficulty. Perhaps it was more of an emotional problem than a physical one.

Unfortunately, Ian had made it clear on countless occasions that *he* alone would decide how much intimacy he would allow. The spontaneous kiss she had given him at the start of this conversation was an excellent example: If she had tried for *two* kisses, he would have withdrawn from her, perhaps even gotten angry, his anger overshadowing even his exhilaration over their victory.

The war was over.

Today she would celebrate *that,* and tomorrow keep working on Ian and Thor.

At Christmas, Mercy gave Ian a new set of buckled shoes, one of which had a built-up heel since his bad leg was now slightly shorter than his good leg. After weeks of assistance from Caleb and Augustus, he could walk with two canes—one on each side—but his gait was woefully uneven. She hoped the built-up heel would help to remedy the situation.

"Thank you, my love," he said, smiling warmly at her in the fire's glow that lit up his bedchamber. Outside, sleet rattled the windowpanes and the wind howled like a demon. "I am certain the shoes will help me walk better, if not with complete security. Tomorrow we will put them to the test. Now, I have a gift for *you.*"

"For me?" Mercy was astonished. Despite how much better Ian was able to get around these days, he still stuck close to familiar surroundings—being more comfortable in his bedchamber than anywhere else. She attributed this to his poor vision and fear that he might fall and injure himself again in less familiar quarters. When had he found opportunity to seek a gift for her—and where could it have come from without her knowledge?

" 'Tis a little something I made for you," he said, extending his hand.

He held a small object wrapped in a square of homespun. Immediately wary lest she offend him in some way, Mercy gingerly accepted the humble offering. Her hands trembled as she unwrapped the gift. *It could not be one of Ian's carvings—could it?* Thus far, he had jealously guarded his creations, refusing to show her what he was working on even when she asked to see it.

"I have made nothing worth looking at yet," he kept telling her. "Until I can show you something I can take pride in, I would rather show you nothing."

She would be so thrilled if he had made her something! Nothing could be more precious than a carving he had done with his own hands.

Her heart fluttered wildly as the gift was revealed. It was indeed a carving—a tiny, delicate horse caught at full gallop, mane and tail streaming behind it. Holding it up to the firelight, Mercy examined it through a blur of tears.

"Ian, it is exquisite!"

Carved from a piece of oak and polished to a high golden gleam, the little horse bore a striking resemblance to Liberty.

"I wanted to carve *you* riding the horse, but I have not enough skill yet," he explained. "So I confined my efforts to capturing your mare. This is my fifth attempt. I would have tried a sixth, but Christmas came too quickly."

"Speak not of skill to me, Ian! This is so skillfully rendered I cannot believe my eyes. The horse is perfect, right down to the tiniest detail."

"Look not too closely, Wife," came Ian's mocking drawl. "If you do, you will see all my mistakes. I have only to hold the piece and I can feel them. Still, I wanted to give you something made by own hands. 'Tis primitive, I admit, but in time—''

"Ian, it is perfect! I will cherish it always. Never have I received a gift that pleased me more." Mercy rose from her chair and hurried to his side to kneel on the floor next to his chair.

"Oh, my dearest love, 'tis so beautiful!" she exclaimed, overcome by emotion. "I had no idea you were so talented. Truly, you are an artist!"

He laughed, but without bitterness. "Mercy, you will struggle to find the sun even on the darkest day. If I loved you for nothing more, I would be your slave for that."

He rested his hand on her head and idly stroked her unbound hair. She still wore it down most days as a subtle signal that she was "available." Instead of telling her to put it up—as he had done that one time—he occasionally seemed to take all his old delight in it and reached out to touch her hair in a brief caress. She considered it a good sign.

"You really think my effort has merit?" he asked. "You are not just saying it to salve my pride?"

"Ian, it is marvelous! How can you doubt it? . . . What does Rufus say?"

Ian laughed again. "Rufus concedes I may have promise as a woodcutter. But I know I will never be as skilled as he is, and *he* claims he will never be as good as the fellow who used to carve masks and other ceremonial objects for his people—before they were enslaved and brought here. Rufus can remember the fellow's work as if he saw it yesterday. The legs of your little horse are crudely done, Mercy. I wanted to show each muscle and bone and sinew, but—"

"You did not need to! You caught Liberty's spirit—no more was needed. The details are unimportant. What matters most is the character, the feeling. . . . Ian, you have a wonderful gift!"

Ian cocked his head, considering. "I never thought about it that way—capturing the spirit and the character. I just assumed that all the details were important. Rufus labors over details."

"I know he does. He tries to show the way things are—the way we see them with our eyes. He does a fine job. But Ian, you gave me Liberty the way I see her with my *heart*. When I witness her galloping free across an open meadow, I get a sudden lump in my throat—and your carving gives me the same feeling."

"You are only saying that because you love me."

"Yes, I love you," she said. "But I am also saying it because 'tis true."

"What an interesting idea!" he murmured, his face and eyes alight. "Trying to capture what the heart sees, rather than the eyes. That is what I want to do with my carving from now on—portray the spirit, particularly the spirit of the horse. When I think of Thor . . ."

The light faded from his eyes. "I would do better *not* to think of Thor."

Mercy almost told him then—almost blurted out that his beloved stallion still lived, and like Ian himself was slowly healing and finding new joy and purpose in life. She quickly bit down on the impulse, reminding herself that it would be better to wait and surprise him. By spring, Thor should be ready—and so should Ian. Spring—the season of new life. The time of rebirth. The awakening of passion and the need to mate. Thor would surely breed Liberty then, and Ian might look at her with new eyes, as well!

"Thank *you*, Ian, for the carving. I mean it when I say I will treasure it always."

"Thank *you*, Wife, for all you have given *me*—especially for your constant, unwavering faith in my abilities, even my newly discovered ones."

"I *do* have faith in your abilities, Ian! *All* of them." She forgot her good intentions then and blurted: "I cannot believe you have truly lost—"

He clamped his hand over her mouth. "Let us not speak of my losses. Tonight, especially, I am looking forward, not back. What more do you want of me? You have me on my feet again—have given me shoes to improve my walk—and I am excited about my carving."

"Yes, and that makes me very happy! But, Ian—"

"But nothing, Mercy. I give thanks for that much, and so must you."

"I do! Indeed, I do."

"Good. Enough then. 'Tis time for bed." He leaned forward and brushed her hair with his lips. "Good night, my love. Sleep well. I will see you in the morning."

She had been dismissed. Sent from his room. But she yearned to remain and pass the entire night in his embrace.

Time. Give him a little more time. By spring . . .

Clutching the little wooden horse to her bosom, Mercy rose to her feet and silently left her husband's warm, cheery chamber to seek her own cold, dark, and lonely one.

The new year of 1782 began with a well-publicized mass exodus of loyalists to Canada. Mercy had to assume that Prudence and Reggie Wharton were among them. Like them, many loyalists had taken refuge in the New England states; now they departed with great bitterness, leaving behind a rejoicing populace.

King George III, however, did exactly as Ian had predicted: He refused to recognize that the war was over and England had lost. Not until Lord North resigned his high office did the king accept that he must allow Parliament to negotiate a peace treaty with the American representatives: Benjamin Franklin, John Jay, and John Adams.

Ian predicted that the negotiations would be long and complicated—which they quickly proved to be. The actual peace talks did not begin until mid-April, and the terms Franklin demanded made Ian shake his head in dismay. Franklin wanted American independence to be recognized, all British troops withdrawn, the Mississippi River declared the western boundary of the United States, Americans permitted to fish on the Newfoundland Grand Banks, and Canada declared the boundary for the Great Lakes.

Those terms were difficult enough, but he also wanted Canada to be ceded to the United States and Great Britain to issue a public apology to the people of the United States.

"If Franklin keeps demanding the impossible, especially the ceding of Canada to the United States, the peace negotiations are likely to last even longer than the war," Ian complained to Mercy.

She silently agreed. At least ships were now running back and forth to England. Without saying a word to anyone, Mercy had sent for a selection of spectacles for Ian. Despite warming weather and the arrival of springtime in Virginia, poor vision kept Ian indoors most of the time. He could now walk short distances with a single cane but continued to lack confidence.

April was rainy, as were the first two weeks of May. When the mud finally dried up beneath a benevolent sun, Mercy decided it was time to get Ian out of the house more— and time to test Thor's training in harness. The stallion would forever bear the scars from the war, but Moses reported that Thor had shown every indication that he was still a stud and was chasing Liberty around the field these days whenever they were turned out together.

The old man had tried putting weight on the stallion's back—only to have him start limping again as a result. Otherwise, Thor appeared in good health and seemed to have no trouble whatever in pulling the light riding chair whenever Mercy hitched him and took him for a drive. It was time to take Ian along for the ride.

"Please come with me, Ian," she begged on a glorious May afternoon when the smell of flowers was enough to make a person's head spin. "We will just take a little turn around the estate so I can check on the fields and see how the crops are coming along. Everything should be sprouted by now, and the livestock have borne their young, so—"

"Go ahead without me, Mercy." Ian barely glanced up from the block of wood on which he was working.

Beside him, Rufus raised his eyes from his own labors and gave Mercy a sympathetic smile.

"Ian, you cannot allow yourself to molder away indoors while a perfectly beautiful spring day goes to waste. I will not budge from this spot until you agree to accompany me."

Exasperation tinged Ian's sigh. Reluctantly, he looked up. "My dear, I cannot *see* all the wonders of the countryside, so what is the point in going? I had much rather remain here and continue working."

His hands caressed the chunk of hickory even as he spoke.

"Are you carving another horse?" Mercy asked brightly, trying not to lose patience.

"All of my carving is of horses. I want to get them right before I move on to something else—which means I will be carving horses forever. I do not really mind, though; horses have filled my life for as long as I can remember. If I cannot have the *real* ones, especially my fiery Thor, my wooden ones will at least keep me from going mad."

"Ian, come for a drive with me. Your carving will be here when you get back—but the lovely flowers perfuming the air and the birdsong you can enjoy without seeing the birds will not. Spend some time with me out in the sunlight. We will go in the riding chair and visit your fields."

"My fields," Ian said. "I had forgotten about them— but then 'tis easy to forget what you cannot see."

Is that why you sometimes seem to forget even me?

"I will describe them to you in great detail. Come with me now. Everything is ready. Besides, you have been working Rufus too hard lately. He needs to rest from his labors the same as you do—and he is older than you so he needs rest even more."

"I suppose you are right." Ian set down the chunk of hickory on his carving table. "Rufus, you are dismissed. Go and take a nap or something. I do forget your age at times. Forgive me for not considering your welfare, my friend. You keep long hours with me—too long, I fear. I must try harder to keep from wearing you out."

"Carving doan tire me none," Rufus protested. "But on such a fine day, I would like to feel the sun on my old bones, Master Ian."

"Then be gone with you! Hand me my cane first, and then go sit in the sun for the rest of the day."

"I will await you downstairs," Mercy said, knowing that Ian did not like to have her watch him make his slow, careful descent down the stairs.

"I will come as quickly as I can—which should be sometime before sunset,'' Ian drawled with his typical dry humor.

Half an hour later they were in the riding chair going down the worn path that wound through the estate. Mercy was reminded of the first time she had taken Ian on a drive about the grounds to show him Collier Manor. She was no less uncomfortable now than she had been then— but for different reasons.

She felt the same sexual tension and uncertainty—the same excitement and nervousness at being alone with him. She was particularly nervous about Thor. Ian had thus far shown no interest in the horse pulling the conveyance; he had probably assumed it was Liberty, though even with his blurred vision he ought to have been able to distinguish between the mare's chestnut coat and the stallion's rich dark brown one.

At first, when he had gotten into the riding chair, Ian had looked almost terrified—a clear indication that he *did* need to get out more. His movements had been stiff and jerky. Now he was starting to relax. At the moment, he had his eyes closed and his face tilted back as if he relished the feel of the warm sunshine on his skin.

He was informally dressed in open shirt, breeches, and his buckled shoes, with his dark hair tied back away from his face. His cane leaned on one thigh. Other than the cane and the suggestion of tension, he looked as fit as ever. The exercise she had insisted upon had strengthened him and kept him fit. He now walked with much less difficulty and hesitation, though he would probably never be able to surrender the cane.

Mercy flicked the whip lightly over Thor's glossy back. The stallion responded by trotting a little faster, but not much. His injuries had affected his gaits and his self-confidence in much the same way as Ian's movement had been compromised. Neither would ever be perfect again, but both had come so far that Mercy was humbly grateful.

"What is wrong with your mare?" Ian suddenly asked, opening his eyes and squinting in Thor's direction. "Oh, this is not Liberty, is it? She always had such a fine floating trot, and this beast is slow and off balance."

"No," Mercy said. "This is not Liberty. This horse is newly broken to harness and recovering from severe injuries. Still, I think he is doing marvelously well, considering all he has been through."

She flicked the whip again, and Thor tried even harder to respond. Lifting his head, he whinnied and surged forward, showing some of his old fire. He actually seemed to be enjoying his work. Mercy was so proud of him! Her heart swelled with emotion. This was even better than she had dared hope for. Then she noticed that Ian was gripping his cane, his knuckles white with strain.

"Ian, what is it?" She slowed the stallion to a walk with a slight fluttering motion of her fingers.

Thor whinnied again—plaintively, and Mercy saw what was ailing him. Despite his blinders, he had caught a fleeting glimpse of Liberty galloping in the field without him.

"That whinny," Ian muttered. "Who *is* this horse? He sounds just like . . . Thor."

"My darling. . . . It *is* Thor."

"Impossible!" Ian raised his cane in agitation. "It cannot be. Thor is dead! Even if he were not, he was never trained to harness."

"He is now, my love. . . . Thor, trot!" Mercy called out, and Thor obediently resumed trotting.

She let him go a short distance and again signaled him for a walk. He was light and obedient in her hands, trying his best to please her. "Good boy!" she praised, delighted and as proud of herself as she was of him. She had done an excellent job of training him, patiently teaching him to respond to the lightest of commands. No one who drove him in the future would ever have to resort to strength to stop him or the harsh use of the whip to urge him onward. He was behaving like a perfect gentleman, his whinny to Liberty his only fault in an otherwise flawless performance.

Then she looked at Ian and her elation vanished. He was sitting absolutely rigid against the back of the riding chair, his teeth locked in a grimace. As she stared at him, her anxiety mounted. Tears were streaming down his cheeks!

"Ian!"

Oh God, what had she done?

Ian did not look pleased; he looked devastated. And she was suddenly devastated, too. Quickly she halted the stallion and wound the lines around one arm of the riding chair. Turning to her husband, she grabbed his hands. They were shaking. His shoulders, head and arms—his whole body—was shaking. Harsh sobs broke from his throat.

She had made a mistake—a dreadful mistake.

Suddenly he reached for her and gathered her into his arms, clasping her tightly against him. She held him as he sobbed brokenly. What he was thinking and feeling, what had precipitated this outburst, she could not guess. Whether it was for good or ill was an equal mystery. She only knew that Ian was weeping as if a great storm had unleashed itself within him. Until it was spent, he could not even speak, much less answer her questions.

Thor stood patiently, never moving except to toss his head from time to time. Once, he stamped his foot as if inquiring when they might be off again. Mercy noticed these things from a distance, so overcome with her own emptying of emotion that she could only hold Ian and wet his shirtfront with her own tears.

"Ian," she finally managed to get out. "Ian, I only thought to please you. Thor's recovery was meant to be a surprise. I am so sorry if I have hurt you. I never intended to do so. I thought if I could retrain him—"

"I know what you thought, Mercy," came Ian's muffled reply. He lifted his head and heaved a long sigh.

"Ian, what? *What? Tell me,"* she begged, dreading to hear his answer. Her life, her happiness, her entire future hung on his response.

CHAPTER
TWENTY-ONE

He took her face in his hands, and the pads of his thumbs traced tiny circles on her cheekbones. "I am thinking that my beautiful, exasperating wife has outdone herself this time."

"Outdone myself? What do you mean?"

"I mean she has given me a gift beyond price. She has restored to me a horse whose death I never stopped mourning—a horse who gave up his life for me and carried me mile after agonizing mile when he himself was wounded and suffering. I have thought of him so often and wondered if there was any way we could have saved him. Naturally, *I* could not have saved him, nor could I bear to know he was miserable. How did you do it, Mercy? What sorcery did you use? . . . And you taught him to drive, yet!"

"My love, *I* did not do it. Nor did Moses. It was Liberty who gave him a reason for living. She stayed with him day and night, encouraging him each step of the way. I tried to kill him that day—I tried! But when he looked at me, I could not do it. So I put him into a field alone with my mare and left Thor to decide for himself if he wished to die or not."

"Apparently, he preferred living."

"Yes, but he was many months healing—just as you were. I despaired he would heal well enough to work again. Moses tried to put young Henry up on him, but Thor goes lame whenever he bears weight. Pulling the riding chair does not seem to hurt him, though; we have gone very slowly. At first he did not take to it. I think it frightened him. Then, as he grew accustomed to hearing the noise behind him—and feeling the weight of the shafts and the pressure of the breast collar . . ."

"He accepted it. Even as I have accepted woodcutting as my new life's work."

"He trusts in his own strength now. Moses thinks he may have succeeded in mounting Liberty! At first he showed no interest in her, at least not in that way. But then—oh, Ian, do you think . . . ?"

"Mercy, Mercy . . ." Ian enfolded her in his arms. "My dearest love, I am a man, not a horse. Do you think I would not resume loving you—*in that way*—just as soon as I possibly could? . . . Do you think I do not lie in bed at night cursing the particular affliction that keeps me away from you?"

"But Ian, you have not tried! We have not tried. How do you know you cannot—"

"Mercy, I *know.*" Releasing her, Ian groaned in frustration. "I need no awkward fumbling in the dark to prove it to myself. To try and fail would be a worse torture than never trying at all. We have friendship, companionship, tenderness, and laughter. That is more than most people have together."

"And we can still have all that even if we fail! But I should like to *try,* Ian. . . . At the very least, I want to be near you at night. To hold you and caress you and—"

"*That* I could never tolerate, Mercy." He leaned back against the seat as if trying to distance himself from her. "In time, I think I will be able to satisfy your needs, if not my own, without thinking of my losses as slurs on my manhood. I cannot do it yet. Forgive me but I cannot. I am still learning to . . . to live with who I am now. I still *despise* this weak, dependent creature I have become, but

I am learning not to dwell on my misfortune. The wood-cutting has helped tremendously—just as you intended."

"Getting out into the fresh air will help even more!" Mercy fervently assured him. "It has helped already. At least we are discussing this. And I finally feel free to tell you how much I hate sleeping apart from you."

"I am sorry, my love." He touched her cheek again. "I wish I could invite you into my bed and satisfy all your yearnings. But I am not strong enough—not yet. Maybe not ever. Thor may be your only miracle, while *I* remain your greatest failure."

"You will never be a failure, Ian Montjoy! You must not say that. If we cannot . . . cannot try yet, I will summon my patience to endure another delay. But I will not give up hoping. I will never stop hoping—or praying. Nearly all that I have prayed for I have received. God has been wonderfully good to me—to *us*. When I think of the many women like Caroline who have lost their husbands and will never again be able to hold them, I realize how fortunate I am."

"Yes, God left you a husband—though he can scarcely be called 'husbandly.' Speaking of Caroline, how *are* your ladies? I have not heard you mention them lately."

"That is because we are all too busy trying to recover from the war to spend time visiting. . . . Oh, Ian! This year when foxhunting season arrives, we can host the Collier Manor Hunt again!"

"Yes. Thor and I can watch from a distance. Rather, *he* can watch. I must content myself with listening to the music of the hounds and the thunder of hoofbeats leaving me far behind."

Mercy bit her tongue in aggravation at herself. How could she have been so thoughtless as to mention foxhunting season to a man who could no longer participate? It was as bad as mentioning lovemaking.

"Oh, perhaps we should not have the hunt, after all," she suggested. "It has been so long since the last one that we have probably all forgotten how to hunt, anyway."

"*You* have not forgotten. It is bred into your bones, Mercy. And you must not forgo foxhunting on *my* account.

'Tis something you truly enjoy, so you must continue doing it whether or not I am able to take part.''

As if she could bear to leave him and go galloping across the countryside without him! If Ian could not foxhunt, she would not.

"We will see," she said, to placate him. "Now, do you wish to take the lines and continue our drive? I will tell you what signals to give Thor."

"No," Ian said. "I am happy to let *you* handle the driving. If I cannot manage it myself, I want no pale imitation of the activity. Still, it greatly pleases me to know that Thor is pulling the riding chair. After our drive, I wish to rub him down. I do not need to see well to do that; just to put my hands on him again will be pleasure enough. Again, I thank you, Mercy. I am more delighted than I can say."

Mercy was delighted also. They may not have gone as far as she had hoped today, but they had gained new ground. All the effort had been worth it. Now that Ian knew Thor was alive and well, he would feel drawn to the stable to check on him every day. He was too much of a horseman to leave his horse's welfare to others. And he would be willing to get out of the house more often to go for drives. These were victories to cherish.

Unwrapping the lines and taking them in one hand, Mercy clucked to Thor, and he moved off eagerly, glad to be on his way. The stallion, at least, exceeded her expectations. Now, all she needed to do was continue working on his master. If only Ian's spectacles would come! Once he could see again, one more excuse for why he could not risk being a man—and a husband—in the fullest sense of the word would be eliminated.

From that day onward, Ian made astounding progress. He continued with his carving—but now only for part of the day. Each day, he ventured outside, usually grimacing in intense concentration, a tactic she had noticed he employed whenever he tried something new or different. Slowly and laboriously, he made his way down to the stable on his own—tapping with his cane and following the exact same route. Once there, Moses would fetch Thor and tie the stallion in the aisle so that Ian could groom him.

Mercy frequently stopped whatever she was doing to go and watch the ritual, for it moved her deeply. She would stand silently in the doorway, too far away for Ian to really see her—or to recognize her if he did see her. There, she would watch him curry, brush, and massage the big stallion's rippling muscles, including his scars, with hands that never failed to be kind and gentle.

Ian touched the horse as if he marveled that Thor still lived. Indeed, his face held a wordless rapture as he ministered to his old friend.

Mercy could not help feeling jealous; she wanted Ian to touch *her* with that same tenderness and awe. Although she sensed a new closeness between them, he maintained his usual distance. Touching *her* seemed out of the question.

Watching him stroke the stallion's glossy neck, she dreamed of him stroking her own breasts and thighs. Witnessing him comb the stallion's mane and tail with infinite patience, never breaking a hair, she yearned for him to comb *her* hair with equal gentleness. Sometimes he just rested his forehead against the stallion's crest, closed his eyes, and appeared to be praying—and Mercy wanted to hold him in her arms and grant every prayer he had ever uttered.

Her longing became an obsession, and at night she dreamed of Ian—hot, erotic dreams that left her quaking and trembling with need when she suddenly awakened. Summer brought sultry, languid nights in which she lay in her bed and feared she might go mad with longing. One night she could stand it no longer and dared to visit his bedchamber once more, only to stand silently in the moonlit room, observing him as he lay sleeping and unaware of her presence.

She managed to restrain herself from getting into bed with him; if he sent her away again, it would cut too deeply. She knew she had to wait . . . wait for him to come to her. Wait for his fears to be conquered. Wait for the pain and the doubts to finally leave him. Wait for the final healing.

But she was losing patience! She had no more miracles to give him. The spectacles might never come—or if they did, might do him no good. Several people had offered him their own spectacles on the chance they would help, but so far none had. Chloe had found a forgotten pair in an old, little-used cabinet and excitedly brought them to Mercy. Neither could recall the former owner. Mercy had rushed to Ian and bade him try them on. They were much too small, barely fitting over the bridge of his nose—and they only made the world look more blurred, not less. Mercy had been crushed.

She took to splashing rose water on herself in the hope that Ian would respond to her scent, if not her presence. Once, she silently entered a room where he could not see her, and he immediately lifted his head. His nostrils flared, like Thor's, and a naked look of longing suffused his handsome features. She derived a perverse satisfaction from the realization that she was not suffering alone. Eventually, *his* passion must reawaken.

Unfortunately, he soon caught on to her ploy and admonished her for it. "Mercy," he said one night after supper which they had eaten in a cloud of perfumed air. "I should like to ask a favor of you."

"What is it, Ian? You know I will do anything for you."

Amusement crept into his blue eyes. He smiled slightly with a hint of masculine triumph. "Really? You will do anything?"

"I can refuse you nothing and well you know it, Ian Montjoy."

"Then I most respectfully request that you cease drenching yourself in rose water morning, noon, and night. The scent has begun to make my eyes water and my nose tingle. I believe I have developed an aversion to it. Before you began using it so freely, I enjoyed it. The elusive fragrance always reminded me of you. Now that it is no longer elusive, it gives me sniffles whenever I smell it."

Mercy was mortified—and annoyed. "Then I will tell Chloe never to make it for me again."

"My thanks to both of you. Too much of a good thing can become a bad thing, you know."

"I quite agree. From now on, I shall perfume myself with stable odors. Will that please you? You seem to enjoy *those* scents well enough these days."

"I relish stable odors. Pray do not put anything suspicious in my soup, however," he said, reminding her of that day so long ago when she had put a horse apple in Reggie Wharton's soup to discourage him. Discouraging a man was easy, she thought. Enticing one was devilishly hard—especially one determined *not* to be enticed.

Not long after that, during a late July heat spell that had everyone looking damp and listless, a letter for Ian came from General Washington. Mercy had written to Martha and let her know what had happened to Ian—begging her to inform her husband so that *he* would know of Ian's fate. She had yet to receive a reply from Martha, but the letter indicated that Washington now knew Ian was still alive and home again.

Picking up her skirts, Mercy flew to the stable where she knew Ian was grooming Thor at this hour.

"Ian, a letter has come from General Washington!" She stopped breathlessly in front of the stallion, who raised his head and eyed her warily.

Ian paused in currying Thor's neck. "Washington? . . . How does he even know I am here? I should have sent word to him long before this, but I never got around to it."

"I wrote to Martha," Mercy explained. "Do you want me to open the letter and read it to you?"

"You might as well. That would appear to be the thing to do at this point," he drawled. "What does my commander have to say to a man who failed to report to him as he should have?"

Mercy tore open the wax-sealed letter and quickly scanned its contents. "He says he is relieved and delighted that you survived the war. He makes no mention of your tardiness in informing him of your whereabouts. He also says . . . Ian! He *begs* you to consider returning to his side if you are at all able. He claims he is beset by problems, not the least of which is an effort by the Army to have him declared *king* of the United States."

"King? Washington will never accept that—my God! That is what this fight was all about."

"That is what *he* says," Mercy confirmed, quoting from the letter. " *'No occurrence in the course of the war has given me more painful sensations.'* However, he goes on to say that there is no money to pay his loyal soldiers and officers—such as yourself—and the Congress claims to be bankrupt."

"Then the individual states should pay the men," Ian snapped, currycomb still in hand but forgotten. "I speak not for myself but for all those who lack a wealthy wife to take care of them when they return home."

The comment made her wince, but Mercy offered no argument. Instead, she read on, summarizing the remainder of the letter in her own words. "The states are refusing to make good on federal promises. Washington has even uncovered a conspiracy among the ranks of the Army to *force* the Congress to respond to their demands. He has taken swift action to keep the angry troops under control, imploring them to act in such a manner that posterity will have no reason to judge them harshly. He says he was making no progress in his pleas until he took out his new spectacles to read a letter from a Congressman assuring them that their complaints would all be settled. 'Twas not the letter itself that moved them, but the sight of his spectacles. He says he told them, *'Gentlemen, you will permit me to put on my spectacles, for I have not only grown gray but almost blind in your service.'* From that point on, their sentiments improved, and they began to heed him."

"Washington cannot see, either?" Ian shook his head in wonderment. "Truly, this war has brought us all to our knees."

"He can see with spectacles! Ian, he says he needs your good advice on how to handle all these difficulties. He begs you to come join him in New York and assist him in squashing these new threats to liberty and strengthening this fragile peace."

Mercy glanced up from the letter just in time to witness a fleeting look of something amazingly close to terror pass across Ian's face. His features quickly assumed a calm, guarded expression, but Mercy knew she had seen *some*-thing, and she could not pretend to ignore it.

"Ian, what is it? It would not be impossible for you to travel to New York, now. Thor could even take you. I would have to go along, of course, or *some*one would—to drive Thor and find the way. We could work it all out. . . . Why are you shaking your head no even as I speak? Washington *needs* you. You could be such a help to him. 'Tis just as I have always said. Your advice is so brilliant and in-formed . . ."

She trailed off helplessly, realizing that he would never go. "Ian, tell me. What frightens you so?"

He turned away from Thor—away from *her,* and limped down the stable aisle. Then he paused and leaned one hand against a post supporting the roof. When he spoke, she could barely hear him and had to step closer.

"Mercy, I never told you what it was like after I was wounded, did I?"

"You said you could not remember much of anything, except when Hiram found you and got you away from the scene of battle."

"I *do* remember *some* things," he admitted. "And others have come back to me in dreams . . . terrible dreams. Night-mares from which I awaken shivering, sweating, and shak-ing so badly that I would be ashamed if you should see me that way."

"Oh, my dearest, is that why—?"

"No. I have not been lying about my impotence and the way it makes me feel. But my dreams are another reason why I dread having you in my bed again—and why I could not *bear* to travel. When I first discovered that I was blind, I was . . . I was . . ."

"You were terrified," Mercy supplied, imagining how awful it must have been.

"Yes." Ian nodded. "Terrified and helpless and certain I was going to die alone in blackness, fear, and pain. I went a little mad, I think. 'Tis why I could recall so little later. I know not how I regained my sensibilities. Suddenly I did, and that is when I blamed poor Hiram for saving me. I am past blaming Hiram, of course, but sometimes that feeling of terror comes back to me—and with it the sense of being overwhelmed, trapped in darkness, and vulnerable unto death."

"*When*, Ian? When does it come back to you?"

He turned to face her, and his sorrow and vulnerability struck her like a blow. "Whenever I venture away from the safe and known. First, it happened only when I left my bed or chair, which I could hardly do anyway because of my physical limitations. Then it kept me in my bedchamber. To descend the staircase, to go out of the house, to go as far as the stable, to go anywhere new or different was an ordeal, a true test of courage. . . . I have been conquering my fears one step at a time. Day by day going a few steps further. Some days it all comes back to me and I find I can hardly go at all. On those days, even the familiar looks impossible, and I must fight just to leave my bed."

"Ian, you never told me! You should have told me all this. Perhaps I could have helped you."

He smiled—his old smile of self-mockery, tinged with chagrin. "My love, 'tis not exactly a thing a man is proud to admit to his wife. To discover that I am such a coward came as a great shock to me. I did not want it to shock *you*, as well. What would you think of me, I often asked myself, if you ever discovered *this* infirmity?"

"What would I think of you? Ian, I think you are the bravest man alive to have coped with this all by yourself! To have kept it secret for so long, to have struggled to overcome it alone, with no help. . . . You *are* the bravest man alive." She went to him, threw her arms around him, and hugged him. "Ian, you should have told me. I would not have thought less of you for it."

"Mercy, I wanted to. But I could not bring myself to do it. I was too ashamed—too aggravated. It seemed to me I should be able to conquer the feeling, but I have not done it yet. I am over the worst of it, but some days remain a struggle. I could never travel. Not when it is sometimes a battle for me to come down to the stable. If not for Thor, I would stay in the house on those days. If not for you insisting that I need fresh air, I would refuse to go for drives around the estate. I never know when the panic will suddenly visit me, making a mockery of all my good intentions."

"How could I not have noticed?" Mercy wailed. "Am I as blind as you are?"

Ian's slow grin emerged. "Well, the one thing I pride myself upon is hiding it. I have gotten rather good at that. For a while, I even managed to hide it from myself. I simply refused to admit to it. But the mere thought of leaving Collier Manor—of going all the way to New York—"

He held out his hand, and Mercy could see that it was shaking. She could *feel* him trembling. Perhaps that was another reason why he spurned her touch; he feared revealing his fear to her.

"You need not go, then. I will write and tell him that your health does not permit travel—at least not yet."

"Do that, my love. I am flattered that the general still thinks of me. Perhaps I will write to him—or you can do it for me. Advice in a letter does little good, for it is often old before it arrives at its destination. Still, I might write."

"I would be happy to copy down all you wish to say."

"Good. We are in agreement, then, that I will not be traveling anywhere."

"Oh, yes! At least you will not be traveling anytime *soon*."

He gave a short, bitter laugh. "You never give up, do you, my love?"

"No, Ian. I never give up."

Ian did dictate a letter to General Washington a week later, and Mercy carefully wrote every word. He suggested that as the troops were discharged, they be given some sort of settlement vouchers or promissory notes for their back pay. Congress could then make good on the notes at a later date, as soon as it was able. He urged Washington to continue resisting any efforts to appoint him to a high office of any kind. No one should be appointed to office, he told the general. Instead, Congress must set itself the duty of deciding how the new government should now function.

Why should it pattern itself on English laws and customs?

he asked Washington. And then he shocked Mercy by suggesting that Washington should resign as commander of the Continental Army as soon as a treaty was formally signed with England.

"Why would you suggest *that?*" Mercy demanded, aghast at the notion. "The general is our foremost leader. True, there are many men of influence I could name—our own Thomas Jefferson, Benjamin Franklin ... but General Washington is the one man known and respected by all. He is a hero whose name will be remembered forever by all people who love liberty."

"That is why I am suggesting it," Ian said. "Go on. Write it."

He waved his hand at Mercy where she sat at the table in the library. He sat nearby, idly scratching the ears of a little gray mongrel dog who had shown up at Collier Manor several days previously and already insinuated himself into everyone's affections. When he stopped scratching the dog's ears, the little fellow shoved his nose into Ian's lap and begged for more. His long tail whapped the floor as he did so.

"Not until you tell me why," she said, unable to write such a thing.

"If Washington resigns and returns to private life, there will be no danger of *any* man being named king or lord or prime minister in our new government. *He* is the natural choice. Therefore, it will *force* the Congress to deal with the issue of finding the best way to run the country—a way that takes into account our notions of freedom for all men."

"And women," Mercy tartly added. "Women must be taken into account also. And slaves. What will the Congress do about slavery, do you think?"

"Nothing," Ian said. "That is too controversial an issue to be dealt with at this time. If we tried to free all the slaves now and give them the same rights as *we* wish to enjoy, we would soon wind up fighting among ourselves ... and we can ill afford to do that, Mercy. Women and slaves will have to wait their turn."

"Their turn!"

"Finish writing the letter, will you? If you wish to add your own views, you must write your own letter."

"Perhaps I shall. 'Tis apparent I still have causes for which to fight."

"There will *always* be causes. 'Tis the way of the world, my love. No sooner do we solve one problem than another appears. Our new government must be able to deal with all the causes of the future."

"Now, that is a worthy sentiment to add. Perhaps you should be writing letters to the members of the Congress also. I hear they are all scattered and hardly know what to do next. At the moment, they seem to be powerless to do anything, as evidenced by their inability to pay our poor troops."

"Perhaps I should," Ian said evenly. "The Congress must find themselves a meeting place and closely examine the Articles of Confederation to see if they will be enough to run a country. If the states all go their separate ways now . . ."

He trailed off, as if thinking.

"We could be as bad off as before the war." Mercy quickly grasped the need for better unity and communication between the states. "Ian, we have just won a war, but already I foresee serious problems."

"So do I," he muttered. "I am certain the general does, also. However, he needs time to rest—to think—to recover from this mighty effort. His resignation would ensure that he has the chance to step back from the situation, at least for a time. The man deserves *that* much."

"So does his wife," Mercy pointed out. "The general has been too long away from Mount Vernon. I will tell him of your suggestion, after all. 'Tis a good one, I believe."

"I am glad you have come to see the wisdom of it."

"I always see the wisdom of your thinking," she retorted. *Except when you deny me your bed.*

She still believed that his thinking on *that* issue was faulty. But until he changed his mind—or something happened to change it for him—she had to respect his wishes. As he leaned down to scratch the little dog's belly, Mercy stole a longing glance at him. He looked as fit and handsome as the first day she had ever seen him. . . . Oh, he was thinner and had a few deep lines in his face that had not been there then—and a few gray hairs—but he still possessed a vitality that radiated from him now as much as when he was younger.

He spent enough time outside now to have gained a bronzed color on his face and hands, and he had as many sun-streaked hairs as gray ones. His walk had improved to the extent that he carried his cane more out of habit than need—except to test the path in front of him.

Oh, how she loved and wanted him!

He glanced up and noticed that her pen was no longer making scratching sounds as she wrote, so she busily returned to her task. *He could groom his horse and pet his new little dog, whom he had named Bother for being such a bother to everyone—so why could he not accord her similar tokens of his affection?*

It was a question she was doomed to keep asking herself until she discovered the answer.

CHAPTER
TWENTY-TWO

"Chloe, where is my husband? Have you seen him? He is usually carving at this time of day. He did not go down to the stable, did he?"

"I never saw him leave, girl. Doan know where he went."

Chloe paused in the doorway of Ian's bedchamber. She held an armload of clean linens, and her face was shiny with perspiration. For early September, it was unseasonably warm. The heat of summer had lingered much too long, and everyone had grown tired of it and irritable.

"Have you seen Bother? That dog has become his shadow. If we can find Bother, we can find Ian."

"Saw him early this morning, but not since then. Got too much to do to be lookin' after little dogs." Chloe proceeded down the hallway, leaving Mercy to shake her head.

Where had her husband gone off to now? Lately, he had grown in confidence—possibly because he had Bother to accompany him wherever he went. He seemed determined to make up for lost time. This was not the first time this week that he had altered his normal schedule. Yesterday he had been late to the noonday meal and then spent all afternoon down at the stable and came late to the evening meal.

Mercy rejoiced in his new independence, though it did provoke her concern. She worried constantly that something might happen to set Ian back, as his broken leg had done. If anything should happen now, when he was finally overcoming some of his fears, he would be a long time trusting in his own resources again. She knew she must be careful not to hover over him, but she meant to keep an eye on him just the same. Her constant vigilance would not die easily, if indeed it ever did die.

She decided to go down to the stable. Until she convinced herself that he was all right, she could never continue with her own chores.

Halfway there, she heard Bother's frantic yelping and the murmur of voices. Fearing the worst, she hurried toward the distant building. Suddenly a man—Moses—leading a horse bearing a rider came around the side of the stable and began to cross the stable yard. Young Henry followed behind them, fairly dancing in excitement, while Bother yapped and nipped at the horse's heels.

Mercy's first thought was that the dog was going to get kicked. Thor would only take so much before he struck out—*Thor! The horse was Thor and the rider was Ian!*

Mercy felt as if she herself had been kicked in the chest. She let out a loud yelp and began running toward the stable. "Ian! Moses! What do the pair of you think you are doing? Ian cannot ride—and Thor cannot carry him. Ian, you must get down at once! You could become dizzy and fall off. Thor could pull away from Moses, and then where would you be? Why, that poor horse could collapse under your weight. He is unaccustomed to it. At the very least, he may go lame again."

By the time she reached them, she was breathless—and amazed. None of her dire warnings had come to pass. Indeed, every single participant in the activity seemed to be doing just fine—even Thor. The stallion was paying no attention whatever to the yappy little dog—nor was he limping. As for Ian . . .

Mercy gazed up at her husband and had to blink back sudden tears. For once, she counted herself lucky that he could not see her reaction. But then he was so engrossed in what he was doing that he barely seemed to notice her. A wide grin stretched from ear to ear, and his face glowed with happiness.

"I had to feel him under me once more, Mercy," he said, proving that he *had* noticed her. "And the feeling is *wonderful*. He is not limping at all. I think the driving has helped to strengthen him, just as walking has helped my leg. It was a chore getting up on him, but—damn! The effort was worth it. Walk a little faster, Moses. If you were not so old, I would ask you to trot."

"No trotting! Ian, you dare not risk it."

Ian squinted at her. "I should think you would be happy to see me up here. I have been wanting to try this for such a long time, but I could not summon the nerve. Now that I am here—Mercy, I feel like a man again!"

"Oh, Ian!" Mercy gave up trying to conceal her tears, and they spilled down her cheeks.

"Well, almost like a man again," he amended. "Restrain yourself, Wife. 'Tis too early to draw any conclusions from this triumph."

Mercy could not stop crying. To see him riding his beloved stallion again evoked emotions she could not contain. Even with Moses leading the horse and Henry staying close by in case he was needed, Ian looked more like his old self than he had looked since before the war. Even Thor seemed like *his* old self. He pranced, rather than walked, showing more than a dash of his old spirit. It was obvious he much preferred being under saddle to being hitched to a cart . . . or perhaps he was simply rejoicing to have his master on his back again.

Ian patted the stallion's neck to calm him. "Look at him, Mercy! He wants to trot. I could stay on him, I think. Moses, hand me the reins and let go of him for a moment, and—"

"No, Ian!" Mercy sprang forward and grabbed the horse's reins from the old man's hands. "You have done enough for one day. You have proved to us and to yourself that you can do it. Wait another day to try the trot. Indeed, you should wait until those spectacles I ordered get here—"

"I doubt they are ever coming, Mercy. Besides, I have

tried a dozen pairs that people have offered me. None have made the world clear again. If I am doomed to see everything in a blur for the rest of my life, I had better get used to it. I *am* getting used to it, little by little."

"If that is indeed true—that you never will see clearly— then it is all the more reason why you cannot go trotting off alone when you know not where you are going. Besides, 'tis enough in one day for Thor to carry you at the walk. To ask more of him might aggravate his old injuries."

Ian's sigh was loud enough to wake a dead man. "You are right, Wife. Somehow you are always right. Take me back to the stable, Moses. I must not abuse my faithful horse."

As the radiance faded from his face, Mercy heaved her own sigh. She cared little for the role of enforcing caution; her natural inclination was to promote the exact opposite, as Ian well knew.

She stood and watched as Moses led the stallion away. It had been right to call a halt to the proceedings, but today marked another new beginning. Another milepost. Ian was conquering his demons, one after the other. She was so proud of him! And eager for him to conquer the few remaining demons he had left.

Another week passed, and Ian rode everyday. Moses or Henry led Thor at the walk with Ian proudly on his back. The sight never failed to bring tears to Mercy's eyes. She could see that Ian was itching to go faster, but refrained from rushing either the horse or himself. She began to wonder if it might be possible for her to ride Liberty and lead Thor alongside the mare. It was still too soon to try such a thing, but if she did not do it this fall, she would have to wait until after the winter, and by then Liberty would be busy with her new foal. Moses and she agreed that the mare *had* to be in foal; she had shown no signs of being "in season" for many months now.

Of course, there would be no need for Mercy to be Ian's eyes if he could see for himself. If the spectacles she had sent for ever arrived and did not solve the problem, she would send for *more*—and keep searching until she found a pair that helped him.

As she returned to the house one afternoon after watching Ian ride, she saw a strange carriage standing in the drive. She quickened her pace so as not to keep any visitors waiting. As she drew closer, a woman and a boy alighted from the conveyance. The woman was so stunning that Mercy inhaled sharply.

She was truly lovely—beautifully turned out in a powdered wig, charming bonnet, and pale blue silk gown, a masterful creation that could only have come from Europe. Dripping ruffles and costly lace, it was obviously cut to the latest fashion. Mercy had no idea what that fashion was—she had not followed the current fashions since before the war—but she had an eye for fine clothing, and the lady's elegant attire was the finest.

Mercy wondered if the newcomers might be lost. Perhaps their driver had stopped to seek directions to some other Virginia estate. The carriage was the sort one could hire in any large city. Perhaps now that the war had ended, the beautiful stranger had come to visit relatives.

Hurrying up the walk, Mercy greeted her just as Chloe opened the front door.

"Hello, there!" Mercy called out. "May I help you? I am the lady of the house—Mercy Montjoy."

"Montjoy?" The woman turned to her, her blond brows lifting in surprise. "Then I have come to the right place. I am searching for Viscount Ian Montjoy."

Up close, the woman was even more lovely than from a distance. Elegance and refinement radiated from every aspect of her graceful, delicate person. Mercy quickly became conscious of her own disheveled appearance. She was wearing plain homespun of a nondescript color, covered with a none-too-clean apron, and her long, tangled hair blew about her in the light breeze coming up off the fields.

"You know Ian?" she inquired with a sudden sinking feeling. The woman's presence at Collier Manor suddenly struck her as ominous.

"If one counts being betrothed to a man as *knowing*

him, then I most certainly do. If that does *not* count—in view of how many years it has been since I last laid eyes on the scoundrel—being the mother of his child most certainly will."

"Being the mother of his *child* . . . ?" For the first time, Mercy took a close look at the boy who accompanied the woman and now stood off to one side, staring at Mercy in a hostile manner.

The boy had his mother's green eyes but Ian's dark hair—not precisely the same shade but close enough to make Mercy's heart race. She searched his small, mutinous face for Ian's regal nose and stubborn jaw, but found not a hint of them. Of course, Ian might have looked different when he was younger. Though he bore little physical resemblance, the boy clearly had his father's air of arrogance—and a suggestion of deep hurt beneath his anger.

"Dear God . . ." she murmured under her breath.

"Oh, I would not bother with prayer at this point, my dear," the woman said. " 'Tis too late for prayer. In any case, it is entirely possible there *is* no God. He certainly never answers any of *my* prayers. Believe me, I prayed plenty eight years ago when I discovered myself alone and with child—and the father of my child had gone off to America, abandoning me to my own devices."

How anyone so beautiful could suddenly open her mouth and become so ugly mystified Mercy and imparted a valuable lesson in human nature: Outward appearances could often be deceiving.

"Come into the house," she grimly invited. "I will send for Ian."

"Do that, my dear," the woman said. "Adam and I will be delighted to see the inside of his father's house. Adam, at least, will be living here from now on. You see, I have brought him to join his father and be educated and groomed to receive the inheritance that will one day be his."

"This house comes from *my* side of the family," Mercy quickly informed her. " 'Tis my family home."

"Yes, but what belongs to the wife becomes the domain of the husband after marriage, the same here as it does in England, does it not? And you *did* say you were Mercy *Montjoy,* so I assume you are Ian's wife—and the reason he never came home to me. Aside from this estate, Ian can still claim his wealth and title in England if he so chooses. The boy could inherit his title, if nothing else."

"The front yard is no place for this discussion," Mercy pointed out. "Do come into the house."

She looked at Adam. *Nor is it proper to discuss the boy's future right in front of him. No wonder he looks so angry! Having this woman for a mother cannot be a pleasant experience for the poor lad.*

She followed the pair into the house and sent Chloe to fetch her husband.

Ian had no idea why Mercy had summoned him, but from the urgent tone of Chloe's voice, his wife wanted him immediately.

"What does she want?" he asked the servant, who seemed to be frowning at him as if he were some sort of vermin she had suddenly discovered. He still had to groom Thor after his ride and was in no hurry to leave the stable unless there was some emergency.

"She jus' said t' bring you at once," Chloe told him, her tone suggesting he was pure evil. "All I will say is you got company, and you better prepare yourself for a big surprise."

Why would Chloe be angry if General Washington—or one of their neighbors—had come to visit?

Ian could not imagine what was wrong. "Moses, see to Thor, will you? I had best get up to the house."

"Yes, Master." Moses stood nearby, ready to take over if needed.

Ian handed him the stallion's lead rope, then grabbed his cane and started for the house. He could walk from house to stable and back again with hardly any misgivings now, and Bother deserved much of the credit for it. The little dog seemed to know exactly where he was going and frisked the path ahead of him, head down, nose to the ground, intent on discovering anything that might prove to be an obstacle for Ian. Once, shortly after his arrival, he had stopped and barked at a turtle Ian would have stepped on; his cane had completely missed it, and it had blended right into its surroundings.

The little dog somehow sensed his impairment and had been eager to offer assistance in exchange for room, board, and affection. Ian firmly believed that *he* benefited most from the bargain; Bother gave him a sense of security that had been sadly lacking up until now. God knows he had tried to keep Mercy from finding out about it, but once he had finally told her, his fears had eased somewhat. Bother's arrival had all but put an end to them, except for the last and final one: his inability to perform in bed.

As he made his way toward the house, Ian hoped he was ready to face General Washington, if indeed that was who had come. Mercy would scarcely be so anxious if it was only some of her lady friends come to visit—and she would not have sent for *him* to help entertain them. General Washington was another matter.

When he got to the house, Chloe held the door open for him. She had hurried ahead and arrived there first. Bother trotted right in—a little gray blur—and promptly headed for the library, not the front parlor. Ian lost sight of him, but Bother suddenly started barking and growling, as if he had surprised an intruder.

"Bother, no!" Ian heard Mercy call out. "Stop it. Whatever is wrong with you? You have never behaved this way before, even with strangers. You must forgive him, Elizabeth. . . . Chloe, come and get this dog."

Elizabeth?

Ian only knew of *one* Elizabeth. But no, it could not be *her*. . . . As Chloe carried a growling, struggling Bother out of the room, Ian walked into the library and tried to identify the three people standing in the room: Mercy, a child, and . . . Elizabeth, the woman he had left behind in England.

Even before she spoke, Ian knew it was she: He could smell the lavender scent she had always favored. She wore pale blue, and he recalled that it was her favorite color.

"Hello, Ian," she said. "Are you surprised to see me? I

imagine you are. Well, I have another surprise for you."
She motioned for the child—a boy—to come to her, and
when he did, she put her hands on his shoulders, spun
him around, and pushed him toward Ian.

"This is your son, Adam. I have brought him to you. It
grieves me to part with him, but the time has come for
you to take over raising and educating him. My own slender
resources do not permit me to provide all that he
deserves."

"Do not make me stay here, Mama!" the boy suddenly
blurted out, retreating behind his mother's skirts. "I care
not if you *are* my father," he hissed at Ian. "I want to go
home—back to England. I left my dog there. Mama would
not let me bring him."

"He was the gamekeeper's dog, Adam, not yours—and
as nasty as that one that was just growling at me," Elizabeth
snapped. "Hush now and greet your father."

She attempted to drag him out from behind her but he
hung back, resisting. *"No!* I do not have a father. I do not
want one. What good is a father, anyway?"

"Adam! We have been over this many times." In a blur
of movement, Elizabeth turned to face her son and seized
his arms with both hands. "Now, you will behave yourself
and *greet your father,"* she ordered. "Or I will make you
sorry you disobeyed me."

Ian was so stunned he could not immediately react. His
mind had gone numb. He felt as if he were watching a
theatrical performance that had nothing to do with him.

"Adam!" Mercy stepped forward. "Let us go down to
the stable. I will show you my husband's—your father's—
horse. Do you like horses? Have you ever been on a horse?"

"No." Adam stopped struggling with his mother.
"Mama says I am too young to think of riding horses.
Besides, there is no one to teach me and no horses to ride.
Mama keeps only carriage horses."

Mercy held out her hand to the boy. "Come along with
me, then. I will show you all of our horses, including my
own mare, Liberty. Your mother can stay here. I am certain
she and . . . and your *father* have much to discuss."

Ian heard the slight tremor in his wife's voice and wished

he could go to her and explain all this—but what could he say? He had never told her he had been intimate with his betrothed before leaving England; it had only happened on the one occasion, and he was not proud of the fact.

Mercy was coping in her usual courageous fashion, but he knew she was hurting. Heat rose to his face; he writhed inside with shame. "Thank you, Mercy," he said. "I would appreciate a few moments in private with Elizabeth."

As soon as he was alone with the woman—the mother of his *son*—he urged her to sit down and himself took a seat before the fireplace. "Now then, Elizabeth. . . . Do tell me how I came to have a son about whom I know nothing."

"I wrote to you," she began, suddenly sounding nervous. "You must not have received my letters."

"You are correct in that assumption. I also wrote to you. Did you receive *my* letters?"

"Not a single one, Ian. This dreadful war ruined everything. When I discovered that I was with child, I tried to reach you. I thought you were staying with a family named McCaulley here in Virginia."

"McCallister, not McCaulley," Ian informed her. "You must not have been listening when I first told you of the family the king had recommended."

"Ian, I was desperate to contact you! But I cannot be faulted for not listening closely when you assured me that you would write to me. I began trying almost immediately after your departure."

"Almost immediately? . . . You knew that quickly that you were with child?" Ian's knowledge of a woman's biology was modest, but he sensed a falseness in her tone and immediately grew wary. He had not written her right away, and by the time he did, tensions between the British and the Americans had risen to the point where the reliability of the mail had apparently been affected.

"Well, I was not certain, of course . . . but then I began to suspect . . . and naturally, I was quite terrified—"

"When was Adam born?" he demanded, his suspicions spiraling.

"Why . . . nine months after you left."

"When exactly?" he pressed.

"Ian, what are you implying?—That Adam is not your son? He most certainly *is*. He . . . he came a bit early. Actually, it was more like seven months after you left. Well, *almost* seven months."

Ian did know that it took nine months for a child to develop in its mother's womb. "And he managed to survive being born so far ahead of time?"

"He . . . he was very big and sturdy. A healthy babe, indeed. Ian, you cannot imagine the shame I endured bearing him alone, while you were off in America! My family banished me to the country. They all but disowned me. I have been living there in wretched poverty and isolation ever since."

"You can still afford pale blue gowns," he said. "And lavender. You cannot be suffering *that* much."

"I have suffered enormously!" she bitterly disputed. "Why did you not write to me, Ian? . . . Have you any idea what 'tis like for a woman to have to bear and raise a child alone in the country, abandoned by her family and all society?"

"I am sorry," Ian admitted. "I should have written sooner—and more often. Had I know you were in this unfortunate position, I would have tried to remedy it. Believe me when I say that, Elizabeth."

"Well, you can remedy it now! I have met someone—a British lord—who wishes to marry me *despite* my shame. The only thing he demands is that I rid myself of any reminders of my . . . my youthful mistakes."

"You mean Adam. You must rid yourself of Adam."

He could just make out her vigorous nod. "Yes. I must rid myself of Adam. I was planning to bring him to you anyway. Had it not been for the war, I would have brought him much sooner. If Adam remains in England, you *know* how difficult it will be for him to assume his rightful place in society. You *must* take him, Ian. You have no choice. You are his father."

"If I am indeed his father, I will claim him and gladly. I would never refuse responsibility for my own son. However, I want more assurances, Elizabeth. I want to know

the day, the date, and the hour he was born. I want to
know precisely how many days after that one time we slept
together that he came into the world."

"You have no reason not to trust me, Ian! I never gave
you cause for jealousy."

Ian paused a moment, thinking back. "No," he said.
"You did not. But we committed to each other much too
quickly—shortly after we met, in fact. And I do recall
hearing some gossip about you and a certain gentleman—
a notorious London rake—which I completely ignored
after I had met you. You seemed so sweet and innocent
back then. Now I wonder—"

"Whatever you heard is not true, Ian! I deny everything.
I was a virgin when we met, untouched until you—you
imposed yourself upon me, and I, being young and foolish
and deeply in love with you . . ."

Now Ian was certain she was lying. He had *never* imposed
himself upon her. 'Twas *she* who had been so aggressive
that night—and so triumphant afterwards. Now he understood why: she needed a father for the child she was already
carrying. *That* accounted for her eagerness to wed and bed
him. When he had insisted on putting off their wedding
until after his return from America, she had set about
seducing him so he would think he was the father of her
child.

"Adam's birth date, Elizabeth. Whatever you tell me, I
shall insist upon verifying with the proper authorities
before I accept him as mine."

"You cannot prove he is not yours!"

"And *you* cannot prove he is, can you?"

In the stable, Mercy watched as Adam ran his fingers
over the scars disfiguring Thor's glossy coat. The stallion
stood in the aisle and lowered his head to nose the boy's
frock coat. Adam did not move away, as Mercy might have
expected. He was far too engrossed in Thor's scars.

"What happened to him?" he asked, frowning. "Did
someone whip him?"

The question startled Mercy. What would an eight-year-old boy know about whipping? ... Nothing, unless he had directly experienced one. Elizabeth's threat echoed in Mercy's head: *I will make you sorry you disobeyed me.*

"No, he got hurt in the war. He carried your father into battle and brought him safely home again, but he was badly hurt doing it."

Your father.

The words stuck in Mercy's throat, being difficult to *think,* let alone say. Ian had not denied the possibility that Adam might be his son, so Mercy had to accept that he had been intimate with the beautiful blond woman who was even now alone with him up at the house. The knowledge twisted her heart, causing a pain such as she had never yet experienced; it was almost too great to be borne. Yet, somehow she must bear it.

Adam's hand moved to Thor's face where the hair had been singed off and had grown in odd-colored, almost white. Gently he patted the stallion's jaw and then his neck—having to reach up high to touch him but showing no fear at how the horse towered over him.

"He is so big," he murmured.

Mercy had to lean down to hear him.

"He is so big and strong. I bet he can go fast, can he not?"

"He used to be able to go very fast," Mercy agreed. "But that was before he got hurt. Now he cannot go as fast. Your father was hurt in the war, too, and he cannot do all the things he used to be able to do, either."

He cannot give me children. But he gave that awful woman a child, a precious little boy she does not appreciate.

Adam turned his serious green-eyed gaze on her. "Did he—my father—kill people during the war?"

"I ... I do not know," Mercy said. "I never asked him. I imagine he must have had to kill his enemies or he himself would have been killed."

"*I* would like to kill someone someday!" the boy vehemently announced.

"Why?" This flash of violence in one so young astonished Mercy. She exchanged glances with Moses, who stood nearby, listening and shaking his head.

"Because," Adam answered, volunteering nothing more.

"Because someone has hurt *you?*" she probed.

Adam looked down at his buckled shoes. When he glanced up again at her, she could see hatred, hurt, and fear shining in his eyes. "I hate my father," he said. "I want to kill him."

Mercy dropped to her knees beside the boy and studied his small, angry face. "Adam, why? You do not even *know* your father. You have only just met him."

"He does not want me," Adam said. "I knew he would not want me. Nobody wants me."

"Oh, Adam!" Mercy slid her arms around the child and drew him close. "That is not true! *I* want you. I have no children of my own, you see, and I have *always* wanted a little boy of my own to love. . . . *You* can be *my* little boy from now on. I will teach you how to ride horses. One day I will even get you a horse of your own. What do you think of that?"

She leaned back to see his reaction.

"Do you mean it?" he asked, anxiously watching her. "I could have my own pony?"

She nodded.

"I . . . I will try hard to be good," he promised. "You will never have to whip me like Mama does."

Mercy took his face in her hands and looked him in the eye. She spoke slowly and carefully so he would not miss a word. "Adam, neither your father nor I will *ever* whip you. At Collier Manor, we never whip anyone—not our people or our horses. Moses, tell him."

"It be true, young master. Nobody gonna get a whippin' here," Moses assured him. "I been here all my life, and I never seen anybody get a whippin' yet."

Adam still looked a little anxious. "My father will not send me away? Mama said he might. She says I am so bad she cannot wait to be rid of me."

"He will not send you away if *I* have anything to say about it." Mercy kissed him lightly on the forehead. "And believe me, Adam, I have *plenty* to say about it. Now, I will show you *my* horse—Liberty. She can go very fast, and in the spring she is going to have a foal."

"A foal!" Adam was much impressed. "Will I get to pet it and ride it?"

"Yes, and yes. . . . But you will not get to ride it right away. You must wait for it to grow up first, and you yourself must learn how to ride."

"I really *am* going to be here a long, long time, then?" Adam inquired, still worrying.

"Adam, I will never let you go," Mercy replied—and meant it, astounding herself with her sudden fierce instinct to protect and nurture this wounded, unwanted child.

All of the maternal feelings she had thus far been denied swept through her with the force of a swift summer storm. This child was now *her* child—hers and Ian's—and she would allow no one to ever hurt him again.

CHAPTER
TWENTY-THREE

Mercy kept Adam down at the stable for more than an hour. On their way back to the house, they witnessed the departure of the carriage—with Adam's mother inside it. It rattled right past them, and the woman looked straight ahead, never so much as nodding at her son or waving good-bye to him. She had simply left without a backward glance!

"Adam, I am so sorry." Mercy again dropped to her knees before the boy. Wrapping her arms around him, she gave him a big hug. His body was limp and unresisting.

"I am glad she is gone," he whispered into Mercy's ear. "I never want to see her again."

"Oh, my dearest Adam! You never *will* have to see her again." Despite a strong urge to weep, Mercy managed to summon a smile for his benefit. "Adam, this is the start of a whole new life for you—with me and your father. You will see; it will be much better than your old life."

Thus far, Adam had not shed a single tear, but now his green eyes suddenly overflowed with them. "I tried to please Mama!" he wailed. "But I never could. I did *try* to be good and make Mama like me. But she never did. Only my nurse liked me—and the butler. They told me things would be better in America, and I should not be afraid. But I am—a little.''

"Adam, they were right. Things *will* be better.'' Tucking his head in the crook between her neck and shoulder, Mercy held the child while he wept for a few moments.

When he finally stopped sniffling, she rose and took his hand. "You must be hungry and thirsty by now. Come, and I will take you to Chloe. She will see that you get something good to eat. Chloe is sometimes gruff, but she *loves* children. She was *my* nurse when I was small.''

"Can I play with the little dog, too?'' Adam asked, taking her hand.

"Of course you may. His name is Bother.''

"Why is he called Bother?''

"Because he is sometimes a—because he is *no* bother at all,'' Mercy corrected herself. "He is a grand little dog whom your father adores.''

"Do you think he will like *me*—when he gets to know me, I mean?''

"Your father? I *know* he will.'' Mercy squeezed his hand. "Indeed, after I take you to Chloe, I am going to find him and tell him what a truly wonderful little boy you are. You can visit with Chloe for a bit and play with Bother, and later, at supper, we shall all sit down together as a family and get to know one another better.''

"All right,'' Adam said.

As they entered the house, Mercy saw two small trunks right inside the doorway.

"Those are my things,'' he informed her.

"I guessed that. I will have them taken upstairs to one of the guest chambers. It will be *your* chamber now.'' She spotted Chloe coming toward her. "Chloe, Adam is hungry. Do you think you can find something good for him to eat?''

"Follow me, young master,'' Chloe said, reaching for his hand.

"Where is my husband?'' Mercy asked before Chloe and Adam disappeared into the depths of the house together.

"Gone upstairs, girl. The driver of the carriage brought him a package from the same ship that carried this boy and his mama across the sea to Chesapeake Bay. Guess that's how the lady knew where to come lookin' for Master Ian. It was right there on the package. When the ship's captain heard who she was lookin' for, he gave her the package to give to Master Ian."

A package for Ian; that could mean only one thing! The spectacles she had sent for had finally arrived. Leaving Adam in Chloe's capable hands, Mercy hurried up the staircase.

The door to Ian's chamber stood open, but Mercy knocked to avoid barging in on her husband unannounced. Before, she might never have thought of it, but now, with this new awkwardness between them, she felt compelled to observe formalities.

"Ian?"

"Come in, Mercy."

Mercy stepped inside the room. Facing away from her, Ian stood at the window with his hands clasped behind his back. On a nearby table lay some wrinkled brown paper and several pairs of discarded spectacles. Her heart sank. Apparently none of them had improved Ian's vision, and he had already forgotten about them.

She decided to be forthright about the matter of Elizabeth and not wait for Ian's explanation—if he had one. She no longer cared what had happened all those years ago between her husband and that awful woman; he was lucky he had not married her. Elizabeth would have made him miserable. All that mattered now was Adam's future—and her own and Ian's.

"Adam and I saw his mother depart, Ian. She went right past us in the carriage and never stopped to say good-bye. She does not deserve a wonderful child like Adam. She abused him and made him feel unloved and unwanted. I have told him I am *delighted* to be his new mother and that we both welcome him and will love him forever. He is with Chloe now, getting something to eat. I just wanted you to know without having to ask that I have accepted Adam as

my own. It will be no chore to raise and mother him, and—
Ian, why are you shaking your head like that?"

She wished he would turn around so she could see his
expression. It was disconcerting to address his back.

"Mercy, sweet Mercy . . ." he said, still shaking his head.
"You are too good—too perfect to be true. I sometimes
wonder if you have even one selfish bone in your body.
Do you never get angry or succumb to despair? Must you
rescue every broken, damaged, frightened creature that
comes your way and attempt to heal it?"

"I am hardly perfect, Ian. I wanted to claw out that
woman's eyes. If she ever sets foot on the estate again, I
will. The way she has mistreated your son is—"

"He is not my son. After you left with the boy, she finally
admitted the truth. Adam's father is an infamous despoiler
of foolish young women. Elizabeth was not the first to fall
prey to his charms; the scoundrel has sired other unwanted
children and refuses to claim a single one of them—hence
her determination to convince *me* that I am Adam's
father."

"But . . . but she left here without him! And—"

"And I *was* intimate with her, Mercy—only once, if that
comforts you any. It was enough to give her reason to
believe I might be persuaded to accept the boy as mine.
I have decided to do just that—for no other reason than
to get him away from *her*. No child deserves to grow up
unloved, unwanted, and branded as a bastard. I could not
find it in my heart to send him away with her. . . . Besides,
I knew I could count on you to feel the same way."

"I do, Ian! Oh, I do!" Mercy walked further into the
room. "Do you know she whipped that poor child—and
told him he was bad? Why, I have no doubt he would grow
up to be a villain if he remained under her influence. . . .
Ian, why are you still standing at the window like that? I
dislike talking to the back of your head."

"Because I wanted to surprise you." Slowly he turned
to face her and looked right at her without squinting. A
huge grin lit his face as he beamed at her through a pair
of gold-rimmed spectacles. "Mercy, I can finally *see* you—

the most magnificent woman with the most beautiful soul
it has ever been my good fortune to encounter."

The spectacles popped off his nose and would have gone
crashing to the floor then, but he fumbled and caught
them just in time. "I need to tie the strings on them to
keep them in place," he ruefully explained, setting them
on his nose again and drawing the tie ribbons back behind
his ears. " 'Tis how they stay on. As soon as I tried them,
I could see everything clearly—for the first time since I
was wounded in the war."

"Ian, 'tis just what I prayed for! Oh, my love, you are
cured of your blindness!" She flew into his arms and almost
knocked him over with the force of her embrace.

"Yes!" he cried, laughing. "I am cured of my blindness—in more ways than one, Wife!"

"How many ways *are* there?" she demanded, and kissed
him before he could answer.

To her surprise and delight, he did not push her away
or attempt to shorten the kiss. Instead, he took her in his
arms and gave her one of his *old* kisses, the kind that made
her knees tremble and her body quake deep inside. For
once, he seemed reluctant to end the kiss—but he did
pause long enough to mutter: "Will my new son be occupied long enough that I dare risk taking my wife to bed
for an hour or two?"

Mercy leaned back to look at him and bumped her nose
on his spectacles. Apparently they would take some getting
used to—not just for him but for her. "Chloe will not let
him out of her sight . . . but oh, Ian, do you mean it? Are
you sure you are ready?"

"I have never been more ready," he whispered. "Even
before I tried my new spectacles, I knew I was ready. When
I saw you take Adam's hand to lead him down to the
stable—take the hand of a son you knew nothing about,
accept him simply because you thought he was mine—
something happened to me, Mercy. In that moment, I
asked myself why I was so afraid. Even if I could not—you
know—*perform*, you would still love me . . . want me . . .
accept me as I am. There was no need for me to be ashamed
or fearful. Your love is big enough to forgive *any*thing. 'Tis

like God's love, or what I have always imagined God's love to be—forgiving, accepting, understanding, never selfish or filled with condemnation and judgment. . . . You would never mock me or laugh at my efforts . . ."

"Ian, how could you ever think I *would?*"

"Because I was blind, my love . . . blind and foolish. Because I wanted to be all things to you—strong and fearless. Able to protect you and make you happy. I wanted to be the man who could stir your passions and satisfy them beyond your wildest imaginings. Because I could not bear the possibility of failing. . . . I may still fail, my love. But at least now I am not afraid to *try.* I have regained my courage. All I can think about now is how much I want you . . . how much I need you."

He took her hand and slid it down between them—pressing her palm against the part of him she had so wanted to caress once more. She touched him with tenderness, awe, and a bit of nervousness. She could tell no difference in him from the first time she had touched him intimately.

"Ian, let me close the door first and then join you in bed."

He nodded. "Close the door . . . and then, take off everything you are wearing. I want to watch you, my beautiful wife. I want to lie on my bed and rejoice as all your loveliness is revealed to me again."

She left him and closed the door while he removed his shoes and stretched out on the bed, waiting for her to come to him. She took her time undressing, savoring the wondrous moments as her husband gazed at her with love and lust shining in his eyes.

"Come here," he said before she had even finished.

She shook her head. Her hair swirled about her nakedness, making his eyes widen and darken with desire behind his spectacles.

"Not until you have done as I am doing," she teased. "I want to see you, too, Ian."

"Why would you want to see a battle-scarred old brute of a man? I assure you the experience will hardly be arousing."

"Let me be the judge of that. . . . Must I stand here the

rest of the day? If we have only an hour or two, you had better hurry . . ."

Grumbling, he complied with her wishes, but then snatched a quilt to toss over his own nakedness while he still ogled hers. She was more than satisfied; everything would be fine. She knew it now. The evidence of Ian's desire for her could not be hidden even with a quilt. He stared at her triumphantly, his eyes glowing behind his new spectacles.

"Now will you come to me, Wife? . . . And will you forgive me for all the wrong I have done you by being such a coward until today?"

"Only if you allow me to kiss and caress you from head to foot, including everything that lies between."

"That is what I intend to do to *you!*" he protested.

"You must allow me first, Ian. I demand the right. I deserve it. You have kept me waiting all this time when we could have been enjoying each other and did not . . . so now you must indulge me."

"Oh, God!" Ian cried, flopping back against the pillows. "Perhaps I should take off my spectacles, so they do not get broken."

"Perhaps you should. Our exercise might become a bit . . . vigorous."

She slid her nakedness on top of *his* nakedness and helped untie the strings to his spectacles. Then she took them off his nose and gently laid them on the seat of a chair drawn close to the bed.

"Now I cannot *see* you clearly anymore," he complained.

"You do not need to see—not when you can *feel* me," she soothed, rubbing her breasts along his bare chest.

"Ah, Mercy!" he cried, clasping her to him.

"I am here, Ian. Right where I belong."

They lingered in Ian's bedchamber until it began to grow dark. Mercy hated to have to get up, dress, and go down to supper, but she wanted to see Adam. She had promised the boy they would have supper together.

"Ian, what will you do about Adam?" she asked, rolling

over and sitting up. "Must we sign papers or something to confirm that he is ours?"

"He *is* ours. I want him to grow up believing that he is my son," Ian said, retrieving his spectacles and tying them in place on his nose. "No one but you, me, and Elizabeth knows anything different. He will be the son we should have had by now anyway. Naturally, it would be nice if we could have gotten to know him better before we decided this—or could have discussed it first—but there was no time for that. I sent Elizabeth away as quickly as I could. She was only too glad to leave. Worry not about *her,* Mercy. We will never hear from the woman again. She is returning to England to marry some British lord."

"Good. I never want to see her again. I never want to *think* about her again. Adam will quickly adjust to being our son. *I* will quickly adjust to being his mother. . . . Ian, you are wonderful for accepting him as your own even when you know he is not!"

"And so are you, my love." He leaned over to nuzzle her neck. "Perhaps we will have a baby of our own one of these days. Whether we do or not, Adam will remain our 'firstborn.' When he comes of age, I will offer him the chance to return to England and assume my title, if he wishes. If not . . . there will be plenty for him to do here."

"Collier Manor is big enough for all of us. Now that the war is over, we can pursue our dreams and make it even bigger and better. You once said you wanted to build your own empire, Ian. Now, it seems, you have your chance."

"Yes, and I can *see* while I am doing it—see my lovely wife with her hair all tousled, her cheeks flushed, and her lips red and swollen from lovemaking . . ."

"Ian, will everyone be able to tell what we have been doing when we go down to supper?"

"I certainly hope so," he smugly answered. "Except for Adam, of course. He is too young to know about such things. My guess is the servants will all know—and rejoice with us. Now, you had better hurry and dress or you may never leave this chamber tonight!"

* * *

At supper, they decided to celebrate Adam's arrival and Ian's improved sight by reinstituting the Collier Manor Annual Foxhunt. It would be held as late in the season as possible in order to give them the maximum time to prepare. Ian wanted to polish his riding skills so he could follow the hunt at a sedate pace, at least, even if he could no longer jump fences or keep up with the hounds on Thor. He also wanted to begin Adam's riding lessons in the hopes that Adam could ride along with him.

"Tomorrow I will send young Henry around to our neighbors with the news," Mercy said. "I will have him inquire after a pony suitable for a young child. 'Tis possible someone might have one. The war took most of the horses in the area, but ponies were not nearly so desirable, and people may have kept them for their own mounts and carriage horses."

"We *must* find a good pony for my son," Ian agreed. "Have you a color preference in a pony, Adam?"

"Ian! Try not to make it any more difficult than it is already. We will be lucky to locate a good pony of *any* color. Besides, a pony's color has nothing to with how well he performs under a saddle or pulling a cart."

"I should like a white pony," Adam solemnly announced. "Or a black one. Brown would be nice, too. The only color I do not think I would like is *green.*"

"Then I think we can accommodate you," Mercy said, laughing. "Green ponies are especially hard to find these days."

Adam burst out laughing, too, thoroughly delighted with his own sense of humor. "I do not like *blue* ones, either."

"Now, Adam. As your new mother has already pointed out, we must not make this any more difficult than it is already. If we find a blue one, it will have to do. Understand?"

"Yes, sir!" Adam chortled, turning his attention to a dish of yellow squash seasoned with honey. Between mouthfuls, he paused to add: "As long as it is not a *wooden* pony, it can be *any* color."

This set him off again, and he could hardly eat, so great was his merriment. Ian exchanged a long, emotion-filled glance with Mercy across the table.

"It has been too long a time since I last heard laughter in this house," he commented.

"Much too long," she agreed. "But I expect we will be hearing it often from now on. . . . Adam, if you wish to feed Bother scraps from your plate, wait until *after* supper."

The mild rebuke sobered the boy, and he sat up straighter, fidgeting on his chair. Bother whined and thumped his tail at the boy's feet.

"If you are finished eating, you may leave the table," Mercy told him. "Feel free to take Bother with you."

"Oh, I will! Thank you!" Adam leapt from his chair and raced from the room, with Bother yapping at his heels. Mercy sat perfectly still, savoring the moment and grinning at her husband, while Ian grinned back at her. They probably looked a little foolish, Mercy thought. Their whole lives had changed in a single day—all because a carriage had rolled up their driveway . . .

"Have I told you how beautiful you are?" Ian asked, his blue eyes dark with desire.

"Yes," she said. "But 'tis not a thing I grow tired of hearing. Go ahead and repeat it if you wish."

"You take my breath away," he murmured. "I cannot stop looking at you. How long before we can put Adam to bed?"

"Soon," she promised. "Am I to assume I will be sleeping in *your* bed tonight?"

He nodded. "Tonight and *every* night for the rest of our lives, Wife."

"Good," she said. "That is what I have been waiting to hear."

The Collier Manor Hunt rolled around quickly, almost before they knew it. By then, the Netherlands and the United States had signed a treaty of commerce and friend-

ship, while British and American representatives in Paris
continued to labor over a peace treaty expected to be
signed at any moment. . . . It was a perfect time for a
resumption of the annual hunt.

On the day before the hunt, carriages rolled up the drive
all day long, disgorging passengers. Tied to the back of
the vehicles were the horses who would be used for the
hunt. Some of the guests came mounted on their hunt-
ers—and Mercy was amazed at the number of fine animals
who had somehow escaped the ravages of war. Naturally,
a few people came mounted on plow horses they had been
teaching to jump, for their fine saddle horses had all gone
for the war effort. A few even came on ponies, and one
arrived riding a mule.

Everyone was in such a jovial mood that laughter and
teasing abounded. It was just like old times; actually, it was
better than old times—except for the number of missing
faces. The war had claimed many victims; others had fallen
prey to old age or disease.

Nevertheless, Mercy had never felt so proud or happy
as when she joined her friends and neighbors on the hunt
field. Ian rode Thor beside her, leading a little white pony
carrying Adam. Eunice's children had long ago outgrown
the pony, so she had sent him back to Collier Manor with
Henry. Adam's riding lessons had begun immediately, and
he had caught on more quickly than Mercy had ever dared
hope.

However, Ian insisted that the boy must stay with him
on this first foxhunt of his young life. Adam was not ready
to try jumping yet, nor could his pony be trusted not to
lose his head and go galloping after the other horses during
the hunt. By next year at this time, Adam should be able
to manage Samuel, as the pony was called, on his own.
Until then, Samuel was firmly tethered to Thor, and the
stallion seemed to relish looking after the feisty old fellow.

"Ian, you will explain all the rules to him, will you not?"
Mercy implored her husband. "I have already explained
them once, but I am afraid Adam may have forgotten them
in his excitement."

"Never get between the hounds and the huntsman,"

Adam recited. "Nor must I ever try to play with the hounds."

"Excellent," Mercy praised. "You remembered the most important things. Hounds are not mere dogs like Bother, but specially trained animals. Why, the hounds we are privileged to follow today are the result of careful breeding for many years. They were bred for nose, the ability to follow the scent of a wily fox; for cry, the quality of their voices when they give tongue; and for drive, the urge to get forward on a line of scent."

"Mercy, you are telling him too much," Ian chided. "After today, he will have a very good idea of the work hounds must do."

"I just want him to love foxhunting as much as I do!" Mercy exclaimed. "Perhaps we should think of obtaining our own hounds, Ian, so we do not have to use a pack belonging to one of our neighbors."

She was thinking of their neighbors the Willardsons, whose hounds they had always used in the past. The death of John Willardson had resulted in the sale of his hounds to another neighbor who lived further away. If they had their own hounds, Adam could learn more about raising and training them. The way the boy loved dogs in general, he was bound to enjoy helping with the care and education of a pack of hounds . . . but then, Adam loved everything about life in Virginia. Since he had gotten Samuel, he wanted to spend all his time on the back of his pony— and when he was not doing that, he was helping Moses care for the rest of the horses. If she wanted to know where Adam and Bother had run off to, all she had to do was check the stable. She could usually find Ian there, too.

"Let us get through today safely," Ian urged. "We must not force foxhunting upon the boy; he must make up his own mind about the sport . . . eh, Adam?"

"Yes, Father," Adam nodded. "I already know I like foxhunting."

So the hunt began—and a long, exciting day it proved to be. As the Master of the Hunt, Mercy had little time to check on Adam, but she managed to do it frequently anyway—checking on Ian at the same time. They followed behind everyone else. Since Thor had the constant company of Samuel, he was not nearly as disturbed about being parted from Liberty and the other horses as he might have been.

The fox that day was a true sportsman, leading the hounds far away from Collier Manor, then doubling back in a most clever manner as he began to tire. Apparently he wanted to go to ground in a familiar place. The hounds finally closed in on him near Mercy's woods, and he dove beneath a fallen tree, whereupon the hounds sensed they had him and began frantically digging to get him out.

Since the hounds were not hers, Mercy could not call them off but must let nature take its course. The fox's fate was in the hands of the huntsman controlling the pack, and everyone milled around on horseback, waiting for the kill.

Just then, Ian and Adam rode up. Seeing what was happening—and hearing the excited cry of the hounds—Ian positioned Thor so as to block the boy's view of the proceedings.

"Father, is the fox under that fallen tree?" Adam asked, his eyes wide as he tried to see around Ian.

Ian nodded. "Yes, the hunt is over now, Adam, and the horses are tired. Thor and Samuel may not have jumped today, but they have worked hard. Let us take them down to the stable."

"That is a good idea," Mercy agreed. "You two go ahead, and I will join you shortly."

"But I want to see!" Adam protested.

"No, Adam. You do not want to see this—" Mercy began.

"But why are the hounds snarling now, and—" In the blink of an eye, he was off his pony and racing on foot toward the fray. "No! They must not kill the fox!"

"Adam!" Ian called out. "Adam, come back here!"

Mercy grabbed Samuel's reins to keep him from bolting. By the time she looked back at Adam, the boy had picked up a stick and waded right into the middle of the pack of excited hounds. Flailing at them with his stick, he tried to defend the fox and drive the hounds away. For a few moments, all was pandemonium—until the huntsman

regained control of the pack and called them away from
the scene, giving the fox a chance to escape.

Mercy saw the flick of his red brush as the wily fellow
leapt out from beneath the fallen tree and dashed into
the woods. The hounds, intent on the huntsman's signals,
never saw him go. By then, Mercy was off Liberty, and Ian
had dismounted from Thor. The two of them stood looking
down at Adam, who clenched his small fists and stared
belligerently back at them.

"You did not tell me they were going to kill the fox!"
He glared accusingly at Mercy.

"They do not usually manage to catch the fox," Mercy
explained. "Sir Fox often lives to hunt another day."

"If the fox must die at the end of the hunt, then I never
want to hunt again!" Adam's eyes filled with tears.

"Then perhaps we should begin a *new* tradition at the
Collier Manor Foxhunt," Ian said, taking his son's hand
to lead him away. "From now on, the fox must *always* be
permitted to escape."

Mercy glanced around at their friends. This was a part
of the hunt she herself had never relished—but then,
the fox often *did* escape. Several people looked ready to
protest, but most were nodding their heads in sympathy.
Mercy was so proud of Adam she wanted to pick him up
and hug him then and there! . . . However, she did not
wish to embarrass him in front of all these people.

Was this the same child who had announced he wanted to kill
someone only a short time ago?

She knew then that Adam's early experiences with his
mother had been forgotten—or if not forgotten, they had
been largely overcome. The boy's natural inclination was
to protect life, not take it.

"You must be proud of your son," one of their guests—
a man—said, riding up to Ian. "He is a brave, compassion-
ate lad. Not afraid to fight for his beliefs."

"I *am* proud of him," Ian responded. "Even if he *did*
get between the huntsman and his hounds," he added,
glancing down at Adam.

Adam gazed up at his father with adoration blazing in

his eyes. "Forgive me, Father. I will not do it again. 'Tis just I had to save the fox."

"I understand, Adam. And you must never apologize for doing what you think is right, even if it means breaking the rules. There are times when rules *must* be broken."

Ian knows all about that, Mercy thought, loving her husband even more. *We all do. Not a single one of us was willing to obey a despot. We simply refused to honor his rules.*

Smiling at everyone, she invited them to return to the stable and afterwards the house, where a feast and a grand celebration awaited them.

That evening, Ian surprised Mercy with the presence of a preacher he had invited to the house to witness a repetition of their marriage vows.

"I know we were well and truly wed before the British and all those loyalists," he said, nodding toward the gentleman in the black frock coat who awaited them in a circle of their guests in the front parlor. "But I thought you might want to redo the thing in the company of *all* our friends, not just the few ladies who barely managed to escape *that* ceremony with their lives. This time, we can really celebrate—our new son, our freedom, our victory in the war and the new era of peace that is beginning . . . a peace in which I now plan to participate, after all."

At Mercy's urging, Ian had finally written to General Washington and agreed to become active in Virginia politics and to take part in the possible drafting of a constitution for the government of the new United States.

"What about my return to your bed? Should we not celebrate that, in particular?" Mercy whispered mischievously, relatively certain that although everyone could see them, they could not hear their conversation. She and Ian stood in the hallway outside the parlor, where Mercy had just descended the staircase and been waylaid by her husband, who was waiting to tell her his surprise.

"We must also celebrate the possibility that next year at this time we will have another son or daughter to take part in the Collier Manor Foxhunt," she added with a sideways glance at her now gaping husband.

"What?" Ian gasped. "Are you certain?"

Mercy laid a protective hand across her still-flat stomach. "As certain as I can be at this early stage. Chloe *insists* I am expecting a child. She says I *must* tell you tonight— and since you are surprising *me,* I thought I would surprise you, as well."

"Hurry up, Mother!" Adam rushed up and took her hand. "The minister is waiting."

"You knew about this, too?" Mercy demanded, glancing from Ian to her pink-cheeked son. "Everyone knew about it but me?"

She glanced at the assembled crowd, which included all of her lady friends, the former Daughters of Liberty, even those who had not ridden to the hounds today. Caroline was accompanied by Squire Landry, and Mercy expected an announcement any day now. Everyone was there but General Washington and the most important Virginia statesmen who were still busy negotiating the treaty with England.

"Father told me," Adam confided. "He said he wants everyone to know how much he loves you, and after you say your vows again, we will all drink a toast—to you and to me!"

"To both of you—my beloved family," Ian confirmed.

"Ian, he is too young for hard cider or other spirits."

"Just this once he may indulge," Ian overruled her. "I am his father. I said so."

Adam beamed at her, so excited he could hardly stand still. "Father says I may hold your hands while you say your vows to each other," he further informed her. "He says I am an important part of this ceremony."

"You are, my dear—a *most* important part," Mercy confirmed. "Shall we go in and do it, then?"

Ian adjusted his spectacles and took her hand and Adam's. "I think we had better. Everyone is waiting."

Mercy drew a deep breath. She felt as if they were starting all over—beginning a new life ripe with promise and over-flowing with the joy only love can bring.

"I am ready," she whispered, barely able to speak for the emotions suddenly coursing through her. She felt as giddy as Adam facing his first big jump.

Ian paused a moment, leaned over, and gently kissed her brow. "Now, *I* am ready, too," he answered, winking at her.

Holding hands, they marched into the front parlor to cheers and applause that shook the rafters of Collier Manor and very likely the heavens above it.

AFTERWORD

When I started writing this book, my intention was to focus on the early foxhunting days of this country and the development of the type of horse used for that sport. Once I discovered that George Washington himself was a Master of the Hunt prior to the Revolutionary War, I was off and running. To me, it made him seem much more human than the figure whose birthday occurs in February and whose face adorns dollar bills.

As the war gradually consumed my characters, foxhunting became less important than the story of the war's impact on two special people—Ian and Mercy. I thoroughly enjoyed bringing to life that era and hope you have enjoyed the result of my efforts. Assuming you did, watch for the next Katharine Kincaid adventure combining history, horses, and that most wonderful of all life's experiences—the love between man and woman. Never forget that love can brighten and illuminate even the longest, darkest days of our lives. Write to me c/o Zebra Books, 850 Third Ave., New York, NY 10022.